INSIDER

ADDITIONAL ROCK STAR
EROTIC ROMANCES
BY OLIVIA CUNNING

 ON TOUR SERIES

BACKSTAGE PASS
ROCK HARD
HOT TICKET
WICKED BEAT
DOUBLE TIME
SINNERS AT THE ALTAR

ONE NIGHT WITH

ANTHOLOGIES

TRY ME, TEMPT ME, TAKE ME
SHARE ME, TOUCH ME, TIE ME
TEASE ME, TELL ME

INSIDER

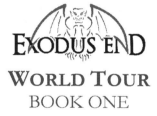

EXODUS END

WORLD TOUR
BOOK ONE

OLIVIA CUNNING

VULPINE
PRESS

CHAPTER 1

TONI PLACED a second wide-angle lens into her gargantuan camera case and shut the lid, locking both clasps with her thumbs. She glanced around her office to make sure she hadn't overlooked anything. It was imperative that she remembered all her equipment. She'd be gone for weeks with no access to any gear she left behind.

"I don't want you to go," Birdie said, grabbing her hand and giving it a hard yank. Toni winced. Birdie never meant to hurt; she simply didn't realize how strong she was.

Rubbing her smarting elbow with her free hand, Toni said, "It's only for a few weeks." Four to be exact, but Birdie didn't deal well with change, and Toni figured it was best to understate her absence. "You and Mom will have a great time without me."

Birdie shook her head. "Who will read me a story?"

"Mom will."

Birdie's face scrunched into a pout. "She doesn't do it the fun way."

Toni tugged one of Birdie's pigtails. She was nine, but emotionally and mentally she was closer to five.

"Maybe you can read it to her, Buttercup. You know every word by heart." Toni must have read *The Princess Bride* to Birdie a thousand times. Her sister never grew bored with the tale. Toni, on the other hand, had started making up weird voices and progressive changes to the story to keep from going insane from the monotony.

"I will try."

Toni smoothed a palm over Birdie's cheek, pausing to rub at a smudge at the corner of her mouth. "Don't forget your chores. I won't be there to remind you."

"Feed the chickens." Birdie smiled that heart-stealing, ear-to-ear grin of hers.

"Good. What else?"

Birdie pressed her lips together around the tip of her tongue and scrunched up her round face in concentration. After a long moment, she said, "I can't 'member."

"What are you supposed to do when you can't remember?"

Birdie's face lit up, and she pulled a piece of paper out of the back pocket of her jeans. "My list!"

"That's right." Toni kissed Birdie's forehead and hugged her tight. "You've got this, Buttercup."

"How many days until you come home?"

"I gave you a calendar. It's on your message board."

"I'm supposed to put an X on each day until I is on the red square."

"Until I *am* on the red square," Toni corrected automatically. She came from a long line of English majors, and she saw how their mother cringed every time Birdie used improper grammar. Poor kid. "Only mark out one day each morning. Don't cheat." Toni made Birdie calendars for birthdays and Christmas countdowns so she didn't have to answer "How many days?" questions every five minutes. Birdie often tried marking out extra days, thinking it would make the anticipated event arrive sooner.

There was a knock on her door and it opened an instant later. Her mom poked her head into the room. "Are you ready?"

"I think so," Toni said, giving her office yet another scan. She couldn't shake the feeling that she was forgetting something. Or maybe she was just nervous.

"Hi, Mommy!" Birdie waved.

"Good evening, Bernadette." Mom immediately turned her attention to Toni. "Julian insisted that he drive you to the rendezvous point. I hope you're not offended that he didn't have to ask for my permission twice."

Toni grinned. Julian would make the trip interesting. And it was probably best for Mom and Birdie to head for home; I-5 traffic could be a bear, and Birdie got antsy on long car rides.

"Also, Susan wants to talk to you before you leave," Mom

added.

Toni's heart plummeted. Her first meeting with Nichols Publishing's newest editor had not gone well. She doubted this one would prove less traumatizing.

"Okay. Thanks." *No thanks.*

"Come, Bernadette," Mom said, holding out a hand. "We're heading for home."

Mom looked as nervous about taking care of her youngest daughter as Toni felt about hanging around with four living legends for a month. It wasn't that Mom had never cared for Birdie before. She'd just never done it without Toni's assistance for more than two days at once. The next four weeks were going to be rough on everyone. But Toni was more than ready for a little adventure. And Birdie had to learn to trust Mom to meet her needs.

"I want to go with Toni," Birdie said, grabbing Toni's hand and shaking her head.

"You can't," Mom said. "Toni needs to get out and gain some experience so she's ready to take over the company someday."

Yeah, about that . . . Toni didn't *want* to take over her mother's company. But who else could? Sadly, Birdie would never be capable of the onerous job, though she could help with many tasks. Dad was gone. There was no one but Toni available to walk in Eloise Nichols's footsteps, and everyone knew how hard her mother had worked to build Nichols Publishing from the ground up. Toni felt obligated to keep the business in the family. But that wasn't why she wanted to go on tour with the most famous metal band on the planet. Nope. Her reasons for touring with Exodus End were entirely selfish. This project would launch her career. The career *she* wanted, not the career her mother wanted for her.

Toni wanted to design interactive electronic biographies about famous people—rock stars, presidents, actors. She hadn't even realized her aspiration until her mom had mentioned the Exodus End project over dinner one evening—Toni had known instantly it was the perfect career for her. She'd majored in all the relevant fields and had loads of experience, she just hadn't been able to figure out how to make her eclectic education and strange skill set mesh into a viable career. This assignment was tailor-made for her, and she was going to blow everyone's mind with her creative genius.

Assuming she didn't pee down her leg the first time she met the band.

"I want to go with Toni," Birdie said. "I can help."

Toni tried imagining her sweet, special needs sister living with a group of raunchy metal musicians for several weeks. Uh yeah, no. Imagining immersing *herself* into the band members' lives was challenging enough.

"Mom needs your help more than I do, Birdie," Toni said. "Who will feed the chickens? Mom doesn't know how."

Birdie chewed her lip, obviously torn between the well-being of their chickens and her desire to be with the sister who'd raised her.

"Okay, Toni," she said haltingly. "I'll help Mommy."

Toni gave her sister another tight hug and a kiss on the forehead. "I'll be home before you know it."

Birdie didn't look quite convinced, but she ambled over to Mom and took her hand. "I'll show you how to feed chickens, Mommy. So next time you can feed them and I can go with Toni."

Mom patted her youngest daughter's back and smiled, but Toni knew the woman wouldn't go within ten yards of the coop. It had been her father's idea to buy the little farm an hour east of Seattle, and after he'd passed away, Mom had wanted to sell it and move closer to the office. But Toni had convinced her to keep their idyllic property. For Birdie's sake and for hers. Anything that allowed Toni to keep the memory of her father alive was worth the effort to maintain and the loss of any chance at a social life.

"Call if you need anything," Mom said.

"I will. Love you both."

"Love you too, Toni!" Birdie yelled in what most would consider an outside voice. But Birdie only had two volumes—loud and whisper.

Toni waited a few moments before collecting her gear and heading to Susan's office. Toni didn't want Birdie to see her again and be forced to go through their goodbyes twice. And maybe if she dawdled enough, Julian would come collect her for their drive to the arena, helping her keep her interaction with her overbearing editor as short as possible.

The ten-yard journey down the hall was just enough to get Toni's heart thudding and her palms sweaty. How could her mom possibly think Toni was capable of being the boss of this place? She'd never been like her ambitious mother. Toni took after her father—laid back, creative, and painfully shy. She hoped her shyness didn't hinder her interactions with the members of Exodus

End. What would she do if she froze up and couldn't say a word to any of them? That would make conducting interviews rather challenging.

Toni took a deep breath and tapped her knuckles quietly on Susan's thick wooden door. Maybe Susan wouldn't hear her knock over the heavy metal music she always blared into her ears via earbuds.

"Come in," Susan called.

Dammit.

Toni eased the door open and peered anxiously inside. "My mom said you wanted to see me before I left."

"I do," Susan said.

Toni pushed her glasses up her nose with the back of her hand.

"Well, are you going to come in or are you going to stand there staring through me?" Susan snapped.

Toni entered the room, deposited her cases, and closed the door.

"Sit." Susan waved to a chair across from her desk.

"I don't think I have time. Julian—"

"Sit!"

Toni perched on the edge of a blue club chair and clenched her fingers into her long skirt. She wasn't sure what it was about this woman that ratcheted her anxiety into the stratosphere. Toni didn't handle disapproval well. She always strived to make everyone happy, and she couldn't figure out how to make Susan happy with her—besides giving up her assignment with Exodus End and allowing Susan to take her place. But Toni refused to back down in this case. She wasn't afraid to go after what she wanted; she just didn't want much. But she did want to make this interactive biography a success, even if it meant telling Susan to go fuck herself. Toni rubbed her lips together. Okay, no, she doubted she'd ever be able to say something so crass to anyone's face, but she'd think it, by God.

Susan slid a legal pad across her desk. "Here are the interview questions I came up with."

Toni read upside down. *Which musician living or dead would you most want to spend a day with?* She blinked hard so she wouldn't roll her eyes. She was pretty sure fans didn't care which musician the members of Exodus End would want to hang out with. She sure didn't. Toni picked up the legal pad, however, and stuffed it into her messenger bag.

"I still don't think you'll be able to handle this job," Susan said.

"I disagr—"

"You'll probably spontaneously combust at the sight of them."

Well, they were incredibly attractive men. All four of them, but—

"And the way you dress?" Susan shook her head. "You won't fit in with a group of rock stars. They're not going to open up to someone like you."

Pressure began to build behind Toni's eyes. "Someone like-?"

"You have absolutely no experience as a reporter. I've interviewed hundreds of musicians over the years. How many have you interviewed?" Susan's voice was beginning to rise, and that scary vein over her left eye bulged.

"Well—"

"Zero! That's how many. You know you wouldn't have gotten this assignment if your *mother* didn't own the company, right? I mean you hardly ever come in to the office . . ."

That was because Toni did most of her work from home so she could take care of Birdie.

". . . and you have no field experience. So what if you can code and do graphic design and write? You can't talk. Journalists have to know how to talk."

She might have talked if Susan had shut her mouth for more than half a second.

"If you can't talk, you can't ask questions. So what good are you?"

Susan actually paused long enough for a response. What good was she? Toni didn't know. She wouldn't know until she tried. But every point Susan made was valid. Toni didn't have any experience interviewing musicians—or anyone famous, for that matter. She wouldn't fit in with the crew on tour with the band or the fans and definitely not four famous rock stars. Toni's chest tightened, and she fought the flood of tears that suddenly burned her eyes. What she needed right now was a pep talk, not to be berated and belittled by a jealous cow.

"Are you seriously going to cry right now?" Susan asked, tilting her head forward so that her silky burgundy hair swung over one sharp blue eye. The silver hoop that pierced the corner of one of Susan's nostrils caught the light and Toni's attention. Susan would fit in better with a rock band. Toni couldn't deny it.

"No." Not at that very minute. Toni could at least hold it together until she found a bathroom before she unleashed a torrent of tears.

"I don't know why I'm so worried that you'll fuck this up." Susan laughed hollowly. "You'll take one look at the tour bus and flee in terror."

Toni lifted her chin, which betrayed her by quivering most annoyingly. "I won't."

"We'll see. You mother already told me that if you fail, I can take back the job I was *hired* to do. I guess I'd better start packing. You'll be home by midnight."

"You only know how to do interviews. You don't know how to do anything else this job requires," Toni said.

"I'll send all the information to you and you can make it pretty and flow together into a book. That's what you're good at."

It was what she was good at. Design. In the past, Toni had been forced to use the information, photographs, illustrations, videos and audio clips that someone else had decided were important for making an amazing interactive book. For this project, she was in charge of collecting everything necessary to capture the men behind the rock stars. And she was determined to wow everyone with this biography. Even Susan. And maybe her mom would realize that Toni was most valuable as a creative asset to Nichols Publishing, not as the head of it. Toni had to get this book right the first time. Mom wasn't big on second chances.

"Call me on Monday to check in," Susan said dismissively. "Unless you're already back in town. Then let me know so I can meet up with the band at their next tour stop."

"I'm not going to fail," Toni said. She lifted her chin another notch. "I can do this."

Susan rolled her eyes and turned toward her computer, dismissing Toni without a word.

Toni scooped herself out of the chair, uncomfortably aware of her trembling knees. If Susan intimidated her this easily, how would Toni ever hold her own with a bunch of cocky rock stars?

She lifted her camera case and slung the strap of her bag over one shoulder. "I'm not going to fail," she said resolutely and rushed out of the office, slamming the door on the corner of her messenger bag, completely negating the finality of her angry exit.

She fled to the bathroom down the hall. Hot tears slipped down her cheeks as she shut herself into the largest of the three stalls. She dropped her case on the floor, then yanked toilet paper from the roll and dabbed at her eyes beneath her glasses. Why was Susan so mean to her? Toni was nice to everyone, whether they deserved her kindness or not. She didn't understand how anyone could say such cruel things to someone else. It was almost as if Susan wanted to rattle her. Wanted her to fail. No one could really be that much of a selfish jerk, could they?

Toni dropped the tear-soggy toilet paper into the bowl and yanked another length off the roll.

"Are you in here, Toni?" a familiar, *masculine* voice called into the bathroom.

"You can't come in here, Julian," Toni called to him. She blew her nose before reaching for more toilet paper.

"Did Susan make you cry again?"

"N-no."

She heard the door close and took a deep, shaky breath, glad Julian had left. She wasn't quite ready to face him yet. Her tears had stopped, but her nose was still running like a leaky faucet. He'd recognize that she was lying as soon as he saw her.

"Toni, she's a horrible jealous bitch," Julian said through the crack in the stall door. "Don't let her hurt your feelings."

"Julian! This is a women's restroom."

"Trust me, honey, there isn't a thing in here that interests me," he said.

She could picture the disgusted sneer on his pretty boy face.

"Except making you smile. Now come on out of there."

"In a minute." She blew her nose again and rubbed her face with the palm of her hand.

"What did she say to you this time?" Julian asked.

"That I'm g-going to f-fail." Toni dashed away a stray tear. God, why did she have to be so soft-hearted? It was a freaking nuisance.

"You aren't going to fail," Julian said. "You're going to kick ass. I guarantee it."

"What if the band members won't talk to me?"

Julian released a soft laugh. "They'll talk. They won't be able to help themselves. Someone has to fill in your long bouts of absolute silence."

She didn't talk much. Especially to strangers. Her stomach

lurched. Everyone around her on this tour would be strangers. *Everyone.*

"I'm terrified," Toni admitted, mostly to herself. But Julian heard her.

"Of course you are. Who wouldn't be? But you're going to get past your fear and you're going to get out there and make a fantastic, exciting life for yourself, because the one your mother made for you just doesn't suit you."

At least someone besides her recognized that.

Toni grinned, feeling loads better, and opened the stall door.

"There's that smile," Julian said, hugging her. "Now hurry the hell up. You have a tour bus to catch and four rock stars to befuddle with your sugary sweetness."

In the company car, Toni snatched the cigarette out of Julian's well-manicured hand and took a deep drag. Lungs burning and eyes watering, she choked before producing a hacking fit that would put a tuberculosis patient to shame. There was a reason she didn't smoke. Well, several actually. But an aversion to choking to death was at the top of her list.

Julian took his eyes off the freeway long enough to give her his what-the-fuck-is-your-problem look before retrieving his cigarette and settling it between his thin lips. "You don't need nicotine, honey," he said around the filter. "What you need is Valium. Or Xanax. Actually, both would do you some good."

"Are you suggesting I need to be drugged?" she asked, giving her mother's personal assistant the evil eye.

Julian was the closest thing she had to a non-blood-related friend. Occasionally he made her leave the house and go out on the town. Unfortunately, they always ended up in gay bars, which was entertaining enough but didn't do much for her romantic prospects. But they weren't crawling through stadium-event traffic to embark on a social adventure. Toni was about to get on the tour bus of the most well-known metal band in the world—hell, even *she* had heard of Exodus End and she mostly listened to classic rock. She'd gone from uncertain to nervous wreck the moment she'd fastened her seat belt. Just thinking about touring with the band made her stomach do summersaults, backflips, and cartwheels. She had an Olympic-level gymnastics meet going inside her.

"Did you remember to shave your legs?" Julian asked. He took a nonchalant drag off his cigarette before holding it between two fingers against the steering wheel. They were inching along the interstate at a snail's pace. She probably could have gotten there faster if she'd walked.

Toni scowled, thinking that was the oddest thing Julian had ever asked her and the man had no filter. "Why does it matter? Did you cut off all my skirts so they barely cover my ass?" Turning her conservative clothing into ho-garb was something he would do.

Julian laughed. "Damn, why didn't I think of that?"

As they neared the Mercer Street exit, Julian switched on his blinker to merge. Space Needle, Science Center, Key Arena Toni read on the directional signs. She was one step closer to her destination. She pursed her lips together to keep her dinner down.

"So did you shave them or not?" he asked.

"Not that it's any of your business, but yes, they're silky smooth. Why?"

"So you *are* expecting to get laid tonight," he said, wiggling his eyebrows suggestively. "I thought your frumpy sweater was a little tighter than usual. Showing off the goods for a change?"

Toni's mouth dropped open in indignation, and she slapped Julian on the head. He had so much product in his black hair that she was sure he didn't feel the blow. "I am not showing off the goods." She crossed her arms over her chest and scowled. "And I have absolutely no expectations in the getting laid department. I just don't like my legs all itchy and hairy in my pajamas."

"You didn't seriously pack pajamas to wear while on tour with a rock band, did you?"

"What else am I supposed to sleep in?"

"Nothing. The wet spot. A puddle of your own vomit. Anything would be preferable to pajamas."

She crinkled her nose at his suggestions. "You're disgusting."

He pulled around the back of the arena, where barricades were set up to keep the public from the tour buses parked near the back entrance. Which reminded her . . . Toni searched through her messenger bag for the packet the band's manager had sent. It included a press pass that would get her past security. Pulling to a halt in a no-stopping zone, Julian shifted into park and turned toward her.

"Disgusting? You know you love me." He blinked at her with sleepy blue eyes surrounded by thick dark lashes.

"Except when I hate you. Which is most of the time." She reached for the door handle, but Julian caught her other arm.

"This is the part where I'm supposed to tell you to be a good girl and to carefully guard your heart, body, and soul from evil rock stars. It's also where I should advise you to stay away from excessive alcohol, drugs, sex, and backstage after-parties."

"But you're not going to . . ."

"Hell no. You need to live it up. Your mother has you so isolated from the outside world, I fear you'll never escape."

"For your information, my mother doesn't isolate me. I isolate myself."

"I'm still surprised she let you take this assignment. It's not like you'll be living in the company of the Vienna Boys' Choir for the next month. I'm sure my life is tame when compared to the exploits of a bunch of rock stars, and she's always giving me that stare of disapproval."

Toni knew that stare all too well. "You know what Mom said when I asked for the assignment? *I suppose it is time you get a life,*" she said, mimicking her mother's typical bored-sounding drawl. But Toni *did* have a life. Being twenty-five and still living at home didn't bother her nearly as much as it bothered everyone else.

"Your mom is right. You do need to get a life."

Toni scowled. Why did everyone assume that because she wasn't some wild party animal or some socialite debutante that she wasn't happy? "I happen to love my life. Birdie means everything to me."

Someone honked behind them. Toni opened the door, but Julian grabbed her arm again to keep her from fleeing.

"Whether you realize it or not, you need more than your little sister to make your life complete. And if you come back from this trip still a virgin, I'm going to do something about it."

She blinked at him. "*You're* going to do something about it? You? The man who fears vaginas?"

"Hey, I'd probably do a better job of it than the last idiot who failed you, but no, I've no plans to contaminate my junk with girl juice."

Toni covered her eyes with one hand as if it would shield her from Julian's crazy schemes.

"If you're still a virgin next time I see you, I will promptly kidnap you, haul your ass to Vegas in the trunk of my car, and buy you a bona fide man-whore to remove your V-chip."

She jerked her hand off her flaming face a gaped at him. "You wouldn't!"

He snorted. "You know I would. And when he's finished with you, he can do me."

Toni shook her head at his ornery grin. "You scare me sometimes."

"I scare me too. But I always have a good time. I refuse to let life pass me by. Now give me a smooch. I think the guy behind me is about to ram the car." Julian presented his cheek, and Toni supplied it with a begrudged peck. "Have fun. I'll call you in a few days to get all the juicy details."

"I wouldn't give you any juicy details even if I had them." She supposed. Heck, she didn't know. It wasn't like she had many juicy details to share. And in those rare incidences that she did, Julian was always the instigator and the star witness.

"We'll see. Text me as soon as you lose your virginity. So, like tonight." He winked at her and shoved her toward the passenger door. "Now go."

So she went with her knees knocking together like a pair of billiard balls. Even with her press pass, it took a bit of convincing to get through security. Apparently no one took one look at her and thought, *Wow, this woman has her shit together. She obviously belongs here.*

By some miracle, she reached her destination without being kicked to the curb.

As Toni stepped onto Exodus End's tour bus, her stomach took residence in her calf-hugging boots. The churning sensation of guilt and worry that had plagued her from the moment she'd left Birdie in the care of her domestically-challenged mother had moved past the lurching flips of her car ride with Julian to what must have been her liver using her stomach as a trampoline as she'd worked her way through security, and now that she'd finally located her home for the next month, the overwrought organ had decided to embark on a skydiving adventure. If this kept up, she was going to need an appointment with a gastroenterologist.

Deep breath, Toni. Susan is wrong. You can do this.

She clutched the strap of her messenger bag and tried to swallow her queasiness. Could she pull this off? Could she spend the next four weeks with one of the most famous rock bands on the planet, or was it possible for a person to die from sheer intimidation? The wall of muscle and mean that suddenly appeared in her path did nothing to put her at ease.

"No fans on the bus," the big guy said, taking her firmly by one arm and spinning her back toward the open bus door she'd just entered.

"I'm not a fan," she blurted, which wasn't exactly true. She enjoyed Exodus End's music and had gained an even greater appreciation for it when she did her background research for this job. She scrambled to grab the press pass on the lanyard around her neck and thrust it in his general direction. It had gotten her through the barricades; surely it would work now. "I'm Toni Nichols. Samuel Baily said to meet up with the bus tonight and join the tour. I was told you'd be expecting me."

She'd made it here, she was living her dream; yet the stars she reached for had never seemed so distant.

The security guard released her arm to take her press pass and scrutinize it. Toni forced herself to meet the suspicious gaze of the giant in a neon-yellow T-shirt as he assessed her press pass and then her. Her press pass again. Her once more. His brown mustache twitched, but the scowl never left his fleshy face. She wondered if fans pretended to be members of the press to get on the bus. This guy obviously wasn't buying her story, even though she was telling the truth. She'd never have been able to muster the courage to actually lie and sneak her way onto a tour bus. Who did that?

"Sam sent you?" he said gruffly. "He didn't clear this with me. He knows he's supposed to clear everything with me. Everything." Big-and-Beefy pulled a cellphone out of his pocket. "Don't move an inch," he demanded as he dialed.

Well, that would be absolutely no problem. It wasn't as if she could walk on the limp noodles that had replaced her legs.

The man turned away, and she stared at the word *SECURITY* printed across the back of his T-shirt while he checked out her credentials with Mr. Baily. Toni figured she should probably be taking in her surroundings and forming first impressions of Exodus End's lavish tour bus, but she feared if she so much as glanced at anything belonging to the band, laser beams would shoot from the security guy's eye sockets and roast her alive.

"Do the guys know she's coming? I don't think they're going to like this much." He paused. "Yeah, *she*. Toni's a chick."

Toni stiffened. The band's manager, Mr. Baily, had assured her mother's publishing house that everything would go smoothly. She'd been told that the guys were excited to be a part of the interactive biography that Mr. Baily had sold to her mom's company for a seven-figure advance. Though Nichols Publishing had a lot of money tied up in this venture, Toni wouldn't be getting rich off book sales. She was just the contract-for-hire writer who also happened to be the photographer, videographer, and programmer for the project. Those in charge were supposed to have cleared everything with the band ahead of time. So what was going on?

A walkie-talkie on the security guard's belt screeched. "Butch, the guys are headed your way," said a voice from the device.

Toni pressed her lips together to stifle a grin. His name was *Butch*? Fitting. A little too fitting.

Butch said goodbye to Mr. Baily and hung up. "Go sit on the sofa until I figure out what to do with you," he said to Toni before reaching for his walkie-talkie.

He didn't *need* to figure out what to do with her. She knew how to do her job. She was supposed to interview the band members. Take note of how they lived while on the road. Get some candid shots of them in their everyday environment. Catch them being themselves in photos, video clips, and audio clips. Then, once she had all the pieces, combine those varied elements into a one-of-a-kind interactive electronic biography. That was what she was *supposed* to do—hang out with the band for a month and become an insider. The hard part would be fitting in with them. She was no rock star. Not by any stretch of her overactive imagination. "Excuse me, but I—"

Butch waved her toward the comfortable-looking leather sofa situated along one side of the bus and spoke into his walkie-talkie. "Send them out." He stomped off the bus, leaving Toni standing there feeling like she'd walked into an episode of *The Twilight Zone* just as the big plot twist was about to reveal itself. The bus was really a spaceship and the band members were actually flesh-eating aliens who'd set her up so they'd have something tasty to snack on while they journeyed to their next destination. *And you thought you were following your dreams, you fool!* It was pretty obvious that Butch didn't appreciate her unexpected appearance. She doubted the band would be any more amicable about her interruption to their lives. Unless they really were flesh-eating space aliens.

Butch's disdain wasn't going to stop her, however. This assignment was important to her. It was the opportunity of a lifetime. She was here to work and to prove her naysayer of an editor wrong. Toni wasn't waiting to start until after Butch decided what to do with her. She was starting now.

Resolve strengthened, Toni headed off the bus to stand next to Butch and observe the members of the band as they made their way from the back door of the stadium to the tour bus.

Butch started when he noticed her standing next to him. She straightened her shoulders and pushed her glasses up her nose. She wasn't going to let some big dude intimidate her. She'd be plenty intimidated when she met the four famous rock stars who were headed in her direction. Make that five rock stars. She'd completely forgotten they'd hired a new rhythm guitarist, Reagan Elliot, to tour with them for the year. A group of yellow-T-shirt-bedecked escorts walked several steps behind the four tattooed hunks and the exuberant woman in their midst.

"This is so much fun," Reagan shouted, hugging the nearest member of her band, who happened to be lead guitarist Dare Mills. Or maybe her choice of huggee hadn't been accidental. The man was exquisite. What woman wouldn't want to hug him? Or more? Toni's face flamed as ideas about what *more* might entail flitted through her thoughts. Not that she'd actually ever experienced *more*. But she knew what it involved. Somewhat.

Dare squeezed Reagan and added an affectionate kiss to the top of her head. "You did great tonight," he said. "The fans already adore you. Aren't you glad you loosened up a little?"

"I've been loose my entire life," she said, which garnered a round of sniggering from her new bandmates. Reagan paused midstride and beamed at the black and red tour bus parked just behind Exodus End's silver and blue bus. "Sinners haven't left yet. I'm riding with them tonight!" She hugged each member of her band, grabbed one hunk of a security guard by the front of his T-shirt, and raced toward the other bus with the chuckling man in tow.

"Your brother is one lucky guy," Steve Aimes, the band's drummer, said, watching Reagan bound up the bus steps of the band that was co-headlining with them on the tour.

"So is her bodyguard," Dare said with a grin.

Toni perked up. She knew Dare's brother was the rhythm guitarist for Sinners, but she hadn't heard that Trey Mills was involved with Reagan Elliot. And what was this about her bodyguard? Was Reagan involved with two men? At the same time? Because who in their right mind would cheat on a man as luscious as Trey Mills? Toni bit her lip, reminding herself that she wasn't here to dig up scandals—and what a scandal *that* would be—but to create a book that made readers feel that they knew the real men behind Exodus End's rock star personas. And she was pretty sure these guys were used to behaving a certain way for the cameras. Surely it would take a while for them to trust her enough to be themselves in front of her. That was fine by her. It wouldn't exactly be a tragedy if she had to spend extra time getting to know them.

Lead singer Maximillian Richardson paused just outside the bus. He had dark brown hair cut in a trendy style, with messy locks on top that begged to be clutched as he used his strong lips on parts below a woman's neck. Max's striking hazel eyes made Toni's toes curl as he looked her up and down. He shifted his gaze to Butch and lifted his eyebrows at him.

"I thought we said to keep the bus empty tonight. We have to head out immediately."

"She's the one writing a book about the band," Butch said. "Sam said he told you about it months ago."

"Book? What fucking book?" Max's face fell and then his eyes widened with apparent remembrance. "Shit," he said, raking a hand through his hair and messing it even more. "I forgot all about it."

"What's going on?" Dare asked.

All four of the men were staring at Toni as if *she* were the flesh-eating space alien. She pasted a hopefully friendly smile on her face and pushed her glasses up her nose before thrusting her hand toward Dare for an introductory shake. Not that she wasn't already shaking. She totally was.

"I'm Toni Nichols. The publisher hired me to write the book."

And perhaps there was a little nepotism at work in the arrangement, but so what.

Dare didn't seem to notice her hand. He was too busy glaring at Max. After an awkward moment, she dropped her hand and clutched the strap of her messenger bag. What would she do if they refused to let her on the bus? Or if they wouldn't answer her blasted editor's carefully prepared interview questions? Or if she got so turned on that she started shedding her clothes in an attempt to seduce one of them? Or all of them . . . She stuck one finger under her turtleneck collar and tugged. Was it hot out here or was it just them? Goodness. What was up with her hormones tonight?

Damn Julian for putting those kinds of thoughts in her head.

"How come this is the first I've heard of this?" Steve asked. His long brown hair—stopping just below his collarbones—hung damp against his bare skin. Toni was uncomfortably aware of the drummer's lack of shirt and his display of abs. Dear lord, the man had a freaking eight-pack. He was close enough that Toni could smell the clean soap scent of a recent shower on him. She was suddenly picturing him in the shower, water cascading over his long lean body. Naked and wet. And . . . and . . . naked. She gave herself a mental shake. She had not expected to react to them this way. Yes, she'd known they were all attractive, but she wasn't the type of woman who lusted after men. Much. Well, maybe she lusted after them, but they never lusted after her in return.

"Shit, guys," Max said. "I have a lot on my mind. Just recovered from my surgery. Had to judge the guitarist contest to find my temporary replacement. Prepare for the new tour."

"Get a manicure," bassist Logan Schmidt added.

"And your hair highlighted," Steve said, fluttering his eyelashes.

Max ignored their taunting. "It's no wonder I forgot about it." He released a frustrated sigh and tilted his head back to stare at the dark sky. "Well, the contract's been signed. We'll have to make the best of this."

"We also have a pact that says no women ride on the bus between shows," Dare said.

"Yeah, all the riding must take place while the bus is stationary," Steve said, making thrusting motions with his slim hips.

Toni scowled with confusion. Riding while stationary was an oxymoron. Her eyes widened when she suddenly realized what he meant by riding. Not that any of them would want to ride her, but uh, yeah, she understood his sexual connotation. And only several seconds late.

Toni looked from one man to the next. She supposed she could offer to follow the bus in a rental car, but how would she really get that insider's point of view if she didn't spend time with them in their element?

"Reagan is a woman," Max pointed out.

"That's different. She's part of the band."

"You can pretend I'm a guy," Toni interrupted.

Five sets of eyes landed on her overly ample breasts. She

crossed her arms over her chest. So maybe she wouldn't pass for a guy, but she knew they wouldn't have any problem treating her like one once they were around her for a few minutes. Men tended to see her as friend material. Only as friend material.

"How long are you staying?" Logan, the golden-haired bassist, asked. Curls framed his handsome face as he tilted his head to look at her. His blue eyes trained mostly on her chest, but occasionally flicked upward to meet her nervous stare. He extended a hand in her direction. "I'm Logan."

"So glad to meet you," she gushed.

She grabbed his hand and shook it vigorously, grateful for his goodwill. When she continued to pump his hand up and down long after was customary, he laughed. "I need that arm to play. Don't dislocate my shoulder now."

Her eyes widened and her cheeks went hot. She dropped his hand and immediately started to rub his arm to undo any damage. Wow, he had nice arms. So hard and smooth and warm. "I-I'm sorry. I'm just really really happy to be here, and I'm so incredibly excited to meet you all. I promise to do a great job. A really great job. The best job ever. You can count on me."

Logan smiled at her as if she were the village idiot. Not that she blamed him. She was babbling like the village idiot.

A sudden commotion near the wall behind the stadium drew Toni's overly divided attention. The buses were parked in a walled alcove, and a barrier had been erected to keep the crowd from harassing the band after the show. As Toni's unexpected intrusion had kept the group outside longer than usual, they'd been spotted by fans leaving the concert.

"Get on the bus, guys," Butch said. "You can figure out what to do with her inside."

"I'll have no problem figuring out what to do with her," Logan said, his lips curving into a suggestive smile. "No problem at all."

Toni stiffened. Was that a come-on? Surely she was imagining things. She glanced at the other members of the band, but no one else seemed to have heard his offhand comment.

"The fans have seen us," Max said.

Dare grinned. "Can't be helped."

All four of them made a beeline for the crowd, their entire security team scrambling after them in a panic. Toni reached into her bag for her small camera and her audio recorder. Most of her gear was in the giant camera case that had been placed under the bus by the helpful security guard who had shown her to the bus, but she didn't have time to grab superior equipment. She switched on the recorder and pinned it to the turtleneck collar of her burnt-orange sweater. She spoke into the microphone as she hurried after the group: "I think they want to interact with their fans. Security doesn't look too pleased with their decision to approach the crowd."

Toni snapped a picture of Steve signing the back of a pretty fan's Drummers Bang Harder T-shirt. The young woman shuddered as he slowly tugged the silver marker tip over the soft cotton. Mr. Abs grinned mischievously as the hand he used to hold the young woman's shoulder stationary inched down her chest. Toni's eyes bulged when his questing fingertips finally reached their target and finding no resistance to his fondling, he cupped the woman's breast, brushing its tip with his thumb. Oh my God. Did he even know this woman? Maybe he did. She didn't smack him. Instead she covered his hand with hers and encouraged him to squeeze her boob while he eased in closer behind her and whispered into her ear. Toni wondered if she should include something like that in the book. She smiled as she imagined the caption beneath such a picture: *Steve Aimes cops a feel while serving his fans*. Or perhaps: *Steve aims to bang more fans than drums*.

The tremulous quality of an unfamiliar voice caught Toni's attention. She tracked the sound to the teary-eyed man standing near Dare Mills and made sure her audio recorder was catching the balding man's conversation to the standoffish lead guitarist. Toni could almost see the invisible bubble Dare had erected around himself. Unlike the swarming fans of the rest of the band members, Dare's admirers kept a respectful distance and had formed a neat line while waiting for the chance to meet him. The only exception was the fan standing to his left, who wasn't in Dare's personal space, but was obviously out of line. Toni couldn't tell if it bothered Dare. She couldn't even tell if Dare was listening to the guy as he signed a CD insert and offered a smile to the giddy fanboy at the front of his line.

"High school," the emotional fan beside Dare was saying. "High school was a nightmare. No one understood my pain. My rage. Except you guys. I must have listened to "Rebel in You" a million times. That song saved my sanity. Probably saved my life."

"Rebel in You" had been Exodus End's first hit. Toni tried to recall the lyrics, but could only remember lots of screaming and angry drumming and wailing guitars. Could one song really mean that much to a person?

"My first job was hell," the guy continued. "Do you have any idea how much shit a yard of cattle produces? I never would have made it through the summer without "Bite" blaring through my headphones."

Each tragedy of the man's life—his breakup with the love of his life, the loss of his mother, the accident that resulted in him being unable to find work—was made tolerable, in his mind, by an Exodus End song. The lead guitarist didn't comment throughout the fan's entire long-winded story, though he did nod occasionally as he simultaneously signed autographs and paused for pictures with others.

Jeez, Dare. The guy is pouring his guts out to you. Are you even listening to a word he's saying? She supposed it was his rock star ego that made the guitarist feel superior to the little people who'd paid for his mansion. Was he really an unfeeling ass? Maybe he *would* have gotten along better with Susan.

"I've been without work for a while," the fan said. "I'm trying to find a decent job, but nothing ever seems to pan out for me. I was so bummed that I couldn't afford to see you guys play live this year, but my bros got me a ticket for the show. It made my year to get to be here tonight. You have no idea how much it means to me to stand here talking to you. I just wish I wasn't such a fuck-up."

Dare's grass green gaze lifted to meet Toni's, and her heart skipped a beat. She hadn't been sure if Dare realized she was recording his apparent disinterest, but with one look, she knew she'd judged him unfairly. He was aware of everything going on around him and in perfect control of his surroundings. It was as if the universe was a slave to his whimsy. He turned to the disheartened fan to his left and grabbed the guy's hand in a tight fist. Dare yanked him forward until their shoulders knocked together.

"Don't let life get you down, man," Dare said as he used his free hand to pat the man's wide back. "Everything will work out. You have to believe in yourself even when no one else sees your true worth."

Surprised by how much she needed to hear those exact words, Toni felt that Dare were talking to her. Why couldn't her editor— or her mother—ever say something like that to her?

The fan beamed, tears in his dark eyes. He pulled a cellphone out of his pocket. "Can I get a picture with you? My friends are going to kick themselves for going directly to the hotel. They'll never believe this shit without photographic evidence."

Dare wrapped an arm around his new buddy and smiled, making a pair of devil horns with one hand while the guy held his phone in front of them and snapped a picture. Dare patted the man on the back before turning his attention to a gushing fangirl.

"Oh God, you're so gorgeous, I'm about to wet myself."

"If I was really that gorgeous, you'd already be wet," Dare said.

Toni snorted in a most unladylike fashion. She had no problem picking up on the meaning of that jest, seeing as Dare's quiet control and amazing green eyes made her wet in uncomfortable places. Toni pulled out a release form and handed it to the long-winded fan. When she explained that he might be included in an interactive e-book about the band, he was very accommodating.

"And I might be in the book? With Dare Mills?" he asked, nodding eagerly.

"No guarantees," she said, "but yes. We can depict you as an anonymous fan or include your name. Just indicate your preference there on the form."

"That is so cool! Definitely use my name. I need this book. When will it be out?"

"Next year." Assuming she didn't mess this up. She glanced at Dare, who was back to pretending detachment, and remembered his words of encouragement. They hadn't been directed at her, but she could pretend they had been. She had to believe in her abilities even when no one else did.

While she waited for Long-Winded—the guy was *still* talking—to fill out his personal information, Toni searched the crowd for her next point of interest. She didn't see the golden-haired bassist, Logan, anywhere, but the band's vocalist was readily identifiable. Toni tucked the completed release form into her bag and started toward Max, who was surrounded by at least twenty fans—all women, all trying to get a hand—or two—on him.

"If they knew what he was really like, they wouldn't chase him like that," someone said in her ear.

Toni turned to find herself staring into Logan's stunning blue eyes.

"I find that hard to believe," she said.

Logan grinned and shrugged. "Believe what you want. He's a complete control freak."

"And that's a bad thing?" She was a bit of a control freak as well. Toni liked things orderly and neat, but Birdie could scarcely function without a smooth routine. Toni fleetingly wondered how her mother was coping with Birdie on her own.

"It is if it gets in the way of my good time."

Logan's smile made her toes curl inside her boots. Why was he looking at her like that? Was he trying to set her panties on fire? If they hadn't already been damp, she was sure they would have ignited by now.

"Logan!" some woman yelled from the crowd. "Logan! Logan! Over here."

"Excuse me, sweetheart," he said and turned just in time to catch the pink-haired woman who launched herself into his arms.

"Why haven't you called me?" she asked, kissing him. Or trying to.

Logan jerked his head to the side so that her mouth landed on his jaw. "Uh . . ."

"He lost your number," Steve said and chuckled.

"You did?" She pouted.

"Yeah, I guess."

"But I programmed it into your phone."

"When was that?" Logan carefully set her on her feet and put several inches between them.

"Last year after MetalFest."

With a wide smile that made his already handsome face even more gorgeous, Logan nodded. "Oh yeah, MetalFest. Victoria?" He lifted both eyebrows hopefully.

She scowled and shook her head.

His eyebrows scrunched together. "Veronica?"

"No. You don't remember me?"

Steve slapped him on the back. "Of course he remembers you. And the six other women he banged that night."

Logan's eyes widened, and he stared directly at Toni. He shook his head, his eyes rolling upward. *I didn't sleep with seven women,* he mouthed, as if the very idea was preposterous. He lifted a hand and splayed his fingers. "Five, tops," he said.

"You bastard!" Victoria-Veronica-whoever screeched. "You had no intention of calling me, did you?"

Steve wrapped his arm around Logan's shoulders and tugged him against his side. Toni snapped a picture, loving the way they were both grinning indulgently. A moment of connection. Brotherhood. She hoped the shot came out clear. It would make a great addition to the book. Damn, she wished she had her Nikon with her.

"Logan always has good intentions," Steve said.

"Thank you," Logan said, and he patted Steve in the center of his bare chest.

"He just never carries through with them," Steve added.

Steve winced and released Logan to rub his ribs where he'd received a sharp elbow for his barb. Logan moved to stand behind Toni and turned her to face Steve, who was already coming after Logan with clenched fists.

"You wouldn't hit a female human shield with glasses, would you?"

"We have to get going, guys!" Butch roared over the crowd. "We'll be off schedule."

"If it were legal, I think the dude would marry that schedule," Logan said as he released Toni and turned toward the bus.

"And have children with it." Steve crinkled his nose in disgust and fell into step with him.

"Even at risk of paper cuts?" Toni asked, scrambling after the pair.

Both men winced and shuddered.

The band members worked at talking their way out of the crowd, signing a few final autographs and saying their goodbyes. Toni was bummed that she hadn't gotten anything on Max. He was the front man, the leader of the group—she assumed. The heart and soul of the band—she assumed. There had to be a reason women swarmed him like ants on a lollipop. Yes, he was gorgeous. Yes, he was tall and built. Yes, his short, trendy hairstyle was trimmed in the perfect style to accentuate his high forehead and angular jaw. And yes, the few golden highlights in his gelled bangs brought out the gold flecks in his soul-stirring hazel eyes, but there must be something deeper to him than his good looks. Maybe it was that gorgeous leather-encased ass of his that made the women go wild. As Toni trailed behind the group on their way back to the bus, she couldn't take her eyes off that nicely rounded hunk of deliciousness. Dear lord, you could bounce a quarter off that thing.

The security guards began to make a human wall between the

fans and the band. And since Toni had been paying more attention to Max's ass than what was going on around her, she found herself on the wrong side of the security team.

"Wait! I'm with the band!"

Butch pursed his lips beneath his thick mustache. He assessed her closely—was he considering whether he could leave her behind? None of the band members noticed or cared that she'd disappeared, so it was Butch's perfect opportunity to ditch her if he wanted. After a long, tense moment, he shrugged and nodded curtly at his men. The crowd yelled in protest when Toni was allowed to follow the band back to the bus while all the other bystanders were corralled to the opposite side of the barrier again.

Two other tour buses, belonging to Sinners, pulled out. Apparently they'd been waiting for the crowd to thin so they could leave. Fans slapped the side of their bus and cheered as it passed. An RV towing a trailer pulled out after the two buses. The words *Aggie's Custom Corsets* were painted in gothic letters across the trailer. Why would Sinners need corsets? Toni could only guess. Maybe if the book on Exodus End was a success, Toni could propose doing one for Sinners. And then maybe she could work with the opening bands, Twisted Element and Riott Actt. She'd originally thought she'd want to switch to an important political figure for her next biography, but this was already too much fun. She couldn't help but dream a little. Okay, a lot. Stars in her eyes over an exciting future following one band after another, she hurried to catch up with Exodus End as they returned to their bus. She needed to do a good job with this first book before she started making plans about additional volumes. She wasn't going to get far if she spent all her time gawking at Steve's abs and drooling over Max's ass and wondering if Logan really had slept with five women in one night. Who did that?

The entire band paused outside the bus door and waited for her to catch up. She wasn't sure if they were being polite—ladies first—or if they always stood outside the door looking lost before they embarked. She stopped next to the group and looked from one man to the next while trying to keep her eyes off Steve's bare chest, abs, and the tattoos that decorated both. At least Max had his distracting ass pointed away from her.

"Do you have luggage?" Logan asked. He placed a hand on the small of her back, and her entire body—from the soles of her feet to the top of her head—flushed with molten heat.

Whoa. What was that? She was much too young to be having hot flashes.

She turned her head and found him staring at her in bewilderment. Did he feel it too? Continual jolts of excitement buzzed through her flesh at the place where his hand touched her body. His eyes, an icy blue with a dark contrasting rim around the irises, held her gaze for an intense moment. Toni's mouth went dry, her palms damp. She couldn't look away. Was he getting closer? Or was she? His breath against her lips made them tingle. Her heart thudded faster. Faster. Blood rushed past her ears with dizzying ferocity. Wait. What was he doing? Was he about to kiss her?

Someone cleared his throat. Followed by someone else. And a third someone.

Toni turned her head to gawk at the other three rock stars. The three who were grinning at Logan and shaking their heads at him.

"I'm sorry. What did you say?" Toni asked. She pressed her fingertips to her face; her skin was on fire. Perhaps she'd contracted malaria, had a fever of 104, and was delirious. A hottie like Logan Schmidt kiss *her*? Yeah, right. No one kissed her unless they were losing at spin the bottle.

"Logan asked if you had any luggage," Steve said.

"I did?" Logan asked.

His three bandmates laughed.

"I think so," Toni said.

"Where is it? We need to get going," Butch said.

"Uh." *Luggage? What's luggage?* Why wouldn't her brain work? She really wasn't an idiot. Usually. Yet she felt as if she'd checked her brain at the bus door. Oh yes, those suitcasey-type things. Her luggage. "Some guy put it under the bus when I arrived."

"You won't have access to it until morning," Logan said. "If you need something to sleep in . . ." His eyes drifted over her frumpy turtleneck sweater, long corduroy skirt, and brown riding boots. He actually made her feel sexy, when she knew she was anything but. "Unless you sleep naked."

"No!" she blurted. Was it possible to die of embarrassment? She hadn't died of intimidation yet, but the combination of the two emotions just might do her in. "I have pajamas in my gym bag. It's under the bus."

Laughing, probably about her wearing pajamas, the guys

headed up the bus steps in single file. Except Logan. He lifted a hand and touched her cheek with his fingertips. His thumb brushed her trembling lips. "A sweet lamb left to fend for herself in a den of wolves. Whatever will we do with you?"

"What do you mean?"

"I'll see you inside."

Minutes after he turned and climbed the bus steps, leaving Toni standing there with her heart thudding and her mouth agape, she could still feel the touch of his fingertips on her lips.

CHAPTER 2

LOGAN GRINNED as he settled on the sofa next to Dare. "Three hours," he said.

Dare chuckled. "Three days," he countered.

"Never," Steve said.

"Never?" Logan said. "Why would you say that?"

"She's a good girl. She won't fall into bed with you in three hours." Steve raked his fingers through his long damp hair and used a band to tie it back.

"How do you know she's a good girl?"

"If she wasn't, she'd have already fallen into bed with me," Dare said and offered a teasing wink.

"Doesn't matter. Good girls are easy," Logan said.

"Logan, don't fuck with her," Max said. "This is business, not for your twisted sense of pleasure."

"I can mix business with pleasure." Logan peered toward the open bus door. Shouldn't Toni be climbing the steps now? He hoped he hadn't scared her away. He found her incredibly attractive. He had a thing for women who understated their beauty, and Toni took understatement to a whole new level. And her rack? God, he could get lost between her enormous tits for hours. He hoped she wasn't wearing a padded bra under that turtleneck sweater. He planned to find out really soon.

Dare thumped Logan on the side of the head. "You're so full of shit."

"Why do you say that?"

"You're talking smack. You like her."

"I don't even know her. How could I like her?"

"Are you talking about me?" a soft, feminine voice said from the top of the bus steps.

Busted.

Logan turned his head and smiled at her. "Of course not."

"Oh," she said, her face falling.

"I already know I like you," he said.

Her hand moved to her mouth. She touched her lips with two fingers, and a pretty blush spread across her face. Sweet, shy, and female, a combination Logan could never resist. Especially the female part. Her fantastic tits were just a bonus.

"Have a seat, Toni," Dare offered. He stood and took a gym bag from her hand. He set it on the floor next to the spot he'd vacated, making it clear that Toni should sit next to Logan on the sofa. Logan loved the guy. Such a thoughtful son of a bitch. Toni's dark eyes, hidden behind a pair of thick-rimmed glasses, scanned the interior of the bus as if searching for refuge. Apparently the seat next to Logan was not it. Dare plopped himself down in the only available recliner and extended the leg rest, as if he had no intention of moving for the night.

"Th-thanks," Toni said, pushing her glasses up her nose with one trembling hand.

Logan wasn't sure what she was so nervous about all of a sudden. She'd seemed perfectly at ease when they'd been interacting with their fans. Perhaps she'd taken his comment about a lamb in a den of wolves to heart. He'd only been teasing, but he found her skittishness endearing in a world where most women threw all inhibitions to the wind when in the presence of any member of his band, much less all four of them.

The bus rumbled as it rolled forward. They were on the road again. Toni's hands flew out as the unexpected movement threw her off balance.

She plopped down beside Logan, perching on the edge of a cushion as if the sofa's back was made of shards of glass. Logan was pretty sure she was looking for the emergency exit. Her gaze settled on Butch, who was standing next to their driver and running over a strict schedule detailing how to get them to their next show in time while making a promotional stop between venues. Their schedule never had an inch of give. Their manager, Sam, was a genius when it came to getting the band the most exposure, but he had the tendency to believe that because they were a metal band, they were made of iron. They didn't require useless things like down time and rest.

"So tell us more about this book," Dare said, which was apparently the exact right thing to say to Toni, because her unease evaporated instantly.

"Have you seen the new interactive electronic textbooks?" she asked, her eager gaze moving from Dare to Max to Steve.

Logan was very conscious of the fact that she didn't look at him once. He'd thought their attraction was mutual, but maybe not. He scooted several inches closer to her because he saw something he wanted and wasn't one to sacrifice his personal needs for the greater good.

"Textbooks?" Steve asked. "Like for school and shit?"

"Yeah, that's usually where textbooks are used," she said, a teasing grin on her lush lips. When no one laughed, her face fell. Logan forced a guffaw about five seconds too late. That got his bandmates laughing. Not at Toni's understated joke. They were laughing at his blatant stupidity. Nothing new there.

"I can't say I've even seen a textbook since high school," Steve said.

"These new interactive ones are amazing. Each topic has videos and pictures and links. It presents the information in a way that gets students who are used to constant entertainment excited about learning."

"So you're writing a textbook about us?" Dare asked, brows drawn together in a confused scowl.

"What kind of textbook would that be? A manual on mayhem and debauchery?" Toni cringed when no one laughed at that joke either.

Logan guffawed five seconds too late again. He was going to have to pay really close attention to what she said to figure out when she was joking. He didn't think she lacked a sense of humor, she just looked serious. She'd definitely fit in better at a library than at standup-comedy night.

"The publishing company I work for designs and distributes these interactive textbooks," she said. "Samuel Baily approached us to make an interactive book about the band, the first of its kind. He's very forward thinking."

That got the band laughing. "You might say that," Max said. "Sometimes he's a bit too forward thinking. He's got every minute of our schedules booked for the next eighteen years. He thinks we're robots or something."

Toni's eyes bulged. "Eighteen years?" she muttered under her breath.

Surely she knew Max was joking, so why did she look so unsettled? Wondering if he could make her blush again, Logan scooted a few more inches closer to her. His knee brushed her thigh, and she yanked on her skirt. Other than her hands and face, not an inch of bare flesh was showing. He wasn't sure exactly what she was trying to conceal. Maybe she wasn't open to his attempts to seduce her. Which made her a challenge. Which, like her tits, he couldn't resist. Or maybe she had a nice boyfriend at home. His loss.

"Speaking of robots," Steve said. "How are the prototypes of our androids coming?"

"Good until they tried to replicate my dick and ran out of materials," Logan said.

Toni's sudden intake of breath made him grin. *That* shocked her? Seriously? Too easy.

"If they ran out of materials, it had to be due to Max's giant forehead," Steve said.

"Or your enormous feet," Max countered.

Toni grabbed a pad of paper out of her bag and started writing furiously. Logan leaned against her shoulder to read what had her so excited. She was writing down their conversation. In the margin, she wrote: *Keep video camera close at hand when all band members are together. They're hilarious.*

He was close enough to feel her body heat and inhale the sweet fragrance of her fruity shampoo. He wondered if she tasted as sweet as she smelled.

"For the record," Logan said in her ear as he pointed toward her notes, "I was the one with the big dick."

Toni leaped from the sofa as if it were on fire. Her gaze darted from one guy to the next, and she pushed her glasses up her nose with the back of her wrist. God, he wanted to take those glasses off, take those clothes off, and do things to her. Naughty, devious, delicious things.

"Um . . ."

The twin bumps poking against her shapeless turtleneck drew Logan's attention. Hard nipples? Did his crassness turn her on? That was all the encouragement he needed to behave inappropriately. Visible nipples also meant that her bra was not padded. There was so much win in that, he should have her name engraved on a trophy.

"What's wrong?" Logan asked. "I won't bite. But I will nibble. And suck. And lick."

She stared at him with her mouth agape and her eyes wide. Her nipples strained against her sweater, begging him to do all those things and more to the tips of those luscious melons.

She glanced down at her tits and immediately crossed her arms over her chest. "Is, um, there a bathroom I can use?"

"At the back of the bus," Dare said, nodding his head toward the end of the corridor.

"Don't take a dump in there," Steve said. "We stop at rest areas to do that business."

Face flaming, she sucked in a deep breath, turned, and sprinted to the back of the bus. She fumbled with the closet door and when it popped open, a stack of towels that had shifted during transit tumbled out and pummeled her in the face.

Logan climbed to his feet to rescue her. He decided to take it easy on her for the moment. He wouldn't want to traumatize her so much she decided to leave. They both bent to pick up the same towel at the same time and bumped heads. They jerked apart and rubbed their heads in unison. Toni looked up at him, her brown, doe-like eyes watery with tears. He wasn't sure if they were tears of pain or humiliation, but seeing them in her eyes did strange things to his chest. He wasn't sure why it was suddenly tight.

"It's okay," he said, deciding that though it was fun to tease her, he'd better tone it down a bit. She obviously wasn't used to it, and he didn't want to harass a woman who wasn't receptive to provocative flirting. He hadn't intended to upset her, just wanted to have a little fun and get under that conservative skirt of hers. "I'll get the towels, Toni. You go ahead and do your business." He opened the bathroom door for her.

She lowered her hand from her forehead to reveal a large reddened bump.

Logan winced and leaned forward to press his lips to the lump. She sucked a startled breath into her chest. Shit. There he went crossing the line again.

"Sorry," he murmured. "I always kiss boo-boos."

"I have a pimple on my ass that needs kissing," Steve called.

Logan closed his eyes and shook his head. "One of the things you should consider stressing in your book is how little *fucking privacy* a man has while on tour with his band."

"I can include that," she said, "but I think fans are more interested in the size of your dick." She backed into the bathroom. "I know I am." She bit her lip before closing the door in his face.

CHAPTER 3

TONI KNEW she had about two minutes to compose herself, or the band was going to think she was taking a dump and smelling up the bus. She wouldn't want to break such an important rule right off the bat. Why was she so off her game? Probably because she'd never expected to be hit on by a man so far out of her league. She cringed at her train of thought. What was with the baseball analogies? She didn't even watch sports.

But she couldn't figure out why the band's bassist kept hitting on her. Not only was Logan Schmidt rich and famous, he was ridiculously gorgeous with all that thick golden curly hair and those sexy blue eyes. And those lips. Dear lord, he'd kissed her bare skin. Yes, it had been her forehead, but it had been skin, by God. Logan must be toying with her for the sheer amusement of watching her behave like a gooftacular reject. There was no other explanation. She relieved her bladder and flushed the toilet before gazing at herself in the mirror as she washed her hands in a marble sink. As she expected, she hadn't suddenly spawned supermodel good looks. Her mouth was too wide, dirt-brown eyes too big, dull brown hair too frizzy, glasses too thick, style too lacking for a man like Logan Schmidt to afford her a second glance.

She wasn't going to let him make fun of her, though. She had to earn their respect as a professional. She was here to do a job, not get hard nipples just because some rock god brushed up against her and told her his dick was big. She checked her chest to make sure her high beams were under control, straightened her spine and exited the bathroom. She hadn't expected Logan to still be in the hall shoving towels back into the linen closet. Her hand moved automatically to her forehead—the memory of his lips brushing against her skin had her belly quivering.

"Do you need an icepack?" he asked, his eyes trained on the lump on her head.

"No, thank you. I'll be fine."

"He's got a head like a brick," Steve said. He was standing a few steps away at a small refrigerator with the door wide open. He grabbed a beer and closed the door.

"Tell me about it," she said.

"Would you like a beer?" Steve asked, tilting a brown bottle in her direction.

"Maybe later. Right now, I'm on duty."

"So tell us more about this book," Steve pressed. "What are we supposed to contribute?"

Max and Dare joined the little huddle in the corridor near the bunks. Four rock stars watched her expectantly. Her deodorant was certainly demonstrating its worth tonight. She'd have to remember to apply twice her usual amount for the rest of her assignment.

"Basically, you just need to be yourselves. The book is intended to be a candid look into your lives."

"Smile!" Logan sang. "You're on candid camera."

Toni laughed. "I promise not to play practical jokes on you." She made the mistake of looking at Logan. He completely shattered her concentration. If she shifted her body a few inches, she could discover firsthand what it felt like to be pressed against that hard chest. More than anything, she wanted to bury her hands in the silky-looking loose curls of his hair and taste his lips.

"It's going to be hard to be ourselves knowing someone is watching us twenty-four seven," Max said. His deep voice was like cool satin caressing the back of Toni's neck. His singing voice was phenomenal and his speaking voice was equally remarkable. It might have been the only sound on the planet that could have broken Logan's spell over her.

She forced her gaze to Max. He was scowling reflectively.

"Hopefully, after a few days you'll forget I'm here," she said.

"Doubtful," Logan said.

The bus lurched unexpectedly, and the driver cursed at whoever had cut him off. "Learn how to drive, asshole!"

Toni took a step backward to regain her balance and bumped into Logan, who was still standing directly behind her. He grabbed her hips to steady her, but there was nothing steadying about the man's hands on her hips. Or the progressively hardening cock prodding her in the ass. From the feel of it, his dick really would run those android makers out of materials.

Instead of pulling away, she relaxed against him. He tensed and shifted her hips a fraction of an inch.

"Fuck, woman," he whispered in her ear. "Don't encourage me. I'm having a hard enough time trying to convince myself that you're off limits."

She was starting to think he really was attracted to her and not just toying with her for his personal amusement.

"Do you have a boyfriend?" he asked.

"Huh?" Why would he ask her that?

"A big, mean-as-fuck, jealous guy who will break my neck with his bare hands if he knew I touched you?"

Toni shook her head.

"A raging case of herpes?"

"Of course not!"

"You're not making this any easier on me."

On him? What about her? She was pretty sure the other band members could hear his whispered questions. They'd definitely heard her blurted reply. She gave herself a shake to clear her thoughts and attempted to ignore the man behind her. Slim chance of that happening.

"I'll also need to interview each of you," she said to the rest of the band, who were watching the two of them with expressions ranging from amusement to bewilderment to annoyance.

"Tonight?" Steve asked. "Probably not a good idea. I'm a bit out of it after a show."

"You're always out of it," Logan said.

"Sorry, but I need to crash immediately," Dare said, stifling a yawn with the back of his hand. "It's been an exhausting day and we have another full day tomorrow." He ticked off events on one hand. "Radio interview, sound check, meet and greet, concert, after-party." He ran out of fingers, so he waved his hands as if looking for extra digits. "And I might need to take a piss in there somewhere."

"You don't have time to take a piss, Dare," Logan said.

"Did Sam forget to schedule piss breaks again? Fuck," Steve

grumbled. "Better start saving our beer bottles. Fair warning, Toni. Never drink out of an open bottle around here."

"Eww." She crinkled her nose.

Dare offered Toni a half smile. His piercing green eyes threatened to melt her into a puddle on the floor. This guy's presence . . . *Just wow.*

"Why don't we start the interviews Monday? We'll have a long boring drive that day followed by two nights in a hotel. We should be more ourselves then."

"That's fine with me," Toni said. "I want you to be comfortable. I intend for this book to reflect what wonderful men you are."

Logan chuckled. "I think you have us mistaken for some other band."

She shook her head. "No mistake."

Toni glanced at the bunks on either side of the corridor. There were only four of them. "So I guess I get to sleep on the couch?"

"Butch sleeps on the couch," Logan said.

"The floor?" She curled her nose. No telling what kinds of things were on that floor. It looked clean, but bacteria were microscopic. She was certain there were innumerable germs embedded in that low-pile carpet.

"You'll sleep with me," Logan said. "You have no other choice."

Toni assessed each member of the band. "Actually, I have three other choices."

Steve laughed. "Ouch! I think you've just been rejected, Lo."

"Not necessarily," Toni said. "I just like to keep my options open." As if even one of these guys would consider her an option. *Right, Toni . . . Keep dreaming.*

"There's a sectional sofa in the back lounge," Max said. "Reagan sleeps on it when she's not jumping Trey's bones on Sinners' bus. You're welcome to sleep there."

Logan's hands covered her ears. "Don't tell her that," he said. "I'm making my move here."

Toni laughed. She was used to being the brunt of jokes. She'd learned long ago that the best way to protect her feelings was to join in on the fun.

"Maybe there's room on that sectional for two," she said.

"We'll make room."

Logan spun her around and escorted her to the back of the bus. Next to the bathroom was a set of sliding doors she hadn't noticed earlier. They were black and shiny and if not for the latches and the seam between them, they would have looked like a solid wall. Logan lifted the latches and slid the doors open to reveal a royal-blue semicircular sectional that ran the entire perimeter of the room. Several guitars hung on the wall above it. Toni stepped into the lounge, her gaze locking on a worn Flying V guitar. In her research, she'd read that Dare Mills used an old Flying V to compose the guitar music for Exodus End. She gaped at the instrument, wondering if it was Dare's legendary guitar. How many amazing and famous songs had been created in this small space on that unassuming instrument?

"Is this where—"

The sound of the doors sliding shut behind her made her heart skip a beat. She turned, thinking Logan had left without even telling her good night, but he was standing just inside the closed doors, looking more like a lion than a wolf with that golden hair, but she was definitely feeling like a feast of lamb.

"This is where," he said.

She'd wanted to ask if this was where the band composed music while on tour, but the words caught in her throat. Why was he looking at her like she was a seven-course meal that he was about to devour? All those things he'd said—the innuendos, the come-ons—he'd been teasing her, right? Like the few guys in her past. Getting her hopes up and then reminding her that she was merely friend material.

Logan took two steps forward, and she found herself wrapped in his arms. Before she could grasp how wonderful it felt to be held by a strong man, Logan's mouth claimed hers and she was lost.

This was not her first kiss, but it was the first time a man feasted upon her mouth as if his life depended on it. His fingers delved into her hair to tilt her head just so. His tongue brushed her upper lip, and her bones melted.

In her inexperience, she wasn't sure how to reciprocate, so she merely accepted his kiss, allowing him to coax her mouth open and slide his tongue against hers. She writhed her hips when an unbearable throb stirred between her thighs. Logan murmured encouragement against her lips when her tormented motions stroked the hard ridge in his jeans.

Did he really want her? It sure felt like it.

Her trembling hand sought the hard evidence of his desire where it rested between their bodies. She half expected him to tell her not to touch him. She definitely didn't expect him to deftly release the buttons of his fly and fill her hand with thick, hot cock. His most private, bare flesh pressed against her palm. Oh, it was so hot. And smooth. And hard.

A distracting throb between her legs had her tugging awkwardly at his length. Toni's face flamed. She didn't even know this man and here she stood with his tongue in her mouth and his cock in her hand. A cock she had no idea what to do with. She'd seen some in pictures and watched a few in action in some second-rate online pornography, but had never actually touched one. Not that she hadn't wanted to; the opportunity had never presented itself. It was presenting itself in abundance now.

He shifted slightly, and everything went dark when he lifted her sweater over her head and tossed it aside. His hands skimmed her bare shoulders as his gaze settled on the tops of her breasts spilling from the top of her black demi-bra.

"Even more beautiful than I imagined," he said.

Did he really mean that? She'd never had a man look at her as if she were desirable. Never felt remotely beautiful until that moment.

His fingers touched the center of her back, and her bra came unfastened. He obviously knew what he was doing, and she wanted him to keep doing whatever it was he had in mind. Kissing. Making out. Sex. Yes. She was ready for any and all of it. When would she ever have an opportunity like this again? Probably never.

He slipped her bra down her arms and tossed it aside. His hands moved to cup her breasts, his thumbs rubbing over their hardened nipples.

"I love big tits," he said. "I could suck on yours for hours."

She cringed at his use of the word *tits*, but suck sounded like a good plan. "Yes," she whispered, "suck them."

"Are you just going to hold it all night?" he asked.

Hold it? Hold what? Oh . . . *it!* She tightened her hand around his penis. What was she supposed to do with it? She'd heard that guys liked to be sucked down there. And stroked. But she had no idea how to do either of those things without looking like the virgin she was.

"Tell me what you like," she said.

"What I like?"

"Yeah, I want to please you." Did that sound too needy? She gazed up at him, hoping to look sexy but figuring she probably looked desperate.

"Sucking your big, beautiful tits will please me plenty."

He backed her toward the sofa, removing his T-shirt as he moved. His chest was covered with intricate gray-scale tattoos. The samurai warrior was so lifelike, she almost expected it to slash her with its razor-sharp sword. Before she tumbled back on the sofa, she fleetingly wondered how much it had hurt to have all of that artwork etched into his skin. She stared wide-eyed when her gaze landed on the enormous cock that protruded from his fly. The thickened tip curved upwards slightly. The darker shaft had a maze of blood vessels straining against the surface. She reached for it with a trembling hand.

"God, that's sexy. Are you doing that on purpose?" he asked.

"Doing what?"

"Acting like you've never been fucked before. Like my dick is the first one you've ever touched."

Her cheeks flamed, and she drew her hand away.

"Whatever," he said, "keep it up. It's a serious turn-on."

Her inexperience was a turn-on? Or him thinking that she was *acting* inexperienced was a turn-on? She would have no problem keeping up the ploy since it wasn't a ruse. But his way of thinking gave her the confidence to not pretend that she knew what she was doing. She was relieved that she could show her sexual cluelessness and turn him on at the same time.

She steeled her nerve and sat upright on the low sofa. She gazed at his cock with trepidation. It jerked, and he gasped.

"If you keep staring at it like that, I'm going to come all over your face."

Did penises really do that? Could he ejaculate just because a woman stared at his cock? Or would he need a little more stimulation? She took a steadying breath, leaned forward, and kissed the swollen head. She gasped, shocked by her brazenness, and looked up at him in apology. "S-sorry."

"For what?"

"Touching you without permission."

"Trust me, lamb, you have permission."

He dropped to his knees in front of her and gazed down at her bare breasts. He lifted his hands to cup them, but hesitated with his palms inches from her skin. Her nipples strained toward his hands, and her back arched involuntarily.

"Do I have permission to touch you, Toni?"

"Yes," she whispered. "Please."

His hands found her aching breasts. He lifted one to his mouth and sucked a nipple inside. Toni's damp panties became instantly drenched. Pleasure radiated out from her nipple and coursed through her body to her lower belly. Something inside her tightened. A spasm gripped the swollen flesh between her thighs, and she called out. Whoa! Had she just had an orgasm? She wasn't sure, but she felt delightful.

Logan shifted his mouth to her other breast, and another spasm caught her by surprise. She reached for his head and buried her hands in his glorious curls as she pulled him closer to her breast. He nipped the sensitive flesh, and her entire body jerked. He soothed the oversensitized nipple with a swirling tongue before sucking with a persistent, hard tug. When he pulled away, releasing his suction with a loud smack, she cried out in protest, and then she moaned when he latched on to her other breast.

One hand moved beneath her skirt to touch her knee and she nearly leaped out of her skin. She clamped her legs together, and her eyes flew open.

"Easy," he murmured.

His mouth on her breast distracted her. Her thighs relaxed. Opened slightly. Logan buried his face between her breasts and then trailed lingering, sucking kisses down her belly. Her fingers clenched in his hair. What was he going to do with her? Would he put his mouth down there? At the thought, a wave of successive spasms gripped her saturated flesh. She cried out again.

"You're so sensitive," he murmured to her belly button. "I can't wait to latch on to your clit. I'm going to suck it until you come so hard you scream."

Toni's knees clamped shut again. He was going to do what to her whozit?

"Are you wet? Tell me how wet you are."

Heart thudding out of control, Toni concentrated on the wetness between her legs. She was so wet her juices had soaked through her panties and dampened her thighs. They even dripped down her ass.

"Very wet," she said on a rush of air.

"Show me." His hand slid halfway up the outside of her thigh. "Open your legs and show me. I want to see you cream for me."

He wanted to see her? Between her legs? The thought definitely had her creaming for him and her heart thudding like a jackhammer.

He lifted her foot off the floor and tugged her boot off. He chuckled when he saw her purple- orange-and-green-striped sock. "Cute," he said. He grinned up at her. She was so caught off guard by how attractive he was, she decided this must all be some vivid wet dream.

"I collect socks," she said. She bit her lip, feeling stupid for sharing something so ridiculous. She did have over seven hundred pairs of socks, but he didn't need to know that or the reasons why. Not now when things were so hot between them.

"You'll have to show them to me sometime." He removed her other boot. That sock was red with black and white spots. "Not matching socks, I see." He chuckled, the deep sound making Toni's belly quiver.

"I have only two feet," she said. "I like to wear as much variety as possible. Doesn't make sense to buy socks and not wear them." And her little sister had all her mismatched sock mates, but Birdie was the last thing she wanted to dwell upon at that moment.

"Lucky me. I have a place for a third sock." When he grabbed his engorged cock and stroked it from base to tip, she laughed at the mental image of that glorious appendage swathed in one of her colorful socks.

"Are you laughing at my dick?" He jerked his chin up in challenge.

She shook her head vehemently. "No. I wouldn't. I just . . . I . . . The thought of it wearing a sock . . ." Her eyes stung as tears threatened to fall. He was going to leave her here alone, wasn't he?

"You sure you're into me?"

She rose up from the sofa and wrapped both arms around his neck. How could he possibly think she wasn't into him? She got sexually excited when he merely looked at her, and she was pretty sure she was having spontaneous orgasms whenever he touched her. "I'm sure."

"You keep closing your legs to me," he said.

Just because she was skittish. "I'm sorry. I thought you wanted me to pretend I wasn't experienced." She'd tie her thighs wide open if need be.

"Is that really why?"

She nodded, knowing she was a terrible liar and that if she spoke, she'd probably blurt out that she was a virgin and the closest she'd gotten to having sex was at a college party when the guy had been so drunk that he couldn't get it up. Or maybe it had been like he'd said and he couldn't get it up because she was too fat and ugly to turn him on.

"I'll pretend to be patient then," he said, grabbing her breasts, "when all I really want to do is fuck you hard and fast. I can't remember the last time I was this turned on."

"I'll show you how wet I am for you now," she said, her belly quivering. Was she really going to show him her panties? She sat back on the sofa, pushed her skirt up, and forced her thighs apart. He shifted back and stared down at the scrap of black lace covering her aching flesh.

After a moment, he lifted her gaze to hers. "Well?"

"Well, what?"

"Are you going to show me?"

She looked down at her exposed panties. "You can see them."

He chuckled. "I want to see your sopping wet pussy, not your panties. I have no interest in panties. What I want is the flesh underneath."

She couldn't stop the blood from flooding her face. She had no voluntary control over blushing. She did have control over removing her panties, though. She reached for the elastic at her hips, and before she could chicken out, Logan covered her hands with his and helped her tug the garment off over her butt. He pulled her panties slowly down her thighs and calves before tossing them aside. He placed a hand on either thigh and forced her legs open wide. Turning her head to the side, she closed her eyes and let him look at her. Her stomach churned with nerves.

"That is pretty wet," he said, "but I think I can do better."

Her thighs tightened as they instinctively tried to close again, but he held them open with his shoulders. His fingers brushed against her lips and spread them further. Oh God! He was touching her. There.

"Do you want me to lick your pussy?"

Lick it? With his actual tongue? Of course with his tongue. What else would he lick with?

Toni swallowed hard. "Yes?" she said tenuously.

"That didn't sound very certain," he teased.

"Yes," she said more firmly.

"Say it."

"Say what?"

"Say what you want me to do."

"Lick my . . . Lick my . . ." There was no way she was saying *that* word. " . . . my vagina . . ." She cringed. He chuckled.

"Your pussy?"

"Yes."

"Yes, what?"

She huffed with impatience. This man was corrupting her in a bad way. "My pussy," she said. "Lick my pussy, Logan."

"My pleasure."

When his tongue touched her exposed skin, she nearly leaped off the sofa.

"Hold still, Toni," he whispered. "You don't have to act quite that skittish. I'm plenty turned on already."

She bit her lip. Just the feel of his breath against her flesh made her pussy spasm with delight. His lips and tongue brushed against her . . . her . . . clitoris. Her *clit*. She took a deep breath. *Just a word*, she reminded herself. And a very sensitive body part. Wowza. It had never felt that good when she'd touched it herself. Logan's tongue flicked repeatedly against her clit until she grabbed his hair in tight fists and held him firmly. Something was building inside her. She needed . . .

"Oh!" Her back arched involuntarily, toes curled, breath came in ragged gasps as pleasure consumed her. "Logan?" She realized she was rocking her hips in time with the movement of his tongue, but she couldn't stop. He sucked her sensitized clit into his mouth, and she exploded. And screamed. The rhythmic clenching between her thighs spiraled outward until every inch of her body was alight with pleasure. Tingling euphoria. Bliss.

She came back to her senses slowly and realized she had Logan in a stranglehold with both legs wrapped around his shoulders and his hair tangled in her fists. She'd been humping his face. How mortifying. She released him at once. "Sorry."

He grinned at her and rubbed his scalp with one hand. "I like that you got so carried away."

She flushed. Again. "You do?"

He nodded. "It makes me think you like what I'm doing to you."

"I do like it."

His gaze never left hers as he asked, "Are you ready for

more?"

"There's more?"

"Take off your skirt."

She hesitated. Was she really going to lose her virginity? To a gorgeous rock god with a huge cock? Nice. That drunk stranger in college who'd made her feel like the homeliest woman on the planet could bite her *fat* ass. Logan Schmidt was going to have sex with her, and she was going to love every minute of it.

She assumed.

She unfastened her skirt, tugged it down her legs, and tossed it aside. Feeling ridiculous in nothing but mismatched socks, she removed those too. She was naked. With a man. And not just any man. *This* man. Somehow she'd imagined sex should always occur in a bed beneath the covers in the dark. But apparently on a sofa in the back of a tour bus with all the lights on worked just fine too.

Toni watched Logan remove his jeans and the rest of his clothes. She couldn't stop staring at his body. The man obviously worked out. Long, lean muscles flexed beneath his suntanned skin with each movement. She wanted to explore every inch of him. With her gaze. And her hands. And her mouth. She covered her tingling lips with the back of her hand, glad he couldn't read her sinful thoughts. How would he react if she acted on impulse? What would he do?

Logan tore open a small square package and unrolled a condom over his massive cock. Oh wow, this was really going to happen. He was going to shove himself inside her and get rid of her blasted virginity once and for all. But how on earth would that thing fit inside her? He was huge! Were all penises that enormous? The ones she'd glimpsed on the Internet tended to be, but she was pretty sure they were enlarged with Photoshop. There was no artificial enlargement going on here. She could see it with her own eyes. Logan grabbed the base and tilted his cock up and down. Toni followed its movement like a drunk taking a sobriety test.

"If you keep looking at me like that, I might think you're only interested in my body," Logan said.

Still unable to tear her gaze from his cock, she said, "I'm sure there are a lot of interesting things about you."

He shook his head. "Nope. Not really."

Toni stretched out on the sofa and spread her arms. "Come."

"I'm sure I will, but I plan to take my time getting there."

He settled on top of her, supporting his upper body on his

elbows. She was distinctly aware of his bare belly against hers, the way the hair on his chest teased her nipples, and that his cock was mere inches from where she wanted it.

He stroked her hair from her face and stared down into her eyes. "What do you look like without . . ."

He plucked her glasses from her nose and set them on the floor.

"My glasses! I can't see a thing without my glasses." She patted his face and chest as if searching for her lost glasses.

He laughed. Not five seconds too late, right on time. "Are you nearsighted?"

"That's an understatement."

"Can you see me?"

She could see him perfectly fine at this close distance. Expressive blue eyes. Strong jaw. Straight nose. Smiling lips. "No," she said, becoming quite adept at lying in recent moments. "Closer."

He moved closer. "Can you see me now?"

"Closer."

When he inched closer, she wrapped her arms around his neck and kissed him. "Mmm," he murmured and kissed her in return. He shifted his weight onto one arm so he could run his free hand up her pliant flesh. Everywhere he touched—breast, side, waist, hip—sparks of excitement danced across her skin. Logan shifted sideways, and she felt his thick cock prod her opening. She kissed him more desperately, her eyes squeezed shut, every muscle in her body tense. *It will be over in a minute*, she told herself. *And then you never have to worry about it again. Just let him in. Let him in.*

"You okay?" Logan's words vibrated against her desperate lips. "You're so tense."

She concentrated on relaxing. She wished he'd just do it already. He surged forward. Her flesh resisted and then gave way. He withdrew slightly and plunged deeper, tearing tender tissue in his enthusiasm to claim her.

Ow! Ow! Ow! Jeezas H Christ, that hurt. Her torn flesh burned so bad, tears flooded her eyes. She gasped brokenly, unable to stop herself from protesting the pain.

Logan pulled his mouth from hers and frowned down at her. She forced the pain not to register on her face and rocked her hips to urge him to thrust. She wasn't sure if that would ease the sting or intensify it, but if she curled into the fetal position and started sobbing, her one-night stand with Mr. Hot Rock Star would be over before he climaxed.

His lashes fluttered as the rhythm consumed him. "Christ, Toni, your cunt is so fucking tight."

Oh, he'd noticed. She grabbed a handful of his hair to distract him. "Do me hard, baby," she said. She'd heard some woman say it on a porno once. It sounded rather ridiculous coming out of her mouth, but Logan didn't laugh at her.

"You want me to fuck you?" he asked, his voice a hard growl that made her belly quiver.

She nodded.

"Say it."

"Fuck me, Logan."

Not her smartest request, she decided, when he dug his fingers into her shoulders and thrust hard and deep. She tilted her head back and squeezed her eyes shut, hoping to keep the tears locked behind her lashes. Damn, that hurt. His lips brushed her jaw, her throat. He slowed his strokes as he kissed every inch of her face.

"Beautiful Toni," he whispered, "you're not enjoying this as much as I am."

Actually, it wasn't so bad now that the initial sting had eased. The slower strokes were almost pleasant. Given time, she might even learn to like it. Maybe. Okay, probably not. Why did women claim to enjoy this? It hurt like hell.

Logan paused and stroked her hip with his fingertips. "Am I hurting you?"

"A little," she whispered.

"You should have said something. Try wrapping your legs around my waist."

She shifted and wrapped her legs around him. "Like this?"

"Just like that. Now stop thinking so much and feel me."

How did he know she was thinking? It wasn't like she could shut her brain off anyway. What kind of ridiculous request—

"Toni?" he murmured. He spoke her name as if he treasured her. Her heart expanded in her chest as if in full bloom. Why was she feeling this way? She knew there was no emotional connection between them. She was just another girl in another place willing to spread her legs for him. She had to remember that. He was her first, so she wasn't sure if she could maintain the same detachment he felt, but she would try. Still, she wasn't stupid enough to think anything would come of this. But at least she wasn't a damned virgin anymore.

Logan caught her gaze. "Be with me."

Oh, he was gorgeous. She couldn't look away. All she could think about was how expressive his blue eyes were and how full she felt with him buried inside her. Full, but no longer in agony.

And then he started to move. Slow. Deep. Gentle thrusts.

Her breath caught and her mouth opened in surprise as sensation flooded her.

There was no pain now. Only exquisite pleasure.

She rocked with him, caught in his sultry beat. As it had before, a need inside her began to build. He gradually increased his tempo. She allowed him to carry her away to a place where carnal desires ruled and there was no room for contemplation.

"That's it," he murmured. "You feel me now, don't you?"

She nodded slightly, still lost in his gaze. Her body lost in bliss.

"Are you with me?"

"Yes, I'm with you."

"I'm with you too. You're amazing inside, Toni."

She bit her lip. She knew he meant inside her body, not inside her heart. Not inside her soul. Not even inside her mind. She wanted only the physical, but found separating the physical from the emotional was a lot harder than she bargained for. Sharing something this intimate, even with a virtual stranger, tugged at feelings she wished she could deny. Toni slipped her hands into his thick curls and urged his sensual mouth to mate with hers. While kissing him, she could pretend that he really liked her. Pretend he loved her. He'd never know. He'd just think she really liked kissing, not that she was pouring her heart into the gesture. *Stupid, Toni. What are you doing?* She kissed him more desperately. Her hands moved to explore his sweat-slick back, his firm ass, and the taut muscles that flexed beneath his skin with each thrust. She wished they could have more than this one time. Wished she could learn how to please him and all the ways her body could be pleased in return. She knew as soon as he figured out she'd misled him, he would be finished with her. But maybe he wouldn't find out. Maybe she could convince him that she was only interested in a sexual relationship and was game for anything. What man would refuse that kind of arrangement?

"You're thinking again," Logan said. "How does a guy get a

brainy woman to stop thinking while he fucks her?"

"I'm sorry. I tend to do more thinking than fu . . . screwing."

He chuckled. "Maybe we can do something about that."

"I sure hope so."

He shifted his body off hers slightly, and his hand moved down between their bodies. She had no idea what his intention was until his fingers brushed her clit.

"Let's disengage that brain of yours." He rubbed her clit with rapid, thought-shattering precision. He rocked his hips, sliding within her slightly as he brought her higher and higher with his touch. It was a moment before she realized she was calling out as her body strained toward something she knew she had to have, at the same time uncertain if she'd ever attain it. She'd brought herself to climax by stroking her clit many times in the past, but her vagina had never been filled when she'd reached orgasm. She'd never been exposed inside and out with a man buried deep within. So when her pleasure peaked and her body clenched around him, pulling at him, drawing him deeper, encouraging him to come with her, she called out to him brokenly, finally understanding what true bliss meant.

Logan shifted his fingers away and rode her climax with rapid thrusts. His body stiffened suddenly, and he groaned. Toni tried to force her eyes open. She wanted to see what a man looked like when her body brought him to his peak, but she still hadn't recovered from her own pulsating orgasm, so she just clung to his shoulders and strained against him as he clung to her hips and let go.

Logan collapsed on top of her, his breaths harsh and ragged in her ear. She held him tightly. Though he was still buried inside of her, she wanted him closer. So close that they ceased existing as separate entities. A part of her wished they could remain like this— naked in each other's arms—for eternity. Damn her fool heart anyway. That wasn't how this worked and she knew it. But he let her hold him as if he instinctively knew that if she didn't hold him against her, she'd completely fall apart.

When his breathing stilled, Logan lifted his head and grinned down at her. "That was fun."

Fun? Well, she supposed it had been fun. It wouldn't have been the first word she'd use to describe it.

"I want a beer," he said. "Do you want one?"

She wasn't much of a drinker, but less than half an hour ago she'd been a virgin, so why not? "Sure," she said.

He pulled out and climbed to his feet. He moved his hand to remove the condom and froze. He had blood—Toni's blood—all over him.

"Are you on your period? I wish you would have told me. We could have at least covered the sofa with a towel."

She should have just continued with her string of lies and gone with *yes, I'm on my period, I'm menstruating like a son of a bitch today*, but instead she shook her head, fighting the ridiculous tears that were suddenly stinging her eyes. "No, that's not it."

Logan's face twisted with horror. "You're a virgin?" It was more an accusation than a question.

"Was," she whispered.

The man should start a new Olympic sport—speed dressing. He'd definitely win the gold. Before she could even apologize for misleading him, he was gone.

Toni rolled onto her side and curled her body into a little ball. What was done was done. She wasn't going to let herself cry over this. Much.

CHAPTER 4

LOGAN DARTED into the bathroom and scrubbed the traces of Toni's blood from his body. A virgin? How could she possibly have been a virgin? She was at least twenty-five. Gorgeous women in their midtwenties with huge tits were not virgins. He was sure of it.

He'd seen the signs, though. So easily believed her lies when she told him her skittishness was an act. Hell, those actions had turned him on and made his dick so hard he could have used it to mine for diamonds. He couldn't deny it.

"Fuck," he growled under his breath.

Now what was he supposed to do? Toni was supposed to tour with them for a month. He wouldn't even be able to look her in the eye. Those big, innocent eyes. His cock stirred just thinking about the way she looked at him with those sweet, trusting eyes.

"Absolutely not," he said to his crotch. "None of that. That pussy is off limits."

At the thought of being buried in Toni's oh-so-tight pussy, his cock twitched with renewed interest. He groaned. This was so not good. He was terrible at telling his cock to behave itself. Didn't matter how much the little head got him into trouble, it ruled him and he knew it. He'd just have to find himself some nice substitute pussy to distract the little head from that sweet virgin he'd just defiled.

Beer. He needed beer. He dried himself with a towel. All traces of her blood were now gone, but he could still smell the scent of her body on his skin. He considered taking a shower, but he liked that reminder of her. And he wasn't going to delve into the reasons why. He should probably be angry with her for misleading him, but in actuality he felt like a total douche for taking advantage of her.

Outwardly decent but inwardly cringing, he left the bathroom and headed to the refrigerator. He paused at the refrigerator door, his hand on the handle, and stared at the sliding doors that he'd closed as he fled the back lounge. He wondered if she was okay. Maybe he should check on her. Nah, she probably preferred some time to herself. Or maybe he was a freaking coward. Beer would help remedy that malady.

"An hour," Steve said. "You beat your own predicted time."

It took Logan a moment to realize he was talking about how Logan had bet that he'd get into Toni's panties within three hours. If he'd known then what he knew now . . . Had to play it up for the guys, though. He had a reputation to uphold. A reputation that currently made him sick to his stomach.

He twisted the cap off a bottle of beer and took a long swallow before locating his wry grin and plastering it to his face. "I told you nice girls were easy."

"You do realize we have to maintain a working relationship with her," Max said. "Sleeping with her wasn't your brightest idea."

That was an understatement. Logan perched sideways on the sofa arm, resting his feet on the cushion, and took another swig of beer and another and another until the bottle was inexplicably empty. His gaze landed on Toni's gym bag, which was sitting on the floor near the sofa. He turned his head to see if she had emerged from the lounge, but the door was still shut. He wasn't sure how to proceed. Should he talk to her? Avoid her? How was he supposed to avoid her for a month? Why did his little head make him do such idiotic things?

A bare foot in the center of his chest shoved him backward. He managed to catch himself before he fell on the floor. "What the fuck?" he shouted at Steve, who was attached to the bare foot.

"You don't look like a guy who just got laid. You look like a guy who committed a hanging offense."

Logan scoffed. "Whatever. It just wasn't that good." Which was a total lie—he couldn't remember a time that he'd enjoyed as much—but how else could he explain his sour mood?

The gym bag near the sofa shifted. He cringed at the sound of dainty feet retreating to the back of the bus. The quiet latching of the bathroom door was like a stake through his heart.

One eye squeezed shut, Logan asked, "Did she hear what I said? About it not being that good?"

All three of his friends looked at the ceiling and nodded. Logan rubbed his forehead with one hand. He hadn't thought it was possible to fuck up this situation any more than he already had. He had thought wrong. With a heavy sigh he climbed to his feet and tossed the empty beer bottle into the bin under the sink.

"I'm going to bed."

"Don't you think you should apologize to her?" Dare asked.

Probably. He had no idea what to say.

"Fuck it, I'm tired."

He stripped down to his boxers and climbed into his bunk. He jerked his curtain closed and stared up at the bottom of Steve's empty bunk. He contemplated turning on the small television that was installed overhead, but then the guys would know he wasn't in his bunk because he was tired, he was in his bunk avoiding Toni. She had to come out of the bathroom eventually.

When he heard her soft voice a few minutes later, his heart rate accelerated.

"Do you have any hydrogen peroxide?" she asked.

"Are you injured?" Dare asked. The concern in his voice made Logan's stomach clench. He better not fucking touch her.

"No, I-I need it to get bloo—um ... a stain out of something."

Logan's ears strained for sound. Rummaging in the bathroom. A relieved sigh from Toni.

"Thanks," she said.

The lounge doors slid shut. Had Dare followed her in there? Logan knew how Dare comforted women. It started out all tender and caring and ended up with the women on their backs and him pounding them. The fucker.

Dare jerked open the curtain of Logan's bunk. He punched him hard in the shoulder, shook his head in disgust, and then yanked the curtain closed again. Logan rubbed his aching deltoid. Yeah, he had totally deserved that. He was sure Dare had put two and two together. Max and Steve were probably oblivious, but Dare was too fucking perceptive for his own good.

"What's going on?" Steve asked.

Logan tensed. All he needed was for his entire band to know

he'd defiled a virgin and was now hiding from her in his bunk.

"Don't worry about it," Dare said.

Logan was one hundred percent certain that Dare was being tight-lipped for Toni's sake, not his. Logan rolled onto his side and stared at the wall. Things were going to become mighty uncomfortable on this bus if he didn't set them right. He had no fucking clue how to do that.

May 2

Dear Journal,

Today didn't go exactly as planned. Apparently the band wasn't expecting me and for a while there, I wasn't sure I was going to get to start the book, much less finish it. But after they straightened it out with their manager and Max admitted that he had known I was coming, I was allowed on the bus and even got some really good material when they ran to interact with their fans behind the stadium.

I can't express how excited I am to be involved with their book. They are all so cool.

Okay, first impressions of the guys.

Maximillian Richardson or Max. He's surprisingly calm. I don't know what I was expecting. I guess watching all that high-energy concert footage gave me a mistaken perception of him. But of the four guys, he definitely seems to be the most . . . What's a good way to describe him? Professional? I guess that's the right word. He's also incredibly gorgeous—especially his ass. Lordie! But he doesn't look like a rocker the way the rest of them do. I could easily imagine him as a high-profile CEO in a tailored Armani suit. I wonder why he chose to become the singer of a metal band. I need to make sure I ask him that for the book.

Darren Mills or Dare. This guy has presence. You can't help but notice him. It's as if a strange gravitational force surrounds him and sucks all attention right to him. The weird thing is, he doesn't seem to do anything consciously. He's not trying to be the center of attention, he just is. He's another one who is knockout gorgeous—honestly, they are all. But he 100 percent looks the rock star part. As if he was born to play the guitar and have millions of fans. Maybe it's the hair. It's jet black and barely touches his shoulders, but I don't think there are many men who could pull off that length. I'm totally jealous of how silky smooth it is, like rich black satin. I need to ask him what conditioner he uses. Maybe it would calm my rat's nest. And he has the most gorgeous green eyes.

Steve Aimes seems like a lot of fun. A bit of a jokester. Energetic. From what I can tell, he really likes women. Really likes women. He's really good looking too. Especially his abs. Oh my God, he has an eight-pack. I thought my eyes were going to fall out of their sockets from staring at them so long. Haha!

Logan Schmidt. I'm not sure I get him at all. Even if he did take my virginity. I still can't believe it happened, but I'll get to that story later. I still haven't fully processed it yet. Logan doesn't seem to take anything seriously. He's this happy-go-lucky kind of guy with a great smile, and he has these amazing blue eyes that seem to stare right into your soul and thick wavy hair that is probably really curly if he doesn't tame it. He also seems to use good hair products.

Note to self: Go to the salon.

Logan reminds me of a surfer dude. He's very tanned—except for where shorts would be—and he's pretty pale down there (yes, I checked when I had the chance!)—but it's not an artificial tan. He looks like he spends a lot of time outdoors. I wonder if he likes to play sports. Everyone knows I suck at sports.

Speaking of things I suck at, we can add sex to that list. Logan said it himself. I heard him telling the guys that it wasn't very good. And what he said hurt, but what hurt worse was I know he's right. I'm not good at it. I assume other people know what to do and how to behave their first time, but I was so nervous and awkward. I'm surprised he was even turned on enough to finish. I'm so glad he did, though. At least I can say I made him come. Or maybe he made himself come. I didn't do much but lie there and moan.

I would like to try sex again. Maybe next time I won't be so weird, and surely it can't hurt as bad the second time as it does the first. I thought my hymen was going to kill me. Literally. And I got blood everywhere. It was so embarrassing to ask for peroxide to clean the blood off the sofa, but the stain is gone. I turned the cushion over to hide the wet spot.

I think Dare might have figured out that I was a virgin.

And all the guys know I had sex with Logan after knowing him only an hour, so I can imagine what they think of me.

For the first time in my life I'm labeled a slut.

Why am I okay with that?

I guess what's done is done. I wouldn't take any of it back.

Except the part where I wasn't any good at it. Maybe I should take lessons. Haha!

I think I ruined any chance I had with Logan. I really do like him. So maybe we can be friends.

Did I really just write that?

To be honest, I don't want to be just friends. I'd much rather be his lover.

Every guy I've ever liked has only wanted to be friends and nothing more. Why can't I have more? Is that too much to ask?

How do I get him to like me? Maybe I should go against my promises to Dad and dress less appropriately.

I dunno.

None of this nonsense I'm writing here will make it into the book, of course. Can you imagine? If my mother read it, she'd have a coronary. She's probably having a coronary right now because I didn't call to let her know I made it to the bus. I'm too emotional to deal with Mom tonight. Maybe I'll call her tomorrow.

I did check my phone for messages and found Susan had already texted me. She asked if I was ready to come home. I didn't bother responding. I guess I understand why she doesn't like me—she really wanted this job—but her reasons don't make her stinging words any easier to take. Julian also texted—*fifteen* messages—starting with *are you still a virgin* followed by *how about now* over and over again. So I texted back *no*. To which he replied *I don't believe you*. What a jackass!

Oh, I almost forgot. I saw Reagan Elliot, but didn't actually get to meet her. She seemed more interested in hanging out on Sinners' tour bus. I thought it was a little strange that she took one of the security guards with her. And based on something Dare said, it sounded as if she was intimate with him. And with Trey Mills. I guess she's cheating on Trey. I can't imagine why she would do that. Have you seen Trey Mills? If he were mine, I sure wouldn't cheat on him. But maybe I'm wrong. I'll be sure to listen for clues if I get to spend any time around her tomorrow.

Now that I'm back here by myself and not distracted by all those virile males, I do miss Birdie. If I were home, I'd be reading her a book right about now. I hope Mom is taking good care of her. I'm sure she's fine.

I'd better try to sleep now since tomorrow will be a busy day. I can't wait to get more stuff for the book! That's what I need to concentrate on. Not my attraction to Logan. Or being terrible at sex. Or anything else. I'm here to do a job and I plan to do it well.

Goodnight, Journal. I'm glad you're here to listen to my silly problems.

Signed,

No-longer-a-virgin,

Toni

CHAPTER 5

ONI'S EYES SHOT open. Something had touched her hair. She could make out unfamiliar shadows in her dimly lit surroundings, but this was not her bedroom. Where was she?

A figure lurked over her, sitting in the space above the top of her head. Toni's entire body tensed. Too terrified to move, she held her breath and squeezed her eyes shut.

"I'm sorry," Logan's deep voice said from nearby. His hand caressed her cheek.

Trembling, Toni let out a breath of relief. It was only Logan, and she now realized she was sleeping on the sectional in the back lounge of Exodus End's tour bus. All that had happened sounded like something she would dream about, not actually experience. No wonder she woke up confused.

Logan scooted along the sofa, took her pillow away, and shifted his thigh beneath her head. His fingers stroked her hair as her head rested on his lap. She couldn't help but relax and be overjoyed that he was with her. Talking to her. Apologizing to her. She couldn't be mad at him. She'd tricked him into taking her virginity, and she was sure the sex *hadn't* been very good for him. She had no idea how to please a man. She was miffed that his entire band knew she sucked in bed, but other than that, she was just glad he was speaking to her. Touching her. Maybe he'd teach her how to rock his world and she could redeem herself.

"I'm sorry too," she said.

His hand paused. "For what?"

"Misleading you. I know you wouldn't have slept with me if you'd known I was a virgin."

He chuckled. "You underestimate your appeal. I told you, you're exactly my type."

"Then I'm sorry I wasn't any good."

"And I'm sorry I'm a fucking liar. It was fantastic, Toni. You, you are fantastic."

Did he really mean that?

"So are you going to be okay?" he asked. "I feel like a complete asshole. I would have done things differently if I'd known it was your first time."

The hand stroking her hair was so soothing, so tender, she could almost imagine being his. She wanted that far more than she should. "Yeah, I'm fine. Really. I'm not just saying that. I wanted you to take my virginity."

His fingertips brushed her neck, and shivers chased goose bumps to the surface of her skin.

"Shouldn't that be something you save for someone you love?" he asked.

She chuckled. "Maybe a few women still think that way. I'm not one of them."

"How old are you?" He stroked a spot behind her ear, and her nipples tightened into hard buds. The flesh between her thighs, which had been tender and sore when she'd fallen asleep, was now hot and achy and embarrassingly damp.

"Are you going to ask my weight next?" she asked.

"Huh?"

"Two things you should never ask a woman: her age and her weight."

"Well, however old you are—"

"Twenty-five," she supplied.

"A twenty-five year old woman with this face . . ." He placed a hand over her mouth and squeezed her cheeks in the most unromantic fashion imaginable. "And these fantastic tits . . ." He reached for a breast but paused an inch from taking it in his hand. Her belly clenched, wanting him to close the narrow gap between their flesh, wanting his fingers against her breast, her throbbing nipple. "Has no business being a virgin unless she's purposely saving herself for marriage or something."

He dropped his hand to the sofa near her arm, and she stifled a moan of frustration. Why wasn't he touching her more? She wanted him to touch every inch of her. "It just never happened," she said. But lord how she wanted it to happen again. She wasn't sure how to convey that to him. Should she just blurt it out? If she did, surely he'd think she was a raving whorebag. "It's not that big a deal, Logan. I'm sorry you found the experience so traumatic."

"Me?" He snorted. "You're the one who should be traumatized. I fuck you—hurt you—then freak out and leave you bleeding on the sofa. That was a very shitty thing to do."

"I'm fine, Logan." *Touch me. Hold me.*

"So you're really cool with it? You're not upset or hurt?"

"Why would I be?" *I don't know how to tell you what I really want.*

He released a long relieved breath. "So we can be friends?"

She stiffened. That was definitely not what she really wanted. *Now* she was upset and hurt. She'd heard the "we can be friends" line from a dozen too many men in her past. And none of those men had ever been inside her.

"Yeah, sure," she said around the knot in her throat. "Friends. What else would we be?"

"You're a sweetheart. I thought you'd bust my balls over this for sure. I'm glad we talked this out," he said. "Sam and the guys would have been royally pissed at me if my perpetual horniness messed up this book experience or whatever it is you're doing."

"Like I said," she said, glad it was dark enough that he wouldn't be able to make out her shell-shocked expression, "no big deal."

He replaced his lap with a pillow and stood. "I owe you some flowers," he said. He bent over her and kissed her cheek. Paused. Kissed the tip of her nose. Hesitated. Covered her mouth with his and kissed her with that deep, devouring hunger that had gotten her so quickly out of her panties in the first place. *Yes, this. This is what I want. Not flowers and friendship. I want passion. You.*

He tore away after a moment, his breathing raspy. "Damn, woman. How am I supposed to keep my dick in my pants if you kiss me like that?"

Before she could respond that she didn't want him to keep his dick in his pants, he left the room and slid the doors closed. She stared into the darkness, a jumbled mess of hormones and emotions and thoughts guaranteed to keep her awake all night.

CHAPTER

6

LOGAN HADN'T SLEPT for shit. First he'd lain wide awake in his bunk for hours feeling like the biggest asshole on the planet. After everyone but the driver had fallen asleep, he'd finally found the balls to apologize to Toni for taking advantage of her inexperience. Then after he'd smoothed things over with her, he'd let his attraction to her get in the way of his judgment and he'd kissed her. After that stupid move, he'd lain awake in bed the rest of the night thinking about her. Dick half-hard. Stomach in knots. Mind tangled with thoughts of her. He surprised himself because only about half of those thoughts had been sexual in nature. He found himself wondering about her life. Her family. Her past. Her likes. Her dislikes. Strange. Maybe he'd try to get to know her a little better. They were supposed to be friends now. Friends talked about boring shit like that, didn't they? Except he didn't think it would be boring in the least. He actually hoped it was boring. Maybe then he'd be able to think about something besides her gentle brown eyes, sweet smile, soft hair, those enormous tits, and that oh-so-tight pussy that had never been filled with any other cock but his.

Logan groaned and tossed his bunk curtain aside. Locking himself in the bathroom, he shaved and then took a long shower, which was sure to catch him grief. They had only a limited supply of water on the bus, and he'd used more than his share. When he emerged from the bathroom in his towel, he felt as human as a sleep-deprived zombie could feel.

A startled inrush of breath came from the open door of the lounge. Those wide brown eyes—now hidden behind a pair of unflattering glasses—took in every exposed inch of his flesh. Sometime during the night, Logan had convinced himself that Toni had given her virginity to him because he'd been available, but there was definitely an attraction there. And it wasn't one-sided. Logan couldn't resist tormenting her. He loved to make her blush. He tugged his towel free and used it to dry his hair. He gave her plenty of time to get an eyeful of his naked body, and then he dropped the wet towel to hang around his shoulders.

"Good morning, lamb," he murmured.

She lifted her eyes to meet his and they widened, as if she just suddenly realized she wasn't invisible.

"Put some clothes on," Butch complained as he fumbled through a cabinet to start a pot of coffee brewing. "No one wants to see that first thing in the morning."

"I wouldn't say no one," Toni said, her cheeks pink. The wide grin on her face was self-indulgent rather than embarrassed. "It does look smaller than I remember."

Logan laughed. "I'm sure you can fix that problem if you try." And by try all she had to do was stand there looking sweet and ruffled.

"I would, but you said you want to be *friends*." She slid the lounge door closed.

"How about friends with benefits?" he called loud enough that she had to have heard him.

"The coffee better be fuckin' ready," Steve grumbled from within his bunk. The man didn't function before ten a.m. without half a pot. "Or Casanova is going to get his face rearranged."

"I think he's more of a John Holmes," Max said as he flipped his body out of his bunk. He froze when his gaze landed on Logan. "Butch is right. No one wants to see that first thing in the morning."

"I'll save it for later then." Logan pulled out the drawer under his bunk to find clean boxer shorts. He decided on a pair of black silk ones. They reminded him of Toni for some reason. Probably because they felt so silky against his flesh. Like her supple, untouched skin.

Deciding that the guys wouldn't want to have to stare at his tented boxers either, he put on a pair of jeans as well.

"Breakfast ETA ten minutes," Cade, their overnight driver,

called from the front of the bus.

Butch reached for the clipboard, pulled off the top page—yesterday's schedule—and consulted the page underneath. He checked his watch and scowled. "Fifteen minutes behind schedule. You'll have to eat fast," he told the guys. "We have to be at the radio station at ten."

Logan went to dry his hair before the rest of the guys started fighting over the bathroom. If he didn't take proper care of his longish waves, they became curls, and then an uncontrollable mass of tangled frizz that put 1970's afros to shame. Max in particular was a bathroom hog, and with the brace on his wrist, it took him ten times longer to get his hair just right. They didn't much care if they looked like shit most days, but when they had a public appearance, they were expected to look presentable. Sam was a real stickler about image. And Logan had been bashed a few too many times by the tabloids for going to events with Brillo-Pad bed hair. He looked forward to the days in their schedule when they didn't have public appearances. On tour, those days were few and far between.

"Is Sinners having breakfast with us?" Dare asked with an exaggerated yawn.

Butch consulted his clipboard again. "Not this morning. I think they have an appearance in the next town over. Sam says we need to spread the awesome around a little."

"What about the radio interview?" Dare asked. He obviously wanted to hang out with his brother. Logan hadn't seen his own brother in over a year, and he was okay with that. They didn't exactly get along. Or even tolerate each other.

"Nope, no Sinners on the radio. And you're on your own at the meet and greet too."

"Stupid me thought I might get to spend some time with Trey on this tour," Dare said with a sour frown.

Logan switched on the hairdryer, calculating how much free time he'd have that day to spend with Toni. He'd definitely make sure he was sitting next to her at breakfast. Then in the limo between their various engagements. Maybe he could hang out with her backstage—or would she be working on her book while they did their events? Perhaps he'd see her more than he thought. He wasn't sure how much they'd get to interact, but as long as she was in sight, maybe he could concentrate on what he was supposed to do instead of wondering where she was and what she was doing.

Hair dry and mostly under control—it was so thick and wavy, it had a mind of its own, and sometimes he had a mind to shave it all off—Logan left the bathroom and knocked on the closed door of the lounge. He figured someone should explain to Toni how the day was going to go, and he volunteered himself before anyone else thought of it.

"Just a minute," she called.

She slid the door open and gaped at his bare chest. Logan was doubly glad that he'd yet to don a shirt and that he'd worked out extra hard the day before. He gave her a moment to stare—because, hey, he liked the attention. The bus engine's pitch lowered as it pulled off the interstate and began to slow.

"We're going to stop for breakfast and then we have a live interview at a radio station. Are you going to tag along and see what that's like?"

She smiled, her wide brown eyes sparking with excitement. "Yep. Can't wait."

He grinned at her like an idiot for a long moment. She really did seem fine this morning and not mad at him. He didn't understand why he felt such relief. He wasn't sure what he'd expected. That she'd hide away and refuse to show her face. Cry for days. Send him scathing looks of hatred.

"You're beautiful," he blurted.

She rolled her eyes and shuffled around him to enter the corridor. She went to talk to Butch, asking him about how the schedule worked. Who set it up? Who enforced it?

"If it wasn't for me," Butch said in his gruffest, most self-important tone, "these four guys would scarcely find the stage, much less tend to all their other responsibilities."

Toni looked impressed, which won Butch over instantly. She was a sly one. Butch knew more about Exodus End than any other person on the planet. If she wanted real dirt on them, she'd charmed the right person. Logan chuckled and rummaged around in his drawer to find a T-shirt. A woman had once told him that blue was his color as it drew attention to his gorgeous eyes. He wasn't sure why that thought crossed his mind or why he had a powerful need to wear blue.

"What are you so cheery about?" Dare asked him.

"It isn't because I slept well." Logan glanced toward the living area where Toni was interrogating Butch without making it blatantly obvious that she was pumping him for information.

"I bet they're really grateful that you're always saving their necks," Toni said with unmistakable earnestness.

Butch actually blushed with pleasure and smiled. "Well, I don't know about that. They think I do it because I enjoy busting their balls."

"He's a total sadist," Max said, offering his coldest smile.

Toni visibly shuddered.

Uh, not happening, Max. Logan slipped his shirt on over his head, kicked his drawer shut, and rushed in the direction of his lamb in conservative clothing. He moved to stand between Toni and Max.

"Funny how Butch forgets about all the times he's fucked things up for us," Logan said.

He wrapped an arm around Toni's waist and, with a stern look, telegraphed signals to Max. *Not to be added to your collection of playthings.*

Max chuckled and shook his head at Logan. Then he put on his wounded animal face and tugged at Toni's sleeve to get her attention. "Toni, would you help me with something?" He rubbed his wrist brace as if he'd suffered a war injury rather than a botched carpal tunnel surgery.

"Depends," she said.

"Could you help me fix my hair? I have a hell of a time getting it to cooperate since I can only use one hand. We're already late. And golden boy was hogging the bathroom earlier."

Women would pay cash money for the opportunity to run their fingers through Maximillian Richardson's hair. Logan watched Toni for her reaction.

"Sounds like a job for Butch," she said.

Logan could have kissed her. If he wasn't trying to be on his best behavior, he probably would have.

Max took her wrist in his braced hand and stroked her fingers with his other. "But these are the hands I want to touch me. So soft and gentle."

Toni stared up at Max as if in some sort of trance. The bus stopped, and Logan took Toni by the shoulders. He turned her toward the exit.

"Too late, Max," Logan said. "We're here. You'll just have to go to breakfast looking like roadkill."

"If roadkill looked like that, I'd get a job with the highway department and bring my own shovel," Toni said under her breath.

Max chuckled, looking very pleased with himself.

Shit! Was she attracted to Max? Was any woman *not* attracted to Max? Logan had to regain Toni's full attention.

"Your hands weren't so gentle last night when they were tangled in *my* hair." The second he said it, he wished he could take it back. While it effectively told Max that Logan had claimed her first, it wiped the smile from Toni's face. She set her jaw in a harsh line. "I *wish*," he added, hoping to play it off as if he'd been joking instead of bragging.

Max and Steve laughed at his misery. Dare gave him the evil eye. Logan was usually so smooth with women. What in the fuck was wrong with him?

"I guess I'm going to breakfast looking like roadkill," Max said. He extended an elbow in Toni's direction. "Care to join me?"

She looked at Max uncertainly for a moment and then slid her hand into the crook of his elbow. Her dazzling smile reappeared.

Logan stifled the urge to say *fuck* repeatedly and followed them off the bus. Their entourage of stage crew, security, and band members meandered toward the restaurant. Toni was asking Max how they'd managed to arrange having the entire place to themselves. Questions Logan wanted to answer for her.

"Sam always does things in a big way. Even before we made it, he insisted on keeping us broke by renting limos and throwing parties we couldn't afford," Max said.

"I'm sure you can afford it now," Toni said.

Max chuckled. "Is that your way of asking how much money we rake in?"

Her eyes widened. "Oh no, I didn't mean it that way at all. That would be crass."

"We can afford it," he said.

Logan really wanted to kick Max in the back of the knee. Why should he get to talk to Toni? Just because he was the lead singer. Bassists were important too. Logan scratched his head. Well, bassists *should* be important. Someone grabbed Logan's arm and pulled him to a halt. Dare's piercing green-eyed gaze made him feel about three inches tall.

"Will you stop?" Dare said.

"Stop what?"

"Toying with her."

"I'm not toying with her." Logan tossed a hand out toward Toni's retreating form. "Max is toying with her."

"Max won't take it too far. You already took it too far."

"Why? Because she was a virgin?"

Dare cringed. "I was hoping my suspicions were wrong."

And Logan had just stuck his foot in his mouth. "Just because I took her virginity—"

"Keep it down," Dare growled. "I doubt she wants you to broadcast that to the world."

"I didn't know, all right? Not until it was over."

"How could you not know, Logan?"

He didn't appreciate being berated and belittled by a bandmate. "I've never had one before."

"Just stop thinking with what's in your pants and try thinking with what's in your head. If you don't stop this now, you're going to hurt her."

"I couldn't have hurt her too much. She didn't cry or anything."

Dare pinched the bridge of his nose as if he was talking to a toddler and his patience was at its limit. "Okay, let me try this again. You know those girls who you sleep with and they think it means you're in love with them?"

"Yeah, naïve girls."

"Who are the most naïve girls on the planet?"

Logan's face fell. "Virgins."

Dare nodded. "So unless you want her to think you're in this for the long run, you have to proceed with caution."

But maybe he wanted to be in it for the long run. Did the month she'd be on tour with them count as a long run? It did for him. "Got it, boss," he said.

Once inside the restaurant, Logan was crushed to find that while Dare had been giving him advice he didn't want or need, Toni had been seated between Max and Steve in a booth at their reserved table. It wasn't that he wasn't happy to see her eating with them. What he didn't like was that she was flanked by two men who weren't him. He was willing to undergo an experimental cloning procedure just so he could sit on either side of Toni. Reagan was sitting across from the trio chattering away about how she won their rhythm guitarist spot in a contest. Toni took notes on a napkin, her expressive eyes wide with fascination. Max was toying with a strand of Toni's waist-length, wavy hair, but she didn't seem to notice. Logan loved how absorbed she got by anything she was focused on. He just wished she was always focused on him.

He slid into the booth next to Reagan, who paused in her soliloquy to give him a hug. "You look tired," she said. She touched his forehead with her fingertips. "You're not getting sick, are you?"

He smiled at her concern. "No. Just didn't sleep well."

"Are we in a hotel tonight?" Reagan asked.

"Nope. Bus again tonight. Hotel tomorrow night," Steve said.

"How did you get here, anyway?" Logan asked Reagan.

"Sinners picked up their breakfast here half an hour ago. They left me here to wait for you lamewads."

Dare slid into the booth next to Logan. He leaned forward so he could talk to Reagan. "I'm surprised my brother let you out of his sight. He knows if he lets his guard down, I'm going to steal you away from him."

Reagan rolled her eyes at him. "As if I would go for a square like you, Dare Mills."

Dare laughed and covered his chest with one hand. "Ow. Wounded."

"He and Ethan were still in bed when I left." She shot a nervous glance at the journalist in their midst. "All the men on Sinners' bus sleep until noon."

There was a tense moment of silence as Toni stared at Reagan, her pen practically quivering with scandal above her stack of napkin notes. Several of the wait staff arrived with their food just then. Reagan released an audible breath of relief.

Toni stared at the servers in confusion. "But we didn't order yet."

"It was called in two hours in advance," a waitress explained as she set a plate in front of Steve.

Today was egg white and veggie omelet day. Tomorrow was fresh fruit, oatmeal, and yogurt day. The next day was scrambled egg whites and turkey sausage with whole grain toast day. Sam fed them more like underwear models than rock stars. *Your bodies are a part of your image*, he'd said as he'd introduced them to their new personal trainer who seconded as part of the road crew. They wouldn't have time for a workout today, but tomorrow Kirk was sure to kick their asses into shape. He always did.

A plate was set in front of Toni. She stared at it as if her omelet was crawling across her plate. "I don't think I can eat this," she said. "It looks disgustingly healthy."

"It's good for you," Max said. "Try it."

"I'd rather have biscuits and gravy."

"Me too," Logan said as his own disgustingly healthy omelet was set before him.

Toni met his eyes across the table and smiled. Logan's heart thudded in response and then galloped in his chest. Dare's warning echoed through his thoughts, but he told it to shut the hell up. He wanted her. He would be proceeding without a modicum of caution.

"So where are you from?" Logan asked, craving her attention.

"A rural area outside of Seattle," she said. "Ever heard of Enumclaw?"

Logan shook his head. "Can't say that I have."

"That's near Mount Rainer, isn't it?" Steve asked.

Toni lit up with a brilliant smile, and Logan wanted to punch Steve. "Yep. I have the most spectacular view of the mountain from my bedroom window."

At the mention of a room featuring Toni's bed, Logan's jeans seemed to shrink a size in the general crotch area.

"I stayed in a cabin there once," Steve said.

"Mountain climbing?" Dare asked.

Steve shrugged. "What else?"

"Steve is part mountain goat," Max said. He only looked up from his self-appointed task of organizing sugar packets by color in the small container on the table when his plate was set before him by the server.

"More like part monkey," Logan said, which earned him a well-placed kick to the shin.

"Do you climb?" Steve asked.

Logan pictured Toni all bundled up like a snow bunny, standing at the foot of a mountain at Steve's side. He didn't like the idea of her having something in common with Steve, and he was very confused as to why he gave a shit.

Toni laughed. "I'm not dexterous enough to climb it. I just like to look at the scenery."

"It is a gorgeous mountain," Steve said. "Not too challenging of a climb, but I wouldn't recommend it for a beginner."

"So what do you do for fun?" Logan asked, trying to regain her attention.

"Me?" Toni met his eyes across the table.

"You're the only one here I don't know well," Logan said.

She shrugged. "Not much. Studying. Reading."

"You study for fun?" Logan had never heard of such a thing.

"I like to learn things." She chuckled. "I guess that's why I kept changing majors. So I could stay in college for as long as possible."

"She's too smart for you, Lo," Steve said. "He barely made it through high school."

School had never been his thing, but he admired those who succeeded at it.

"Some people are good at school," she said. "Some people are good at other things."

She ducked her head, and Logan noticed the blush spreading up her throat and face. She peeked at him from beneath her long lashes, and he could only hope that she thought he was good in bed, because he very much wanted to impress her with his skills.

"What did you major in?" Logan asked.

She laughed. "The more appropriate question is what *didn't* I major in?"

He reached across the table and took her hand. He needed to touch her. Needed all the other jack-offs at the table to disappear so he could have her all to himself. "So what didn't you major in?"

"Physical education."

He grinned. A subject he excelled at. Getting physical. "I have some expertise in that subject if you'd like lessons."

"Ugh." Reagan groaned. "Will you stop with the lame come-ons? I'm trying to eat my disgustingly healthy breakfast."

Toni squeezed his hand. "If I ever decide I need more physical education, I know who to ask."

He grinned. "I'm more than happy to teach you all I know. What kind of things can you teach me?"

"Nothing physical." She laughed. "I started as a pre-law major, tried Russian literature for a while, then changed my focus to computer programming and graphic arts. At the end of my second sophomore year, I decided I liked to write, so I switched to a double major in English and journalism. I ended up with a pretty worthless liberal arts degree."

"Do you have a hard time making up your mind about things?" he asked.

She shrugged and poked at one of the avocado slices on top of her omelet. "Not really. I just have so many interests."

"Am I one of your interests?"

"Ugh!" Reagan cried and started hitting Logan repeatedly in the arm. "I can't take it. Stop hitting on her at the breakfast table."

"I think you're the one hitting on *me*," he complained, unable to avoid her blows since he was trapped in the booth by Dare.

"Logan," Toni said, "you can hit on me later. In private."

He grinned. "Can do."

She tore her gaze from his, and he released her hand so he could concentrate on his breakfast.

"So," she said, shoving the avocados aside and poking at her spinach and tomato omelet with her fork. "I did all the background research on how the band formed and everything, but I'd like to hear you guys tell it. I don't want my book's introduction to read like a Wikipedia entry. I'd love some insider information that has never been shared with the general public before."

"The band was started by Dare," Steve said.

"Why didn't you start a band with your brother?" Toni asked Dare.

Logan had always wondered why Trey and Dare were in different bands. They both played guitar, but Dare had always played lead and Trey played rhythm, so it would make sense for them to be in the same band.

"Because Trey sucked," Dare said.

That earned him a smack in the back of the head from Reagan. As Logan was sitting between them, he got caught in the crossfire. "Hey, now. Watch it."

"Trey does *not* suck." Reagan chuckled and rolled her eyes to the heavens. "Okay, he does—in the best possible way—but the way he plays guitar doesn't." She blew out a flustered breath. "What I'm trying to say is he's amazing at both sucking and playing."

"Now who's getting inappropriate at the breakfast table?" Logan said.

"I said he 'sucked.' Past tense," Dare said. "Trey didn't figure out how to produce a unique sound until he was sixteen and then he really only sounded good with Sinclair. Trey and I never had a complementary sound, not even when my mom first taught us to play folksongs on acoustic guitars. Our sounds competed rather than complemented each other. It sounded like shit when we played together."

"So no chance you'll ever play in a band with your brother?" Toni asked.

"I wouldn't say no chance, but fairly slim. We both love where we are now. Why would we change bands?"

"So Steve joined the band next?" Toni asked. "He answered your ad in the LA Times for 'a drummer who isn't afraid to break sticks and heads.'"

Dare chuckled. "He wasn't the only one who answered that ad."

She sat up straighter and gazed at Dare in rapt attention. Logan had a million stories that weren't public knowledge. If that was the best way to get her attention, he was happy to supply her with enough insider information to fill a semi-trailer full of napkins.

"How many answered it?"

"Just three," Dare said. "The first guy, who is now the drummer for Waylaid, thought I meant he had to know how to fight. He was more interested in breaking human heads than drum heads."

Steve laughed. "Are you serious? You never told me that. Is that the only reason you picked me?"

Dare shook his head. "I picked you because your wife was hot."

Steve's smile faded. "Well, that's the only thing she had going for her."

Damn it, Dare. Really? They all knew how maudlin Steve got when his thoughts turned to his ex-wife. There was no reason to bring up Bianca at breakfast.

"I thought maybe she had some hot friends she could introduce to me," Dare said.

"You fuckin' liar," Max said, shaking his head at Dare.

Dare turned his attention to Max, who sat at the opposite corner of the table. "Why do you say that?"

"You told me that when Steve auditioned, every hair on your body stood on end and you knew you were in the company of greatness."

Dare chuckled. "How drunk was I when I said that?"

"That's the story I heard too," Logan said.

"Yeah, well maybe." Dare shrugged. "It was fifteen years ago. I tend to forget the details."

Toni was scribbling furiously on her napkin, drawing little boxes with words and linking them to other boxes with arrows. Logan tried to read it upside down, but couldn't figure out what all the boxes were about.

"So a drummer and guitarist does not a band make," Reagan said. "Who was next?"

Steve kicked Logan under the table. Logan tore his gaze from Toni and found Steve grinning at him as if he were dumber than a rock. "Uh, Steve asked me if I was available to start a new band," Logan said. "I wasn't actually—I was playing with Last Cannibal—but the lead guitarist was a tool, so I decided to give Exodus End a try. Steve and I had both been playing the Southern Californian club scene in different bands for a couple of years, so we partied together a bit. We never played together until Exodus End, though."

"Last Cannibal broke up as soon as Logan left. He was the only one in the band who knew what he was doing," Steve said.

Logan shrugged. "That's because the rest of them were too lazy to schedule gigs. When you're first starting out, you have to network constantly. They wanted to skip directly to the after-parties."

"Logan got us most of our gigs when we first formed," Dare said. "If he wasn't such an awesome musician, he'd have made a great manager for some lucky band."

"I hated doing that shit," Logan said. "A necessary evil to get noticed."

Logan glanced at Toni and found her gazing at him with adulation. Awesome. *Keep talking me up, guys.* He was all about getting noticed. Always had been.

"So when did Max join?" Toni asked.

"We've been through a couple lead singers," Dare said.

Logan tried not to feel too bitter about that since he'd been the band's first and shortest-lived vocalist.

"It's hard to find the right voice sometimes," Dare said. "You know after a few shows if they're right for the band or not. Since they get most of the attention and glory—"

"But have the easiest role," Steve interrupted.

Max leaned across Toni to shove Steve halfway out of the bench. He was the only one who'd finished his breakfast. That explained why he'd been so quiet throughout their story.

"—you have to find someone who can sing and incite a crowd," Dare continued. "Especially if you plan to make it as a live band. Plus he played bad-ass lead guitar."

"Wait," Toni said. "I thought that until he hurt his wrist, he played rhythm guitar."

"If that's what you want to call it," Dare said.

"When we first started we had two leads," Max said. "The record label made us tone our sound down a little. Have you heard our first album?" he asked Toni. "The one we produced ourselves? It's hard to find. We only pressed a few hundred copies. But we sounded quite a bit different then. Very guitar heavy."

"I don't think I've heard any of your early work," Toni said. "Is there any chance we can share some of it in the book?"

She was so excited her voice squeaked. If Logan hadn't already been crushing hard on the woman, that little sound of joy would have done it for him.

"Maybe," Dare said. "We'll have to check with Sam. We have to worry about record contracts and no-compete clauses and all that legal bullshit. That's why we never rereleased that album digitally."

"Oh," she said. "Well, I hope we can at least share some clips, but if not, I'd really like to hear it just for personal enjoyment."

"It's not as polished as our record label stuff. You might not like it," Max said. "Two lead guitars is a bit overpowering."

"Sinners pull it off in their solos," Reagan said. Her entire body was quivering with the excitement of possibility.

Logan wrapped an arm around her shoulders and squeezed. "Now don't you let that boyfriend of yours give you any ideas. We stick with what works for us, not what works for Sinners."

She sighed in disappointment.

"She wants to play lead so bad she can taste it," Max said with a soft laugh.

"Sorry, Reagan, that's my gig," Dare said. "You'll play lead in your own band someday. You're too good not to."

This seemed to placate her for the time being. Logan loosened his hold. Toni released a loud breath. Hmm . . . Did she not like it when he hugged Reagan? Or was she sighing in relief for some other reason? Logan rubbed Reagan's bare arm and watched Toni for her reaction. Her eyebrows drew together in a harsh scowl. So she didn't like him to touch Reagan. That was a certainty. The elbow jab to the ribs told him Reagan wasn't much appreciating his familiar fondling either.

Logan dropped his arm and located his fork. He picked the tomatoes out of his omelet, eating them one by one, before he repeated the task on the avocado slices. He liked the components separately, but wasn't a fan of their flavors blended with eggs and spinach.

"How did you know Max was the right singer for the band?" Toni asked.

"The first night Max sang onstage with us, we all got laid," Steve said.

"Weren't you married at the time?" Toni asked, her doe-like eyes wide.

"Yep," Steve said with a curt nod. "Bianca had stopped fucking me regularly by then, so when she jumped me backstage that night, I knew Max had what it took."

"To get you laid?" Max frowned.

"To get us *all* laid," Steve said.

"Max does get the ladies hot and bothered," Dare said.

"You all get the ladies hot and bothered," Reagan said. "Frankly, I don't see the appeal."

Knowing she was teasing, Logan grabbed her thigh just above her knee and squeezed repeatedly until she was thrashing about in the booth and laughing. "Reagan lies," he said. "She's totally boy crazy."

"I totally see the appeal," Toni said.

"Are you hot and bothered, Toni?" Max said near her ear.

She stared at Logan as she said, "You have no idea."

CHAPTER 7

TONI TRIED NOT to geek-out in the limo, but it wasn't easy to play it cool. Especially since Logan had taken the seat next to her and she could feel his body heat from knee to shoulder. Every time he moved, his scent engulfed her and it was all she could do to keep herself from burying her nose in that tight blue T-shirt and inhaling his subtle cologne like a cocaine addict.

She'd gotten lots of great material for her book at breakfast. She hoped she'd be able to share some of Exodus End's earliest songs as part of the introduction. She was already thinking of ways to connect the MP3s to the stories of the band's inception. Maybe different songs could play in the background as a reader made their way through the book. She wasn't sure if using their recorded music was possible. Their record label probably held the rights to all the band's songs tightly within its grip.

"Toni?" Logan's voice caressed the back of her neck. The sensation snaked down her spine and made her nipples tingle. That morning she had purposely chosen to wear a thick button-down blouse that didn't hug her breasts. Not because she didn't want to attract the man's attention, but because her nipples were like beacons every time he was near and it was embarrassing.

"Yeah?" she asked, looking up into his blue eyes.

"Nothing," he whispered. "I just wanted to say your name."

Her breath caught.

Okay, she needed this man in a bad way. She didn't care if he was playing her. Didn't care if he had only one thing on his mind.

Didn't care if he never wanted a relationship. She could deal with all of that when the time came. What she couldn't deal with was the thought of never again feeling his warmth against her naked skin or his thick cock driving into her body.

"Logan?" she whispered.

"Yeah?"

She glanced around to make sure no one was listening. The rest of the band members were talking about football, a subject that had never appealed to Toni, but was apparently something that got Reagan amped up. An avid Chargers' fan, she looked ready to throttle Steve, who claimed to be a Raiders' fan. Or maybe he was just pretending to get her all riled and animated. They seemed to like her that way.

While everyone's attention was elsewhere, Toni slid her hand over Logan's knee to press against the inside of his thigh.

"I've been thinking about what you said about my lack of . . . physical education." She moved her mouth closer to his ear so no one would overhear what she was about to say. "Do you think you could teach me things?"

The muscles beneath her fingertips clenched. "What kind of things?"

"Um, I don't know. Maybe we could start with . . ." She searched her brain for something that he would probably like if she had any idea what she was doing. ". . . how to suck . . . uh . . . give you a blow job?"

Logan choked and then went into a coughing fit that drew everyone's attention.

"Are you okay, dude?" Steve asked.

Logan nodded vigorously. "I'm fine," he sputtered between wheezing breaths. "Choked on my own spit."

"Smooth," Steve said with a laugh.

When Logan finally settled, he squeezed Toni's hand. "Damn, woman," he said under his breath, "are you trying to kill me?"

She closed her eyes to keep the threatening tears from spilling. "I understand," she whispered.

"You understand what?"

"That you don't want anything to do with me."

He knocked on her skull with his knuckles. "I thought you were supposed to be smart up here."

She opened her eyes to find him grinning at her. "What do you mean?"

He leaned close and whispered, "I'll teach you anything you want to know. When would you like to start?"

Now, her body demanded. Unfortunately, her brain didn't agree with that degree of spontaneity and inhibition. "As soon as we can be alone," she whispered.

"Do you want to skip the radio interview?"

Yes, her body demanded. Unfortunately her brain realized they both had a job to do and that job didn't include her learning how to give oral pleasure.

She sighed. "We can't."

He echoed her sigh. "You're right. After the interview we have to travel to the venue for tonight's performance. Once we get there, there'll be sound check, then a meet and greet, dinner, and then the show followed by the after-party. Maybe I can call in sick. The band doesn't really need a bassist. We're highly overrated."

She chuckled at his willingness to teach her. She was starting to believe she'd had an excellent idea. After he taught her how to please him with her mouth, she could request additional tutorials. Then maybe when they parted, she could find a boyfriend. Though she'd really like to be Logan's girl, she knew he'd lose interest in her pretty quickly. And that was understandable. They were from completely different worlds. And she wasn't exactly the kind of woman who rock stars dated. Or judging from past experience, the kind of girl who *anyone* dated.

"Are you laughing at me?" he asked.

She tried to stop grinning like a fool, but couldn't help it. "Nope. I'm just glad you agreed to this."

Now he was the one laughing. "Yeah, teaching you to suck my dick is such a hardship." He stroked her hair from her face with one hand and kissed her temple. She smiled in bliss until she noticed everyone was now staring at them. Dare in particular looked pissed.

Reluctantly she tugged away from Logan and sat with her hands in her lap. Her behavior obviously disturbed them all. She wouldn't want to do something to get herself booted from their entourage. She was here to work, after all, not get involved with their bass player.

"How do you guys do all this day after day?" Toni asked. "You must be exhausted."

"We run on pure adrenaline," Dare said. "That's why we crash so hard at night."

"The guys get every fourth day off," Butch said, as if that was pampering them.

"And I will not be moving from my hotel bed for a full twenty-four hours," Logan said. He leaned closer to Toni and whispered, "I hope you'll join me."

She flushed. She couldn't help it. She would very much like to spend twenty-four hours in bed with him but couldn't fathom what they could possibly do to entertain themselves for that long. Watch TV? Maybe he had some ideas.

"What are you thinking?" he asked.

"That I wouldn't know what to do with you for twenty-four hours."

He grinned devilishly. "I need far more than twenty-four hours to do all the things I want to do with you."

His lips brushed the side of her neck, and she sucked in a shaky breath.

"Mmm," he murmured. "There are so many things I want to show you, Toni. Teach you."

"Yes," was the only word she could manage.

"Logan," Reagan said, "will you give the woman some breathing room? She looks a little overwhelmed."

Toni wanted to hide under the seat. She hadn't realized all the limo occupants were staring at them. And here she'd been contemplating ripping off her shirt and clinging to Logan's thick hair as he sucked her throbbing breasts. She forced her body to move so that there were several inches between them.

Logan scowled at Reagan. "Seriously? If Trey was here, you'd be all over him."

"Well, he isn't, so it's a nonissue."

"You'd better get that stiffy under control before we get to the radio station," Steve advised, shaking his head at Logan's disgrace.

"I was working on that before Reagan interrupted."

Toni's gaze dropped to Logan's crotch. Oh my, he *was* hard. She had no idea what possessed her to grab it right there in front of everyone. Logan produced a sound, half groan, half whimper. He covered her bold hand with his and squeezed.

The limo pulled to a halt. The rest of the band scrambled out as if the car was on fire. Had she embarrassed them? She'd certainly embarrassed herself.

Logan was still holding her hand against the hard, thick ridge in his pants when he headed for the door. "I'll be there in fifteen minutes," he called, yanked the door shut, and locked it.

Turning to Toni, the sole occupant in the limo, he said, "You're in trouble, lamb."

Toni swallowed. "I'm sorry. I don't know what came over me. I just . . . wanted it."

She ran her hand up and down the length of his penis beneath the denim. She still wanted it.

"You can't grab it like that and not expect me to fuck you immediately."

Her mouth went dry and she forced her gaze to his, seeking the daring she hadn't realized dwelled within her. "Maybe that's why I grabbed it. So you'd f-fuck me." She couldn't believe those words had escaped her mouth. Saying them caused moisture to surge from her suddenly throbbing pussy. The tender soreness there had been distracting her most of the morning, but now something entirely more distracting was building between her thighs.

"Take your panties off."

She glanced around. The limo was empty and the windows were tinted black. Still . . . "Here?"

"Give them to me."

She hesitated and then reached under her skirt and slid her panties down her thighs. She handed them to Logan and stared at him with wide eyes.

"Are you wet?"

"I don't know."

His hand slid up the inside of her thigh. She tensed.

"Let me," he said, his voice low and completely in control. She got lost in his gaze and opened her thighs as far as she could in her knee-length skirt.

His hand moved higher. Higher. His fingers brushed her slick folds, and she gasped.

"Yes," he said. "You are. Tell me that you're wet."

"I'm wet, Logan. For you."

"Damn, what that does to me," he groaned under his breath. He teased her opening with one fingertip until she was rocking her hips against his hand.

"Oh." Her pussy clenched, begging to be filled. "Deeper, Logan. Inside."

His finger slipped inside her a mere inch. He caught her gasp in his mouth as he kissed her deeply. That was the only thing he was doing deeply. She rocked her hips against his hand, urging him to plunge his finger into her.

He tore his mouth from hers and buried his face in her throat. "You deserve better than this," he murmured. "You deserve better."

She squeezed her eyes shut. *Please don't reject me, Logan. Not now. I couldn't bear it.*

"Forgive me, lamb," he whispered.

Her heart panged unpleasantly. Breath strangled in her throat. *Then don't hurt my feelings. I'll have nothing to forgive.*

He rubbed his lips over her cheek. "Forgive me for not being strong enough to wait. All I can think about is how much I want to bury myself inside this sweet, wet pussy."

He slipped his finger deep, and she shuddered with bliss. He wanted her. Maybe as much as she wanted him.

"You deserve to be treated with gentleness. And patience."

"No," she sputtered. "That's not what I want."

He lifted his head to look at her. "It's not?"

She shook her head. "I like that I turn you on. That you've talked me out of my panties and have your finger inside me in the back of a limo. I even like that everyone knows what we're probably doing in here."

He stared at her wide-eyed. "You do?"

"Yeah. There's only one thing I'd prefer over this."

"What's that?"

"That you had more than your finger inside me. Please tell me you have a condom with you."

He grinned crookedly. He reached into his back pocket and produced a condom. He held it between two fingers to display it for her.

"I was hoping I'd need this today."

"Show me how to put it on you," she said, shifting on the seat so she could see what she was doing.

He knelt on the floorboard between her feet and reached for his fly.

"Let me," she said. She really did want to learn how to turn him on. "Is it better if I unbutton these slowly and tease you, or just yank it open and plunge my hand in there as if I can't wait to hold your hard penis in my hand?"

"Don't call it that," he said.

"What?"

"Penis. It sounds too . . . fifth-grade sex-ed."

"What should I call it?"

"Dick."

She shook her head. She didn't like that word much.

"How about cock?"

"Okay," she said. "Can I grab your hard *cock* now?" It felt strange to say the word. Strange and liberating. "I want your cock in my hand. In my . . . vagina."

"Pussy. You want my hard cock deep in your pussy."

She stepped it up a notch. "In my *cunt*." Her face was flaming. Every inch of her on fire with excitement. Who knew being bad could feel so damned good?

He groaned. It was the only encouragement she needed.

Toni unfastened the button at his waist and then jerked the rest of his buttons open and reached in his open fly to free his cock. She held it loosely in both hands and stroked its length reverently.

"Oh. You're so hard." She tightened her grip and stroked him again.

He sucked a breath through his teeth.

She looked up at his face. He had one eye closed and his mouth open. She couldn't tell if she was hurting him or annoying him or if he liked it.

"Am I doing it wrong?" she asked. "Show me."

"You're doing it perfectly," he said. "I need you to stop, though, because I'm about to come. I'm not sure what it is about you that gets me so worked up so quickly. But just hearing you say the word *cunt* has me ready to nut all over your pretty face."

She smiled. Her ability to excite him so thoroughly gave her an odd sense of empowerment. "Will you show me how to put the condom on you? I want you inside me now." She paused and looked up at him uncertainly. "If that's okay."

"It's definitely okay."

He showed her how to tear open the package, slip the condom over his cockhead, pinch a reservoir at the tip, and unroll it down his shaft. When she had it in place, she looked up at him for approval.

"How was that?"

"You got the job done," he said.

"Next time," she said, "I'll do it sexier."

He practically tackled her to the bench seat. She tensed when she felt his cock probe her opening. Would it hurt again? Mentally, she knew it wasn't supposed to hurt after that first time, but physically, her body remembered what if felt like for her tender tissues to give way to his hard flesh. He slid into her slowly, backing off several times and claiming her deeper with each forward thrust.

"Why are you doing that?" she asked.

"Doing what?"

"In and out like that."

"I'm using your lubrication to make this easier, honey. If I just ram it in, it'll hurt you." He stroked her hair gently. "I want it to feel good for you this time."

"It felt pretty good the first time," she said.

He kissed her gently. "I know you're lying. I hurt you. I won't ever hurt you again. Unless you want to get a little rough. Do you like it rough?"

Rough? She wasn't sure if she'd like rough, but how would she know unless she tried it? "Maybe. I don't know. We'll have to try it and see."

Logan pulled back again and then buried himself to the hilt with one hard thrust.

"Oh!" she gasped. No pain at all, just a delightful sense of fullness.

"Did you like that?"

"Oh yes!"

"Then you like it rough." He dropped his head to her shoulder and began to thrust his hips. Within seconds she was lost in a sea of pleasure. She strained against him, her fingers clinging to his hard chest, her legs tangling around his hips. Her back arched in complete surrender and she couldn't stop herself from chanting his name.

"You feel so good," he murmured into her neck. "So good, Toni. I need more time with you. More time. I want to fuck you slowly for hours."

He grabbed one breast with his hand, pinching at her nipple with the same cadence as his thrusts. She only wished she was naked, so she could experience the full sensation.

"Later," she promised. "We'll take our time later." Right now she liked the urgency and the passion that ignited quickly between them and threatened to explode.

Logan shifted and slid his free hand between her legs to stroke her clit while he thrust into her. Her fingers gripped the edge of the seat as her pleasure intensified.

"Come for me, baby," he whispered. "Don't hold back. Come for me."

She didn't know how to hold back. Or how to come for him. Everything her body was experiencing seemed completely involuntary to her. The throb between her thighs built into an intolerable ache. She writhed against his hand, until the building pleasure burst. Her body went taut and she cried out, shaking with bliss. Logan thrust deep and held himself buried within her, stroking her clit so fast as he came inside her that she couldn't stop shaking. She forced her eyes open so she could watch his face as he found release. His eyes squeezed shut and his mouth dropped open as his entire body shuddered in ecstasy. She would love to see that pleasure-contorted face on a regular basis.

Logan's hand went still and he collapsed. She held his weight against her, enjoying the solid feel of his body on hers. After he caught his breath, he pulled away to look down at her.

"I needed that," he said. "Next time it will be all for your pleasure. I won't let myself get so carried away."

As if she was going to argue with that.

"And then the next time, you'll teach me to suck your cock, right?" she said.

He groaned and wrapped both arms around her to give her an enthusiastic hug. "Woman, you're going to get me hard again if you aren't careful."

Was that supposed to be some kind of warning? She took it as more of a challenge.

CHAPTER 8

IN THE RADIO STATION'S SOUND BOOTH, LOGAN TRIED to pay attention to the interview, but his gaze kept falling on Toni, who was concentrating on recording the interview for her book and jotting notes. She obviously wasn't nearly as distracted by him as he was by her. Didn't seem fair.

An elbow to his ribs turned his attention to the host, who was gazing at him expectantly, waiting for an answer. "I'm sorry, what was the question?" Logan asked.

"Are you still participating in freestyle motocross?"

"When I have time," he said. He almost left it at that, but saw that Toni now had her undivided attention on him and looked interested in what he had to say. "I've been jumping and racing bikes since my teen years," he said. "I still love that adrenaline rush. If the music career hadn't worked out, I'd probably have had the opportunity to go pro."

"Much as I'd like to see you do tricks on a dirt bike, I'm not the only one glad the music career did work out," the host said.

Logan chuckled. "Oh, I'm glad too, but a guy needs something to fall back on."

"He's always been the daredevil of the group," Dare said. "Last time he won a bet, he made us all go skydiving. Not my idea of a good time."

"You had fun," Logan said. "Don't lie."

"*You* had fun," Dare insisted. "I dry humped the ground when the horror ended."

"I thought skydiving was great," Steve said.

"You don't have a lick of sense either," Dare said. "Logan jumps out of planes, Steve scales mountains."

"What do you do with your free time?" the host asked.

"Relax."

"Dare likes the water," Max said. "If he's not on the beach, he's in a pool or a hot tub."

Logan watched Toni scribbling notes like a woman struck by sudden inspiration. She had a huge smile on her face. Logan wondered what was going on in that head of hers.

"Reagan, what do you do in your free time?"

Up until this point, no questions had been directed toward her. She hesitated, probably under the assumption that she wasn't going to have to participate in the interview. "Uh. My boyfriend?" she blurted.

The guys laughed and she grinned.

"There's a rumor going around that you're dating one of the guitarists of Sinners, Trey Mills."

Reagan chuckled warily. "Ha, yeah, rumors," she said noncommittally.

When it was obvious that he wasn't going to get a more concrete answer from Reagan, the host asked, "And what does Max like to do?"

Steve pounded Max on the back. "You'd have to censor his reply." All the members of the band shared a knowing chuckle, except Max, who glowered at Steve.

Toni stopped writing to stare at Max with her head tilted to one side. Logan waved at her to get her attention back on himself. She wasn't quite ready for the kinky stuff Max enjoyed. Maybe in a few weeks they'd move on to more adventurous acts, but she was still fairly innocent. He wouldn't want to push her too fast. Toni lifted a hand of recognition in Logan's direction, blushing furiously under his obvious interest. She ducked her head, licked her upper lip, and tucked her long hair behind her ears.

Damn, she pushed every one of his lust buttons. And she wasn't even trying to. Twenty minutes ago, that demure sweetheart had fucked him in the back of a limo on a busy street. He needed to get his act together and treat her better, or she was going to find someone else to teach her things. The very idea of another man touching her had him clinging to his thighs to keep his hands from balling into fists.

Another elbow in his ribs, allowed Logan to catch the tail end of the radio host's question.

". . . concert tonight?"

"Oh, yeah. Can't wait. The fuckers in this town know how to party." He made a set of devil horns and his rock-on face.

Everyone in the room stared at him as if he'd sprouted purple fur on his eyeballs and then burst out laughing.

"What?" he asked. "What did I say?" He probably shouldn't have said *fuckers* on public radio, but he was sure some intern with fast reflexes had bleeped it out.

"He asked if you'd heard that a church group was protesting the concert tonight," Dare said.

Smooth, Logan. "Don't you think our fans should party with those effing protesters? Bring them over to the dark side?" Were they buying his attempt to cover up his slip?

His bandmates rolled their eyes at him, but the radio host took a liking to his idea. "KY101 will be there to get in on the action."

"Free backstage passes to any fan who can get a protester to agree to come backstage with them," Logan said, knowing he was taking this too far, but hell, he'd already fucked up, might as well make it an epic fail.

Max covered his microphone with one hand. "You're gonna get someone killed," he whispered angrily at Logan.

Shit, Logan thought. There he went acting and not thinking again. "Not by force or gunpoint," he said into the microphone in front of him, knowing how dedicated some of their fans were and the lengths some of them would go for a backstage pass. "The protester has to legitimately want to come backstage because you convinced them that we're awesome. And not Satanists."

"Logan, I'm going to kick you in the teeth if you don't shut up," Max whispered harshly.

Logan produced his toothiest grin, knowing Max was all talk.

"You heard it, folks. If you can get a protester to agree to go backstage after the show . . ."

Logan glanced at Butch, who was standing in the corner scowling at the schedule he had clipped to a clipboard. "Before the show," Logan said. They didn't need any protestors at their after-party.

"Before the show," the host echoed.

"At the meet and greet," Dare said, as if struck by sudden

inspiration.

Max nodded slightly, no longer looking like he wanted blood on his hands. Logan's blood. Logan should have been paying attention to the interview instead of the sexy woman in nerds' clothing who was grinning again as she wrote notes on a legal pad. If she was amused by him acting impulsively stupid, she'd have no problem being continually entertained. He could only concentrate on one thing at a time, and the woman had his full and undivided attention.

"Thanks for having us," he heard one of his bandmates say.

Was it over then? That hadn't taken very long. He would have been better off staying in the limo with Toni for the duration. For more than one reason. After the customary words of appreciation and handshakes with their hosts, Logan scrambled to open the door for Toni and stayed by her side as they were escorted to the elevator. Butch joined the band and Toni in the elevator car. Reagan was holding her security guard's hand—Logan thought the dude's name was Ethan, but he wasn't good with names.

"I'll catch the next one," Reagan said. So sweet that she wanted a moment alone with her second boyfriend. Logan wasn't sure how the woman could date two guys and keep them from killing each other in a jealous rage, but the three of them seemed to have it all worked out. No way Logan would ever let another man touch the woman he loved. Or even lusted. As soon as the elevator doors slid shut, Logan was bombarded with accusations.

"*This* is why we are agreed not to let women on the bus. Exactly this," Max said. "None of the rest of us have this problem. It's you. You have the attention span of a goldfish in heat."

"What in the fuck were you thinking, dude?" Steve asked.

"He wasn't thinking," Dare said. "At least not with his brain."

Logan didn't mind be called out by his bandmates. He'd fucked up, he owned that. He did mind them busting his balls in front of Toni. Not cool.

"You don't think it's a brilliant promotional scheme?" he asked, still trying to play it off as if he wasn't flying by the seat of his pants.

"Do you?" Butch asked. "The fans are going to be pissed off at those protesters anyway, so you draw further attention to them by having them seek them out and convince them to come backstage?"

"The media will be all over it."

"He's right," Toni said. "Something like that might make national news."

He could have kissed her. Knowing that would lead to a tight fly, however, he settled for placing a hand on her lower back.

"You expect us to believe that you didn't come up with that idea just to cover your ass?" Max stared at the ceiling of the elevator car and shook his head. "I can't wait to hear what Sam has to say about this."

"We don't have to tell Sam," Logan said. He'd faced their manager's wrath plenty of times in the past. Pissed-off-Sam was not one of his favorite people.

"Logan's right," Toni said. "I'm sure this will turn out in your favor and Sam will end up thinking Logan's idea was brilliant."

Logan rubbed Toni's lower back. He definitely wanted to kiss her—and *more*—now. He wasn't sure how she expected this fiasco to turn in their favor, but he hoped she was right.

The elevator door opened and several flashes went off in their faces. Logan blinked his blinded eyes and instinctively wrapped a protective arm around Toni.

Butch cursed under his breath as he plowed through the pack of photographers and led the band to the limo parked outside. "I said no fucking paparazzi today. Get those fucking cameras out of his face." Butch growled as he shoved a camera out of Max's face and pushed the singer into the car.

Once they were all inside, the limo couldn't leave no matter how much Butch roared in fury. They still had to wait for Reagan, who'd taken a different elevator to the lobby.

Toni cringed as the car rocked back and forth. Hands slapped the sides of the limo. Faces pressed against the glass. Steve flipped them off. Average day on the road. Logan sank back against the seat and rubbed his eyes with the heels of his hands. His lack of sleep was definitely catching up with him.

The noise outside suddenly intensified when the door opened and Reagan dove into the car with her bodyguard in tow.

"I had to bring him with," Reagan explained. "There was no way he could get me in the limo and then force his way to the other car."

"It's fine," Butch said. "I could probably use some backup." He lifted the phone receiver and spoke to the driver. "Take us to the venue."

"I thought we would go back to the bus," Toni said. "I'd like to rest for a few minutes before the meet and greet. Take a shower. Change clothes. Breathe!"

"The bus will meet us there," Logan said. "Are you tired?"

"I've never been more exhausted."

"The fun's just getting started," Max said. "I can't even imagine what this meet and greet is going to be like." He glared at Logan, who was silently praying for a lack of bloodshed between their fans and the protesters.

"Do you think anyone will notice if I skip it?" Dare asked, crossing his arms over his chest and giving off that "go away" vibe he'd perfected years ago.

Hoping to ignore the animosity in the car, Logan wrapped an arm around Toni's shoulders and tugged her closer. "Why don't you close your eyes for a moment? I've got you."

"I'm not used to this much excitement," she said, relaxing against his side, her head against his shoulder. "I'm a reclusive book geek, you know."

"I read a book once," Logan said.

"It was called *Fast Sluts, Slow Rides*," Steve said.

Toni chuckled. "I think I've read that one."

"Did it have a happy ending?" Steve asked.

"Yeah, the kind you pay extra for at a massage parlor," Toni said.

All the limo occupants laughed. The tension between the bandmates eased. Logan knew they would forgive him sooner or later. It wasn't as if he fucked up everyone's life on purpose. He didn't mean to cause trouble. Things just sort of happened that way for him.

His guilt diminished, Logan relaxed against Toni and closed his eyes. Something about her excited him and soothed him at the same time. He wondered if she'd stay on tour longer if he refused to be cooperative during his part of the interview. Because one thing was clear. He wanted her to stick around.

CHAPTER 9

INSIDE THE ARENA, TONI EXITED the bathroom of the women's dressing room with a towel around her head. The entire room was filled with flowers and chocolates, stuffed animals and leather apparel. With the exception of the leather, it looked like Valentine's Day had thrown up in the place. Apparently Reagan had a lot of admirers. She was sitting in her bra and panties on the arm of a sofa with her bare feet on the sofa cushion, tinkering with an electric guitar. She'd strum a few notes, pause, try a few other notes, nod, jot something down on her knee with a pen and go back to strumming.

Toni was just happy to have one of the members of the band to herself. Perhaps she could stage an informal interview. Logan didn't count. When she was alone with him, the last thing on her mind was asking questions of a nonsexual sort. Technically, Reagan was only a temporary part of the band, but that didn't mean she didn't deserve a chapter in the book.

Toni plucked a card from a bouquet of two dozen long-stemmed black roses. Toni had never seen black roses before. They were a bit macabre for her tastes. The card read,

> You're a goddess. I love your guitar work. I hope I get to see you in person tonight.
>
> Your devoted fan and fed-up vocalist looking for a new guitarist for his band (hint, hint),   Shade

"Who's Shade?" Toni asked.

Reagan looked up from the scribbles on her knee. "Huh?"

"These roses." Toni pointed at them with the card and then realized she probably shouldn't have read it without permission. "They're from some vocalist named Shade." Toni hurriedly stuck the bit of card stock back on the plastic card pick. "Sorry. I didn't mean to pry."

Reagan shrugged. "I have no idea who Shade is, so you aren't prying."

"Do you always have this many flowers in your dressing room?"

The guitarist glanced around as if noticing the flowers for the first time. "It gets more excessive with each tour date. I donate them to the local nursing homes and they distribute them. I think Claire catalogs the cards and sends thank-you notes where appropriate."

"Claire?"

"One of Sam's personal assistants. I'm pretty sure he has one for each band he manages." She laughed. "I don't know, I just play guitar. All that logistical bullshit is beyond my perception."

Toni moved to sit on the opposite sofa arm and added her bare feet to the cushions. "Are you writing music there?"

Reagan glanced down at the ink spots on her knee. "Uh, yeah. Trey and Dare have been encouraging me to find my own sound. I haven't found it yet, but I'm trying."

"Are you dating Trey?"

Reagan's head snapped up, and she stared at Toni suspiciously from beneath her long dirty-blond bangs.

"It's none of my business," Toni said. "Just so you know, I won't include stuff like that in the book. I'm not paparazzi, so you can trust me. I'm not out to ruin lives. I was just curious."

"I'll tell you about Trey if you tell me what's up between you and Logan," she said.

Toni's faced warmed. She wished she didn't blush so easily. "Uh . . ."

"Did something happen last night that you want to share? The guys are all acting weird today. Logan, yeah, that's to be expected, but even Dare is acting out of sorts. He has this overprotective thing he does, and I notice he's been extending that in your direction." Reagan pinned Toni with a pair of inquisitive blue-gray eyes. "Do you know Dare from before?"

Toni shook her head. "No. I think he knows about my, uh, my newfound maturity."

"Huh?"

"Logan and I, well, we . . ."

"Fucked?" Reagan lifted her brows and nodded as if to say, *obviously*.

Toni's face flamed ten degrees hotter. "Uh, yeah. We did. And I happened to be a, a virgin." The last word was scarcely a whisper. How mortifying to tell someone like Reagan Elliot that she'd held on to her V-chip until she was twenty-five.

"That son of a bitch!" Reagan set her guitar down and stood on the sofa. "I'm going to kick him in the nuts."

"No. I wanted to do it. He didn't coerce me or anything."

"You aren't one of those crazy bitches who pokes holes in condoms to trap a rich man by getting pregnant, are you?" Reagan asked.

"What?" Toni felt like her eyes were popping out of her head. "Who would do something like that?"

And even if she wanted to—and she *didn't*—she couldn't get pregnant for months anyway. She'd just gotten her regular birth control shot a couple of weeks ago.

"You'd be surprised." Reagan sat on the sofa arm again, looking slightly less irrational.

"I wanted to have sex with him because he wanted to have sex with me. And, well, he's incredibly attractive. If I hadn't been a virgin, no one would have thought twice about it."

Reagan snorted. "Including him. You do know he's a total player, right?"

Toni didn't know. She didn't know much about him that couldn't be read on Wikipedia. "I guess."

"He's been acting odd too, though. I thought maybe he was still trying to get into your panties and that was why he was so attentive and distracted, but if he's already been in them, maybe he likes you."

Toni's heart thudded in her chest. "Do you think so?"

Reagan's eyebrows lifted. "I don't want to get your hopes up too high, honey. I remember the guy who took my virginity. When he dumped me, I thought I'd die. Broke my heart into a million little pieces."

"Sorry to hear that."

"That was years ago." Reagan shrugged. "I got over him soon

enough."

Toni didn't want to think about getting over Logan. She prayed it never came to that.

"So is he good in bed?" Reagan asked.

Toni paused. Should she tell Reagan the details? Did it go against some code of bedroom ethics she was unaware of?

"I think so," Toni said hesitantly. "I don't really have anything to compare to."

"Does he make sure you come first?"

Toni's face flamed and she nodded. "He did both times."

"Then he's ahead of most of the pack. Don't let him get away with mediocrity just because he's your first and he knows you've never had better. If you're not sure about the girl side of things, you can ask me. I have plenty of experience." Reagan laughed. "I probably shouldn't be telling a journalist that."

Toni bit her lip. She didn't want Reagan to feel that she had to watch what she said around her. She'd really like a female friend to talk to about such things. The only person her own age that she hung around with was Julian, and he was a guy. A gay guy, true, but still a guy.

"Things like that won't be in the book," Toni promised. "It will mostly be about the music and hobbies and stuff like that."

Reagan chuckled. "But sex is my hobby now that the guitar-playing hobby is my actual job."

"So is Trey good in bed?" Toni did want to know the answer to the question, but she was mortified that she'd actually asked.

"The best," Reagan said with a breathy sigh. "He's a pleasure seeker who gives back more than he takes. What could possibly be better?"

"I'm not sure. I do like it when Logan gets so worked up by me that he can't keep his hands to himself."

"You definitely have the guy out of his head."

"So is that why you think he might like me?"

Reagan stared at her for a long moment. Toni guessed she didn't want to hurt her feelings by telling her the truth. There was no way in hell that Toni would ever mean more to Logan than a temporary plaything. She might as well face facts.

"He definitely lusts you," Reagan finally said, and then she shook her head. "I've only known him for a short time, so I can't be sure, but usually when he gets what he wants—"

"Sex?"

"Yeah. As soon as he gets laid, he's no longer interested. But he seems to still be interested in you." Reagan reached over and patted her knee.

"And how do I keep him interested?" She'd never had a man interested in her before, so had no idea how to proceed.

Reagan laughed. "Whatever you're currently doing seems to be working."

"I asked him to teach me how to do sexual things. He seemed interested in that." But she wasn't sure that was all she wanted him to be interested in.

"Of course he's interested in that." Reagan set her guitar aside, laced her fingers together, and set her elbows on her knees, looking like she planned on sitting there talking to Toni for hours. "I miss talking to my girlfriends back home," Reagan said. "I love the guys in the band, but they don't talk about this kind of stuff with me."

"It would probably give them perpetual boners."

"Or embarrass them. Or gross them out. They think of me as their kid sister."

Toni highly doubted that any man could think of Reagan as a kid sister. She had a natural sexiness that even a straight girl could appreciate.

"So how long have you been touring with Exodus End now?" Toni asked, ready to turn the subject to something she could actually write about in the band's biography.

"Three-ish weeks."

"How are you holding up? I never knew how exhausting this lifestyle could be. I haven't even been following the band for twenty-four hours and I'm ready to keel over."

"I'm having a great time," Reagan said. "I love every minute of it. And we do these things in spurts. Usually two days of insanity, a day of travel, and a day to recuperate. Rinse and repeat. Sometimes we do two shows in the same stadium, two nights in a row. Sometimes we do two shows in adjacent cities, but we almost always do shows two nights in a row. Trey claims that we're slackers—taking two days off for every two days on. His band usually tours constantly. If they're not playing, they're traveling. They don't have as many public appearances as Exodus End does, though, so we have to make time for that stuff too."

"The band seems to have accepted you as one of them quickly."

Reagan nodded, her smile stretching from ear to ear. "I pinch myself every day. They've been amazing."

A knock sounded on the door, the doorknob turned, and the door opened a crack. "Are you naked?" a deep voice called into the room. "Please say you're naked."

Reagan grinned. "Not yet, but I have company."

Toni hopped off the sofa. "I'll go."

"Is it my favorite company?" Trey Mills said as he let himself into the room. He was already dressed to go onstage, and Toni couldn't stop her heart from skipping a beat. "Oh," he said. "Company I don't recognize."

"This is Toni. Remember I told you someone was writing a book about Exodus End?"

"And you're chatting with her in your underwear?" Trey asked.

"If I was going to seduce her," Reagan said, "she'd already be naked with her legs wrapped around my neck."

Toni's couldn't bring herself to meet their eyes. Reagan had been joking about that, right? Toni had never considered doing anything sexual with another woman, but now she wondered how a woman's touch differed from that of a man.

"I need to get to the meet and greet," Toni said, rushing into the bathroom to collect her socks and boots. She sat on the toilet lid to put them on.

She could hear Trey's deep voice and Reagan's answering laugh. Were they laughing at her? Probably. She'd made a fool out of herself. Toni secured her hair back with a blue scrunchy that matched her blue blouse which matched one of her socks. Her other sock was gray and matched her long skirt. She looked like she should be shelving library books, not going to a metal band's meet and greet. Perhaps she should've splurged on new clothes for this assignment. She might not stick out like a poodle in a pack of Rottweiler's if she tried to fit in a little better. She glanced in the mirror and pushed her glasses up her nose. She hated wearing contact lenses, but maybe . . . She turned her head this way and that, making kissy faces at herself in the mirror. Maybe she wasn't as plain as she thought. Maybe she was actually pretty. Maybe if she put on some makeup and sexier clothes, Logan would start thinking of her as more than a friend. More than a temporary sex partner.

And maybe she should worry about her job instead of what

she looked like. She'd never really cared about such things before. And Logan seemed to be attracted to her regardless.

He'd been the one to show her to the women's dressing room so she could take a shower. He'd even stolen a kiss before claiming he needed to catch a nap on the bus or he'd be worthless that night during the concert. She wondered if he was still sleeping. And how much he'd mind if she woke him.

A naughty idea forming in her head, she hurried out of the bathroom and found Trey kneeling on the floor between Reagan's legs with a sucker stick protruding from between his lips. He had both hands wrapped around Reagan's upper thigh and was asking her about the notes she had drawn on her leg.

"I'm going back to the bus," Toni said when neither of them noticed that she'd entered the room.

"Okay," Reagan said. "We can talk more later."

"Thanks," Toni said, feeling intrusive.

She slung the strap of her messenger bag over her shoulder and left the room. The tour's regular security guards now recognized her and let her pass without accosting her, but the stadium's security stopped her several times as she made her way outside to the area where the buses were parked.

By the time Toni entered the bus, she'd almost convinced herself that she shouldn't bother Logan. That he did need to sleep and he'd probably be mad at her for waking him. She was thinking that until she found that he was alone on the bus, unconscious in his bunk, wearing nothing but a tangled sheet. She took a moment—a long moment—to admire the smooth skin of his naked back, the tattoo inked on his shoulder, the bit of naked buttocks exposed above the edge of the sheet, the bend of one bare leg, the muscular arm half obscured by his pillow, and all that golden hair surrounding his peacefully sleeping face. He had a half smile on his strong lips. She wondered if he was dreaming about something nice. She could only hope that it was her.

She continued to admire him until nothing could have stopped her from climbing into that bunk next to him and molding her body to his hard-muscled form. He started awake with an inrush of breath through his nose and lifted his head to see who had climbed into bed with him. Toni doubted she was the first to force her attention on the man, and would probably not be the last, but the smile he gifted her pushed those thoughts aside.

"Is it time to get up?" he asked, rubbing one eye with a

knuckle and yawning.

She shook her head.

"Good," he murmured before tugging her against the wall of his chest. His hands slid down her back and grabbed her ass to pull her more securely against him.

She lifted a trembling hand to caress the warm skin along his side. She'd never really touched a man before. She wanted to experience all the differences between his body and hers with her hands and when she got up the nerve, with her lips.

"Can I touch you?" she asked.

"Isn't that what you're doing?" he said in a drowsy voice.

"Everywhere?" she clarified.

"Mmm," he murmured. "I think I'm going to like this."

"Will you tell me what feels good for you?"

"If you pay attention, it should be obvious."

She smiled. Finally, something she excelled at. "I'm good at paying attention."

He scowled. "I'm not. The only thing I'm good at is being a fuck-up."

She rubbed his worried brow with her fingertips until his flesh relaxed beneath her touch. "You're not a fuck-up, Logan. You're . . ." *Wonderful.* She sighed internally, not wanting him to know how infatuated she was with him already. Or maybe her jumping into his bunk with him was a dead giveaway.

"Prove it. Name one thing I've done in the past twenty-four hours that wasn't impulsively stupid."

"Impulsive, yes, stupid, no. You're a creature of instinct."

"So now I'm a creature?"

"A man," she corrected. "A sexy one who I can't stop thinking about, even though I know I should be paying attention to my work."

"I have the same annoying problem when it comes to you."

"You don't have to say things like that to get into my panties," she said with a grin.

"But I do to make you smile." He kissed her, and she melted against him. His lips moved to her jaw. "Besides," he whispered, "it's true. Why do you think I shoved both feet in my mouth at that radio interview?"

"Because you were looking for new adventures with religious zealots?" she teased.

"Because I wasn't listening. I was too busy watching you." He lifted his head and looked down at her. He grinned crookedly. "See, when I tell you things like that, it makes you smile."

"It also makes my heart pound," she admitted.

He shifted down her body to rest his head against her chest. She wondered if her heart was pounding hard enough to damage his hearing. She lifted a trembling hand and placed it on his head, allowing her fingers to toy with the silky strands of his hair. They lay like that for a long while. She breathed in his scent, which clung to the pillow beneath her head and the entire space of his bunk. She relished the weight of his head on her chest and the feel of his fingertips pressing into either side of her ribcage. Toni's eyes drifted closed as her thoughts found rare tranquility.

"Didn't you come into my bed with plans to seduce me?" he asked.

She laughed. "I'm not very good at it, if you can't tell."

"No, I *can't* tell, and I have the hard-on to prove it."

Her heart leaped against her ribcage. She didn't know if she'd ever become accustomed to such shocking statements.

"Will you let me suck it?" she asked.

He laughed and lifted his head. She forced herself to look down and meet his gaze. He had every reason to laugh at her; her attempts to be sexy were ludicrous.

"Will I *let* you suck it?"

"If you're afraid that I'll hurt you . . ." She broke eye contact by tipping her chin up. "You'd probably prefer someone who knows what she's doing. I understand." She attempted to squirm out of the bunk, but he moved to cover her body and pinned her to the thin mattress beneath him. He grabbed her wrists and held them down on either side of her head. A thrill of unexpected excitement coursed through her body and settled as a throb between her thighs. She'd thought that being held down would be terrifying, but it was actually thrilling. Maybe someday she'd get up the courage to ask him to tie her to the bed.

"And I thought I was the stupid one." He shook his head at her. "I never have a problem brushing off a woman I'm not interested in. I know how to say no. If I wanted someone else, I'd say so. The only woman I want is you."

"Even though I'm inexperienced?"

"Hell, I think it's because you're inexperienced. It's refreshing. Even other women who don't have much experience sure don't make it known."

Toni gasped as realization dawned. "Oh. So I should pretend I know what I'm doing and muddle through it."

He kissed the tip of her nose. "Nope. You should keep doing exactly what you're doing."

"Then please stop making this so hard. I don't like it when you laugh at me."

"I'm not laughing at you, lamb. You make me feel happy."

Her heart skipped a beat. It seemed to be doing that a lot lately. Maybe she should visit a cardiologist. "I do?"

"You also make me talk too much. I'm going to shut up now and *let* you suck my hard-as-granite cock."

He kissed her breathless and then rolled onto his side against the wall. She stared into his dreamy blue eyes for a long moment and then glanced down to see if his cock was as hard as he claimed. Not so unfortunately, she got distracted by his muscular chest. Palms flat against him, she explored the hard contours of his pecs. She found his abdomen to be equally mesmerizing and continued to stroke his skin until she noticed his breath was hitching. When she tugged the sheet off his hip, she recognized his predicament immediately. Long, hard, and impressively thick, Logan's cock strained toward her. There was no way on earth that she could suck that entire thing into her mouth. She glanced up at him uncertainly, but he had his eyes closed and his lower lip trapped between his teeth. Toni longed to snap a picture of that face. Dear lord, if she included a picture of him like that in her book, every woman who saw it would need a change of panties.

Her gaze returned to his cock. This she was not willing to share with the world. Even though she knew it wasn't feasible, she wanted him all to herself. Her fingertips touched the hard length of his cock, and it jerked. Startled, she drew her hand away. Was it supposed to do that? Had she hurt him? Maybe she shouldn't be so bold. Logan produced a sound—half pleasure, half torture—but remained still.

Toni scooted lower on the bed until his navel was at eye level. She kissed his lower belly, delighted by the quivering quality of his flesh beneath her lips. She touched his cock with her fingers again, and Logan drew a shaky breath into his lungs. Did he like that? She thought so, but she couldn't be sure. She was tempted to ask him, but remembered that he said she'd know what he liked if she paid attention. Steeling her nerve, she bent her head and drew her tongue over the enlarged head of his cock.

"Toni, please," he whispered.

Please? Please what? She licked him again and waited for his reaction. She liked how a few touches had his breathing labored and his muscles taut. She felt powerful and a little sexy. And really horny. His hand moved to the back of her head. The muscles in his arm tightened, but he didn't press her forward to force her mouth to take him, though she was pretty sure he wanted to.

As she worked up the nerve to go for it, Toni trailed her fingers down his thick shaft, tracing a vein just beneath his satiny skin. When her fingers brushed over the wrinkled skin of his testicles, he sucked in a deep breath. She wondered what he would do if she . . . Toni shifted lower and kissed the loose flesh beneath her exploring fingertips. She kissed his balls the way he kissed her between her legs, with coaxing lips and slight flicks of her tongue. He squirmed, his hands moving to the sheet beneath him, which he clung to with clenched fingers.

Encouraged that he seemed to enjoy her experimentation, she drew the flat of her tongue over the bulge of one nut and then sucked on it gently. She'd known that this area of a man was incredibly sensitive to pain, but she hadn't been sure if that was true for pleasure. The deep moan of bliss her lover—*her* lover—produced exhilarated Toni. What other sexy sounds was the man capable of producing besides making a bass guitar purr?

Her hand circled his shaft, and she lifted her head to stare at his huge cock. It was already seeping fluid. A single drop glistened in the narrow slit at the tip. Toni decided she'd much rather have its lengthy thickness pounding into her hot and achy pussy, but she'd told him she wanted to suck him, so she wasn't going to change tactics now. *You can do this, Toni.* She used her hand to direct him into her mouth. Her first taste of him wasn't what she expected. Salty. Musky. She wasn't sure if she could take an entire mouthful of his cum. Was she supposed to swallow it? Spit it out? What was the proper procedure the first time you sucked a guy off? Toni decided she needed more experienced friends who would tell her these things. Maybe Reagan would give her advice if she asked, but she couldn't tell Logan to hold on for a moment while she ran to ask Reagan if she should swallow.

His fingers untangled from the bedclothes and he stroked her hair gently with one hand. "Feels good, baby. You're so beautiful. I'm crushing so hard on you right now."

Okay, she would totally swallow. Now she just had to excite

him enough to get the opportunity. She drew him deeper into her mouth. Deeper. Deeper. Triggered her gag reflex. Drew away abruptly, choking and retching in a most embarrassing fashion.

Her stomach still clenching with spasms, she buried her face in the mattress beside his hip. Humiliated, she prayed an alien would beam her onto the mother ship and fly her to a distant galaxy.

Logan touched the back of her head. "Are you okay?"

"Don't laugh," she pleaded, her voice muffled by the bedding.

"I'm not laughing. You don't have to deep throat it. The head is the most sensitive part anyway."

She knew that. Everyone knew that. Okay, so maybe she hadn't known that. But now she did.

"Do you want to try again?" he asked. "Or can I rip off your shirt and fuck your gorgeous tits?"

Her eyes widened. What? How would that be any fun? Or even possible? She lay there for a while trying to picture how one had her tits fucked.

"Toni?"

She lifted her head to look at him. "You can fuck my tits some other time," she said. "I'm going to try the blow-job thing again."

He bit his lip, and she could tell he was trying really hard not to laugh. She slapped his belly and eyed the thing that had tried to choke her to death.

"Would you hold it against me if I gave you some instructions?" he asked.

"I'd be relieved actually." Perhaps he would save her from embarrassing herself again.

"Hold the base with one hand," he said.

She shifted into a more comfortable position on her knees and one elbow, and used her free hand to grab the base of his cock.

"Not quite that tight," he said breathlessly.

"Sorry." She loosened her grip.

"Perfect. Nothing hurts worse than a pair of sharp teeth scraping over the surface of your cock."

"Nothing?"

"Few things," he amended. "So keep your teeth covered with your lips, like this." He demonstrated by drawing his lips in over his teeth.

"Have you done this before, Logan?"

He laughed. "Uh, not personally, no."

She mimicked his teeth-covering technique and looked at him for approval.

He stroked a stray piece of her hair behind her ear. "Have I mentioned that I'm crushing on you hard?" He snatched her glasses off her nose and set them down on the bed beside him.

She nodded, still making her I'm-about-to-suck-your-cock face.

"Go ahead." He nodded toward his lap.

Her shoulders tense with nerves, she directed him into her mouth, but didn't make the mistake of shoving him down her throat this time.

"Can you take it a little deeper?"

She took another inch of him.

"That's perfect," he said. "Are you okay?"

"Mmm-hmmph." She became aware of her saliva dripping down his shaft and onto her hand.

She released his cock to wipe her hand on the sheet and tried to suck her spit back into her mouth.

"Don't try to be neat," he whispered. "Slobber all over it. Sloppy and wet is sexy."

If he said so. She returned her hand to his shaft, cock head pressed against the roof of her mouth, teeth properly covered by her lips, and waited.

"I'll tell you how I like it best, but if it's too much of a challenge, don't worry about it. I'll like anything you do."

She was definitely up for a challenge, as long as it didn't involve his cock all the way down her throat.

"Suck as you pull back, hum as you go down. Not too deep. Don't choke yourself."

She felt awkward doing the motions at first and had to think really hard about what she was doing—especially the hum thing—but as she got the hang of it, she became aware of how vocal Logan was getting. He definitely liked this.

"Pull back just a little more," he gasped, "so your lips bump over the rim—Oh God, just like that."

His excitement was infectious. Her hips began to writhe involuntarily. Her panties were entirely drenched, her pussy a throbbing, swollen, far-too-empty place of longing.

"Rub . . . Rub your tongue . . . against . . . when you go

down."

She worked her tongue against him.

"Fuck yes, baby! Just like that. Faster now."

She was doing it. She was pleasuring him.

"Hey, Logan," someone called from the front of the bus. "The meet and greet is about to start. Are you coming?"

"Almost," he called, his back arching off the bed. "Almost."

He patted Toni on the back of the head—a signal she didn't understand—and then exploded in her mouth, bathing her tongue with thick, salty fluids. She swallowed, still using the techniques he'd showed her, until he finished spurting and cursing under his breath.

She released him from her mouth, the muscles in her face and throat aching, but damn if it hadn't been worth it. She had totally gotten him off. He'd come. In her mouth.

He lifted his head off the pillow to focus on her. "Did you swallow that?"

Still gasping for air, she nodded.

"Fuck, woman."

He grabbed her and tossed her onto her back on the bunk. *What?* He shoved her skirt up around her waist and grabbed her panties in one hand, yanking them down her thighs. He pulled one leg free of them before spreading her legs wide, climbing between her thighs, and thrusting his still-hard cock deep into her hot, wet cunt. She cried out in excitement—twisting in spasms of delight, her pussy clenching around his driving cock. As his erection subsided, he pulled out in frustration and slid down her body. Two fingers plunged into her pussy, and his mouth latched onto her clit. He quickly worked her into a frenzy, his fingers thrusting in and out of her, his lips and tongue massaging her clit until she was rocking against his face and calling his name. She exploded like a supernova, her entire body engulfed in mindless pleasure. As she drifted down from the stratosphere, Logan moved to wrap her in a tight embrace.

"I can't wait to keep you in my hotel room for an entire day and show you all the dirty things I want to do to this body," he whispered.

Eyes wide, Toni's body stiffened. She wasn't sure if she should be excited or nervous by the prospect.

"Your pussy tastes so sweet," he said. "I'm going to start you off by licking it for hours."

Okay, excited it was.

CHAPTER 10

CHAOS.

Toni had expected the meet and greet to be thrilling, but things had gotten completely out of hand. Her idea of making this a media event had only added to the mayhem. The band didn't seem to mind the extra attention, or maybe they were used to the insanity, but security was struggling to keep those with legitimate VIP passes separate from those trying to sneak in separate from those who had heard the radio broadcast and had a protester in tow separate from the press. It was a valiant effort, but they ended up with a big mix of crazy. Toni had no hope of keeping up with most of it, so she decided to stick near Logan, who had taken it upon himself to screen the fans with protesters. Toni had her camera rolling and her voice recorder running and was doing her best to get the blasted release forms signed by anyone who might end up recognizable in her footage and jot down notes at the same time. While Toni was the Queen of Multitasking, everything started to run together in an indistinguishable mix of unfamiliar faces and garbled words. She hoped events weren't always this overwhelming for the band. How did they put up with this day after day?

"So have you ever actually listened to any of our songs?" Logan asked a woman holding a sign that read *Exodus End Should End Now.*

"Our church group has studied your lyrics," she said, her eyes bugging out of her head as they shifted from Logan to Max, who was laughing at something a fan said, to Dare, who had a three-foot circle of space around him and a completely inapproachable look on his face. The church woman actually squeaked in terror when the sexy lead guitarist's eyes met hers.

"We have lyrics?" Logan glanced at Toni. "Is that what you call the words Max belts out?"

The woman tore her gaze from Dare to look at Logan. "What?"

"I don't think this one is acting," Logan said to Toni. He'd already discovered three of the "protesters" had been fans in disguise. It hadn't been difficult. Eventually they started gushing about being in the presence of musical greatness.

"Why does your church group study Exodus End's lyrics?" Toni asked, stuffing a release form into the woman's free hand.

"Its evil message corrupts our children."

"Can I ditch the lady now?" asked the fan who'd somehow talked her into joining him backstage. Maybe he'd succeeded because he was a boy of fifteen or so who had the most innocent-looking face. Well, except for the nose, eyebrow, and lip piercings. "She's nucking futs." The woman gasped and the kid glared at her. "What? I said 'nucking futs.' Clean out your ears, old lady."

"How did you get her to come backstage with you?" Logan asked.

"I told her I wanted to be saved. Can I go talk to Mills now? He's my idol."

"Good luck with that," Logan said. He slapped a backstage pass into the kid's hand and nodded in Dare's direction.

Logan tilted his head at the church lady and scratched his jaw with one finger. "So which songs did you analyze? I'm trying to remember which ones have an evil message."

The woman glanced nervously at Toni. Toni was sure it was because she looked "normal."

"Isn't he gorgeous?" Toni asked her.

She looked at Logan. Really looked at him. Her expression softened. "Maybe if he cut his hair," she whispered out of the corner of her mouth.

Logan laughed. "I cut several inches off of it just a few weeks ago, but I'm not going any shorter. The ladies like to pull it when . . ." He lifted his eyebrows suggestively, and Toni finally found a woman who could blush more crimson than she did when Logan teased.

"Well, I never," the lady gasped, a hand trembling at her neck.

Logan scowled. "That's unfortunate. You really should. Not that I'm volunteering. I'm thinking about getting a steady girlfriend." Logan moved his gaze to Toni. "A sweet girl who gets easily embarrassed. Has brains. Mismatched socks. And big boobs." He held his hands out two feet in front of his chest. "Really stacked."

Toni smacked him in the arm, but her heart was smiling. She'd never expected him to consider her girlfriend material. She tucked the idea in the back of her mind. She'd get all goofy about it later when some stranger wasn't shaking her head in disapproval.

"Did your whole congregation come to protest the concert?" Toni asked the woman.

She shook her head. "Some of 'em don't blame the band for Jeff's suicide, but that sweet boy changed when he started listening to Satan's music."

Toni's heart rose to her throat. "I'm so sorry. Did you know Jeff well?"

She nodded curtly. "He was my grandson's best friend. At least when they were boys. They grew apart in junior high. Didn't even talk to each other in high school. Our Timothy still cared, though. He still cried when he heard the news after Jeff shot himself. Thought maybe he could have been a better friend to Jeff. And then maybe Jeff wouldn't have . . ." The lady broke off, pulled a tissue out of her pocket, and dabbed at her eyes. She noticed that Toni's eyes were also leaky, and she reached into her purse to offer a second tissue to the bleeding heart beside her. Feeling foolish but no less empathetic, Toni dabbed at her eyes with the proffered tissue.

Logan reached out and squeezed the woman's shoulder. "My condolences. I know how hard this is."

"How could you possibly know how hard this is, *rock* star?" she sneered.

"When Vic killed herself, I thought the pain of her loss would kill me too."

Vic?

Logan glanced at Dare, who was talking to the kid with the shiny new backstage pass.

The woman covered Logan's hand and squeezed. "I'm sorry about your . . ."

"Friend," Logan said. "She was our lead guitarist's high school sweetheart. They dated into their twenties, so we all knew her well. Everyone thought Dare would marry her someday. When she lost the baby . . . The doctors said her hormones were off balance and that's why . . ." Logan swallowed and closed his eyes.

How had Toni missed that in her research? She wrapped both arms around Logan and hugged him as hard as she could. Dare Mills was next on her list.

"If it makes you feel better to have someone to blame, I completely understand," Logan said to the woman. "I can't hold that against you if it makes your grief easier to bear."

"That boy," she said, nodding at the young Exodus End fan she'd accompanied, "he reminds me a lot of Jeff. I guess that's why I followed him in here." She smiled as she watched the kid chatter excitedly with his guitar hero. "He looks happy to be here. I'm glad I could give him that."

"Well, since you're here, you might as well have a beer. I promise we won't sacrifice any goats in honor of Satan tonight."

She laughed. "It's not nice to poke fun at a helpless old lady."

"Helpless? I don't see a helpless old lady. Though you must be terrified to be in the same room with Max, and who can blame you."

Toni chuckled and finally released her hug. Logan wrapped an arm around her to keep her from moving away.

"Which one is Max?" the woman asked.

"That tall one over there in the leather pants."

The woman craned her neck and gasped when she caught sight of Max in a crowd of female admirers. "The tall one with the short hair?"

"Yeah, he's our lead singer. He comes up with most of our evil lyrics."

"Now that one is easy on the eyes," she purred.

Toni bit her lip so she wouldn't laugh.

"Go introduce yourself," Logan suggested. "He'll get a kick out of it."

"I think I will," she said, stopping to grab a beer out of the nearest cooler as she wandered off in Max's direction.

"I didn't think I'd ever get rid of her," Logan said before stealing a kiss. Someone lifted their cellphone to take a picture. Logan spun toward the camera and pulled Toni behind him. She understood why he wouldn't want anyone to have photographic evidence of him kissing her, but it still made her chest ache and her ire rise. She pulled out of Logan's grasp and marched toward Dare. She still owed him a hug. She couldn't imagine how hard it would be to lose an unborn child and have the baby's mother commit suicide over the tragedy. No wonder he tried to keep strangers at a distance.

CHAPTER 11

LOGAN SPUN around, wondering why Toni had suddenly stomped off in the opposite direction. Had she wanted her picture all over the Internet with speculation about why he'd been kissing her in public? Kissing her in front of everyone hadn't been his brightest move, but he couldn't help it. He liked to kiss her. And he didn't mind who knew it. Yet he knew how brutal people could be to the significant others of famous people, so he wanted to protect her from the bullshit. Hadn't she recognized that? Where in the hell had she gone? He scanned the room for a mane of thick brown hair.

When Logan spotted her with her arms wrapped around Dare, his jaw dropped in disbelief. Dare knew that Logan liked her. Where did he get off putting his hands on *his* woman? Maybe Mr. Know-It-All wanted to prove to Logan that he wasn't ready to commit to her. Maybe Mr. Can-Do-No-Wrong thought this would make Logan give up on her. The bastard.

Logan stalked across the room and shoved Dare in the shoulder. "Get your fucking hands off her, Mills."

Dare looked at him as if he were speaking Klingon. "What?"

"You heard me. Don't touch my woman."

Dare blinked especially hard. "Your *woman*?" He grinned wickedly and then tugged Toni closer. "I think she missed your memo. Looks like she's with me."

Logan's arm moved of its own volition. He honestly hadn't meant to punch Dare in the face. It didn't actually register that he'd hit him until Logan drew his stinging knuckles away from the nose they'd connected with. Before Dare could retaliate, Toni had Logan by one ear and jerked him down to her level.

"What is wrong with you?" she bellowed.

He'd never seen her angry before. Why was his fly suddenly so tight?

"Me? You're the one hanging all over Dare."

"I'm going to fuck you up later, Lo," Dare said. He held his head tilted backwards with the bridge of his nose pinched between two fingers. One of the security guards was forcibly directing him toward the bathroom.

"I wasn't hanging all over Dare," Toni said. "I was hugging him."

Logan pulled her hand off his ear and straightened to his full height. He crossed his arms over his chest and glared down at her. "Same difference."

"It is not the same. At all. And since when am I *your* woman?"

"Since I popped your cherry."

She gave him a frosty stare. "I would have let any member of your band *pop* my cherry," she said. "You know that, right? I just wanted it over and done with. I didn't care who did the deed."

His heart twisted in his chest, cutting off his ability to take a decent breath. She couldn't mean that.

He glanced around at their spectators. Maybe the meet and greet wasn't the best place to discuss this. He grabbed her arm and tugged her toward the bathroom. He'd forgotten that Dare was already in there until he was confronted by a pair of grass-green eyes above a freely bleeding nose. No way was he confining himself with that caged tiger.

"Did you come to apologize?" Dare asked as he stuffed a tissue up one nostril. "It won't save you. I'm still going to fuck you up."

"Actually, I forgot you were in here," Logan said.

"Figures." Dare shoved him aside and left the room. The roadie, who went by the nickname T-Bone, grabbed the first aid kit and scurried after Dare.

When they were alone, Toni yanked out of his hold. "Why are you acting like such a jerk?"

She thought he was a jerk? Ouch. "I-I don't know." He'd never felt so confused before in his life. And worried about what someone else thought of him. And afraid that he'd done something that she'd never forgive him for. He was less concerned about Dare fucking him up than he was of Toni's disapproval.

"How could you think I'd mess around with Dare? Especially right in front of you?"

"I didn't just think it, I saw it."

"I was *hugging* him, Logan. What you said about him losing his baby and the mother committing suicide, it made my heart ache and I needed to hug him."

So she'd been behaving like a first-class sweetheart and he'd been behaving like a first-class asshole. "It wasn't even Dare's baby. It was Max's."

Toni stared at him open-mouthed for a long moment before licking her lips. "I thought she was Dare's girlfriend."

"She was."

Toni sucked a deep breath into her chest and blew it out with a fierce scowl.

"That better not end up in your book," he said.

She shook her head vigorously. "I won't put anything in the book that could potentially hurt one of you." She lowered her head. "Or all of you."

He believed her. If she'd told him that pigs had finally evolved wings, he would have believed that too. "I'm sorry for being a jerk," Logan said. "I just . . ." He stared at the wall behind her. How could he put this? "I didn't like seeing another man with his hands on you."

"Obviously." She chuckled, and he shifted his gaze to hers.

She was smiling. He felt as if the weight of the world had lifted off his shoulders.

"You don't hate me?"

"Why would I hate you? I'm your woman, aren't I?" She tilted her head and winked at him.

He grinned, his head swimming with happiness. "Yeah."

"Go talk to Dare."

"Do I have to?"

"You sucker punched him in the nose, Logan. Don't you think you at least owe him an apology?"

He took a deep breath. "Yeah. He's going to kick my ass, you know."

"You probably deserve that. But I'll kiss it and make it better."

"I'm going to hold you to that."

"So you'd let me?"

"Let you what?"

"Do things to your ass."

Logan gawked at her.

She lowered her eyes. "Forget I asked that."

"Depends on what you have in mind. No strap-on dicks allowed in my bedroom."

She laughed. "Why would I use a strap-on . . ."

Her eyes widened when she apparently figured it out. She was still so innocent and he was so enjoying making her naughty. Logan stroked her hair from her lovely face and tucked it behind her ear. He stared down into the inquisitive brown eyes hidden behind thick glasses and couldn't help but smile. It was a permanent condition when she was around. What was it about this woman that had him in knots? God, he hoped he didn't fuck things up with her. Yet he figured it was inevitable. He tended to fuck up everything eventually. Except his music. It was the one thing he had under perfect control, but maybe that had more to do with his bandmates, the crew, and his anal-retentive manager than it had to do with anything he did. "You're beautiful. We'll try things—some of them so naughty your glasses will steam up." He kissed her forehead before leaving the room to seek his well-deserved ass-kicking.

Pissed off and out of sorts, Dare had let his guard down and was completely surrounded by a collection of lead-guitarist worshipers (mostly male) and rock-star-dick worshipers (mostly female). Logan knew exactly how to earn Dare's forgiveness. Free him from the hell of adulation. At least Dare considered that hell. Logan wouldn't mind a little more of it.

"Hey, Dare," Logan called over the crowd. He had no chance of making his way through the flock of admirers. "We need you in the dressing room. Pronto."

Dare gave him a measured look. He obviously knew Logan was lying. Now he just needed to decide which was the lesser of two evils—fans he'd allowed to get too close or one of his best friends who was currently on his shit list. Logan thought Dare had decided to take his chances with the crowd until he lifted one finger, said, "Excuse me," and the crowd parted before him like the Red Sea.

Dare stalked toward the dressing room which was labeled Band ONLY—No Guests, and Logan followed him, hoping there were witnesses present behind that closed door in case Dare actually killed him. He was such an easygoing guy until someone pissed him off.

Dare stormed into the dressing room, and Logan closed the door behind them. They probably should have knocked before barging in. A rhythmic pounding of flesh on flesh came from the couch on the opposite side of the room. Logan couldn't see anything but one feminine foot poking over the back of the sofa, but he could hear a whole lot.

"Yes, Steve. Oh yes!"

Well, that explained where Steve had been during the meet and greet. His head appeared above the sofa back, and his confused gaze shifted from Logan to Dare.

"What the fuck happened to you?" Steve asked as he took in the bit of bloody tissue Dare had shoved up one nostril.

"Logan." Dare pulled the tissue out of his nose and dabbed his nostril on the back of his hand to check if it was still bleeding.

"Don't stop, baby. I'm almost there," crooned a woman from somewhere beneath Steve.

Steve continued to stare at his bandmates, but he was moving again. The sound of wet pussy getting pounded was unmistakable. "Did you punch him or what?"

"Yeah," Logan said, raking a hand through his hair. "I didn't mean to. Well, yeah, I did. I overreacted when I saw Toni hanging all over him. I thought he was making a move on her. I'm sorry I hit you, Dare. I overreacted."

"Logan is stupid over a woman," Steve said. "Now his ignorance knows no bounds."

A hand with long hot-pink fingernails moved to Steve's hair. He flinched as she got a handful and pulled.

"Ouch. Don't yank."

"Then stop talking. I can't concentrate."

"Me neither." Steve shifted and moved to kneel on the sofa, his elbows resting on its back and his fingers linked together.

"I didn't mean you should stop," the woman protested.

Steve ignored her. "So are you going to hit him back?" he asked Dare. "Because that's something I'd like to see."

"No," Dare said. "I have a better way to get back at him."

A chill raced down Logan's spine. He had no doubt that Dare was capable of ripping his guts out if he had a mind to. "Just hit me. Get it over with."

Dare chuckled coldly and then let himself out of the dressing room without another word.

"Shit," Logan said. "What do you think he's going to do?"

"I'd keep a close eye on Toni if I were you," Steve said. "You know if he shows the slightest interest in a woman, her panties are around her ankles in less than five seconds."

"He wouldn't do that. He knows I like her."

"Are you sure? I think he's pretty pissed off at you."

Dare wasn't someone you wanted to piss off. And Logan had decked him in the nose. In front of a crowd of people. Logan rubbed his forehead with one hand. So what should he do about this? It was too late to take it back. He guessed he'd just follow Steve's advice and keep an eye on Toni. As if that would be a chore.

"Can we finish now?" an annoyed voice said from the sofa.

Steve rolled his eyes at Logan and then disappeared from view again. Logan let himself out of the dressing room before their porn sounds gave him wood.

Keeping an eye on Toni turned out to be easier said than done. He didn't want to be blatantly obvious to everyone in the room that he had the hots for her. Not with members of the press for the entire city of Eugene, Oregon, watching his every move. At least Dare didn't seem to have Toni on his agenda. For now in any case. He had regained his sphere of cool, and everyone was keeping an appropriate distance from the guitar god. Logan spotted Toni talking to the church lady, who was trying her damnedest to gain Max's attention. Toni had a camera in one hand and a tape recorder in the other and was spouting off questions he couldn't hear over the din of conversation. Logan decided it was his best bet to find something else to occupy his time.

Beer worked.

He grabbed a bottle from the nearest ice chest and leaned against a wall. It didn't take fans long to notice he was alone. A particularly talkative young woman decided his ear was free and spent the next twenty minutes telling him about every band she'd ever seen in concert. "Exodus End is the best, of course. I'm looking forward to Sinners' show tonight too."

"Great band," Logan said. He deliberately drained the rest of his beer.

"I think I'll skip Riott Actt, though. I don't know any of their songs."

"You really shouldn't. You'll regret it someday."

At a raucous round of laughter from Max's general direction, Logan straightened and craned his neck to see what fun he was missing.

"I want to talk to the cleavage cam next," someone insisted.

Cleavage cam?

Logan decided he'd done his duty for the evening. He handed his empty bottle to the blabbering fan and went to investigate the cleavage cam. That sounded right up his alley.

He wasn't sure if Toni had come up with the idea of holding the camera between her luscious breasts or if Max had put her up to it. Whoever had come up with the idea had made Toni a complete hit with every male in the room. All in good fun, but if any of them put their hands on her . . .

Logan took a deep breath. Why was he so insistent on claiming her as his alone? He definitely liked the idea that no other dude had ever been inside her, but that couldn't possibly be the only reason he was so wrapped up in the woman. So protective of her. Overprotective. He couldn't help himself. He squeezed through the crowd until he stood beside her.

"I'm Dennis Brown. I won my guest pass from a radio show. I've been an Exodus End fan for fourteen years and I saw my first Ex-End concert with my parents when I was ten." The fan spoke into the microphone clipped to Toni's shirt.

Ugh. He'd seen his first show when he was ten? That made Logan feel old. But thirty-two wasn't so old, was it?

Not if he had a say in the matter.

Logan was glad to see that not much of Toni's considerable bosom was actually showing. Her shirt was buttoned around the camera so that the lens protruded from her cleavage, but those perfect breasts of his, of *hers,* were out of view. He suddenly had a powerful need to stir her up a little.

He leaned close to her ear and whispered, "I think you should keep that camera rolling while I fuck you later."

Her face reddened as he knew it would, but she whispered, "I think all the jiggling would make anyone who watched it motion sick."

He chuckled. Okay, yes, he liked that he had been her first and that he was her only lover, but he liked her quick wit even more. He loved how she'd get all embarrassed but still said things he didn't think would ever come out of her mouth.

"So whose idea was the cleavage cam?" he asked.

"Mine. It's impossible to get anyone's attention when Max is around."

"Tell me about it," Logan grumbled.

"So I figured if they wouldn't talk to me, maybe they'd talk to my boobs. Okay, who's next?" she called out.

Logan leaned toward her chest. "I'm Logan Schmidt, and I've been a fan of Toni's boobs for almost a day now."

She laughed and slapped him on the shoulder. "Don't tease."

"Who's teasing? They're amazing." He moved his mouth close to her ear. "I can't wait to squeeze them together around my cock and fuck them until I come all over your chest."

"Oh! So *that's* how a guy fucks tits," she blurted loudly. Very loudly.

Everyone within earshot burst out laughing. She stood perfectly still for a long moment. Logan feared she'd need CPR if she didn't take a breath soon. He didn't know CPR, but he was definitely ready for some more mouth-to-mouth with her.

"Everyone knows that," she announced after an uncomfortably long minute and laughed. And laughed. And laughed some more until Logan decided she was on the verge of hysteria.

He lifted her hand and kissed her knuckles. "Come on, sweetie," he said. "Let's take a little break outside. You look like you need some fresh air." She looked like she needed a psychiatric evaluation, but there was no way he was stupid enough to say that.

Toni swallowed hard and nodded vigorously. Holding her hand securely in his, Logan led her to the back of the stadium near where the buses were parked. He lifted her to sit on a loading dock and stood in front of her knees, waiting for her to say something.

"I'm so sorry I'm stupid about this stuff," she whispered. "I didn't mean to embarrass you."

"I'm not embarrassed," he assured her. He was smitten by her. He even thought she looked beautiful under the orange glare of the streetlights.

She smiled softly and shook her head. "You don't have to lie to save my feelings, Logan. I'm a big girl."

"I'm not lying." He lifted her hand from her lap and kissed her wrist. "I wish I could fast-forward time a couple of hours so the show would be over and I could teach you more about making love," he said. *And you can teach me how to love someone.*

She wrapped her arms around his head and hugged him to her abdomen. "Why are you so nice to me?"

His chuckle was muffled against her belly. "I have ulterior motives."

"Such as?"

"Making you mine." *Shit.* Why had he said that? He was showing his cards much too soon.

She slapped his shoulder. "Don't say it if you don't mean it."

He wished he could say he didn't mean it. He didn't particularly want to be so far gone. Ah, what the fuck—he liked her. A lot. She was just going to have to learn to live with it. If he could admit it, surely she could accept it.

"I mean it, Toni." He untangled his head from her grasp so he could look up at her. "I really do like you. And it isn't just lust." For once in his dick-led life. "I can't stop thinking about you. Even when you're not in my bed, you're in my head. It's driving me crazy. I'm not sure how to handle it."

She smiled, and he saw her feelings displayed clearly in her eyes. "You're going to break my heart someday." She released a sigh and stared over his head as she spoke. "I really like you too, Logan. But maybe it's best if we pretend the only thing between us is lust. If I fall for you . . ." She shook her head and closed her eyes.

"You don't trust me with your heart."

"Should I?"

He wanted to say she should, wanted to say that he'd never hurt her, but he, more than anyone, was aware of his track record with women.

"That's something you'll have to decide on your own."

She gnawed on her lip and nodded. "I do trust you with my body," she said. "That's a start, isn't it?"

"A perfect start." For something he hoped never had to end.

Not sure why his train of thought was making his heart thud harder than it did when he dove out of perfectly good airplanes, Logan lifted Toni from her perch on the loading dock and set her on her feet. Perhaps being alone with this woman wasn't the best idea. She made him say things and feel things that he just wasn't ready to face.

"I better get back to the meet and greet," he said. "Do you want to go back with me?"

She sucked in a deep breath and released it slowly.

"I think I'll go hide out in Reagan's dressing room for a little while, if that's okay," she said after a moment.

Logan shrugged. "It's not my dressing room; you'll have to ask her." He tilted his head toward her, deciding she looked a little pale. "Are you feeling okay?"

"I think I'm bewildered," she said, and huffed out a laugh. "But I'm pretty sure it's from being alone with you."

"I'd apologize, but I'm not the least bit sorry that I have that effect on you."

She laughed and grabbed his T-shirt in both hands, tugging him close. "If you really want to make my head spin, you should try kissing me."

"That sounds dangerous," he said, folding her in his embrace and pulling her body against his. He wasn't satisfied until she moved her arms around to his back and there wasn't an inch of space between them. Even then, he wished they were skin on skin.

"I'm sure this much dizziness *is* dangerous," she said as she relaxed against him, her full breasts pressing into his chest. "But I'm willing to hazard the vertigo."

"I do love a risk taker," he murmured.

He claimed her mouth in a heated kiss, doing his best to make the earth move topsy-turvy beneath her feet. His world hadn't been steady since the moment she'd try to rip his arm off by enthusiastically shaking his hand. But he'd always liked a little mayhem in his world.

CHAPTER
12

*L*OGAN LIKED *her.*

Lost in thought, Toni stumbled against a wall on her way to seek sanctuary in Reagan's dressing room. Toni wanted to have faith in Logan's words, but something inside her just couldn't believe that gorgeous, rich, famous, and charming specimen of a man would want anything permanent to do with an unworldly, unexciting, and chubby specimen of a woman. She understood that he must have a thing for virgins and that for some reason he'd latched on to the idea that being the first to conquer her pussy meant he could stick his flag in it and claim it as his, but his feeling of conquest would wear off eventually. She was sure of it. She was terrified of letting herself feel too much for him. She had to work with these guys for four weeks, and if Logan ripped her heart out, would she be able to continue to immerse herself in his world?

This was why she never should have gotten involved with him in the first place. She could try to excuse her behavior by claiming it was her inexperience that had made her fall into the sack with him so quickly, but that was a lie. She knew exactly what she'd been doing. It had been a not-so-momentary lapse of judgment that on a personal level she embraced. On a professional level, however, she wanted to kick herself in the ass.

She should be following the band around right now, interviewing fans, getting inside the backstage scene, but she was utterly overwhelmed by the chaos. She was a solitary creature by nature; she hadn't a clue how the band members and crew dealt with this insanity day after day. Night after night. Dare had somehow mastered being alone in a crowd, but the rest of the band were constantly on. It was exhausting to watch, much less being caught up in the whirlwind. Maybe hanging around with Reagan in her dressing room for a few minutes before the show started would allow Toni to collect her thoughts.

Toni wondered why Reagan had been conspicuously absent for the entire meet and greet. The guitarist didn't seem the reclusive type. Maybe because she was a temporary band member, she didn't feel part of the group. She hadn't ridden on the bus with the guys the night before and had only been with them when required by obligation. Was it because she wasn't welcome? Or because she didn't want to be with them? Toni's journalistic senses were tingling. Something seemed off about the newest member of the band.

Steve stepped out into the corridor and nearly careened into her. He grabbed her shoulders to steady her, and she smiled up at him in gratitude.

"Where's your Siamese twin?" he asked.

"Huh?"

"Logan. The man who's been bodily attached to you since you boarded his bus."

The two of them weren't that bad, were they? "I think he's at the meet and greet." Toni glanced behind her. She couldn't see the area where everyone had congregated, but the din of conversation and laughter traveled the length of the corridor.

"Without you?"

She turned back toward him and lifted her eyebrows. "Is that a problem?"

Steve shook his head. "Nope. Just surprised he trusts Dare not to scoop you up when he's not paying attention. Catch you later."

Dare? Before she could ask what he meant, Steve and his long legs had already traversed half the hallway. He even managed to twirl a drumstick in one hand while walking.

Shrugging to herself, Toni bypassed the dressing room that Steve had just exited and paused outside Reagan's door. She knocked and waited.

"Occupied!" Reagan called from within the confines of the room.

"Very occupied," a deeper voice said. Toni was pretty sure the voice wasn't Trey's. Was Reagan's sexy bodyguard inside with her? Toni leaned closer to the door, listening, trying to let the sounds of the milling crowd down the hall fade into the background.

Someone touched her back, and she jerked away from the door, her face flushed with embarrassment. She'd been caught snooping.

She turned slowly, one eye closed as she forced her gaze up a pair of long legs encased in leather, up a stark white T-shirt and a strong neck to a familiar handsome face surrounding a pair of striking emerald-green eyes. Dare. Did he know his brother's woman was cheating with another man? And how had Steve known Dare would show up when she was alone? She wondered if she should be worried or intrigued.

"Oh, hey, Dare," she gushed. She pushed her glasses up her nose with the back of her wrist. "I was just hoping to interview Reagan for the book, but I think she's busy."

He grinned crookedly. "She's always busy with Trey."

Trey. *Yeah, we'll go with that. Reagan is busy with Trey.* And maybe it *was* Trey in the room with Reagan. He had been with her the last time Toni had seen her, but she definitely didn't remember his voice sounding so baritone.

"You don't like crowds either, do you?" Dare asked. His green eyes softened when he smiled. "Now that Steve's out of the dressing room, I think it's empty. Would you like to get away for a few moments?"

He stepped over to the band's dressing room and opened the door. "Anyone in here?"

"I'm almost dressed," a woman said from inside.

"Why don't you like crowds?" Toni asked Dare as they waited for the woman to put on her shoes and leave.

"Don't know," he said with a shrug. "I just like my interactions with others to be more intimate."

Even with the swollen nose, he was still easily the best-looking man she'd ever stood in a hallway with. Which reminded her . . . "I'm really sorry that Logan hit you on account of me. I guess I shouldn't have hugged you like that."

He grinned. "He's being a complete ass. Guess you bring that out in him. But I'll get him straightened out for you."

"What's that mean?"

Green-eyed gaze boring into hers, he licked the corner of his mouth, and she felt suddenly light-headed and dizzy. Holy father of hot men.

"Nothing," he said. "How about that interview? I seem to be currently unoccupied."

"Now?" she blurted. She didn't have the mental capacity of a gnat at the moment, and her list of questions was on the bus, so she wouldn't even be able to fake her intelligence.

"If you'd rather wait . . ." He waved a hand. "I just thought we could both get away from the crowd for a moment and get to know each other better."

She really should be working. And she supposed getting to know Dare Mills *was* working. She loved this job. "I guess I can ask a few warm-up questions."

The corner of his mouth twitched upward. "Good."

Why was he looking at her like that? As though he was touching every inch of her body in his thoughts. And why did she have the sudden urge to peel her panties off? She wasn't sure if being alone with him was the best idea. He wouldn't try anything, would he? And if he did, would she have the backbone to turn him down? Surely she wasn't that despicable. She liked Logan way too much to mess up their growing relationship by fooling around with Dare.

As if Dare could possibly be interested in *her*. Right.

Yet she couldn't help but dwell on what Steve had said right before he'd walked away.

The gorgeous woman who'd been Steve's pre-show entertainment passed through the door that Dare was holding open with one masculine hand. She paused and wrapped both arms around Dare's midsection, giving him a tight hug. He half-heartedly hugged her back with his free arm.

"I don't suppose you're interested in sloppy seconds," she said, just loud enough for Toni to hear.

"Not at all," he said.

"Is Logan around?" she asked.

Toni stiffened.

"I think he's hanging in the commons."

"I love it when you guys come to town," the black-haired beauty said. "I will get into your pants one day, Dare Mills."

"Not tonight. I have company." He lifted an eyebrow in Toni's direction.

Toni's heart produced a thud so hard, she jumped. What did he mean by that?

The woman slipped her arms from Dare's waist and turned to give Toni the twice over. She obviously didn't think much of her competition. "Hmm," she said. "Interesting choice."

She sauntered off, probably in search of Logan, whom she apparently believed was fair game. Toni wasn't sure if she had the right to be jealous. She and Logan had openly admitted to *liking* each other, but neither of them had committed to anything. One thing was for sure: if he messed around with another woman, Toni wouldn't be sharing his bed again. She crossed her arms over her chest and glared after the woman. Logan wouldn't sleep with her, would he? Toni honestly couldn't say she knew for a certainty.

"You have nothing to worry about," Dare said and held his free hand out to the open door to beckon her inside. "You're much more interesting than she is."

Dare entered the room behind her and while she was glancing around for the best place to conduct their interview, she heard the unmistakable click of Dare locking the door behind them.

CHAPTER 13

LOGAN DECIDED that Toni had been interviewing Reagan for far too long. He didn't want to get in the way of her work, but he couldn't help but want to be with her. There was something about her that made him notice her. And when she was missing? He couldn't seem to notice anything else. He stretched to his tiptoes and scanned the room, looking over the tops of heads for one very specific one. How could she not be done with her interview? What the hell could possibly be so interesting about Reagan?

Logan went still when his gaze landed on their sassy little guitarist. Reagan was standing against the wall chatting very animatedly with Steve and the same woman who'd tried to talk Logan into joining her in the dressing room not ten minutes ago. When he'd refused, the brunette decided to hang out with Steve. Logan really didn't want to have to interact with the pushy woman again, but if Reagan was back from the interview, then Toni should be as well.

Attempting nonchalance, Logan approached Reagan and waited for her to look at him before asking, "So how did the interview with Toni go? Should we be worried about all the terrible things you said about us?" If pretending indifference didn't work, he was all about demanding to know where Toni was and when Reagan had last seen her. He didn't care if the knowing smirk on Steve's face spread from here to Nebraska.

Reagan's slim brows drew together over her grayish-blue eyes.

"What interview? She took a shower in my dressing room a couple of hours ago, but we didn't talk much. I wouldn't call it an interview."

Logan's stomach dropped. "She said she was going to your dressing room to interview you about twenty minutes ago."

Reagan grinned. "I bet she was the one who knocked when I was busy with, uh, my makeup. I haven't seen her."

"I saw her down by the dressing room," Steve said, his smirk at least halfway to Colorado at this point.

"That nerdy girl?" asked the dark-haired beauty who was plastered to Steve's side. "With the glasses?"

Logan didn't particularly appreciate such a lackluster description of the woman who had him completely out of his head, but he nodded.

"She was with Dare. They were headed into the dressing room for a little alone time."

Logan's heart dropped to join his stomach in his shoes. Another scan of the room told him exactly what he feared: the other conspicuous absence in the room was Dare. And Dare was on a mission to get back at him for hitting him in the nose. Sweet, sweet Toni didn't stand a chance against the guy's libido if he set his sights on her. And if the guitarist *was* seducing the innocent young woman that Logan had taken advantage of the night before—as well as most of today—Dare was about to suffer injuries a lot more severe than a bloody nose.

CHAPTER 14

TONI TURNED to face Dare, a little thrill of panic spiking though her heart. He smiled reassuringly, but she didn't feel reassured. She wasn't accustomed to being locked in rooms with men she scarcely knew.

"Why did you lock the door?" she asked.

"So we wouldn't be bothered."

"I'd feel better if it wasn't locked." She didn't really think Dare was the type of man who would harm a woman, but she wasn't the first woman to think that about a deranged lunatic, a serial killer, or a throat-slitting rapist.

He didn't unlock the door, but instead crossed the room to pour a drink. "Would you like something?"

"I'd like to unlock the door."

He filled a lowball glass with amber whiskey and set the bottle aside. "If it makes you that uncomfortable to be alone with me, please unlock it. I didn't mean to alarm you. I just figured Logan will interrupt us before we even get started and you'll never get any work done."

She wasn't exactly alarmed. She felt no malice from the mysterious guitarist. She just thought it was weird that he'd lock the door in the first place. She studied him. She was starting to think Dare's behavior had nothing to do with her and everything to do with Logan. "Why would Logan interrupt?"

The door handle jiggled and there was a loud knock on the door.

"Right on cue," Dare said, one corner of his mouth lifting sardonically. "He's entirely predictable."

"Toni?" Logan called from the corridor. "Open this goddamned door." The jiggling became incessant rattling. The knocking became pounding. "Toni!"

"Should I open it? He sounds mad." Toni said.

"Of course he's mad. He thinks I'm fucking you. That's because he never uses his head and always jumps to conclusions. Then he acts on his false impulses and punches people in the nose." Dare pointed to his swollen face. "Case in point."

"Toni!"

Toni frowned at him. "So you lured me in here to get back at Logan?"

"Maybe," Dare said, taking a swig from the tumbler in his hand.

"Toni, please," Logan cried, sounding desperate now.

"He punishes himself. It's not like I'm a big enough ass to actually make a move on the woman of one of my friends," Dare said. He sat casually in a club chair, crossed his long legs at the ankle, and took another sip of his drink. "But I am enough of an ass to make him believe that I would. He'll think twice before sucker punching me in the face again."

"I'm going to let him in," Toni said. She understood that Dare was pissed at Logan. She couldn't blame him for wanting to teach Logan a lesson, but she couldn't stand the thought of Logan thinking she'd toss her skirt up at the first sign of interest from an attractive man. Oh wait, she had done that. With Logan. He knew firsthand that she was capable of unleashing her inner slut.

Toni unlocked the door with trembling fingers and it flew inward, almost banging her in the face. Logan looked from Toni, fully clothed and obviously not violated, to Dare, who was sitting across the room completely apathetic and looking rather bored.

"What's going on in here?" Logan demanded.

"She was going to interview me for the book when you so rudely interrupted," Dare said.

"Is that so?" Logan said, his eyes narrowed.

Toni nodded. "Yeah, that's right. What did you think was going on?"

"I thought," he said. "I thought . . ." He looked down at Toni and swallowed hard. "Ah hell," he grumbled and stormed off, slamming the door behind him.

"You sure you want to deal with that?" Dare said. "The guy runs on instinct. He doesn't know how to be rational."

And that was half his allure.

"I'm sure," she said as she flung open the door to go after him. She glanced toward the common area, but saw no sign of him. She looked in the opposite direction, toward the exit, and caught a brief glimpse of blue T-shirt turning the corner. Her boot heels clicked on the tiles as she raced down the hall after him. She caught up with him only because he had to wait for a roadie pushing a giant black case before he could get through a door.

"Logan."

He didn't even glance at her. "Can you let me feel like an idiot in private?"

"No. I think you should face your idiocy in front of me."

He scowled, and then his face softened and he laughed.

"It could have been worse," she said. "Dare could have punched you in the nose."

"I'd have preferred that and he knows it."

"We weren't doing anything."

"So why did he make sure Steve's chick saw you together? And why did you lock the door?"

"He locked it. Apparently, so you'd think we were doing something. I was about to unlock the door when you started banging on it. I told him I didn't feel comfortable being alone with him in a locked room."

"So he *was* going to try something on you. I'll fucking punch him in his other nose."

He swung around, but Toni pushed both hands against his chest. "First off, he only has one nose. And secondly, I don't think he was going to try anything. I wasn't sure at first. I thought it was strange that he wanted the door locked, but he really was just passive-aggressively kicking your ass."

Logan raked a hand through his hair, disheveling golden curls. "I'm sure he's saving the real ass kicking for later."

She couldn't stand the fact that he was upset. "Logan, I know we haven't known each other long—"

"Are you sure?" he interrupted, pushing her glasses up her nose for her. "It feels like I've known you forever."

"I'm not the kind of woman who would sleep with you twice . . ." She paused. "Three times? Does a blow job count as sleeping with you?"

"Even if it was in your mouth, I came inside you," he whispered into her ear. Her vaginal walls contracted to remind her of her current unfortunate emptiness. "It counts."

The rising ridge against her lower belly told her that he was as affected by his whispered words as she was.

She continued with what she had to say before three sexual encounters became four. "I'm not the kind of woman who would sleep with you *three* times and then have sex with some other guy in the same day. Who does that?"

He chuckled. "You'd be surprised. A lot of women behave differently around famous people. Especially if that famous person is the lead guitarist of Exodus End."

"I'm not like that," she insisted.

"Toni, you don't have to explain yourself. You didn't do anything wrong."

She looked into his eyes and tried to keep her wits about her. Not an easy task with those baby blues wreaking havoc on her thoughts. "I know. I just . . ." She sucked in a deep breath. "This is going to sound ridiculous and naïve and probably a little desperate, but I need you to know that as long as I'm in your bed, I will not allow another man touch me. No man. Not even Dare Mills."

"Not even if I talk Steve into having a threesome with us?"

Her jaw dropped, and Logan chuckled. He hugged her against him again and rubbed her back soothingly.

"I'm just trying to get a rise out of you, lamb," he said. "I won't even ask him, because I know he'll say yes." His body shook against hers as he laughed.

"People don't really do that kind of thing, do they?" she said, her gaze darting from one uninterested passerby to another. "Not really."

"Some do."

She couldn't even figure out the logistics of that. Did the men take turns? Or use different orifices? Her head was spinning at the very idea. "Have you done it?"

"Maybe."

"You have!" She pushed away from him and stared up at him with wide eyes.

"More often with two women than a woman and another man, but yeah, I have. More than once."

Holy shit!

Toni buried her face in his neck. What kind of man had she

gotten herself tangled up with? A worldly one. So how could she possibly keep his interest if things like threesomes and fucking women's tits and getting blow jobs were common occurrences for him? She didn't know how to do any of that stuff. Well she did have a bit of experience with blow jobs now. But she was sure her single attempt had been less than exciting for him. He'd had to tell her what to do, for fuck's sake.

"I'm sorry if that disgusts you," he whispered in her ear. "We don't have to do anything as wild as that."

"I'm not disgusted," she assured him. "I just feel so . . . so, well . . . so virginal!"

"You're not virginal—we took care of that last night, remember? You're just inexperienced."

That didn't make her feel better. She needed to educate herself about these things. Maybe it was time for an internet search with the adult filter off.

"Toni?" he said after a moment.

"Yeah."

"What you said about not letting a man touch you?"

"I meant it," she said, tugging away so she could look into his eyes again.

"Yeah, I believe you. I just . . . I want to promise the same to you."

She almost choked on the happiness welling in her chest. "Really?"

"Yeah. I promise not to let any men touch me."

She snapped her mouth shut as her happiness burst into despair. He was making fun of her? She'd meant that pledge from the bottom of her heart.

"But I need to be honest with you," he said.

She wasn't sure she wanted him to be honest with her.

"I've never been good at monogamy. Probably because I've never had anyone expect it from me."

She wanted him to be faithful to her, but she was too afraid to press the issue. She wasn't prepared to lose him entirely. They hadn't forged a strong enough bond to declare themselves in a committed relationship. She knew that much.

Logan stared down at her as if challenging her to demand his fidelity. Was it because he wanted an excuse to dump her or because he wanted someone to draw a line he may or may not cross?

"Hey, Logan!" one of the roadies called to him. "Mad Dog has been looking for you."

"I'll be right there," Logan said. He glanced down at Toni. "Do you want to meet a legend?"

Toni slipped a hand into her pocket and silenced her phone. "Maybe later. I need to go back to the bus for something."

"Will it require you to be naked?"

Toni shook her head at him. "Is that all you think about?"

"Absolutely."

Twenty minutes later, Toni closed herself in the lounge area at the back of the tour bus and pulled her vibrating cellphone out of her pocket. It had been ringing nonstop the entire time she'd made her way through the backstage area of the arena to the bus. She knew it was her mother; no one else would call her over and over again. Text her repeatedly? Sure. But not call. And there was no way she was talking to her mother in front of Logan or backstage at a metal concert. Her mother could be overprotective—stifling even—but Toni didn't want her to go into cardiac arrest with worry. And Toni couldn't help but wonder if there was an emergency involving her sister.

"Toni, is everything okay?" her mom asked as soon as Toni accepted the call.

Toni felt guilty for being responsible for the anxiety in her mother's voice.

"Everything is fine here," Toni said. "Is something wrong with Birdie?"

"She's a little whiney about you being gone, but she's okay. I've been worried sick over you. You're usually so good about calling."

"I'm sorry I didn't call sooner," Toni said. "I've been busy working. Actually, I need to get back."

"You're still working? At this hour? Are you running yourself ragged?" Mom asked.

"A little, but it's going well," Toni said. "I can't talk long. I need to go back to the arena. They haven't performed yet, and I want to make sure to record some footage of the concert."

"When you didn't call last night or all day today. I was picturing you dead in a gutter."

Mom often pictured Toni dead in a gutter. Toni wasn't sure why a gutter always featured in her untimely end.

"Nope, not dead, Mom. If I ever find myself dead, I promise

to call you from the gutter immediately."

"That's not funny."

She imagined Logan would have laughed at her joke, no matter how inappropriate.

"Is Birdie around?" She knew her sister would be upset if she found out Toni had been on the phone and she didn't get to talk to her.

"I'll put her on."

Toni pulled the phone away from her ear in preparation of Birdie's greeting.

"Toni!" Birdie shouted. "I miss you!"

"I miss you too, Buttercup," Toni said and then pulled the phone away from her ear again. Birdie had never quite grasped the concept of indoor voice.

"I fed the chickens all by myself!"

Toni smiled, her heart instantly warming at the sound of her little sister's pride and exuberance. "I told you that you could do it."

"But I spilled a lot of the food in the shed."

"That's okay; you'll do better next time."

"Will you read *Princess* to me now?"

"I won't be home tonight, Buttercup. Mom will read to you."

"She doesn't do it right."

Toni turned their nightly reading of *The Princess Bride* into somewhat of a theatrical production, having a lot of fun with it.

"Birdie," Toni said in a chastising tone, "that wasn't nice."

"I's sorry, Mommy! You are a good reader!" And Toni knew that Birdie was hugging the dickens out of their mother, because she had to be the most affectionate kid on the planet.

"We'll be fine, Toni," Mom said. "I can handle her."

Toni wanted to believe her, but she had a difficult time trusting Mom's ability to properly care for Birdie for more than a few days. Mom hadn't signed up to be the single parent of a special needs child, and for a long time she wouldn't have anything to do with her youngest daughter. Toni had been almost fifteen when her sister was born, and she'd practically raised her. Toni didn't regret her home-schooled high school years or missing out on the normal things teenage girls did. She didn't regret getting the bulk of her college degree online and only commuting to campus to take required labs. Being there for Birdie while Mom ran her little publishing empire had been worth Toni's personal sacrifices. But now that she was out in the big wide world, she had to admit she felt a little lost. She already missed the cozy security of home. She knew how to be Birdie's caregiver and she was good at it. She wasn't sure she'd figured out her new role in life or if she ever would.

There was a knock at the door, and she heard the sounds of it sliding open. She whirled around and cringed at seeing Logan's face, visible between the sides of the partially open door.

"Dinner," he mouthed when he noticed she was on the phone.

She nodded. "I have to go," she said to her mom. "I just wanted to let you know I'm okay and not to worry."

"You know I can't help but worry. Will you call tomorrow and talk longer? I want to hear all about your first day on the job."

All about it? There was no way Toni would be telling her even half of what had happened to her in the past twenty-four hours—most of it centering around the gorgeous man now eyeing her suspiciously.

"I'll try, but can't promise. I'm going to be really busy."

"Well, goodnight then, Antonia. I love you."

"I love you too."

She hung up, surprised when Logan shoved the door wide.

"Who were you talking to?" he asked, crossing his arms over his chest and glaring at her with accusation.

"Uh, not that it's any of your business but—"

"Do you have a boyfriend?"

Toni closed one eye and shook her head, wondering where that idea had come from.

"Because I just heard you tell him that you love him."

"And won't you feel like an ass when you find out that I was saying that to a her, not a him?"

"You're a lesbian?" he blurted.

She snorted. "Not that I'm aware of. I was talking to my mother."

He dropped his arms to his sides. "You're right," he said, shaking his head at her.

"About what?"

"I do feel like an ass."

"Good." She began searching through her bag for a better camera. The one she'd been using backstage didn't take high quality pictures like her old Nikon. She'd also brought a newer model—a better, more expensive model. But she preferred the camera she was accustomed to using.

"Are you coming to dinner?" Logan asked.

"I really need a few minutes of peace and quiet before the show. I'm sorry I'm not more sociable." She'd have plenty of time to capture footage of concerts and behind the scenes events like dinner. She wasn't used to all the people and the constant activity. She was an introvert to the nth degree and could only stand the chaos for so long. She was used to having as much alone time as she liked, and when she wanted human contact, she spent the bulk of her existence with her younger sister.

"So you don't want to eat with everyone?" Logan asked.

"I'd rather not."

"Okay." He turned on his heel and left her standing gaping after him.

Well, that had been strange. Maybe he was just in a hurry. She knew she'd thrown off his tight schedule by being a constant distraction. She should probably feel a bit guiltier about that.

A while later, as she was switching out the memory card in her camera, she heard a loud thud from somewhere inside the bus. She'd expected to be alone until the concert began. Her heart rate kicked up, and she searched for something she could use as a weapon. She attempted to lift a lamp from an end table and found that it was fixed to the surface. Before she could reevaluate her plan, she was assailed by the most delicious smell of garlic. Her stomach growled and her mouth watered at the thought of food.

A moment later, Logan entered the lounge.

"I hope you like braised chicken and steamed asparagus," he said.

"You brought me dinner?" she asked, half incredulous, half touched by his gesture.

"You said you didn't want to eat with the others. Plus it will give us a few moments alone together." He grinned, his blue eyes sparking with mischief.

"So there were ulterior motives involved," she said, not minding in the least.

"A few," he admitted.

He touched the side of his hand to her chin and tilted her face upward. He kissed her until her knees went weak and she transformed into an unfamiliar creature of sexual need. Her hands trembled as she lifted them to his shoulders and held on to the only thing solid in her world at that moment. Him.

He tugged his mouth away slowly, his lips clinging to hers. She sighed at the deliciousness that was Logan Schmidt's kiss.

"I thought maybe we'd share a little tongue action next, but I'm not sure you can handle it." His teasing chuckle was tender and made her flush with joy.

"We'll never know unless we try." Her fingers dug into his shoulder to urge him closer.

"When you're right, you're right," he said and kissed her again. When his tongue caressed her upper lip, a jolt of excitement shook her to her core. Toni concentrated on his technique, so overwhelmed with pleasure and need that she didn't give as much as she received. She could imagine—almost *feel*—the tug of his lips and stroke of his tongue against the molten, throbbing flesh between her thighs. His tongue touched hers and she moaned, her clit tingling so distractingly that she rubbed against his leg.

"Easy," he murmured. "It's just a kiss."

Maybe for him it was just a kiss, but for her it was the epitome of sensation.

"It makes me want you to kiss me there," she whispered, her face warming from either her boldness or her desire or a combination of the two.

"Where do you want me to kiss you?"

"Under my skirt."

He smiled against her lips. "There's a lot of territory under that skirt," he said. "You're going to have to be more specific."

He was going to make her say it? She took a deep breath. "I want you to kiss my pussy."

"You want me to kiss it like this?" He kissed and suckled and licked her lips, drawing excited gasps and encouraging moans from deep with her as she imagined him doing the same to her downstairs area.

"Yes."

"Do you want my tongue inside you? Fucking you?" He traced her lips with his tongue and then invaded her mouth, thrusting in and out in shallow strokes that just teased her tongue.

"Yes. Please."

"And is this what you want me to do to your clit?" He caught the tip of her tongue with his lips and latched on with a gentle suction as he rapidly flicked his own tongue against the bit of flesh he held trapped in his mouth. Her clit throbbed in time with his motion until she couldn't stand it any longer and pulled free of his demonstration.

"Yes," she said firmly, holding his gaze so he'd know she was serious.

"Maybe later." He released her and approached the dining table. "Let's eat. Our food's getting cold."

"Logan!" She took several steps in his direction.

He glanced up from the foil he was pulling from a small metal pan. "Yes, Toni?"

She crumpled her hands in the hem of her button-down cotton shirt and tugged. She wasn't used to asking for what she wanted. It made her chest tight and her stomach churn.

"I thought we were going to . . ." She glanced sidelong at the open door to the lounge. "You know."

"Fuck?"

Her heart produced a hard thud at all that word implied. "Yeah, that."

"I can't miss dinner," he said. "My blood sugar will drop while I'm onstage and I'll black out. As delicious as your pussy tastes, it doesn't supply sufficient calories."

Flooded with concern over his wellbeing, she asked, "Are you diabetic?"

"Nothing that serious," he said, removing foil from a second pan. "I just expend a lot of energy onstage. Sometimes I overdo it."

"So you've blacked out before?" She moved in close beside him, stifling the urge to cling to him.

He nodded. "A few times. It freaks everyone out. Delays the show. So as much as I want to fuck you right now . . ." He grabbed her hand and pressed it against the hard evidence of his desire. ". . . I need to eat first."

"I'm sorry. I didn't mean to be a bother. I just got a little worked up when you kissed me."

Logan chuckled. "A bother? You're kidding, right?"

He wrapped a lock of her hair around one finger and tugged. "You are no bother," he said. "What you are, Miss Nichols, is a distraction."

"Isn't that the same thing?"

He shook his head. "I wouldn't want to be around a bother. I can't stop thinking about or wanting to be near a distraction. Does that sound like the same thing to you?"

She flushed with pleasure, still not used to the idea that a man as fun and gorgeous and amazing as Logan Schmidt liked her at all, much less liked her enough to find her distracting.

"You're a distraction to me too," she said.

"Do you think we can stop distracting each other long enough to eat?" he asked.

"I'm not sure," she said with a laugh. "We'll see how it goes."

The braised chicken was rather dry and tasteless. The steamed asparagus was overripe—woody and stringy. The garlic mashed potatoes would have been better drowning in butter, but the company was delicious, so Toni very much enjoyed her meal.

"So you're a bit of a mama's girl, I take it," Logan said as he shoved his asparagus to one side of his plate and plopped a second helping of potatoes beside it.

"Not really. She just worries about me." Toni didn't want to share the personal details of her humdrum life. Even though he could probably tell she hadn't had a typical life, she didn't want Logan to know how completely sheltered she'd been.

"Daddy's girl then?"

"Not since he passed away."

"Sorry," Logan said, frowning at his asparagus. "I didn't realize."

She waved a dismissive hand. "Of course you didn't realize."

"Tell me about him."

Her heart rose to her throat and settled there as a huge lump. Her father been gone over a decade, and she still found it hard to talk about him.

"Daddy was the nurturer in the family. While my mother went off to build her career, he did the majority of the child rearing. So we were rather close. He died when I was fifteen."

Toni had been gutted. Just thinking about it now brought tears to her eyes. A few months after Daddy's passing, Birdie had been born, and it was as if he'd left Toni a precious gift to treasure in his place. Her mother had been angry with him for leaving her to raise a newborn by herself. Birdie hadn't been part of her plan and neither had becoming a widow in her midforties. It just seemed natural that Toni would take on a parental role with her little sister.

"He must have been young," Logan commented, reaching across the table to squeeze her hand.

She pressed her lips together and nodded. "Forty-six."

"An accident?"

"Sudden catastrophic heart attack," she said, images of the paramedics trying to resuscitate him on the front porch swarming her thoughts. "He was such a good person. I guess he gave too much of his heart away and didn't keep enough of it for himself."

"Which means any man in your life has huge shoes to fill," Logan said, watching his fork as he pulled parallel lines through his mashed potatoes.

She smiled, wondering if he meant to hint at something that involved him personally or if he was just making a comment.

"Enormous shoes," she admitted.

"How am I measuring up so far?" He lifted his gaze to hers.

"You're getting there," she said. "I'd say you're currently around a size sixteen basketball shoe."

He grinned at her, looking rather pleased with himself. "I'm that good, am I?"

"Well, considering my daddy wore clown shoes . . ."

He laughed and squeezed her hand again. "I've got a way to go then." He speared his asparagus with his fork and shoved it into his mouth, not bothering to chew and swallow before he continued asking questions. "And your mother? Does she always keep close tabs on you?"

"She's not used to me being gone." Toni stared down at her food. She'd known she'd eventually have to find a life for herself—and she was excited to be exploring the world outside her tiny sphere of comfort—but she couldn't stop the guilt from clawing at her belly. What if something happened while she was gone and she wasn't there to protect those she loved? Like she hadn't been there when her father collapsed. He'd been lying on the porch for almost an hour when she'd found him after school. He might have been saved if she'd been there with him when his heart had betrayed him. How would she ever live with herself if something happened to her mother while she was gone? Or to Birdie? Birdie had been born with a congenital heart defect, so it was probably only a matter of time—

Logan interrupted her upsetting thoughts. "So you live with her?"

"Who?"

"Your mother."

"Yeah." Why was he so interested in her mundane life? She should be the one doing the interview here.

"This would be a lot easier if you volunteered information," he said.

She glanced up from her plate and found him grinning at her. "Sorry. I'm just kind of confused as to why you'd want to know about my life."

"Because I like you."

"But I'm not interesting at all."

"I think I'm capable of judging that for myself."

She took a deep breath. "What do you want to know?"

"Everything," he said. "But focus on you instead of your family."

"On me?" She hadn't focused on herself much since her father had died. With the exception of trying to find her way through college. "I had a very normal childhood growing up in a suburb of Seattle. The only real difference was that my mom was CEO of a publishing company and my dad stayed at home with the kids. Well, kid. I was an only child until I was fifteen."

"So you have siblings?"

"A little sister. She wasn't planned. My mom thought she'd finished going through menopause and then whoops. I guess there was still one viable egg in there after all."

Logan's forehead wrinkled in concentration. Doing math, she presumed. Everyone did math when they found out her sister had been born after her father had died. "So your sister was born . . ."

"A few months after my father passed away. He never got to meet her."

"That must have been hard on you and your mother."

"Mom isn't really the maternal sort, and that was okay when I was growing up, because I had Dad, but Birdie—"

Logan's eyebrows shot up. "Birdie?"

Toni laughed. "We both have formal, rather elegant names. My full first name is Antonia and she's Bernadette, but Toni and Birdie fit better."

"I'm sorry, I didn't mean to interrupt. You had Dad, but Birdie . . ."

She couldn't believe he seemed so interested in her family. "Mom didn't know what to do with Birdie. Actually, I don't think she even wanted Birdie at first. Birdie was born with Down syndrome, and Mom seemed to think she was being punished. First losing her husband and then her baby being imperfect in her eyes."

"That's really sad," he said. "For your sister."

Toni's lips trembled as she forced a smile. "Birdie never knew how Mom felt about her in the beginning." And she never would. But Toni knew and it still broke her heart. "So I switched from public school to home school in tenth grade and stayed home to take care of the baby."

His eyes widened. "You did? That's a pretty selfless thing for a teenager to do."

She shook her head. "I didn't miss high school at all. I was my little sister's universe for the first five years of her life, and I didn't have to put up with mean boys anymore."

She pressed her lips together. She hadn't meant to let that last part slip out. Logan was just so easy to talk to. He listened. He seemed to care. She said things to him only her journal knew about.

"Boys were mean to you?" He chuckled. "They probably just liked you and didn't know how to express it."

She rolled her eyes and shook her head at him. "I think I know the difference between flirting and bullying, Logan."

"Did that sound like I was undermining your pain and suffering? Because, you know, I like you and I'm not sure how to express it." He poked the back of her hand repeatedly. "So poking you and pinching you and shoving you into walls won't get my point across?"

She flushed with pleasure and laughed. "No, keep doing what you're doing."

"Okay, so then what? You went away to college, and your mother figured out how to raise her own kid."

Toni shook her head. "No. I completed most of my degree online and continued to raise Birdie. I did my classwork while she was at school and we had the afternoons and evenings together."

"And then after college you got a job . . ."

She knew he was trying to lead her somewhere, but couldn't figure out where. "I did freelance work for my mother's company."

"Following bands around the country?"

She laughed. "Uh, no. This is the first assignment I haven't been able to do from home. Until now, I've done almost all of my work remotely. Online."

"Oh," Logan said, slapping his hands on the table and making Toni jump. "Now I get it!"

Toni covered her racing heart with one hand and scowled at him. "You get what?"

"I couldn't figure out how a beautiful, intelligent, funny,

loving, sweet, sexy woman like you hadn't already been snatched up by some lucky bastard."

Her breath caught. She wasn't used to anyone—much less gorgeous men—saying such wonderful things about her. Logan almost made her feel that they were true.

"Their loss is my gain," he said.

"My gain," she corrected. She wasn't sure if he'd still be interested in her if she hadn't been a virgin their first time together; he seemed really wrapped up in knowing he'd been her first. Her only. "So where did you grow up? Where do you live now?" She already knew his answers. She'd researched it all before she'd met him. But it would be far more interesting hearing it from his delectable lips.

"Born and raised in Phoenix, Arizona."

"Is that why you're so hot?"

He grinned at her compliment. "It must be. My parents divorced when I was still in elementary school. I lived with my dad. My brother with my mom."

He didn't look at her when he said it. She wasn't sure if he was hiding his emotions from her or if it hadn't been that big a deal to him.

"I moved to Los Angeles right after high school. I heard that's where all the ladies who were willing to have sex with mediocre bass players lived." His gaze lifted to hers.

"Did you find what you were looking for there?"

He winked. "In abundance."

"How did you get into motocross?" She'd been dying to ask him about it during the radio interview, but somewhere in the hectic activities of the day, the topic had slipped her overstimulated mind.

"Racing or freestyle?" he asked.

"I'm not really familiar with the sport. What's the difference?" She picked at her chicken, not hungry any longer, but she wanted to extend her alone time with Logan for as long as possible, so she pretended to still be interested in her meal.

"Racing is just going as fast as possible without crashing into anyone or anything."

She held his gaze. "Have you ever crashed?"

"Plenty of times."

Her heart rate kicked up a notch, the way it did when her sister stood behind a horse or stumbled on the stairs. "Were you hurt?"

He shrugged. "I lived. But I'd say freestyle is the more dangerous of the two. I started freestyle when racing became too boring."

"Boring?"

"I'm a bit of an adrenaline junkie."

If that were true, she'd never be able to keep his attention. She was the epitome of boring. The very definition of predictable.

"Want to see something cool?" he asked, pulling out his cellphone.

"Um." She had no idea what to expect. "I guess so."

He slid around the table and scooted in close beside her. She was so conscious of the feel of his body and his attention-shattering scent that she forgot she was supposed to be looking at something on his phone.

She looked down. The view of a wide green river caught her attention. "I'm ready," his recorded voice said from off-screen.

"It's a lovely view," Toni said.

"It's about to get real," he said.

"No fear," the recorded Logan yelled.

She heard a soft grunt from his footage and then suddenly the river was getting closer at a dizzying rate. She heard him yell in exuberance, but she didn't see him hit the water. She slapped her hands over her eyes so she didn't have to watch. She knew he'd survived the ordeal—he was sitting right beside her. But that didn't stop her from cringing when she heard the splash, the sound of a cord recoiling, and then more excited shouts from the man she barely knew.

"You missed the best part," Logan said with a soft chuckle. "I didn't get hurt."

"But you could have!" She still hadn't removed her hands from her eyes.

"I could get hurt standing in the middle of an open field."

"True," she said, "but the odds of that happening are a lot less."

"You can't live your life by the odds, lamb. Besides, bungee jumping isn't all that dangerous. Do you want to see something really dangerous?" he asked, tugging at her wrist.

"I'd rather not," she said.

"Ah, come on. You already know I didn't die."

She lowered her hands and looked up at him. He really did

seem to be excited about this stuff. Maybe she was overreacting. She glanced down at his video screen, and stretched before the camera was a spectacular view of a cerulean blue ocean. A waterfall spilled from the ground beneath the shot, water thundering over rocks on its way to the sea.

"I'm not going down that way," yelled a voice on the recording. Steve's face came into view as the camera turned in his direction.

"Then why in the hell did you climb up here?" Logan said onscreen. Toni couldn't see him, but he sounded close.

"Up is my thing. Down is yours," Steve said.

"How do you record the footage?" Toni asked, leaning closer to the screen for clues.

"I'm wearing a headcam. Maybe you'd like to borrow it while you're following the band around. It would free up your hands for taking notes on napkins."

He laughed—and she knew he was laughing *at* her—but a headcam was a wonderful idea. Why hadn't she thought of it?

Toni gripped his wrist excitedly. "Could I really borrow it?"

"Sure. Now you have to watch." He nodded toward his screen.

"You're not really going to jump, are you?" Steve asked on the video.

"No fear," Logan yelled, and suddenly the waterfall was the only thing in sight and seemed to slow until it stood still. Or maybe it was just falling at the same rate as the man who'd just jumped off the cliff. There was a brief glimpse of the craggy rocks sending water spraying toward the camera, then the rapidly approaching surface of the water below. Toni didn't see the rest—she covered her eyes again—but over the rumble of the falls she could hear Logan yelling exuberantly.

"What a rush," Logan said beside her. "I need to do that one again."

There was a tremendous splash and gurgling sounds as water closed in around him. Toni didn't uncover her eyes until she heard the distinctive sound of him surfacing and taking a deep breath.

"Fuck yeah, that was awesome!" he yelled on the video as the camera, with its view now partially blocked by water droplets, panned far, far, far up the waterfall and cliff face. "Come on, Steve. Get your ass down here!"

"You're insane!" Toni heard Steve yell from a great distance.

His voice was nearly drowned out by the sound of the waterfall. "*I'm* insane!" And then there was a loud whoop as Steve launched himself over the cliff.

Toni covered her eyes again. Yes, she knew that Steve hadn't died that day either, but holy shit, he was almost as fearless as the man beside her. And here she was practically afraid of her own shadow.

She heard Steve screaming in terror all the way down, heard his entry splash. When he surfaced, he coughed several times and then yelled at Logan, "That fucking hurt like hell!"

Logan just laughed. "If I told you it hurt, you never would have jumped. But it was fun, right?"

"Spectacular," Steve said.

Logan shut off the video. "You can uncover your eyes now," he said into her ear. His tone revealed his amusement at her terror.

"You could have died!" And she did uncover her eyes. So she could slap him on the chest.

"But I didn't."

"Jeez, I must bore you to tears," she whispered, not sure she actually wanted to voice that thought aloud.

"Do I look bored?" He grinned at her crookedly.

"Maybe not today. Maybe not tomorrow."

"Maybe never," he interrupted.

He slid out of the booth. A gasp escaped her as he hauled her to her feet and into his arms.

"School is back in session," he said.

Yes, school. She was good at school. "What am I going to learn now?"

"How to be on top so I can watch your luscious tits bounce while you figure out how to ride me for your pleasure." His fingers moved to the top button of her blouse and unfastened it.

"You are *quite* the sweet talker," she said with a laugh.

"Just telling it like it is." He unfastened another button and slid a finger into the cleavage he revealed. "Should we hook up the cleavage cam or the headcam?"

Face flaming, she shook her head vigorously. "Neither!" She could only imagine how embarrassing it would be to watch herself having sex. Logan released another button and slid a hand into her half-open blouse to cup her breast. She glanced over her shoulder nervously, looking to see if the bus was still empty. Even though it was, the knowledge didn't put her at ease. Someone could walk in at any moment.

"Still skittish," he murmured.

He leaned in to steal her lips in a thought-shattering kiss. And if he was so fearless and reckless, why did he like her skittishness? Shouldn't a thrill seeker, such as Logan, be attracted to boldness? She didn't get it. But then shouldn't she be attracted to shy, awkward men? And she totally wasn't. Perhaps opposites really did attract. But were two people so different capable of creating a lasting relationship?

Did it matter? God, he was a good kisser.

By the time he drew away, she didn't care if he stripped her naked and fucked her right there on the dining room table. Instead, he took her hand and led her to the lounge. With his free hand, he switched on the light and closed the door.

Anticipation made her belly quiver, her nipples tighten, her pussy throb. It also robbed her of all patience. She reached for the hem of his T-shirt and tugged upward. Before, she'd always allowed him to take command of every situation, but at that moment, she wanted her hands on his body even more than she wanted his hands on hers. She sank down to suck kisses on his lower belly. His muscles tightened beneath her seeking lips. When she nipped the fold of skin at the top of his belly button, he jerked. She slid a hand up the inside of his thigh and on upward to the thickening ridge of his cock. If his excitement was any indication, he didn't mind her taking liberties. Were his nipples as sensitive as hers? She supposed she'd just have to experiment to find out.

With her free hand, she shoved his T-shirt higher, exposing his hard chest and the beguiling cut of his pectoral muscles. She flicked her tongue over the tiny bead of one nipple and sucked it into her mouth. He didn't seem to mind her exploring, but he wasn't trying to dry hump the nearest leg, as she'd likely be doing if it was her nipple in his mouth.

She released her suction and tilted her head to look up at him. "Does that feel good?"

"Truthfully?" He touched the top of her head gently, staring down at her as if afraid she couldn't take his criticism.

She nodded.

"It's okay," he said, "but if you want to suck on something that will make my knees weak . . ."

His hand pressed down on the top of her head. She immediately understood what he was suggesting, but she now felt confident enough to play coy with him.

"Here?" she said, sucking on a patch of skin over his ribs.

He squirmed and chuckled. "That tickles."

She looked up, trying to see his face, but mostly saw the crumpled fabric of his T-shirt. Reading her mind, he yanked his shirt off over his head and tossed it aside. He stared down at her, watching her closely.

She held his gaze as she licked and nibbled, kissed and suckled his ticklish flesh. She knew it was ticklish because every few seconds his body would jerk and he'd laugh.

"I'd give you an A for your sexsational technique," he said.

Sexsational? Now he was making up words?

"But if you want extra credit, you need to move it a bit lower." He pressed on her head again.

She shifted lower, doing things to his navel that she wished he was doing to her drenched pussy.

Impatiently, he yanked his pants open and his cock sprang free, eager for attention. Her eyes widened in surprise when he shifted and used one hand to direct his cockhead into the cleft between her breasts.

"That should help him pass the time while you continue to drive me insane," Logan said.

Toni laughed and squeezed her breasts together with her upper arms. He released a huff of air and rocked his hips slightly. She pushed his pants to his knees so she could explore his ass with both hands while she teased his navel with her mouth. She couldn't see his face anymore. Instead of looking down at her, he had his head tilted back. The motion of his hips intensified, and she couldn't begin to fathom what fantasy world he was currently emerged within. She only knew that she wanted to join him there.

She finished unbuttoning her shirt and removed her bra. She looked up to find him staring down at her. He gave her no instruction on how to proceed, so she cupped her breasts and squeezed them together and around as much of his length as would fit between her boobs, with the head pressed firmly against her breastbone.

"Like this?" she asked, trying to figure out how either of them would derive pleasure from squashing his cock between her boobs.

He chuckled. "Not usually, lamb, but I'm always up for new experiences."

Frustrated, she leaned away and rose to her feet. "How am I

supposed to get anything right if you don't give clear instructions?"

"Sometimes it's best to just experiment and figure out what *feels* right."

"You don't need to experiment," she said, crossing her arms over her chest. "You already know how to do all this stuff."

"You're wrong."

She raked a hand through her hair until her fingers got stuck in a tangle. "What's new?"

He caught her shoulders in his hands and stared down into her eyes. Whenever he did that, her heart danced in her chest and her breath caught. Her tummy fluttered. The soles of her feet tingled. It was the most bizarre set of sensations she'd ever experienced.

"I *do* need to experiment to discover what you like," he said. "But we're always so rushed."

She knew that this time was no different. Soon he would have to go to back to the arena to perform. Very soon.

"I'm sorry you didn't pick a better teacher," he said.

She stared at him in wide-eyed shock.

"I take that back. I'm not sorry at all that you picked me. I'm sorry that I'm so infatuated with you that I'm incapable of doing a good job instructing you."

Toni had never experienced being dumbstruck until that moment. She hadn't actually understood what the feeling encompassed. Her brain seemed to completely shut down on her, and she literally couldn't figure out how to form words or make her mouth move to speak them. Hell, even primitive brain functions like breathing had become a challenge. Logan was *infatuated* with her? Infatuated? With *her*?

"Fuck. That's not what I'm trying to say either," he said, his gaze sweeping to the ceiling before boring into hers again. "Maybe after I blow this load you've worked up inside me, I'll be able to say what I'm trying to say, but with you looking up at me all beautiful and bewildered and topless, I can't think of a goddamned thing but pounding you raw, sweetheart."

"Yes." She was surprised she could even muster that little word.

What little breath she'd managed to hold onto left her lungs in a whoosh when he tackled her to the sofa. His hands yanked at her skirt, her panties, somehow managing to remove both before he spread her legs wide, grabbed his cock in one hand, and pressed it into her slick opening.

"God, yes." He groaned as he sank into her heated flesh.

Toni gasped brokenly as she discovered firsthand what it meant to be pounded. Each time his cock drove into her body, the impact sent waves of excitement vibrating through her clit. Every few strokes he bumped against something inside her that hurt, yet she craved that short burst of sensation. Wanted every stroke to bang her there so she could feel how deep he was buried within.

Some annoying, logical part of her brain engaged suddenly, and she knew she had to stop him.

"Logan!" she said, shoving against his chest with all her strength. "Stop!"

"I'm sorry," he said, backing out slightly. "I didn't mean to bump your cervix that hard."

He altered his motions from pounding to grinding, which did things to her clit that made her bones turn to butter and her thighs tremble.

Is that what he'd been banging into? Her cervix? She was momentarily placated as she puzzled over her anatomy and then she remembered why she'd tried to stop him in the first place.

"Logan!" she shouted. "Stop!"

"Please don't make me stop," he said against her throat. "Anything but that."

"You aren't wearing a condom."

"I'm aware of that. You feel so good." He groaned, thrusting into her gently. Hoping she wouldn't notice?

"You have to wear one."

"But you said I could pound you raw."

"Yeah, I liked being pounded hard like that. But put a condom on first."

He snorted on a laugh. "Your inexperience is going to kill me."

He pulled out slowly, sucking a breath through his teeth as he withdrew. Was he in pain?

"What does my inexperience have to do with anything?" she asked.

"Raw means without a condom."

"It does?"

His head was resting on her chest, his wet cock against the inside of her thigh. He nodded. "What did you think it meant?"

"Well." Her face had already been warm from their sexy

exertions, but it flamed all the hotter as she struggled to tell him. "I thought it meant you'd do it to me until my vagina got sore."

"Do what to you?"

"Pound me."

"Well, I guess since you didn't know any better, we'll have to settle for your definition this time. But next time you say I can fuck you raw, it'll be without a condom."

With a huff, he rolled onto his side and kicked off the jeans that had scrunched down around his ankles. He reached down and pulled a condom from his pocket.

"Do I need to worry about diseases?" It was a horrifically embarrassing question, but it needed to be asked. He'd been inside her without a condom, and she knew he'd been with other women. A lot of other women.

"You should always worry," he said, "but I assure you I don't have any STDs. What about you?"

"How could I? I was a virgin."

"I don't know what kind of toilets you frequent," he said.

She wrinkled her nose in disgust. "I don't have anything."

Logan squirmed to squeeze in beside her on his back. He handed her the condom. "If you insist I wear this, you have to put it on me."

She lifted the small square package and stared at it. She supposed she did need to practice this technique more than once. She scooted off the sofa to kneel on the floor beside his hip. She was taken aback by how swollen and dark his cock was. She didn't remember it ever looking so, well, so *angry*. It probably was upset for being stopped by her *coitus interruptus*. His length was also wet and slick. She stifled the urge to lick him clean, deciding it was weird to want to know what her own fluids tasted like.

She tore open the condom package and pinched the ring of rubber to pull it out.

"Are you ready?" she asked.

His cock twitched, and he gasped brokenly when she touched it. Her hand was trembling as she slowly unrolled the condom down his length. "Is there a way to do this sexier?" she asked. The action felt awkward to her, so it must feel awkward to him too.

"Baby, anything you do with my dick is sexy. Don't worry about it."

He reached for her, using impressive strength to assist her from the floor. She looked down at him anxiously, not sure what was expected of her.

"Have a seat," he said with a suggestive grin.

When she turned to sit on the sofa beside him, he stopped her with a hand on her butt.

"I meant straddle my hips and bury my dick in whichever hole suits your fancy."

"Oh."

He centered himself on the sofa cushions so she could climb on top of him. "Should I take my boots off?" she asked as she hovered above him, her knees pressed into the cushions on either side of his hips.

"I honestly don't care."

He lifted his butt off the sofa and prodded her with his cock.

"Put it inside you before I die," he instructed.

"I wouldn't want that to happen." How ironic would it be if he survived jumping off cliffs and racing dirt bikes only to die from lack of sexual fulfillment?

She squirmed around, trying to get him to line up properly. Her aim was atrocious. He poked her here, then there. Everywhere, it seemed, but the proper entrance. And as far as she was concerned, there was only one proper entrance.

"Just use your hand." There was a hint of frustration in his tone—not that she blamed him. But she'd figured using her hand was somehow cheating.

She reached between her legs to guide him to her. Her breath caught as she slowly sank down and filled herself with him. She squirmed until he was buried as deeply as possible and then looked down.

"Now what?"

"You're in charge, lamb. Do whatever feels good to you."

She straightened her hips and sank down on him again, watching his face for signs of pleasure or distress. She didn't want to squash him.

"Toni."

"What?"

"Don't think so hard about it. Your only goal is to use me to get yourself off."

"What about you? I want it to feel good for you too."

"Don't worry about me. It already feels good. Getting off is never ever a problem for me."

Her motions were slow at first as she tried different angles.

She eventually discovered a rocking motion that rubbed her clit against him on the down stroke. Her mouth dropped open as her pleasure built quickly. Yes, she thought. *Oh yes, right there.* And then she was moaning the same words, completely oblivious to everything but the pleasure between her thighs. She cursed the betrayal of those thighs when they began to tremble with fatigue. She was definitely using muscles she'd never used before.

Logan's hands grabbed her ass, supporting her laboring motion as she sought her release. She forced her eyes open, thinking she ought to thank him for his assistance and found him watching her bouncing breasts as if hypnotized.

Her hands moved to her tits. She cupped them and gave them a firm squeeze. Logan licked his lips and she pinched her stiff nipples. She gasped brokenly as her pussy clenched unexpectedly.

"I'm coming," she shouted. "Oh God. Oh God."

Her body stiffened as she let go and though she wanted to keep riding him as she found release, her thighs refused to move.

"Don't stop," Logan pleaded.

She didn't want to stop, but her body gave her no choice.

Logan sat up and wrapped his arms around her back. Sitting with her breasts squashed against his chest, Toni held him in her arms and legs, quivering against him as her orgasm subsided. Somewhere in her hazy thoughts she realized he hadn't come yet and holding onto him so tightly wasn't assisting his release, but she couldn't help herself.

"You did great," he whispered in her ear. He rotated his hips, rubbing against her overly sensitive clit. She shivered. She couldn't stand any more pleasure. "Do you want me to take over, or do you think you have the strength to finish me off?"

She was exhausted, but she wanted her actions to give him release. "I'll do it."

"Maybe try putting one foot on the ground," he suggested. He rubbed the leg that was closest to the edge of the couch.

Good plan. Maybe she'd be able to move if her leg was extended. She reluctantly released her leg lock on his hips, wondering if her boots had caused him any injury. Wincing, she straightened her leg, and he shifted so that he was on the very edge of the sofa. She began to move again, slower this time. Logan captured her mouth in a lingering kiss, his hands skimming over her back and buttocks. The tips of her breasts rubbed against his chest as she rose and fell.

"Do you need me to go faster?" she asked when his mouth moved from her lips to press butterfly kisses over her throat.

"I just need you."

She rode him slowly, pausing between each down stroke and rocking her hips to deepen the connection between them.

"You're a natural," he murmured, his breath warming her bare breasts.

He lifted his head to stare at her, blurry-eyed, for a long moment. "Unfortunately, we don't have much time left," he finally said. "I do need it faster in order to come. Work it, girl."

She smiled, realizing he was feeling more than he was letting on and that he wasn't quite ready to come to terms with what was growing between them. He might not speak many tender words to her, but she felt his affection in his kiss and in his touch, in those rare moments he wasn't trying to be cute or funny.

"Then give me some room to work," she said.

He grinned and reclined back. With one foot on the floor and one knee on the sofa, her motions were a bit off center, but Logan didn't seem to mind. If the way he kept moaning her name was any indication, he rather enjoyed the way it felt to be driven into her at an angle. Within moments he grabbed her hips and pulled her down onto him as he shuddered beneath her.

She'd done it. She'd made him come. Next time, she hoped they'd manage to find release together.

Exhausted, she collapsed on top of him. Her legs quivered uncontrollably from overexertion as she labored for air.

Once she caught her breath, she shifted to lie against his side and rested her head on his chest. She was bone weary but satisfied. And almost giddy with happiness. She never would have guessed that sex could be so fun. Empowering even.

Stroking her tangled hair with one hand, Logan said, "We'd better get dressed. The show starts soon, and any moment now they'll be sending Butch to kick my naked ass out of bed."

"I thought I'd stay on the bus during the show," she said, tilting her head to try to see his face. Mostly she got a view of the underside of his chin. "I can get some work done." That was a lie. She just wanted some down time to herself. Though she had to admit down time with Logan outstripped being alone by a light year.

"You don't want to see me perform live?" he asked, lifting his head to scowl down at her.

"I saw hours and hours of live footage while doing research for the book, Logan."

"That's not the same," he said, squirming from beneath her head and rising to his feet. "Not the same at all."

She gaped after him as he opened the sliding doors and strode confidently into the corridor with his ass displayed in all its naked glory. Toni rose to her feet, reached for a throw blanket, and wrapped it around herself, noting the wet spot on the sofa. She cringed and flipped the cushion over before stumbling after Logan. Was he mad at her? She wasn't sure if she could handle his ire, not after they'd shared such passion together only moments ago.

Logan shut himself in the bathroom before Toni caught up to him. She stared indecisively at the door. Should she knock? Barge in? Wait until he came out?

"Um, Logan," she said to the door. "I'll go if you want me to go."

"It would mean a lot to me," she heard him say.

Well, in that case, of course she'd go—frumpy clothes, frizzy hair, frayed nerves and all.

CHAPTER 15

L OGAN OFFERED Toni a wink and a smile before he slipped the strap of his five-string bass guitar over his shoulder. She smiled back, her ever-inquisitive eyes darting away to observe the ordered chaos of the roadies making final preparations for the band's stage entrance. He couldn't deny that he preferred her attention to be focused on him. He entered the door that led to the area beneath the stage and decided that this was something Toni would want to put in the book. Few people had ever seen the underbelly of their new stage setup, which was rigged so that the band members rose from beneath the stage in grand style.

"Hey, Toni," he called over the din of the waiting audience and the commentary of the stage crew.

She whirled around to look at him, and her eyes widened when he waved her toward him. She glanced around before she headed toward him. Was she embarrassed to be seen with him or what?

"Do you want to see what's under here for your book?"

She craned her neck to peer into the darkness under the stage. Paths were marked off by dimly lit strips so that each band member could find the appropriate spot to stand for his entrance. A faint blue glow surrounded the drum kit far to the back of the area, but otherwise, it was inky black beneath the stage.

"I don't think there's enough light for pictures," she said.

"You could write about what it's like to stand under the stage and wait for the show to begin," he said. "It's pretty trippy."

She nodded and ducked her head to enter the small door. Steve had already taken his spot behind the drum kit, but the rest of the band hadn't found their places.

"Are you sure it's safe for her under here?" Steve asked.

Logan squinted in his direction, not sure how Steve could see a damned thing in the low light. He decided Steve must have the eyes of a nocturnal owl.

"I'll keep her safe," Logan said and settled a hand at the base of Toni's spine to lead her down his lit path to the platform he rode just in front of the drum kit. She'd probably get better insight for her book if she hung around with Dare or Max or even Steve—Logan was only the bassist, after all, and his entrance was even less impressive than newcomer Reagan's—but he hadn't brought Toni here to aid her career. He'd brought her because he had a very unusual desire to be near her as much as possible.

"Did you turn on your video camera?" he asked.

"It's rolling," she said, adjusting the headband she wore so that the borrowed headcam was at the side of her head and would see what she saw. Or couldn't see in the case of the darkened area beneath the stage.

Logan helped her step up onto his platform and moved to stand behind her. She jumped when his guitar bumped against her rear and produced a low tone. His amplifier wasn't on yet, so at least the sound didn't radiate out into the arena.

He couldn't seem to stop his hands from sliding up her body to cup her huge tits and give them an appreciative squeeze.

She slapped at his hands. "You can't do that here," she said in a loud whisper.

"Why not?" he murmured in her ear. "No one can see us."

Her shyness fueled his brazenness, and he ran his hands down her sides just so he could slide them up under her shirt and touch the bare skin of her smooth belly.

"Logan, I'm here to work, not play," she admonished.

"But the show is our playtime," Logan said.

"What?"

"The band. We work damned hard at interviews and signings and meet and greets."

"That's working hard?"

He chuckled. "Yeah. We always work hard at all that bullshit, so we can play hard on stage."

"So you don't take the stage performance seriously?" With

that question, Toni sounded like any number of reporters who'd interviewed him throughout his career.

"We take our playtime very seriously. If we aren't having a good time, the crowd easily picks up on that and they don't have as good a time either."

"I can understand how that would be true for you, but Dare and Max seem pretty serious about every aspect of Exodus End."

Logan scowled. Was she insinuating what he thought she was insinuating? "So you don't think I take the band seriously?"

"Not as seriously as the others do."

He supposed he had been slacking off most of the day, but it was because Toni kept distracting him with her wit and her smile and her sweetness and her glorious tits—he gave them another appreciative squeeze beneath her shirt.

"That's your fault," he said.

"My fault?" Her exasperated tone made him grin.

"Yep," he said. "You're hell on my concentration, baby. Even now I'm thinking of what your tight pussy feels like around my dick."

"Logan! The camera is rolling."

He chuckled. "You don't think the world wants to know what a fantastic little pussy you have?"

"I don't care what the world wants, *I* don't want them to know," she said, squirming out of his grip.

He allowed her a few inches of space and moved his hands to his bass, fearing she'd take a tumble off the edge of his platform if she got too wiggly.

"Come to think of it," he said. "I don't want anyone to know that but me. So I ask that you delete the footage of me praising your perfect pussy."

She bopped him in the nose as she tried to cover his mouth and missed in the darkness. "Stop talking about it."

"For now," he said. "But later, when I have you bent over the arm of the sofa and I'm buried inside that hot, slick piece of heaven, I'm going to tell you all about it."

Her shuddering intake of breath made him grin. He didn't know why it was so much fun to get her flustered, but he couldn't stop himself.

"Will you tell me how it feels to have my dick inside you?"

"No," she squeaked.

His grin widened. He'd have her singing his praises by the

time he finished with her. It was a challenge he couldn't resist.

"Are you already under here, Lo?" Max said from Logan's right.

"Yeah. Just waiting for you guys."

"He's under the stage," Max called to someone. To Logan he said, "We thought you'd wandered off to get some pussy again."

Toni gasped, and Logan cringed.

"I have all the pussy I want right here," he said.

His eyes had adjusted enough to the darkness that he could make out Max standing under the center of the stage on his platform, but he couldn't see his expression.

"You brought Toni under here?" Max asked.

"She's filming."

"Hi, Max," she said quietly. She squeezed Logan's arm at the same time. He wasn't sure if the gesture meant she was nervous or appreciative. Damn this darkness.

"Toni's under here too!" Max called to someone. "Reagan was looking for you," Max said. "She thought you might want to ride up to the stage with her."

"She's riding me," Logan said, his slip not the least Freudian. He'd meant it to sound sexual. Especially since now he knew how good she was at riding him. If they'd had more time, he'd have let her ride him all slow and sensually for hours. He couldn't wait to sequester her in his hotel room.

"You're way in the back, Lo," Reagan said from the darkness on the other side of the stage. "She won't get good footage back there."

"Maybe I can ride with you next time, Reagan," Toni said. "I'm not sure what to expect."

Her tight grip on Logan's forearm made him feel like she wanted his protection, and he was proud to offer it willingly.

"Stand behind me," he said, "and hold on. Steve will go first. My platform jerks a bit when it first starts to rise, so brace yourself." He was already used to the stage setup since they'd performed about a dozen shows with the new hydraulics. He'd almost fallen on his ass the first time he'd ridden the platform up to the stage.

"Okay," Toni said, her voice small, her grip tight.

"About halfway up, we'll be completely surrounded. Like we're in a metal tunnel. So if you're claustrophobic—"

"I'm not."

He was. But just a little.

One of the stagehands appeared beside him with a flashlight so he could turn on Logan's amp and connect his ear feed. "You're live," he said. He gave him an earplug for his other ear and even provided Toni with a pair.

"One minute," he heard Mad Dog, their front of house sound engineer, say through his earpiece.

"One minute," he whispered to Toni, who couldn't hear Mad Dog's raspy instructions.

Toni pressed her face into his shoulder. He could feel the trembling of her body behind him. "It's okay," he said, though she probably couldn't hear him through the earplugs.

The stage shuddered as Steve banged out the intro of "Ovation" and his glowing blue platform began to rise at the rear of the stage. As the drum kit slowly rose into view, the crowd erupted into cheers that shook the arena. Logan patted Toni's hip to remind her that they were next and tugged a guitar pick from the tape stuck to his stock. His fingers found his strings automatically. He started playing on his cue—filling the drum progression with the low tones of the bass intro—and braced his feet for the jolt he knew was coming as a door above him slid open and the platform he and Toni were standing on began the slow ascent to the stage. After the initial lurch, the ride was smooth and steady. Toni's death grip on his arm loosened when she seemed to realize he needed that arm to play. To Logan's right, Reagan's platform was rising from the floor as well. The crowd watched in hushed awe.

Still beneath the stage, Max chanted the beginning of the song, his voice deep and raw with an edge unique to Exodus End.

Rise from the ashes.
Rise above it all.
There's a sea of fists before you.
Demanding one final call.
It's not over yet.
Though the curtain went down.
They want more.
More!
Stand before them.
Give it your all.
They own you.
What!
Own you.

It's your ovation.
No!
Their ovation.
Give it to them.
Give it to them.
Give it to them nowwwwwwwwww.

The crowd sang along with Max, as did Logan. He couldn't help but rock his body to the beat. Music lived inside him, and it was during concerts that he let it burst free.

There was a loud bang as flames and sparks announced Max's platform shooting him out of the floor like a cannon. He leaped onto the stage and landed with what Logan had started referring to as the "cool stick-it landing." Not as graceful as a gymnast's, but a thousand times more metal. From his crouch, Max slowly rose to his full height, lifting his arm in the air to rouse the crowd as he carried the final note of the intro.

Dare's rise to the stage was announced by the wail of his guitar. The crowd erupted once more as the powerhouse that was Darren Mills made his first appearance.

"Gets better every night, guys," Mad Dog said into the feed. He sounded strangely emotional about the fact. "Logan, move forward, the crowd can't see you back there."

Like anyone came to an Exodus End show to see him. But Logan obeyed, glancing over his shoulder to make sure Toni had found a safe place. She was standing next to the drum kit, staring up at the flailing arms of Steve Aimes with her mouth hanging open. Yeah, dude was wicked fast, but no need to gawk.

Logan squelched the annoying pangs of jealousy twisting his gut and headed to the front of the stage for a little fun. He especially liked toying with Reagan because the woman was sexy as sin and every dude in the arena had a boner over her. Logan was sure they were all picturing themselves as him—leaning up against her back while holding his bass guitar at a ninety degree angle from his crotch and playing it suggestively. Or maybe they were stroking something other than a guitar neck.

Logan laughed when Reagan pretended to slap his face for being vulgar, before she got down and dirty with her own guitar. The male fans in the audience obviously appreciated her efforts to entertain them. Their fans had always been excitable, but they were really giving the security guards a run for their money these days in their heated attempts to get onstage. It had to be the addition of

Reagan to their mix. Logan wondered if they'd keep her even if Max was able to go back to playing guitar. The band hadn't discussed the possibility yet. Max was still a bit sensitive about the topic.

When the song ended, the crowd cheered their enthusiasm, and Max waited for them to calm down before greeting them. "How are we feeling tonight, Oregon?"

If their screams were any indication, they were fueled with almost as much adrenaline as Logan was.

"Who's the geek?" someone in the front row yelled loud enough to be heard over the waning cheers and through the band's earpieces.

"Geek?" Max said and turned to look behind him. He smiled when he spotted Toni. "Oh, that's just Toni. She's capturing footage for a band videography."

Logan beamed with pride, but his smile faded when Toni paled, covered her lips with trembling fingertips, and fled the stage. He scowled at Max, having half a mind to give him a black eye to match Dare's bloody nose.

"Where the fuck do you get off calling her a geek?" Logan yelled.

Max raised an eyebrow at him. "I didn't call her a geek."

"Yeah, you did." Well, he might as well have.

"Why do you care so much, Logan?" Reagan teased from the microphone Dare used to sing harmony.

"Because," he said, still struggling to bury his sudden rage. "She's sensitive and gets her feelings hurt easily."

"Or maybe it's because you like her," Reagan egged him on.

"What is this, junior high?" Max grumbled.

"I think he likes her tits," Dare said with a wry grin.

"If you like tits, check these out," yelled some male fan standing behind a woman squashed against the barrier fence. He then lifted the woman's shirt to display her rather impressive rack. The woman struggled to lower her shirt before slapping the shit out of the guy.

"That was uncalled for," Max said to the guy and shook his head at him. "If she wants to show us her tits, that's one thing . . ."

Which of course prompted the chesty woman to give them a second eyeful.

"I've got something in my pants I want to show Reagan," a different male fan yelled and grabbed at his crotch.

"Not interested, honey," Reagan said.

That didn't deter the guy. "I'd like to put it in your—"

"Hey!" Dare yelled down at the dude. He shifted Reagan's body behind his back and pointed an angry finger at the fan. "That's no way to talk to a lady."

Max sagely segued into the next song before things got really out of hand. Normally Logan would have joined in on the confrontation and tried to escalate it all in good fun, but he was worried about Toni. He hoped she wasn't too upset over being humiliated. How could anyone mistake her for a geek? Was it her glasses? He didn't get it. She was perfect. And if he hadn't had a concert to perform, he would have gone after her and told her exactly that.

May 3

Dear Journal,

I don't fit in here. Not that I expected to. But I honestly didn't realize how different—how weird—I really am. And I don't mean just different from the band. I'm not even slightly normal. A stranger called me a geek in front of more than ten thousand people and instead of standing up for myself, I ran back to the bus to write about it in my journal. Who does that?

Why is it so easy for me to write down how I feel but so hard for me to say it?

I should have stayed. I was right there in the middle of it all, getting great footage for the book, and I panicked.

I'm not sure I'm doing a good job. I could use a little feedback. I really need to call Susan and talk to her about my progress and see if she has suggestions—Mom is going to be so mad at me for not checking in with my editor today—but the woman makes me nervous. She's so loud. And those text messages she keeps sending aren't putting my fears at ease. Six of them today. All asking if she should come take my place or if I was on my way home. I know she wanted to do this project and she's made it perfectly clear that she thinks the only reason I was allowed to do such an important job is because my mom owns the company. But I'm qualified for this job. I have all the education and skills to pull it off. I know that, even if no one else does.

So why do I feel like I'm doomed to fail? Maybe because I've been having so much fun that it doesn't feel like work. Or maybe it's because I feel so alienated. No one is making me feel that way—I'm doing it to myself. I realize that. But knowing I'm my own worst enemy doesn't make me feel any better.

Enough about my stupid insecurity.

I'd rather talk about more interesting people.

I'm really confused about Reagan. She was flirting with and

kissing on Trey Mills—he saw her in her underwear—so it seemed like she was in a relationship with him. But she also keeps flirting with and touching this other guy—some really dark and gorgeous security guard (I need to find out what his name is)—and I thought it was harmless, but I heard him in the dressing room with her and I think they were having sex. So is she cheating on Trey or is she cheating on the security guard or is it possible to have more than one lover at a time? I don't know how anyone could keep up with more than one man. I'm having a hard enough time keeping up with Logan. He mentioned today that he's had sex with more than one person at a time, so I guess it happens. I just don't think I'd be able to do something like that.

Oh Logan. He's so . . . alive. I don't think I've ever met anyone who approaches life the way he does. Balls out and full throttle. Haha! He does some crazy stuff, like bungee jumping and freestyle motocross and who knows what else. I'd never be able to do any of that stuff. But it's pretty impressive that he does. I wish I was as brave as he is.

I'm learning so much from him about sex. And he's really nice to me and patient and doesn't make fun of me when I don't know what I'm doing, but I don't think he has the same feelings for me that I have for him. His actions confuse me. He's very possessive—he even punched Dare Mills because I hugged him. And he said he liked me, but he also said that he couldn't be trusted to be monogamous.

Maybe asking him to teach me how to be a good lover was a mistake. I'm obviously not good at keeping emotions out of a sexual relationship. I know when we have to part ways at the end of this job that never seeing him again is going to be unbearably painful, but that doesn't stop me from going back for more.

I still haven't gotten to talk much to Steve and Max. I did talk to Dare for a while this evening, but mostly because he was trying to get back at Logan for punching him. Dare seems like a really nice guy, but I don't think I'd want to get on his bad side. I wonder if Dare knows that Reagan is cheating on his brother. Would he tell Trey if he knew? I don't want to cause problems, so I don't think I should ask him, but I do think I would want to know if Logan was sleeping with other women. There's definitely plenty of opportunity for him to do so.

It would be nice if I had someone to talk to about all this. I'm so mixed up right now. Do I even have a right to demand he has sex with no one but me? If he did stray, I'd want to know because I think fidelity is important.

And then I guess we'd have to part ways. Would I be able to give him up?

Why do I always get so hung up on could-happens and planning my reactions to potential occurrences? I wish I could be more like Logan and not worry about such things. I guess he has more to teach me than just sex.

The rest of the day was busy and tonight I need to go through my notes and footage so I can get organized and figure out what other clips I need to gather at the next show.

Tomorrow is a travel day and I start the one-on-one interviews with the band members. I hope they trust me enough to give me some good insight into their lives.

I'm intensely curious about the woman in Dare's past who took her own life and was apparently pregnant with Max's child. Her name was Vic. I don't think it's proper to ask about her. It's too personal to put in the book anyway.

But I can't help but be curious.

It's suddenly quiet in the arena. I think the concert is over. I better pull myself together before I have to face the band again.

Good night, Journal.

Hopelessly confused about Logan's feelings,

CHAPTER 16

TONI STARTED when the sliding door banged open. She shoved her small pink journal into her messenger bag and looked up, surprised to see a winded, sweaty, red-faced Logan staring at her with wide eyes.

"Are you okay?" he asked, breathless.

She wrinkled her brow and glanced sideways. "Uh, yeah," she said. "Why wouldn't I be?"

"You ran off early in the show and never returned. I thought . . ." He wiped a hand over his face. "I'm not sure what I thought. I'm not used to worrying about other people, but apparently I begin to think they died or something."

"In a gutter?"

"Obviously in a gutter. Where else would you die?"

She chuckled, flattered that he'd been worried about her. "Nope, I'm not dead. In a gutter or otherwise. I just needed to be alone for a while."

"Why?"

"I take it you don't hang around with many introverts."

"You mean like Dare?"

Toni shrugged. She guessed that Dare was the most introverted of the band, but if he was considered introverted, then she was mega-advanced introverted. "I guess. I just get overwhelmed when I'm around too many people."

"So I should leave you alone?"

"No," she said and shook her head. "It's only long

interactions with crowds that bother me. I enjoy intimate gatherings."

He grinned suggestively and wiggled her eyebrows at her. "I enjoy intimate gatherings as well."

He closed the door behind him and crossed the room. He took the bag from her lap and set it on the shiny round white coffee table before the deep blue sectional. She crinkled her nose at him when her senses were bombarded by the musky, strangely erotic scent of his body. Why was the flesh between her legs suddenly throbbing? Could the scent of his sweat really turn her on?

"You're all sweaty," she protested when he pulled her to her feet and grabbed her ass to press her up against him—belly to belly.

"And you're about to get that way."

He kissed her neck, and an excited breath escaped her. Obviously encouraged by her response, he moved his mouth to her throat to suckle there, his tongue swirling in chaotic patterns against her tender flesh. Good God! Why did that feel so good? Logan's mouth was on her neck, not at her breast, not between her thighs, and yet Toni was paralyzed by pleasure.

"Mmm," Logan murmured against her throat. "I think I've discovered a new erogenous zone."

He nipped her skin, and her entire body jerked. "Oh!" she gasped.

"Got yourself a vampire fetish?" he asked with a chuckle.

"What?" she managed to say. "No, of course not. Vampires aren't real."

"But I'm all about bringing your fantasies to life, babe. If you want to be banged by a sparkling dick, I'll go get the glitter."

She shook her head slightly, confused. She had no idea what he was referring to. "Wait. What? Why would your dick sparkle if you're a vampire?"

"I'm a modern-day vampire. The kind that sparkles in the sun instead of bursting into flames."

She laughed. "You've seen *Twilight*?"

He arched a brow at her. "Do I look like the kind of guy who would watch that girly shit?"

She bit her lip, not sure if she'd insulted him.

"Yeah, I've seen it," he said. "Twice."

"Twice?" She didn't know why the admission surprised her so

much.

"I watch all kinds of movies. The bus gets pretty boring, you know. But don't tell the guys what I'm watching on my phone. They think I'm looking at porn."

She laughed and hugged him. "You're full of surprises."

"Do you like surprises?"

"I like *your* surprises," she gushed. "I love everything about you."

His teasing smile faded, and his blue-eyed gaze locked on hers.

Crap! What was she saying? She was sure to push him away if he had any idea how much she already liked him. "I mean, I like everything about you as a *friend*," she said.

He blinked, and his gaze shifted to her forehead. "Yeah," he said flatly. "Friend."

Did he not even want her in that capacity?

He took a deep breath, and his hands tightened on her ass. "So do you want the sparkle treatment or just plain dick?"

She laughed, glad the moment of tension between them had faded. She really needed to watch what came gushing out of her mouth. "Plain dick is fine."

"Good, because I think we're out of glitter and I need to be inside you right now."

Toni flushed with pleasure. She'd never felt truly wanted before. People in her life needed her regularly—her sister, her mother, and she supposed even her editor, though there would be no admittance of that by Susan—but no one except Logan had ever made her feel the heady rush of being wanted. Or of wanting. She was certain his wants were purely sexual, but she wanted more than his body. She wanted his heart. The realization terrified her because she knew it would never belong to her in the capacity she desired and she was only setting herself up for heartache.

"Take your clothes off," he said.

"Aren't the others—"

"Toni."

The mere utterance of her name in that tone made her throb with want. Maybe even need.

"Yes?" She looked up at him, and he removed her glasses, tossing them on the sofa.

"Take your clothes off."

Her fingers trembled as she lifted them to unfasten the

topmost button of her blouse. She stared at his slightly blurry shoulder, unable to meet his eyes, though she wasn't sure why she was so embarrassed after all the intimate moments they'd shared over the past day.

"Look at me," he demanded.

Her fingers went still on her buttons, and she forced her gaze to his. Her heart fluttered at the smoldering intensity in his pale blue eyes.

"Take your clothes off," he repeated again.

She lowered her gaze and unfastened another button.

"Can't you look at me and take your clothes off at the same time?"

She shook her head. "I can't do anything but stare when I look at you," she admitted, her blush spreading down her throat. "My fingers won't work."

"Try. I want you to see how much you turn me on."

She so admired him for knowing what he wanted and being able to ask for it. Would she ever be that bold? Or would she always be the one being told how to act and respond? Not that she minded. It was strangely exciting to be told to undress.

She forced her gaze upward to meet his and somehow found a steady enough hand to unfasten the button between her breasts. Logan's gaze darted down to her cleavage, now on display, and he licked the corner of his mouth before gnawing on his lips as if placating them from the feast he denied them.

A bit more confident in her actions—seeing that he was affected by her body, even if he seemed to be calling all the shots—she released the next button and the next. When she ran out of buttons on her blouse, she unfastened the one at the waist of her long skirt and then slowly unzipped the suddenly constrictive garment. The skirt slid from her hips to land in a heap at her feet. Logan was still staring at her cleavage. She was used to people staring at her boobs. They were enormous by any standards, but she wasn't used to liking the attention they garnered for her. She typically tried to hide them, though even the loosest sweaters became form-fitting on her and all her button-down shirts had to be tailored so they didn't gap between her boobs while simultaneously billowing like a circus tent around the waist.

"Do you like them?" she asked, glancing down at the swell of her breasts above the cups of her not-so-sexy bra. She'd usually went for comfort and durability in the undergarment department, but she was suddenly longing for something skimpy, lacy, and red to show off what Logan obviously considered her best feature. So strange that she wanted to fuel his desire when she'd spent her life trying to understate her natural assets.

"What?" he said, his eyes flicking up to meet hers briefly before focusing on her breasts again.

"My boobs. Do you like them?"

He shook his head slowly, never taking his eyes off her cleavage. "Like is not a strong enough word."

She grinned and reached behind her back to unfasten her bra. Logan groaned when she slipped the straps from her shoulders and tossed the garment onto the back of the sofa. Her nipples were already stiff from the excitement his riveted stare offered her. Their sudden exposure to the chill in the room hardened them to uncomfortable points.

"Touch them," Logan whispered. All the command had gone out of his tone. His words were more a plea than a request.

"You touch them."

And he did. His hands cupped her heavy breasts, lifting them, massaging them, allowing them to drop, pressing them together. He couldn't take his eyes off them. She felt a strange rush of empowerment.

"Take your clothes off," she demanded. Her confident tone didn't give away the twinges of nerves in her belly. She wasn't sure what she would do if he refused. Should she play hard to get to gain his cooperation? She would definitely be playing. But she didn't need to worry. He released her breasts long enough to hastily shed his clothes and then filled his palms with them once more, his thumbs and forefingers pinching at her nipples. Her body jerked as pleasure radiated through her breasts and down her belly. She gasped in surprise when her pussy throbbed with anticipation.

Logan prodded her in the hip with his stiff cock. "Touch it."

She almost told him to touch it himself, but somehow the thought of watching him rubbing the length of his cock with the same hands he had on her breasts was far naughtier than touching it herself.

"You're blushing," he said, and she lifted her head to find him grinning at her. "What are you thinking? Dirty thoughts?"

"I can't say," she said, her heart suddenly thudding.

"You can tell me anything."

She wet her lips and stared at his shoulder as she said, "I was thinking about you touching yourself."

"Masturbating?"

Her eyes widened, and she shook her head. "No, just touching it. Not, not making yourself . . ." She swallowed hard as she remembered the look on his face when he came. "Do you do that?"

He chuckled. "Sometimes. Do you want to watch me jerk off, Toni?"

She wasn't sure if she'd be able to handle it. And wouldn't he be embarrassed for her to witness something so shameful? She hadn't realized she'd asked the question aloud until he answered.

"You think it's shameful?"

She stared up at him, not sure how to respond. Didn't he think it was shameful?

"You masturbate, don't you?"

"Of course not!" she said. But her denial was a complete lie. She masturbated on occasion, but she didn't want anyone—not even Logan—to know she was so desperate for sexual release that she gave it to herself.

"You're kidding."

She shook her head vigorously, though she couldn't meet his eyes. She knew he'd see right through her lies.

"Not even in the shower?"

"Sometimes it feels good when I clean myself down there." She covered her mouth with her hand, unable to believe she'd just told him that. Next she'd be telling him about her infatuation with the massaging showerhead.

"So you never had an orgasm before I gave you one?"

"Um . . ." she said, frustrated by the entire conversation. Yes, she'd had orgasms, but after being with him and seeing how explosive getting off could be, she wasn't sure those little ripples of pleasure she gave herself—or the showerhead gave her—really counted.

He gaped at her as if he were talking to the biggest idiot on the planet. "You really don't know how to get yourself off?"

She shrugged. "Nothing prepared me for the things you do to my body." That was not a lie, at least.

"Don't you talk about these kinds of things with your girlfriends?"

"I don't really have any female friends my own age." Even

Julian was several years older than her and even though he was gay, he was still technically a guy. It was embarrassing for her to admit how abnormal her social life was, but she honestly didn't have the opportunity to interact with many people. And she'd certainly never had a close enough relationship with another woman to discuss the ins and outs of masturbation and orgasms. Did women really talk about such things?

"What about the Internet? Surely, you've watched some porn."

Toni scowled at him. "Of course I've watched porn. What do you think I am, a nun living in a cave?"

Logan's jaw dropped, and then he laughed before hugging her closer. "Lord, woman, I do love you." She felt his heart thud hard against her chest. "I mean as a friend."

"Stop doing that!" she demanded.

He released her so abruptly that she had to take a step backward to regain her balance.

"Did I hurt you?"

She covered her aching heart with one hand. "Yes, it does hurt. I'd rather you never say it than have you keep saying it and then take it back."

He covered his mouth with one hand, a worried crease above his brow.

"I understand that you probably say I love you to every woman that you, that you *bang*, but—"

"But I don't. I haven't said it to anyone for a very long time. I don't know why it keeps slipping out."

At first Toni was stunned that he hadn't said it to every woman he'd ever had sex with. And then she was strangely jealous of every woman he *had* said it to in the past. Because he'd probably meant it then. And he obviously didn't mean it now.

"You've been in love before?" she asked, a hint of accusation in her voice.

"Well, yeah, what do you think I am, a nun living in a cave?"

She laughed and shook her head at him. He was about as different from a nun in a cave as Toni was from him. "What was her name?"

He grinned crookedly. "It's not important. Besides, I can't remember it with your bare tits jiggling so enticingly before my eyes."

He stepped closer and cupped her breasts in his hands once

again.

"My tits do not jiggle," she said defensively.

He shook his hands back and forth, proving that her tits did in fact jiggle.

"*Logan.* Stop."

He stopped and caught her gaze with his. "Why?"

"Because."

He lifted an eyebrow at her.

"Because it's not sexy."

"It's sexy to me," he said. And to prove it, he lowered his head to draw the flat of his tongue over her nipple. "Besides, sex isn't always sexy. Sometimes it's messy. Sometimes it's fun. Sometimes it's boring."

"Boring?" She couldn't imagine sex ever being boring. Truthfully, it was the most exciting thing she'd ever done.

"If you allow it to become too monotonous."

"I won't."

"I'm going to hold you to that," he said. Then he and sucked her nipple into his mouth. She clung to his head, delighting in the gentle tug at her breast.

She gasped when he released her abruptly and spun her to face the opposite direction. He took her hands in his—his palms against the backs of her hands—and coaxed her into touching her breasts.

"If these were mine, I'd never get anything done," he whispered into her ear. "I'd play with them constantly."

"They are yours."

He went still, and she held her breath as she waited for his response. "Open your legs, Toni," was not what she had expected him to say.

She spread her legs, and he shifted behind her so that his cock slid between her thighs.

"Now close them."

She scrunched her brow in confusion, but she did what he said. He hadn't steered her wrong yet.

"Your body is so soft," he said, and she stiffened at the sudden pain in her heart. She'd always considered her soft chubbiness one of her failings. "It feels spectacular." He worked his cock between her thighs, his breath hitching in her ear. She squeezed her thighs together, and he gasped. "This needs to be about your pleasure too," he murmured before directing her palms down her belly. "I'll show you how to touch yourself."

"I know how to do that," she admitted, but somehow as he pressed her finger into her cleft and rubbed it against her clit, the movement was far more pleasurable and exciting than any of her previous attempts at self-gratification.

"So you lied to me?" He sounded more amused than angry. "You've gotten yourself off in the past?"

"I'm sorry. I was embarrassed." And now she was mortified.

"Don't be. I'm actually relieved that you do it. Show me how you touch yourself," he said.

"I couldn't," she protested, jerking her hand from his grasp.

He caught her wrist and coaxed her hand between her legs again. "Make yourself come on my dick."

"What?"

"I know you feel it nestled there between your legs. Come on it. Make it all slippery."

"Logan!"

"And after you come on my dick, I want you to come on my face."

"How would I do that?"

"By sitting on it."

"I'll suffocate you!"

His chuckle was deep and sexy. It made her entire spine tingle. "It's a risk I'm willing to take."

She'd been so distracted by his words that she'd temporarily forgotten he was holding her hand between her legs.

"So how do you touch it, Toni? Slow and hard?" He massaged her clit with her own fingers, rubbing in hard, languid circles. Her pussy tightened, but she shook her head. "A little faster?" He directed her fingers to move against her clit more rapidly.

"Oh!" She gasped as need began to build within her. "Faster," she heard herself say.

"Show me." He released her hand, and she took over, rubbing her clit with every intention of getting off. That freed Logan's hands to massage the aching globes of her breasts.

"Sometimes I pinch one nipple really hard when I'm coming," she admitted, having no idea why she felt inclined to reveal that very intimate detail about her masturbation sessions. Hell, five minutes ago she wouldn't even admit to touching herself and now she was volunteering the details.

"Show me how you get off, Toni."

"Yes," she whispered as her peak approached. She rubbed her clit faster and gripped one stiff nipple between her thumb and forefinger. "Yes," she cried more loudly, twisting her nipple viciously as her pussy clenched with the first tease of orgasm. "Yes!"

Logan thrust behind her, driving his cock into the cleft between her thighs as she bucked with release.

"To hell with this," he muttered.

Toni sucked in a breath of surprise when she found herself bent over the sofa arm. Logan grabbed the lobes of her ass in either hand, spread her cheeks apart, and rammed his cock into her still clenching pussy.

"God, yes," he groaned, thrusting deep and withdrawing before thrusting deep again. "I shouldn't have done that, but it's so hot and tight. I want it just like this." He massaged her ass cheeks together as he pumped into her.

Toni was still trembling in the aftermath of her orgasm when she realized something.

"Logan, are you wearing a condom?"

He cursed under his breath and pulled out. "Whoops."

Whoops? "Logan! This is the second time today."

"I'm sorry. I was lost in the moment. The sight of you. The sounds you make. The way you feel. Won't happen again."

He stepped away and headed for the door, which he slid open and stuck his head through. "Can someone shoot me a condom?" he called to the bus occupants.

Toni's eyes widened. Could he be any more embarrassing?

"Get your own damned condom," she heard Steve say.

Logan huffed with impatience and opened the door wide enough to slip out into the corridor. Not only was he naked, but his dick was rock hard and still wet with Toni's fluids.

"What the fuck, dude?" said a voice Toni wasn't familiar with. "I'll get you a goddamned condom. Put that thing away!"

"You know you want it, Zach. But you can't have it. It's all for Toni."

Zach? Zach Mercer, the drummer of Twisted Element? Toni hoped the entire band wasn't on the bus. She'd never be able to look any of them in the eye when she interviewed them for her "How Other Band's See Exodus End" chapter.

"Who's Tony?" Zach sounded surprised. "You like guys?"

"Toni's a girl," Steve said.

"My girl," Logan said.

Yep, it was official. Logan *could* be more embarrassing. Toni buried her face in the sofa cushions and groaned.

"Are you coming to the after-party?" Zach asked.

After-party? Their day wasn't over yet? Toni was ready to crawl into bed for fourteen hours of sleep.

"Have you ever known me to miss a party?" Logan said.

The door slid on its track and bumped shut. Toni turned her head to make sure Logan hadn't brought along spectators to prove she was, in fact, a girl. Thankfully he was alone and devastatingly naked. He had a strip of condoms in one hand and his dick in the other. And she'd been right. Seeing him touch himself had her all sorts of flustered.

"Damn, woman," he muttered, his gaze trained on her ass, still up in the air since she hadn't moved from her bent-over-the-sofa-arm position. "No wonder I can't think straight when you're near. That pussy is a work of art."

Instead of trying to hide her "work of art," she spread her legs wider and wiggled her hips. She was surprised by her lack of inhibition and by how much she appreciated his crass compliment. She was rewarded for her brazenness when Logan dropped to his knees behind her and buried his face in her ass. His tongue plunged into her throbbing pussy. The tip of his nose touched her asshole. She gasped as the ring of muscle tightened involuntarily and began to throb with unexpected desire. His fingers dug into her hips and his tongue slid up to her still virginal back hole. Her hips bucked as he flicked his tongue, barely touching her there, but she was so shocked by his unexpected action she couldn't breathe.

"Don't, Logan," she said in a panicked gasp of a voice. "Not there."

He licked her gently again. "It doesn't feel good?"

"It feels weird," she said, which was true. His tongue traced a circle around the perimeter of what she'd always considered an exit. "And good," she admitted.

"Have you ever been taken in the ass?" he asked.

Her face flamed, and she buried it in the cushions so that her next words were muffled. "No. I thought we'd established that I was a virgin."

"Yeah, well, there are women who get fucked daily in the ass and claim to be virgins because they've never given up the pussy."

Were there really? Was he pulling her leg? "That doesn't count, does it?"

"Not in my mind," he said. "So this hole is virginal too?" he said before licking her ass again.

"And it's going to stay that way!" She tried to squirm away from his mouth, but he had a firm hold on her hips.

"For now," he said agreeably and rose to his feet.

He released his hold on one hip, and she trembled as she felt the head of his cock being rubbed the length of her slit. She tensed when the tip of his condom brushed her saliva-wetted ass.

"Logan!" She tried covering her butt with one hand.

"I'll never do anything you don't want me to do," he said before he slid the rigid length of his cock into her pussy, claiming her deep and slow.

"Yes," she gasped, not sure why her ass was tingling with neglect, as if it wanted to lose its virginity too. That was not happening on her watch.

"One day soon, you're going to beg me to claim every inch of you."

Nope. Wasn't going to happen. But she wasn't about to relieve him of his fantasy when he was working his magic on her pussy. And she didn't have the mindset to protest when his thumb began to rub her back opening in the same slow churning motion of his hips.

"Move with me, baby," he murmured. "Let yourself become a part of our rhythm."

He was doing spectacularly on his own; she didn't want to get in the way of his skill. Yet she also wanted to be a good lover, and she supposed there wasn't much good in just standing there taking all he had to give.

Her first attempts to move felt awkward. She rocked her hips front and back and was rewarded for her uncoordinated effort by his cock falling free of her body. He didn't criticize, just found her again and used gentle squeezes on her hip to give her cues on when and how to move. Within a few strokes, she found that rhythm he'd referred to. The churning motion of her hips became more exaggerated as her confidence grew. Logan's groans of pleasure added to her own bliss. She was so going to high-five herself later for being the cause of his obvious enjoyment.

"Oh God, Toni," he said, "you're going to make me come so hard if you keep doing that."

Well then, of course she'd keep doing it. Their bodies were rubbing together so perfectly that his balls ground into her clit each time he thrust into her. Her own groans echoed his as she stopped worrying about what he was doing and concentrated on finding pleasure.

"Fuck, woman," he said, stretching his hot body over her back. "Up, up, up. Your pussy feels too good in that position. I can't take it."

He eased her upright. Toni's head swam at the sudden change of position. She made a grab for the back of the sofa as he lifted one of her knees onto the sofa arm and shifted so that he could thrust up into her. Once she had her balance, she began to move with him again. He held her breast, massaging and tugging her nipple as she bounced on his cock faster and faster. Her pleasure built until orgasm was just within reach, but she couldn't figure out how to tumble over the edge.

"Logan," she said, her legs starting to tremble from all the unfamiliar activity. "How do I?"

"How do you what, baby?"

"How do I come?"

"Touch yourself."

"What?" Why would she do that when she had a man at her disposal? Wasn't the whole point of having a lover so she didn't have to get herself off?

"I'd do it for you, but I don't have a spare hand at the moment."

Her hand was trembling as she slowly slid it down her belly. When her fingertips brushed her clit, her body jerked. "Harder," she demanded, wanting him to roughen his touch on her aching nipple. His thrusts grew harder. Faster. Harder. Her fingers stroked her clit, and she cried out as she exploded instantly.

"Keep it up until I finish," he said in her ear.

Oh, but she couldn't. It was too much. She wasn't used to the added stimulation of a cock thrusting into her as she came. The pleasure was intense. Overwhelming. Her entire body was shaking with pleasure.

"Rub it out, baby," he demanded. "Don't stop."

Her fingers began to move against her clit, sending her into a state of euphoria she hadn't known existed. She was only partially aware of being pressed face down on the sofa with her hand trapped beneath her body so she could keep touching herself and of the loud cries of pleasure bursting from her throat and Logan's answering cries as he worked toward his own orgasm. She was fixated on the intensifying and receding waves of friction as her pussy clenched rhythmically on Logan's hard, thick cock. Her body began to twitch as she rubbed herself and rubbed herself and he fucked her and fucked her. His strokes stilled suddenly when he shoved into her balls deep and shuddered against her with a loud cry. She slowed the rapid stroking of her clit and groaned as her body shook with continued waves of pleasure.

"Best. Pussy. Ever." Logan punctuated his words with hard thrusts.

She laughed softly, still shaking. He collapsed on her back.

"Was it good for you?" he asked with a self-serving chuckle.

"Not bad," she teased.

"Not bad? Damn, woman. I thought your pussy was going to suck my dick clean off my body you were coming so hard." He kissed her shoulder, nuzzled his face into her hair, and gave her breast a gentle squeeze.

"Did it hurt?" she asked.

He laughed. "In that way you think you might die from too much pleasure."

"That's how it was for me too." She shifted her hand out from under her body. It was slick with her fluids.

"Just so you know—since you're not very experienced and all—what we have here isn't normal."

Great. Something else that was abnormal about her. "I'll do better. You just have to teach me what to do."

"Better? Woman, if you do any better, they're going to have to check me into a hospital."

She'd always imagined she'd feel some profound, psychological connection with her partner after sex. But lying squashed under Logan's hard and heavy naked body, absolutely nothing insightful stirred her soul. Nope, the only emotion washing over her was exquisite joy. And maybe a little love.

Okay, a *lot* of love. Overwhelming, tummy-fluttering, breath-stealing, thought-shattering love.

At least she thought that was what she was feeling.

But she wasn't foolish enough to tell him that.

CHAPTER 17

LOGAN JAMMED his foot into his shoe and tied his laces. He scowled at Toni, who'd managed to get one leg in her panties, but was now lying on her side on the sectional, her face squashed and her eyes closed.

"Come on," he said. "Get dressed. The party has started without us."

"I'm not going," she murmured. "Too tired."

He took her foot in one hand and slipped it through the empty leg hole of her panties, which he didn't notice were wrong side out until he had them drawn up to her knees.

"You have to come," he said, removing her underwear and turning them right side out before starting over. "I want to see what you're like when you're drunk."

She opened one eye to look at him. "This is pretty much what it looks like, but with more vomiting."

He was hoping that pouring a little alcohol down her throat would loosen her up a little. Open her shell.

"Don't you need to see what an after-party is like for the book?"

"Yeah," she said.

Ha, he knew he'd get her to accompany him somehow.

"But not tonight," she said. "I'm exhausted. I need sleep."

"So you'd rather stay here on the bus by yourself than go to a party with me?" Was he pouting? He was pouting. What the actual fuck?

"Actually, I'd rather you stay here with me." She patted the sofa cushion beside her.

"Fuck, woman," he said with a crooked grin. "And I thought *I* was the horniest person on this tour."

"Not for sex," she murmured, her voice slurred. "For sleep."

"You just have to stay for a little while."

"An hour?" she bargained.

An hour? How much partying did she think she could accomplish in an hour? He supposed she wasn't used to keeping up with him. Yet. He'd let her get off with an hour this time, but he'd keep her out until dawn at the next party. The woman needed to get out and have a little fun. Under his supervision, of course. He didn't want any other man to discover what fantastic blow jobs she gave.

"Fine," he said. "But I'll probably stay out later than that."

She rolled over and tugged her panties up her thighs, and then continued to lie there half asleep. By the time she was dressed and the two of them left the bus, they'd missed out on at least an hour of fun.

The bar the tour had *borrowed* for the evening's festivities was jam-packed from wall to wall. Those who couldn't get inside were having their own little party in the parking lot. He lifted a hand to people he recognized as they called out greetings to him. Logan scarcely noticed the two members of the security team who escorted them from the bus to the bar entrance. He was so used to them being there in his shadow, that it was natural to be followed. Toni kept glancing back at them, though, as if they were stalkers, not protection. There were plenty of yellow shirts mixed with the crowd inside as well, but they were there to make sure their employers didn't get hurt, not to get in the way of their good time.

Logan took Toni's hand and led her through the crush of bodies. He knew almost every person in the place, so he got stopped often on his way to the bar.

"Who is this?" Matt Chesterfield asked, his British roots made apparent by his accent.

"This is Toni. Toni this is—"

"Matt Chesterfield," Toni said, reaching out to shake Matt's hand. "Lead singer of Riott Actt."

Matt raised an eyebrow at Logan. "Girlfriend?"

Logan's brow crumpled. Why would he think that? Sure, he and Toni were holding hands, but Logan always had a girl or two on his arm and no one had ever mistaken one of them for his girlfriend. "No, just friends. She's writing a book about Exodus End. I figured she'd want to see what one of these after-parties is like."

"Nice to meet you," Toni shouted over the raucous noise of the crowd and the music blaring in the background. "If you're interested in having an interactive biography written about your band—"

"What's that?" Matt shouted, leaning closer to her and turning his ear in her direction.

"I said," she shouted louder, "if you're interested—"

A nearby explosion of laughter cut off her words.

"Sorry?" Matt asked.

Toni shook her head. "We'll talk some other time!"

Logan tugged her through the crowd once more, introducing her to anyone of interest. Matt wasn't the only person who mistook Toni for his girlfriend. Logan was getting really annoyed by the fifth time he had to correct someone. "No! We're just friends!" he yelled at Twisted Element's lead guitarist.

"My apologies," Brent said, holding up both hands in surrender, though a brown beer bottle was hooked in one.

Toni offered Brent a weary smile.

"What do you want to drink?" Logan shouted at her over the ruckus.

She pressed her hands to her temples and shook her head. "Is my hour up yet?"

"You're not having fun?"

She looked like a wilted flower—still beautiful, but fading fast.

"This isn't really my thing," she said, "and I'm tired."

He rubbed her arm. "You can go back to the bus if you really want to."

He wanted her to say, *I'd rather stay here with you*, but she perked up immediately at his suggestion to leave. "Thank you," she said with a relieved sigh.

He tugged her back through the crowd toward the exit, not sure how anyone would willingly give up partying with over a dozen rock stars to hang out on a boring tour bus.

Once outside, Toni sucked in a deep breath of the cool night air.

"I'm going back inside," he said. "Can you make it to the bus by yourself?"

She glanced across the parking lot to where the bus was parked under a collection of street lights. "Yeah."

He kissed her cheek, knowing that if he drew her into his arms and kissed her the passionate way he wanted to kiss her, *everyone* would mistake her for his girlfriend. "I'll see you later, okay?"

She stared up into his eyes for a long moment as if she wanted to say something, but turned away instead. "Good night."

She was a couple of yards away when he nodded at the nearest security guard so he'd follow her and keep her safe from the drunks in the parking lot. She started when she noticed the yellow shirt trailing behind her, but she offered him a timid smile and continued toward the bus.

Ensured of Toni's safety, Logan returned to the bar.

"About time he ditched the stiff," Logan heard Steve yell as soon as he got inside. "I thought maybe he was too pussy whipped to have any *real* fun tonight."

Pussy whipped? Please.

"Sorry to keep you waiting," Logan said, lifting a hand toward the bar and finding it immediately filled with his usual drink—a Godfather. He chugged it in two gulps and extended his arm for a refill.

"This is Candace," Steve introduced the gorgeous blonde on his right. "And Tonya," He nodded to the equally gorgeous black woman on his left. "Oh, and you met Stacia earlier." The same brunette Steve had banged backstage. She must be exceptional if he hadn't ditched her yet.

"Ladies," Logan said, lifting his fresh cocktail in their direction.

After the hi's and great-to-meet-yous, Stacia moved to stand so close to Logan that her breast was pressed firmly into his arm. "What are you having?" she asked, eyeing his drink. Her perfume assailed his nostrils, and his nose twitched.

"If he had half a brain, he'd be having you," Steve said and lifted his glass at her.

If he hadn't just finished with Toni, yeah, it probably would have been Stacia. But he felt absolutely no interest in her, and he could only attribute his disinterest to having already had sex a handful of times that day. With the same woman. Which rarely happened.

"It's a Godfather," Logan said. "Scotch and amaretto."

"Can I taste it?"

Knowing he could have as many as he wanted, he handed his drink to Stacia. She lifted it to her ruby lips and sipped, her eyes smoldering into his as she licked the rim of his glass. "Mmm," she purred.

Okay, normally if a hot woman pressed her tit into his arm and made out with the glass he'd just sipped from while producing those kinds of sounds and offering him *come over here and fuck me* glances, his dick would have been bursting through the zipper of his jeans. But he didn't feel so much as a tingle down below. There was some weird shit going down here. He must be getting old or something.

"It's good, right?" Logan said.

"Strong," she murmured. She rubbed her boob into his arm as she turned toward him and tried to hand the lowball glass back to him.

"You keep that one," he said, extending a hand toward the bar for a fresh drink.

Reagan appeared unexpectedly beside him and practically shoved Stacia to the floor in her quest to get in next to him. Definitely some weird shit going down here. Reagan had never come on to him before. And it soon became apparent that she wasn't coming on to him now as she jabbered about the concert and how she'd twisted her ankle in her damned high-heeled boots and how she wasn't going to wear them anymore. She was going to wear her combat boots. Fuck Sam's idea of feminine beauty. Blah blah blah. Eventually Stacia got tired of standing behind Reagan and making huffing sounds with her arms crossed. She wandered off to find less annoying company.

"Cock block," Reagan whispered in Logan's ear and then danced away.

What did she mean by that?

He glanced over at Steve, who was making out with the two women he'd introduced earlier. Hell if Logan could remember either of their names. Normally Steve's behavior would have gotten Logan in the mood to one-up his bro and make out with *three* women at once, but he didn't see a single woman who interested him, much less three of them.

Weird, *weird* shit going down here.

He begged his leave from the horn dog across from him and sought less promiscuous company. But Dare was with his brother—coming between that pair was an exercise in futility—and Max had disappeared for the evening. Maybe Max had already gone back to the bus. Maybe Logan should go back to the bus as well. Not to be with Toni. Just because this party was kind of dead. He usually had a lot more fun at these things. What the hell was wrong with him tonight? Maybe he was just tired. Or maybe he needed another drink. Or maybe he missed Toni.

Nah. He just wasn't drunk yet. Though he usually didn't drink enough to actually get drunk. He only drank until he mellowed.

A hush fell over the bar, and Logan turned to see Steve standing on a table and searching the crowd. "Logan!" he yelled. "Where the hell did you run off to, bro?"

Someone shoved Logan in the back, and he stumbled forward, his movement catching Steve's attention.

"There you are. Candice and Tonya have agreed to a little game of double or nothing."

"I don't want to play. Pick someone else." Why didn't he want to play? It was his favorite game of all time, and the rewards were guaranteed to blow his mind. Or his load. Mostly his load.

"Awww, I think someone is pussy whipped," Steve called to the bar patrons, getting everyone in the place chanting: "Pussy whipped. Pussy whipped. Pussy whipped."

"Fuck you," Logan shouted over the chanting. "You're going down, Aimes."

A knot formed in Logan's gut as Steve's two women removed their tops and lay on their backs, head to head across the wooden bar. They were still wearing their bras—which was a bit of a relief—but Toni wouldn't like him playing this game. And she really wouldn't like it if he won. The prize was a threesome with the two ladies. Logan wasn't sure if Steve would purposely throw the game so Logan had to admit he didn't want to bang the two hot chicks or if Steve honestly wanted a competition. Dude was almost as competitive as Logan was.

"Logan," Reagan said, tugging on his arm. "Don't hurt her. She's such a sweet girl."

He pretended he didn't know Reagan was talking about Toni. "I'm sure they're both sweet girls," Logan said, "which is why they agreed to fuck the winner of this game. They won't be sweet when I'm finished with them."

Many of the male patrons at the bar cheered his boasting.

Once Trey had collected his cock-blocking pest of a girlfriend and the game had been set up, Logan stood next to the knees of one participant and waited for the festivities to begin. He couldn't make it obvious that he was losing on purpose; he'd never live it down. At the very least, he had to make it look like he was trying.

"Go!" Steve shouted.

Logan leaned over the woman's crotch, used his teeth to pick up the shot glass balanced on her pelvis, and tilted his head back to pour tequila down his throat. He swallowed, dropped the glass on the floor and bent over the woman again to lick the salt off her belly. He took the next shot glass off her stomach, which was a challenge because she was fighting a case of the giggles. Logan dropped that glass as well and fished the lime from between her tits with his mouth. Good thing she was relatively flat-chested, so it didn't take too many swipes of his tongue to retrieve the green wedge. He bit into the lime and spit out the rind, wincing at the tartness on his tongue. He then snorted the bump of cocaine off her collarbone. Logan stood abruptly, smacking himself in the eye when the rush went straight to his head. He produced a full-body shudder and peeked at Steve's progress. Steve was still trying to get the lime out from between his girl's tits. Probably because he was doing more licking than lime seeking. Damn. Logan rubbed his nose and sniffed, shooting a second rush of exhilaration up into his brain. Whoa! Good shit. He didn't do coke often—he was hyper enough without it. But how was he going to lose if Steve was so far behind? He had only one task left to complete.

Carla—was that even her name?—lifted a maraschino cherry toward him with her fingertips. Normally when he played this game, he licked and sucked the woman's fingers as he attempted to get the cherry in his mouth, but in this case, he went after it with his teeth. He groaned when the first cherry fell to the floor and she had to grab a second cherry out of the bowl near her hip. He caught a glimpse of Steve snorting his bump of coke—*finally*—and going after a cherry without pause. That meant they were neck and neck. Logan might not have to throw the game after all. Holding the second cherry between his teeth, he moved to stand over the woman's face. The idea was to get it from his mouth into hers without touching her lips. Which was way easier if he got up close and personal, but he dropped his cherry from full standing height and cringed as it fell toward her wide open mouth in a perfect trajectory. Shit! Why did this chick have to have a mouth like Steven Tyler? It was like dropping the cherry into a kiddie pool.

The cherry hit her tooth and for a second he thought it might bounce out of the gaping orifice. But no, in it went. The riveted crowd cheered.

His stomach dropped into his shoes.

Well, fuck. Now what was he supposed to do?

"That was a close one!" Steve said, coming over to pound Logan on the back. "But I won again. You suck at this!"

Wait? He'd lost? Woo hoo!

Uh, he meant *damn*. How had he lost? He'd been so far ahead before that first cherry had gotten away from him.

"I'll get you next time," Logan said, punching Steve in the shoulder several times.

Steve leaned in close to Logan's ear. "You would have won *this* time if you weren't so *pussy whipped*."

Logan shoved his laughing opponent out of his face. "Whatever."

He was relieved when Steve left with his two happy prizes. No one else would bother him about his disinterest in chasing skirts tonight. He thought about going back to the bus and crawling into bed with Toni, but even the small dose of coke he'd snorted made him way too fucking hyper. He'd never be able to sleep and would disturb her rest. So he burned off some of his excess energy by making an ass of himself on the dance floor. And then he burned off some more by talking like an auctioneer to anyone who would listen and to several people who weren't listening. By the time he finally settled down, the bar was mostly empty and it was well after three a.m. Normally the cops would have come to make everyone go home after two. But police tended to look the other way when Exodus End was out on the town. Unless Steve stirred up a fight or someone was rushed to the hospital with alcohol poisoning or a drug overdose. Such things didn't happen as much as they used to. The band members were slowing down now that they were all in their thirties.

"We're like a bunch of old ladies," Logan said to a lamp post as he stumbled back toward the bus.

One of the security team stopped him from walking into a fire hydrant. "I got this," he assured the guy and patted him on the chest. "Do you think Toni is sleeping?"

"I don't know, sir," the man said. He had a buzz cut and deeply tanned skin. But Logan mostly noticed his yellow shirt. That meant he was one of Logan's own and he could trust him. "It is very late."

"I think I'll wake her up." He lifted his T-shirt to his nose and sniffed. "Does this smell like women's perfume?" He offered the shoulder area of his T-shirt to the security guard, who was now walking beside him with his arms out, as if trying to save a toddler from falling on the cement and cracking open his skull. Perhaps Logan was stumbling to his left. But just a little. "Smell it. Smell it."

The guy took a whiff. "Yes, sir. It does smell like perfume."

"Shit. She's going to think I've been messing around with other women. I didn't though." He patted the guy's arm. "Why didn't I?"

"I don't know, sir."

"Fuck it." Logan stripped his T-shirt off over his head and tossed it on the ground. "Burn that," he said.

"Yes, sir."

Another of the security team that was trailing Logan picked up the discarded shirt.

"I'm tired." Logan felt himself fading. He just hoped he blacked out on something softer than the sidewalk.

"Would you like to go back to the bus, sir?"

Logan scowled. "Isn't that where I'm going?"

The guy somehow managed not to laugh. "No, sir." He nodded in the opposite direction. "The bus is that way."

Logan turned around, squinted down the sidewalk, and recognized the bus almost a block away under a bunch of bright street lamps.

"So it is." He turned on his heel and started toward the bus. Again. "I think I might be drunk."

"It's a possibility, sir." Logan knew they hired a lot of military veterans to serve on their security team, but why did this guy keep calling him *sir*? It made him feel old.

Logan ambled toward the bus, his thoughts—as always—on the woman he'd met the night before. "Do you think she really is my girlfriend?"

Enough people had certainly mistaken her as important to him.

"Who's that, sir?"

"Toni."

"I'm sure I don't know, sir."

Logan sighed. "I'm sure I don't know either."

CHAPTER 18

"**O**N YOUR FEET, SOLDIER!"

Toni sprang from a dead sleep to her best impersonation of an army private standing at full attention—complete with salute—before she realized she wasn't dreaming. There really was a blurry drill-sergeant type standing over the sofa.

"Not you," the very large, very muscular man said to a half-groggy, half-terrified, completely confused Toni. "I'm going to make bread pudding out of your doughy boyfriend here."

Doughy? If Logan was doughy, then Toni was a bag of jumbo marshmallows.

"Go to hell, Kirk," Logan muttered before he buried his head under his pillow.

Toni doubted he'd even been asleep three hours. He apparently thought it was his job to be that last person to leave an after-party. When he'd crawled onto the sofa and passed out next to her, it had been after three.

"Wrong answer. Everyone else is already in the gym," Kirk said. "Get your lazy ass out of bed before I embarrass you in front of your girlfriend."

Surely he meant Logan's *just*friend.

It wasn't even fully light outside yet, Toni realized as she blinked at the open doorway and out the just visible windshield. The bus door stood wide open and a cool breeze blew down the corridor, chilling her bare legs. She tugged on the hem of her sleepshirt, glad she'd decided to pull it on when she'd gone to bed the night before. Otherwise she'd currently be in the buff while she continued to salute Drill Sergeant Kirk. Feeling ridiculous, she dropped her arm, and then she found her glasses on the coffee table. She stuck them on her face and gawked at the giant of a man—he had to be at least six foot eight, with the shoulders of a gorilla and biceps bigger than her head. She was sure he could crush watermelons between his enormous thighs. The giant yanked the blanket off Logan and tossed it on the floor.

"I'm not embarrassed," Logan said to Kirk as his pillow was snatched away and thrown across the room. "She's already seen me naked."

"But has she seen you hogtied and physically carried out of the bus before?" Kirk shouted.

Logan smirked and opened one eye to look up at the man towering over him. "Is that a threat, Captain Kirk?"

Toni pressed her lips together so she didn't laugh as she pictured the hulking muscle man in a Starfleet uniform. In her mind's eye, it was several sizes too small and bursting at the seams.

"How many times do I have to tell you I was an enlisted man, not an officer?" Kirk asked. Well, he actually yelled it. Toni wondered if the "inside voices" speech she used with Birdie would work on him.

"Sorry. I keep forgetting," Logan said, sitting up and rubbing his eyes with the heels of his hands. "Go back to the gym and torture the other guys. I'll be there in a minute."

"If I have to come back to get you, I'm getting out my cattle prod," Kirk said.

"Promises, promises."

Kirk turned and seemed to actually see Toni for the first time. His scrutinizing gaze traveled down her body and back up again. He frowned and offered her a curt nod. "You should come with him."

She crossed her arms self-consciously over her not-even-close-to-rock-hard abs. "I was planning on it," she said, wanting some candid shots for her project. However, she had no plans to work out and make a fool of herself in front of the fine specimen of a man on the sofa who was currently stretching like a sleepy cat and muttering negative slurs against the effects of alcohol.

"Good." Kirk left the room, his footsteps surprisingly light as he jogged the length of the bus and down the steps.

"So that's the band's physical trainer, I take it?" Toni said.

"No," Logan said, his tone thick with sarcasm. "He bakes us cupcakes."

"Mmm, caaaake," Toni said in the voice of a zombie craving brains. She wished Kirk really did bake cupcakes. Her sweet tooth hadn't been satisfied once since she'd stepped on the bus. She was surprised by how healthy these guys ate. But then they probably wouldn't look so fit and delicious if they subsisted on beer and Cheetos.

"Caaaake," Logan copied her.

"Do you guys always exercise and eat well?" she asked as she found a pair of yoga pants in her bag and slid them on over her sleep shorts. She figured she could dress comfortably while following the guys around in the gym and no one would notice. She changed into a clean shirt as well.

"Only when we're under Sam's thumb," Logan said. "You'll get to watch me lounge around and binge on junk food tomorrow."

His day off. She smiled, looking forward to having his undivided attention and no social engagements. She couldn't really complain anyway. He'd done a remarkable job of spending time with her, even though he was so incredibly busy with the tour. Well, except for leaving her alone while he'd stayed at the party. She wondered if he'd had fun while she was sleeping like a rock.

"Assuming I can lift my hands as high as my mouth after Kirk is finished with me," Logan added.

With a sigh, he stood and made a pit stop in the bathroom—taking a lengthy pee with the door wide open. The man had no boundaries. He then swallowed a few painkillers with a sports drink he grabbed out of the fridge—still deliciously in the buff—before putting on a pair of tight briefs.

"Gotta keep the boys from flopping about," he told her with a wink. He covered his black underwear with a pair of shorts, and they sat side by side on the sofa to put on their socks and trainers.

"Pink and blue zigzags today," Logan said as he waited for her to grab her camera and other equipment.

"What?"

"Your socks."

She hadn't paid attention to what she'd put on.

"Do you approve?" she asked, snuggling into his side when he wrapped an arm around her and directed her toward the door.

"Seeing what socks you're wearing is like getting an extra little surprise every time I get you naked."

"You don't have to get me naked to see my socks," she reminded him as she stepped in front of him so she could take the narrow stairs to the ground.

"But I prefer it that way."

Logan shivered when he stepped off the bus. He hadn't put on a shirt. And Toni couldn't resist running a hand over his gooseflesh and the taut nipples that were now begging for her attention.

"Why is it so damned cold?" Logan rubbed his hands briskly over his upper arms.

"Probably because the sun isn't even up yet."

"Yeah, well, most of the gyms will only accommodate us taking over their facility if we do it in their off hours. So we get to work out at oh dark thirty."

Toni wrote a note on her hand about asking Butch how they coordinated gym time. Sounded like a huge hassle just to exercise.

"Can't you work out at the hotel or something?" she asked.

"We do. But every three days, Kirk insists on free weights."

"Of course he does," Toni muttered under her breath. The man could probably deadlift a tank.

The gym was a surprising flurry of activity. She'd anticipated seeing the band members of Exodus End, but most of the crew—including Butch—and two members of Sinners—lead singer Sed Lionheart and the short guy with spikey blond hair, whose name and instrument escaped Toni at the moment—were already working up a sweat. There were a couple of women she didn't recognize on the elliptical machines. Toni was pretty sure the one who looked like a supermodel was Sed Lionheart's wife. Reagan wasn't with the other women. She was curling a set of large dumbbells and making faces at herself in the mirror that spanned one large wall. Her hunk of a tall, dark, and handsome bodyguard was keeping a close eye on her while he performed squats.

Toni turned on her video camera and waited for some magic to happen. She didn't have to wait long.

"Behold!" Logan said raising both arms in the air and flicking his wrists to wave his hands down at himself. "Lo."

"I think you mean lo and behold," Dare said as he slid a black disk labeled 25kg on the end of a weight bar.

"Prepare to be shocked and amazed," Logan continued. He

spun in a slow circle as he scoped out the room.

Toni couldn't help but giggle at his attention-seeking theatrics.

"We're all amazed that you're here," Max said as he pulled his chin over a bar. "What time did you get to bed?"

"Three a.m. Five. I don't know."

"Did Kirk have to carry you off the bus again?"

"Shut up," Logan said in Max's direction. "He's only done that once."

"For being late, you can drop and give me twenty," Kirk shouted as he handed an upside-down Steve a weight to hold against his chest as he did inverted crunches. That would explain Steve's eight-pack, Toni mused as she snapped several pictures of said eight-pack.

"Twenty?" Logan said. "Is that all?"

"For your cockiness, make it thirty," Kirk said.

"You're boring me, Kirk." Logan rolled his eyes and examined each person in the room. "I challenge you," he said, pointing at the bleach-blond man from Sinners, "to a push-up duel."

"Me?" the guy said, looking flabbergasted.

Dare grumbled, "Here we go again," before he used his teeth to tear the tape he was wrapping around one hand and wrist.

Sed burst out laughing and pounded his bandmate on the back. "Go kick his ass, Jace."

Jace Seymour. Sinners' bassist, Toni recalled suddenly. Apparently her body was out of bed while her brain was still asleep. Jace was the smallest guy in the place. Toni wondered why Logan had singled him out.

Logan rotated his arms in wide circles and then stretched them over his head, jogging in place next to a mat as he waited for Jace to join him.

"What's a push-up duel?" Jace asked as he stepped next to Logan.

"A game I never lose," Logan said.

"A game that everyone he usually trains with refuses to play," Dare corrected as he lay back on a weight bench and carefully wrapped his hands around the silver bar above his face.

"That's because you all know I can't be beat."

"I'm pretty sure Jace will make you eat those words." Sed crossed his arms over his broad chest and beamed at his bandmate with something that bordered on fatherly pride. Toni made sure she caught the look with her camera.

"How does this work?" Jace asked. He didn't have Logan's swagger, but the determination in his stance was unmistakable. He didn't look the least bit intimidated.

"We do sets of thirty push-ups," Logan said.

"Thirty?" Toni cringed. Her arms and chest were aching just thinking about it. She doubted she could do three.

Jace nodded without batting an eyelash, and flexed his fingers.

"On the second set, you call out a modification for the next thirty. I call out a modification for the third set, you for the fourth, and so on until one of us collapses. Or rather, until *you* collapse."

"Got it," Jace said. He dropped to the mat without hesitation.

"Which one of you dumbasses can count to thirty?" Logan asked.

"I *think* I can count that high," Sed volunteered with a crooked grin.

Logan got into position on the mat parallel to Jace. Sed counted out reps while the two men completed push-up after push-up in perfect form. Strangely, the guy most into the competition was Kirk, and he was obviously rooting for the opposing team.

"Hey, Logan," Kirk said, "don't you know smaller guys are better at this sort of thing? They don't have to push up as much weight."

"That's why"—Logan lowered his body to the floor—"I picked"—up again—"him." And down. "No one"—up—"ever really"—down—"challenges me."

"One of these days, someone is going to knock you down a peg," Kirk said.

"Not today."

Neither man had broken into a sweat when Sed reached thirty and Jace called out, "Right leg up."

"Too easy," Logan claimed as he lifted his right foot off the floor and continued into the next thirty push-ups.

Toni squatted down in front of Logan so she could get a close-up of his face. A bead of sweat ran down the side of his neck. The muscles of his arms, shoulders, and chest strained with each repetition. Toni had never realized how beautiful a push-up could be. She was pretty sure she was sweating far more than Logan was. She wasn't sure if this footage would make it into the book, but she was positive she'd review it regularly.

Sed reached thirty again. Toni peeked at Jace, who had sweat dripping onto the mat beneath him, but still wore the same focused and determined look on his face as when he'd accepted Logan's challenge. Toni decided that Logan had indeed chosen a worthy opponent and might soon find himself knocked down a peg. At least she thought that until Logan called out his modification.

"Clap between reps."

"Ah, shit," Jace muttered. But when Sed started back at one, he pushed off the mat with the force necessary to lift his hands high enough off the ground to clap.

Toni gawked at them, vaguely aware that the gym had fallen silent as everyone had stopped their own workouts to watch the competition. As they were all cheering for Jace, Toni shouted, "Come on, Logan! You can do it!"

He tilted his head to offer her a smile and a wink before turning his concentration back to his task.

Both men were laboring hard by the time they reached thirty. Logan nodded in Jace's direction. "Impressive," he said. "Most guys kiss the mat by the fifth rep."

"I always do," Steve said and laughed.

"So what's next?" Logan asked.

Jace could scarcely catch his breath enough to say. "One arm."

"Left or right?" Logan shifted from his left arm to his right arm without wavering.

"Right," Jace said.

"But that's the arm you were shot in," Sed protested. "Are you sure you're up for that?"

Toni sought and found the bullet scars on Jace's right shoulder and arm. She snapped a couple of pictures, making a mental note to find out what had happened to him.

"Nope," Jace said. He lifted his left hand off the floor. "Gonna try it anyway."

"Someone needs to shoot Logan so it's a fair match," Steve said.

Logan lifted his left hand off the mat and gave Steve the middle finger. He kept that finger extended through the entire thirty, one-armed push-ups. Jace's arm was shaking so bad by the final repetition that Toni was sure it would give out on him, but he managed to keep going. His relief was tangible when he was finally able to set his left hand back on the mat.

Everyone cheered and clapped for him, even Toni.

"Are you done?" Logan asked. Sweat glistened on his bronze skin and wetted the golden curls around his face and neck.

"Not yet," Jace said.

"Well, that about kicked my ass," Logan said, shifting to his left arm and rotating his right. "Time for a set of girl push-ups."

Jace laughed and set his knees down on the mat. Toni wondered if Logan had picked so-called *girl* push-ups more for Jace's benefit than his own. She was pretty sure Jace's right arm had been worked to the point of exhaustion and one more clap repetition would have flattened him, resulting in a sure win for Logan.

After thirty more reps, which everyone in the room counted off, Jace said, "Feet on a bench."

"You're trying to kill me, aren't you?" Logan said. "It's not bad enough that you tried to take my job."

Take his job? As bassist of Exodus End? Surely Logan was joking.

The two bassists pulled their mats across the room to a bench and got into position with both feet on the seat and their hands on the mat.

"Just making sure you get in a good workout," Jace said with a devilish grin.

After several reps, it was apparent that Jace's right arm was physically incapable of contracting. Toni had never in her life worked out to exhaustion. She tended to stop when she got a little winded. Jace shifted to put all his weight on his left arm. In a few reps, that arm was shaking too. Logan was showing signs of fatigue as well. In any case, he was too tired to talk smack and had his full concentration on lowering and raising his body.

Jace released a growl of exertion, which gave him the perseverance to do one more push-up before he ended up sprawled face down and panting on the mat. Logan did a final rep to claim his victory and collapsed beside Jace. Both men laughed as they tried—and failed—to get off the floor.

"I'm tempted to call that a draw," Logan said, his voice muffled since his face was pressed into the mat.

"Don't you dare," Jace said, between gasps for air. "I'll get you next time."

"Are you okay?" Toni asked as Logan lay on the floor long after everyone had returned to their respective workouts.

"I can't move my arms," he said.

"Me neither." Jace chuckled and rolled onto his back to stare at the ceiling. "Good thing we don't have a show for a couple of days."

"Not that it's a huge deal if a couple of bassists don't show up for a gig," Steve said from a nearby weight bench.

Battle of the Bassists. Toni gave the event a title in case it made it into the book.

"It's not naptime, Schmidt," Kirk yelled from across the room where he was spotting Max through his bench presses. "You need to work your lower body. I want you to do squats until your ass catches fire."

"That won't take long," Toni said quietly. "His ass is already exceptionally hot."

She glanced up and grinned when Logan and Jace both burst out laughing. The two men assisted each other to their feet, whacked each other enthusiastically on the back, and knocked their knuckles together in parting.

"Respect," Logan said.

He turned, searching for the squat station. Therefore he missed the open-mouthed look of astonishment followed by the wide smile on Jace Seymour's face as he walked away. Toni, however, recognized it. She wondered why someone as young and successful as Jace coveted Logan's validation. She supposed most bassists would look up to Logan Schmidt, the musician. He was phenomenally talented and one of the best-known bassists on the planet. Yet he was so easygoing and personable, she tended to forget he was famous. She tilted her head as she trailed after him, seeing him in a new light. Sure, he could be a bit cocky, but all things considered, he wasn't like most celebrities. But then maybe most celebrities weren't the stuck-up, egotistical jerks they were portrayed to be by the media. Or maybe they were. Whatever the case, she was going to make sure that these four men—and Reagan too—were shown in their true colors.

"Hey, Toni!" Reagan waved her over from across the room. "Come over here and get a dose of estrogen. Hanging out with all that testosterone will grow hair on your chest."

"Is that why you keep stealing my razor?" her hunk of a bodyguard said. He then glanced wide-eyed at Toni before dropping his weights with a loud clang and dashing out of the room.

Okay, weird. Toni should be about as intimidating as a gnat to that guy. Why would he run from her?

"I'm working," Toni called back. As if watching four hot guys lift weights was actually work.

"Don't worry," Reagan said, "we have a good view of them in the mirror over here."

"Yeah, we do!" one of the other women said.

"Ah," Toni said, heading toward the cardio area, curious to meet a few rock stars' wives and/or girlfriends. "But can you *smell* them from over there?"

"Not yet," Reagan said. "And trust me, that's a good thing." She crinkled her nose in disgust.

Toni stopped next to Reagan's elliptical machine and waited for introductions. There were two other women working out—one with burnished brown hair, the other a strawberry blonde.

"This is Myrna, Brian Sinclair's wife." Reagan introduced the stunning brunette who was running at warp speed on the treadmill to her left.

"Nice to meet you," Toni said, bobbing her head to try to meet the woman's gaze.

"Likewise," Myrna said in a huff of breath.

"Can you believe she just had a baby a few weeks ago?" Reagan asked.

"You look great," Toni said, meaning it.

"Thanks," Myrna huffed. "I need to keep in shape to ward off all the pretty young thangs trying to get their hooks into my husband."

Reagan rolled her eyes. "Puh-leaze," she said. "That man loves you so blindingly, it hurts my eyes to look at you two directly."

Myrna smiled, but didn't slow her pace.

"Sinclair doesn't work out?" Toni asked. She still hadn't had the chance to meet the renowned guitarist. An oversight she hoped to remedy soon.

"He has Mal," Myrna said. "When I'm finished, we'll switch out." She increased the incline on her treadmill.

So apparently keeping a rock star's romantic interest involved having buns of steel. Toni eyed the stair climber with dread.

"This is Jessica Chase," Reagan introduced the blonde—another stunner, one who made Toni feel like a Walmart shopper who'd accidentally stumbled onto Rodeo Drive. "She and Sed

Lionheart are getting married in a couple of weeks."

"Gotta fit in that dress," Jessica said as she wiped the sweat from her face with a small white towel.

"I'm sure you'll look gorgeous."

Jessica ran a hand over her lower belly. "Maybe if Unborn Sed would stop insisting I need to put mayonnaise on everything that goes into my mouth. I don't even *like* mayonnaise."

So the small bulge in her lower belly was a baby. Was that how she'd managed to get someone like Sed Lionheart to commit? Not that Toni was considering doing that to Logan.

"So I guess Logan finally has a date for the occasion," Reagan said. She offered Toni a suggestive wink.

"Me?" Toni sputtered. She clapped a hand over her suddenly thundering heart.

"Who else? You are his girlfriend, aren't you?"

"Not really. No." She'd thought that maybe she was until Logan had debunked that myth half a dozen times at the after-party the night before.

"So you haven't spent every moment of the last two days with him?"

"Well, yeah."

"And he isn't so possessive of you that he immediately wants to fight every man who so much as glances your way?"

"I guess, but—"

"And he left the after-party alone last night *because*?"

Was that unusual for him? "Um."

"Because Reagan is an excellent cock blocker," Jessica said, reaching out a fist to knock her knuckles against Reagan's.

"So why is he so jealous?" Reagan pressed.

"He's just—" Just what? What was he exactly? "He thinks he has a special claim over me." And only because she'd been a virgin. Not because he was romantically jealous. She was sure of that much.

"And that's why he can't take his eyes off of you," Reagan said.

"Right."

Reagan shook her head at Toni. "Girl, we need to have a long talk."

"About?"

"About using your power to get what you want."

And what did she want exactly? Toni glanced over her

shoulder to find Logan watching her as he continued his squats.

Logan. That was what she wanted. *Who* she wanted. And not just as a temporary sex coach. Or a *just*friend. As her forever.

"I would appreciate some advice," Toni admitted.

She wasn't the only woman in the room being closely watched by a man. Sed always had at least one eye on Jessica and now that Reagan's bodyguard had returned to the gym, he was doing a poor job of pretending he wasn't watching her. Perhaps it was time for Toni to employ her cleverness.

"Maybe you can give me some pointers on how to catch the attention of *that* guy," Toni said, nodding in tall, dark, and obviously smitten's direction.

Reagan's eyebrows arched. "What guy?"

"That guy over there who keeps staring at us." And by us, Toni meant Reagan, but the woman's reaction was priceless.

"Ethan?" Reagan squeaked and almost face-planted on her treadmill.

Finally! A name to go with the face. And the body.

"Yeah," Toni said. "He's quite attractive." In an I'll-rip-out-your-spine-and-use-it-to-stir-my-coffee kind of way.

"I think he's taken," Myrna said, snorting on a laugh.

"*Really* taken," Jessica added.

Reagan cringed and shook her head at both women.

"He does appear to have a crush on Reagan." Toni sighed as she continued to try to work some information out of the tight-lipped woman.

"What makes you say that?" Reagan said, her grayish-blue eyes locked on her treadmill display.

"Well, he watches you constantly."

Reagan laughed. "He *is* my bodyguard. That's his job."

Touché.

"Besides, I thought you liked Logan," Reagan said.

"I do," Toni admitted. She so much more than liked him. "I just figure he'll tire of me sooner rather than later."

"Oh, honey," Jessica said. "We really do need to have a long talk with you."

Myrna shut off her machine and slowed to a walk before hopping to the floor. "It's been lovely," she said, "but I need to get back to Malcolm. My boobs say it's feeding time."

"It was great meeting you," Toni said. "Maybe you'd let me interview you about what it's like to raise a child on the road with a rock band."

Myrna smiled. "You'll have to read my book to find out," she said. "I should have it finished in about eighteen years or so."

So that would be a no on the interview.

Toni set her equipment down—she wasn't getting any work done anyway—and took Myrna's spot on the treadmill. She set a brisk walking pace. She and Birdie often took their border collie for long walks, so she was used to this level of exercise. All the strength training and weightlifting going on across the room was far beyond her current ability. But it was fun to watch in the mirror in front of her treadmill.

A few moments later, a pair of men entered the gym. She immediately recognized the black spikey hair and tattoos of Brian "Master" Sinclair, and his laughing partner in crime was none other than Trey Mills.

"I'm surprised he's out of bed," Reagan said with a self-satisfied grin.

"Where Brian goes, he goes," Jessica said.

Ethan's attention had finally shifted from Reagan, but he didn't look pleased to see the new arrivals. Maybe he was jealous of Trey's relationship with Reagan after all. Strange thing was, Ethan's cold stare of animosity wasn't aimed at Trey, the man competing for Reagan's affection. Nope, he directed all his rancor in Brian's direction. Toni knew there was a huge story in all this somewhere. She had to keep reminding herself that she was there to write a candid interactive book to make Exodus End look good, not stir up gossip about their newest and likely temporary bandmate.

Trey parted ways with Brian and offered Ethan a sexy smile that probably melted the guy's tennis shoes to the mat.

What? If Toni had been confused by the dynamics before, she was now completely flabbergasted. She'd hung around enough gay guys to know that look. She certainly hadn't expected to see it here.

Trey made his way toward Reagan and climbed onto the front of her treadmill, leaning forward and offering her his sensual lips in a pucker. Toni had no idea how Reagan managed to kiss him without knocking their teeth out.

"What are you doing out of bed?" Reagan asked after their mouths parted.

"I was lonely." He pouted in a way that made Toni wish she could take that loneliness away. "And Malcolm was screaming his little head off for his breakfast. Can you believe Brian wouldn't let me give the baby a sucker to shut him up?"

"That asshole," Reagan said with a laugh.

"Are you done in here?" Trey asked. "There's a bed on the bus with your name on it."

"Aren't Eric and Reb hogging the bedroom?"

So that was where Sinners' drummer was. All other band members were accounted for.

"Maybe your big, tough bodyguard over there can convince the perpetual newlyweds that it's our turn to rock the bus."

Reagan grinned. "I think he might be able to." She shut off her treadmill and hopped off. "We'll talk later, okay, Toni?"

Toni was surprised that Reagan knew anyone but Trey existed.

"Okay."

"I'll offer you a few pointers on how to get what you want."

"Thanks."

Well, that should be some valuable information. Toni was pretty sure that Reagan Elliot was a master at getting *every*thing she wanted out of life.

INTERVIEW
WITH
MAXIMILLIAN
RICHARDSON

TONI FIDDLED with her recording device, not because there was anything wrong with it, but because this was her first official interview with one of the band members and, frankly, she was intimidated by Max. He'd never really done anything to unsettle her per se. There was just something about him that was a little raw. A little dangerous. A lot sexually charged. She wasn't even sure she would have recognized the feelings of unease as awareness of his masculinity if she hadn't spent so much time in Logan's company. But while Logan's prowess was in your face, Max's existed on a deeper instinctual level. It was as if her lady bits knew he'd make gorgeous, healthy babies and wanted a piece of his genetic material.

And why was she fixated on his allure? They weren't here to discuss how mind-bogglingly attractive he was or how he was a perfect physical specimen of a man. They were here to discuss his part in Exodus End and maybe, if he trusted her, some personal fragments of information to add to her book.

"You look more nervous than I feel," Max told her in his consistently subdued voice. The only time she ever saw him excited was onstage. She wondered if he was naturally quiet or if he just saved up his energy for performances. Was he this calm when off tour? She added a couple of question to her list. She didn't have to wonder—she could ask.

Toni glanced up from her recorder and the pages of neatly written questions on her lap to Max's face. He was staring at her questions, trying to read them upside down. She shifted the legal pad against her chest to hide the words, and his hazel eyes lifted to meet hers. She hadn't noticed how much green was flecked inside the light brown irises. Maybe his green Save the Wails T-shirt brought out the brighter hues in his eyes.

"You're nervous?" she asked.

His laugh was soft and low-pitched. "I have no idea what you're about to ask me." He raked a hand through his hair, drawing her attention to his wrist brace. She had several questions about his surgery but was really wondering how it felt to watch Reagan play guitar in his place. Would he tell Toni something like that, or were those feelings too personal?

She grinned at him. "I guess you'll have to wait and see."

She switched on her digital recorder and set it on the shiny white surface of the coffee table.

"I'm surprised Logan let you talk to me in private," Max said, his gaze on the stack of neatly folded blankets behind her. She'd hoped he wouldn't notice that they were sitting on her makeshift bed—the one that Logan had shared with her the night before. She flushed as she recalled all the dirty things they'd done on this very sofa. She was still tender between her legs, so all she had to do was shift slightly to be reminded of how it felt to have him deep inside her.

"He didn't want to leave us alone together," she admitted. "But I reminded him that I had a job to do and that if he wouldn't allow me to do it, then I'd have no reason to stay."

"So you have him figured out already," Max said with a chuckle. "I guess he isn't very mysterious, is he?"

Would it be wrong to pump Max for personal information about Logan when she had no intention of including it in the book? This was supposed to be a formal interview, but how could she resist learning more about the man she loved—as a *friend*— from those who'd known him almost half his life? "Why do you say that?" she asked, hoping he didn't recognize her eagerness.

"Logan isn't very good at hiding things, so I guess it's only natural that he says exactly what's on his mind and puts his true self on display. I don't know how he gets away with it. Maybe it's because he's the bassist and there's less pressure on him to maintain a certain persona."

"The way there's pressure on you?"

Max shrugged. "I guess."

"Who puts the most pressure on you? Your band? The fans?

Your manager? The media?"

"Myself mostly, but yeah, I feel it from every direction."

Toni leaned closer, interested in his unexpected response. "Why do you put pressure on yourself?"

"If I tell you, I'm sure you'll slant it in such a way that I end up looking bad."

She was surprised that his lack of trust stung her feelings. She'd come into this experience expecting the guys to be cautious around her—especially at first. She supposed Logan was to blame for her thinking she'd already gained their friendship and trust. Perhaps his throwing caution to the wind and being open and honest with her was more unusual than she'd realized.

"I would never do that," Toni said, touching the back of his hand to press her point. "I'm here to write a book that shows all of you in the best possible light. My goal is to make you human, but not bad. Or scandalous. Or weak. But real."

"That might be even worse," he said.

"How so?"

He glanced away as if searching for the right words. "When the world believes you are the persona you display to the public, that perception allows you a certain layer of protection. So you feel like the criticism and hate isn't directed at you—not the real you— it's directed at the man they all think you are, who isn't really you at all. Otherwise . . ." He shook his head slightly, his hazel eyes dark with gloom.

She'd never thought about that side of fame. Accepting criticism was hard, and feeling that someone hated you was completely demoralizing. She didn't know if everyone took such things personally, but for Toni, negativity never just rolled off her back. It stuck deep in her heart. She fixated on it until even the smallest negativity sometimes blotted out all the good around her. So she understood why someone in the spotlight would need separation between the cruelty of the outside world and their day-to-day reality. But much of the world thought this man was the moon and stars, so that had to feel good. Didn't it? Or did he only apply the praise to his public persona and not to the real him as well?

"Is it the same for the adulation?" she asked. "Do you also keep that at a distance from the real you? Or do you allow that to touch you?"

His gaze shifted back to her. "Why don't we start on the

questions you brought with you?" he said. "I didn't intend to get this personal."

"I could shut off the recorder if you don't want it on the record," she said.

He shook his head. "Just ask me something else."

But her prepared questions seemed so superficial in comparison to what they were talking about. Regardless, she forged ahead. Susan wanted certain questions answered, and Toni had a job to do. As a for-hire writer, she knew the book wasn't truly her own, even though she would place her personal stamp all over it.

"When did you know you wanted to be a singer?"

Max grinned, some of the tension releasing from his broad shoulders as he answered a question he'd no doubt been asked a thousand times before.

"I never wanted to be a singer," he said. "I just wanted to play guitar."

"Oh." Her gaze dropped to the brace on his wrist.

"The band decided that out of all of us, my voice was the least offensive to the ear, so they made me sing."

Least offensive? "You have a spectacular voice," she said, knowing she was gushing, but anyone who listened to him knew that he'd been born to sing.

"Thank you," he said, the fingers of his right hand toying with the brace on his left wrist.

"Will you ever be able to play guitar again?" she asked. She could practically feel the sense of loss in him. She'd always been very sensitive to the feelings of others, so much so that her empathy was sometimes crippling. At the moment, her eyes were prickling with threatening tears, and he hadn't even told her how he felt about losing his ability to play. She just had to look at him to know he was struggling with it.

"I hope so," he said. "Even if I never regain enough strength and mobility to return to the stage, I hope to at least be able to play for fun. I do miss the feel of the strings beneath my fingers." He grinned. "I guess it's a good thing my voice was the least offensive. If I couldn't sing, I'd be entirely out of a job."

"I thought they hired you to be a singer. At breakfast yesterday they said your voice got them all laid."

Max laughed. "Their perception of that audition and my perception of it are a bit different."

"How so?" she asked, riveted by his every word and recalling that he hadn't weighed in much on that breakfast conversation.

"They were looking for a guitarist/potential singer. I was actually auditioning just to be their second guitarist. I only sang because it was required. Before that, Logan was singing for them."

"No shit!" she blurted.

"He has a decent voice," Max said. "It just didn't have the unique grittiness they were looking for."

Toni was going to ask Logan to sing for her the next chance she got. She wondered if he'd indulge her curiosity.

"Does it bother you that Reagan has taken over as guitarist for the tour?" Another question that was very personal. She wasn't surprised when he paused for a long moment before answering.

"Reagan has a bright future," he said. "If her personal life doesn't destroy it."

Now Toni was the one to pause as she contemplated his response. "Why would her personal life destroy it?" she asked when she couldn't decide what he meant. She figured it had something to do with Trey Mills. Maybe. And her bodyguard. Likely.

Max shook his head. "I shouldn't have said that. I usually don't talk this freely in interviews. Next question."

Toni smiled. Did that mean he trusted her? She returned to her list. Maybe he wouldn't notice she wasn't following her scripted questions if she pretended. She could read a few from the list and then sneak in a few of her own.

She read the first question that Susan had insisted she ask each band member. "If you could spend a day with any musician—living or dead—who would it be and why?"

"I spend every day with musicians, so why would I want to hang out with another one?"

Surprised by his answer, she glanced up from her legal pad and found him grinning. "Are you teasing me, Mr. Richardson?"

"I couldn't help myself. I've been puzzling over what Logan sees in you for days. You aren't exactly his type, you know?"

She'd been puzzling over it as well, so Max's criticism didn't hurt her feelings. Much. "What's his type?"

"Fast and superficial."

Her face flamed. Well, she definitely fit in the "fast" category. She'd known Logan all of an hour before she'd succumbed to his charm and tumbled into his bed.

"There's an uncommon warmth about you," Max continued.

So he'd noticed her blush, had he?

"A recognizable depth. Thoughtfulness. You seem to care deeply about . . ."

She met his eyes, and his brows lifted.

" . . .everything?"

"Doesn't everyone?"

He laughed cynically. "No, sweetheart. It's rare in this dog-eat-dog world." He leaned forward, his head cocked slightly as he appraised her. "So now I can't help but puzzle over what *you* see in Logan."

Flustered by his compliment, Toni pushed her glasses up her nose.

"He's fun and caring and considerate," she said.

"Logan Schmidt is caring and considerate?" Max asked, his eyebrows arched high. "Are we talking about the same guy?"

"He is to me. He brought me dinner last night. I didn't even have to ask."

"I guess you bring that out in him." He smiled softly. "John Lennon."

She blinked at him. "Huh?"

"I'd spend a day with John Lennon."

"Oh!" She'd forgotten she'd asked him that question. "Why?"

He lifted an eyebrow at her. "Because he's fucking John Lennon. I met the rest of the Beatles at various charity events and award shows. I'd dreamed of meeting the band since childhood and, well, John was murdered before I got the privilege."

"You couldn't have been very old when he died."

"I was in elementary school. I didn't take the news well. I refused to get out of bed for days. My mom was so worried, she took me to a psychiatrist." He tilted his head at Toni. "I'm not sure why I'm telling you this. I've never told anyone that before."

"Do you mind if I include it in the book?" This was exactly the kind of thing she wanted to include. Scraps of their lives that had never been shared with the world before.

"You could leave the part about the shrink out." He worried his wrist brace again, avoiding her gaze.

"I'll leave it out," she promised.

She read the next question on her list. "What's your favorite part of being a rock star?"

"Being interviewed by pretty journalists."

Of all the amazing things that touched his life on a daily basis, *that* was his favorite? After gawking at him for a moment, Toni realized that he was teasing her. Flirting with her? She dismissed that thought as soon as it occurred. There was no way Maximillian Richardson was flirting with her. The man dated supermodels and A-list actresses.

"I was under the impression that you didn't like to be interviewed."

"Depends on who's doing the interviewing." The smoldering look he offered would have sent her panties flying across the room under normal circumstances, but she'd given control of her panties to Logan, and she wasn't about to lose them so easily this time.

She narrowed her eyes at Max. He wasn't flirting, she realized. He was trying to redirect her questions by being distracting. And the man wrote the book on distraction. She'd have to word her questions cleverly if she wanted to milk real answers out of him.

Her next question was supposed to be: *Where do you see yourself in five years?* She could only imagine how he'd twist his response to that one. But she didn't want to lead his responses by having her questions be too precise. She wanted her questions to be open-ended. And she wanted his answers to be insightful. She just had to figure out how to keep him talking freely.

So instead of asking Susan's questions, Toni set the legal pad aside.

"You come across as a man who likes to have things all planned out," she said.

Max stared at her discarded pad for a long moment. "I do?" he asked, still looking at the bright yellow paper.

"Pretty much Logan's exact opposite," she said, grinning indulgently. "If you prefer, I'll give you the list of questions and you can plan your answers. We can reschedule the rest of this interview for a later time."

Max released a sigh. "You'd do that?"

"Why not? I don't want to make you uncomfortable."

"I'd appreciate it," he said, his shoulders sagging for the first time since he'd sat down beside her. She'd thought he just had really good posture.

Max leaned forward to rise, but Toni placed a hand on his knee. "Could you help me figure out what to ask your bandmates? I'm afraid I botched my first interview pretty badly."

"Nah, you did fine. It isn't you, Toni. It's me."

She chuckled and pushed her glasses up her nose. "That's

what they all say."

He sat back against the sofa cushions, making every posture-stickler mama on Earth proud once again.

"I'm interviewing Steve next," she said, consulting her notepad. "Is there a reason no one calls him Stevie? He seems like a Stevie to me."

"You should ask him," Max said.

"Do you think he'll answer questions about his ex-wife?"

"Which one?"

Toni shifted her gaze to his. "He has more than one?" She hadn't run across that in any of her research. Maybe Max was messing with her. But if he wasn't, what a scoop that would be.

"You'll have to ask him."

Oh, she definitely would. "After Steve, I'm supposed to interview Dare."

"Good luck with that," Max said.

"Please don't tell me he's even more tight-lipped than you are."

"Okay, I won't tell you."

Crap. "Did you really get his girlfriend pregnant?" She wasn't sure where that question had come from. It popped out of her mouth as if she had some sort of journalist Tourette's syndrome.

Max's normally tan complexion went pale. "Who told you that?"

"So it's true?"

"Has Logan been flapping his lips? I'll beat his fucking teeth in. See how well he talks after that." Max shot to his feet and stormed toward the door. His expression showed his anger, but it was the tangible look of loss that crumpled his strong features into a mask of desperate longing that had Toni's heart in a vice.

Whoa. She'd never seen the man display that much passion offstage. She hurried after him and grabbed his arm, thinking Logan looked good with teeth. She wouldn't want him to get them beaten in just because she'd asked Max the wrong question.

"I won't tell anyone," she said. "I should have never asked you that in an interview setting. I should have never asked you period."

Max stood with his palm flat on the door. His breathing was deep and irregular, but at least he was willing to hear her out.

"I apologize," she continued. "Don't make Logan pay for my mistakes."

"You're not really sorry," he said. "You just want to save your boyfriend's teeth."

"That's not true. I am sorry. I'm sorry when anyone feels pain. And I don't know if you loved her or only shared one night of passion, but her losing your baby, her taking her life, it had to hurt you. There's no way such losses couldn't have hurt." Her heart was twisting so hard in her chest, she could scarcely breathe.

"I did love her," he said flatly. "And instead of breaking it off with Dare, she convinced me to keep our affair secret so she could spare his feelings. When she got pregnant, she told him I raped her."

"What? If she was going to lie, why didn't she just tell Dare the baby was his?"

"Because the two of them weren't having sex. He thought she was a virgin and wanted her to stay that way until they got married."

"Did he believe that you raped her?"

"Of course he believed her. Vic meant everything to him. They'd been dating since they were in the ninth grade. When Dare found out about us, he tried to tear me to pieces. Almost killed me. And then he quit the band. He was still going to marry her, because he thought she was the helpless victim and I was a villain. And then a couple of weeks later, Vic lost the baby. She blew her brains out on a rainy Thursday in her old bedroom at her parents' house. In her suicide note, she told Dare the truth. After several months, Dare and I made amends as best we could, but he's never been the same since then. *We've* never been the same. So do I hurt?" He took a deep shuddering breath. "What do you think, Miss Journalist?"

Toni didn't bother trying to stop the tears from streaking down her face. She pressed her forehead into the center of his broad back and slid her arms around his waist to hug him from behind. He covered her hands with his, squeezing her right with one strong hand, his wrist brace—reminder of something else he'd lost—pressing against her left.

After a moment, he said, "You're the first person who doesn't think I'm a giant ass for sleeping with Vic."

"You're mistaken," she said. "You *are* a giant ass for sleeping with Vic. You should have waited to have sex with her until after she broke it off with Dare."

He released a breathy laugh. "Fair enough. Then you're the

first person who hasn't sided with Dare."

"I'm not siding with either of you. This is really about me," she said, sniffling. "I can't stand to see anyone hurting. Please tell me that look on your face is gone."

"What look?"

"The one that screamed your world had just ended."

He squeezed her hand even tighter. "You really are a sweetheart."

"Of the sappiest design, I'm afraid."

She released her hold on him and pulled a tissue from a box on the end table. She dabbed at her tears and blew her nose.

She stiffened when Max tugged her against him and wrapped his arms around her back. "Is the look gone?" he asked, leaning so close she could feel his breath on her lips.

Her heart thudded so hard against her ribs, she thought it was surely bruising itself. "If you kiss me right now, I'm going to kick you in the nuts."

He laughed and gave her a squeeze before releasing her. "I can't say I'm not tempted," he said, "but I learned my lesson about fooling around with a bandmate's girl."

Toni stepped back. The man smelled like heaven, and all the heat coming off his hard-muscled body was suddenly addling her senses. Maximillian Richardson was tempted to kiss *her*? Seriously? He had to be messing with her.

"Just to be clear," he said, "you are involved with Logan, right?"

She pressed one palm to a hot cheek. Okay, she was definitely feverish. That would explain the sudden weakness in her knees. "Right."

"Let me know when his boyish charm starts to get old," he said, the intensity in his hazel gaze sending butterflies flittering through her belly. "I'll show you how a real man treats his woman."

"Logan's a real man," she blurted.

Max chuckled and slid the door open. "Don't forget to give me a copy of those questions."

She was still gaping at his back when he shut the door behind him. It took her several moments to figure out why he wanted a copy of the questions.

Why did these men turn her into a fricking idiot?

CHAPTER 19

L OGAN WAS BROUGHT to a sudden halt by Steve's foot in his stomach.

"Stop pacing," Steve said from his reclined location on the bus's common area sofa.

"Why did she have to shut the door?" Logan grumbled. "It's not like we don't already know everything there is to know about Max." Including how he liked to steal other band members' girlfriends and knock them up. "He better keep his hands to himself."

"You're being ridiculous," Steve said. "If she spreads her legs for him, then she's not worth your time. Isn't that right, Dare?"

Dare glanced up, his attention diverted from the glow of his tablet computer's screen. He scowled slightly as if in pain—and perhaps he was hurting since the bridge of his nose was all bruised. "Some women are worth any hardship," he said quietly before returning his attention to his computer.

Yeah. Exactly. And Toni was one of those rare women. But Logan much preferred not having to brave any hardship. He liked how easily they'd come together. Life was fucked up enough without having to worry about heartache. Or hardship. Or Max using his smooth moves on an innocent young woman who happened to rock Logan's world. "He better keep his hands to himself," Logan repeated. Then he flopped onto the sofa next to Steve's enormous feet. Steve nudged Logan in the arm with one big toe.

"What's so great about her anyway?" Steve asked.

Logan turned his head and squinted at the lounging drummer, trying to decide why Steve wanted to know. "You better keep your hands to yourself as well," he said.

"And whatever you do, don't let her hug you." Dare pointed at the bridge of his nose without looking up.

"I apologized for that," Logan reminded him.

"And I've decided not to kill you unless you break Toni's heart," Dare said, his voice unsettlingly calm. "Then it's on."

"And why are you so protective of her?" Steve asked Dare. "You barely know her."

"She reminds *me* of Vic," Trey said from his seat at the dining table.

Logan was surprised the guy could talk after all the making out he'd done with Reagan all morning. Every time Toni had entered the room, the two of them started going at it like a pair of horny toads. Logan understood the need to physically express admiration for a woman, but it seemed that those two were up to something. Reagan had insisted that Trey ride with them today. And that bodyguard of hers was nowhere to be found. Logan was pretty sure Reagan was trying to hide her weird relationship with two guys by overcompensating with the one she was willing to flaunt publicly. That had to be rough for the other guy.

"She doesn't look anything like Vic," Steve said.

Dare didn't respond, but he'd gone very still.

"Not the way she looks," Trey said. "The way she is. You know what I mean, don't you, Dare?"

"No idea." Dare stood from his recliner and headed toward the bathroom.

"She's nice," Trey said, catching his brother's arm as he walked past. "A real sweetheart."

"Sorry, I don't see it," Dare said. After brushing Trey's hand off his arm, he entered the bathroom and closed the door.

"He does see it," Trey muttered. "That's why he's so broody."

"So Vic is . . ." Reagan prodded, shaking her head at Trey.

"One of Dare's many ex-girlfriends." Trey leaned over to steal a kiss. "Why did you make Ethan ride in the van again?"

"I think Toni suspects something."

"So?"

"So, she's a journalist. If the truth about the three of us gets out, my reputation will be destroyed."

"Your reputation?" Trey said. "What about *my* reputation? When you're a metal guitarist, sleeping around is expected. But being gay?" He shook his head.

"I'm trying to protect you as well."

"Maybe I'm tired of hiding our relationship. You know this is killing Ethan."

The door at the back of the bus slid open, and Reagan grabbed Trey for another round of making out. Logan hopped to his feet, examining Max for signs of seduction. His clothes were still in place, hair not mussed by exploring fingers, lips not swollen from passionate kisses. Logan released a relieved huff of air.

"That was quick," Steve commented. "Maybe this won't be so bad after all."

"We have to reschedule a second interview later," Max said with a mischievous grin directed toward Logan. "Toni got so hot and bothered sitting next to me that she couldn't concentrate."

Logan reminded himself that Max was just fucking with him and that he shouldn't punch him in the nose. Besides, his bandmates were now expecting him to hit them if they messed with Toni. It was unlikely he'd be able to sucker punch another one of them.

"Well, I'd better help her with that then," Logan said, "before we set Aimes loose on her."

When Logan tried to brush past Max in the corridor, Max caught him by the arm. "If you break her heart, I *will* fuck you up," Max said.

"Why does everyone keep thinking I'll break her heart?" Logan said, punching Max in the shoulder to encourage him to release his arm.

"The bigger question is," Steve said, "why do you guys care so much?"

It was unusual for his bandmates to give a shit about another guy's romantic interest. But then, Toni was unusual. At least in their circle of acquaintances.

Once Logan gained his freedom from Max's loose hold, he slid open the door to the back lounge and found Toni typing furiously on her laptop.

"Are you busy?" he asked. She was obviously busy. What he really meant was stop being busy and pay attention to me, please.

She glanced up from her laptop screen. Her cheeks were streaked with tears, and the tip of her nose was doing its best impression of Rudolph the reindeer.

"What's wrong?" he asked, torn between wanting to comfort her and wanting to yell at Max for upsetting her. The need to touch her proved victorious. He sat beside her on the sofa, closed her laptop, and set it on the table.

"Logan," she chastised. "I was in the middle of something."

"Yeah," he said. "My lap."

He tugged her to sit on his thighs and wrapped both arms around her. He doubted he'd ever get used to his all-encompassing need to touch her, to hear her voice, see her smile. He wasn't the kind of guy who got wrapped up in some woman. But apparently he was the kind of guy who got wrapped up in *this* woman.

"Why were you crying?" he asked, pressing a kiss to her head when she relaxed against him.

"It's nothing," she said. "Just something Max said."

"Did he hurt your feelings again?"

"Again?"

"Last night," he reminded her. "When he called you a geek."

"I told you that didn't hurt my feelings."

Yep, that was why she'd fled the stage. No hurt feelings there. He wasn't buying it.

"And he didn't call me a geek. He just didn't deny it. But no, he didn't hurt my feelings. He told me about Vic."

Logan was surprised that Max would bring up Vic in an interview. Unless . . . "Did you ask him about her?"

"I know I shouldn't have, but I'm naturally curious."

"Toni, you can't include anything about Vic in your book. Promise me."

"I promise I won't. I didn't ask him for the sake of the book. I asked him as a friend."

A friend? Max didn't have friends of the female persuasion.

"Toni, don't let your guard down around the guy. He's a total player."

"Like you?" She turned her head to grin at him crookedly.

"Exactly like me," Logan said. "When it comes to women, the dude has only one thing on his mind."

She laughed. "So he *is* like you."

"I'm being serious here." Which was why he slid his hand to her full breast and gave it an appreciative squeeze. His cock stirred to life, and he shifted her slightly so he could feel her soft ass against his perpetual arousal.

"Obviously," she said, a hint of laughter in her voice. She squirmed against him, sending unexpected waves of pleasure coursing down his length. "Can you send Steve in? I'm ready for him now."

"What? You'd better only be ready for me."

"I'm always ready for you," she said, "but I have to work. I'm not even sure why you came back here. I told you I didn't want to see you until it's your turn."

"It sounds like you're letting the guys take turns screwing you," he grumbled.

"Well, I do want this book to be authentic. That would be the fastest way to get to know all of you."

Even though he knew she was teasing, his heart shuddered with a painful lurch.

"Don't even joke about that, Toni."

"You don't think a chapter on what it's like to sleep with each member of the band would make the book an instant best-seller?"

"Probably, but I don't give a fuck about the success of the book."

She turned to sit sideways across his lap and buried a hand in his hair. She stared into his eyes until his throat tightened with emotion. "You can trust me, Logan. I'm not going to hurt you."

"That's not what I'm worried about." He was such a fucking liar. "I wouldn't want them to taint your sweet, clean pussy. It's mine."

Her eyes narrowed. "Oh, really?"

"Yeah."

"I guess I'll just have to blow them instead." She shrugged and slid from his lap. "Go get Steve for me," she said, and then she opened her mouth wide, stretching her jaw.

Twinges of anger made his hands clench. "You're not blowing anyone but me."

"What do you care?" she spat. "I'm just your friend, right?"

"Yeah," he said.

"And all you really care about is that you're the first guy to stick his dick in me."

It wasn't true—not even close to true. He cared so much about her that it scared the shit out of him. Which was why instead of telling her how he really felt, he stood from the sofa and crossed the room. He slid the door open and called into the corridor, "Hey, Steve. Toni's ready to give you your blow job now."

"Take it easy on her," Max said with a wink. "Her throat's probably still sore after the one she gave me."

Logan glared at him, annoyed that his attempts to get a rise out of Toni had backfired. At that moment, he hated every asshole in his band.

INTERVIEW
WITH
STEVEN
AIMES

"**I** WAS PROMISED a blow job," Steve said as he plopped down on the sectional and spun to lie on his back, his bare feet on the cushion and his fingers at the waistband of his jeans.

"Knock it off," Toni said, her cheeks flaming with embarrassment.

"So you'll suck Max's d—"

"I didn't suck Max's anything," she insisted.

"That's not the story he's telling."

"Yeah, well, he's lying."

"You could try playing along," Steve said, his grin appearing upside down to her. "We just like fucking with Logan's head, you know. I didn't mean to insult you."

"I'm not insulted," Toni said. Well, maybe she had been, but she wasn't telling him how easily rattled she was. It was bad enough that Logan realized it. "I'm just trying to be professional for this interview."

"Is the tape rolling?" Steve asked, eyeing her recording device on the coffee table.

"Yeah."

"Oh. Well, start asking your questions, then. I promise to keep my dick in my pants for the duration of the interview."

She couldn't tell if he was joking or not. He didn't really think she was giving out blow jobs during the interviews, did he? "Uh, *thanks*?"

Toni was determined to stick to her script this time. Even

though her scribbled note about Steve's second ex-wife kept drawing her attention as if it were flashing in neon lights. Despite her interest in tales that had no business in the band's interactive biography, she started with the first question.

"If you could spend a day with any musician—living or dead—who would it be and why?"

"Zach Mercer."

"Weren't you with him yesterday?"

"Yep. And I'd be hanging out with him today too if I didn't have to be here for this interview."

He didn't sound pissed or annoyed—just stating a fact—but Toni had to dig. She couldn't help herself.

"Are you two really close?"

Steve tilted his head back on the sofa cushion so he could look up at Toni, who was seated at the top of his head. "You don't believe that rumor, do you?"

"What rumor is that?" She honestly had no idea.

"That we *like* each other."

Confused, she scrunched her brow. "If you're friends, you obviously like each other, right?"

"You have no idea what I'm talking about, do you?"

Not a clue, but she decided he'd talk more if he thought she knew what he was alluding to. "I didn't think you'd want anything about that rumor on record." She glanced pointedly at her recorder.

"Actually, I would like to go on the record about that rumor. I don't know if Zach is gay. I don't really care if he is. He's a cool guy. But I'm absolutely not gay. I've been married, for Christ's sake."

"Twice," Toni said, knowing he was off guard and that it was the perfect time to get answers.

"Exactly. So just because I get a little touchy-feely when I get drunk doesn't mean I like to have butt sex with my friends. Understand?"

"Perfectly."

"Just because assholes like to take pictures of me hanging on Zach at an after-party and post said incriminating pictures all over the Internet with memes about drummers banging each other, doesn't mean it's true."

"Right," Toni agreed. She hadn't seen the pictures or the memes he was referring to, but she was definitely going to look this up as soon as possible.

"And just because his hand was down my pants and I had a huge boner, that doesn't mean I'm gay. Any guy would get hard under the expert tug of Zach Mercer's hand."

Toni's eyes were about to pop out of her head.

Steve snorted and burst out laughing.

Toni's face went slack when she figured out she was being had. Well, two could play at that game. "I'll be sure to make it perfectly clear in your section of the biography that even though you like hand jobs from Zach Mercer, you draw the line at butt sex."

She'd expected her threat to calm Steve down a bit, but he just laughed harder. "Good one, Toni. Now, when I tell Zach about this, you'll back me up, right?"

"Back you up?"

"He's the one who posted the photo. Several fans said it looked like his hand was on my dick and let's just say my drunken expression looked rather *enthusiastic*. Then someone captioned it with *Mercer takes Aimes in his own hand*. Damn thing went viral, and I've been catching hell for it ever since. I've been trying to think of a way to get back at him. If he thinks you're going to address it in an actual book, he'll think twice about ruining my life."

"So this incident ruined your life? How so?"

He rotated into a sitting position and placed his bare feet on the edge of the coffee table. "Do you always take things so literally?"

"Not always." But usually.

"It didn't ruin my life, but it does annoy me."

"You don't think it's funny?"

"At first it was hilarious—it's amazing how many different ways people come up with to caption a photo—but now it's just annoying. Pretty much anything that goes viral online ends up being annoying, and when you're the brunt of the joke and you can't defend yourself—"

"Why can't you defend yourself?"

"If you feed the internet trolls, they grow and reproduce. Best to let them starve. Eventually they find something else to obsess over."

Toni nodded. "So are you mad at Zach for making the image public in the first place?"

"How was he supposed to know people would take it the

wrong way?" Steve closed his eyes and laughed. "Okay, he totally knew people would take it the wrong way and have a good time with it. He just had no idea how far they'd take it."

"So tell me about your ex-wife." The interview had already derailed. No sense in trying to get it back on track now.

Steve's head swiveled, and he scowled at her, but she sat poised with pen in hand, pretending she was supposed to ask about personal matters.

"Nothing new to tell there," he said. "Everyone knows it was a messy divorce. Bianca almost bankrupted me in the settlement, and she loves telling the press what an impossible asshole I am."

"I wasn't referring to that ex-wife." Everyone knew about his divorce from America's sweetheart. The mess had been in the tabloids for months and was still good for an occasional stirring of shit. "Unless you want to tell your side of the story."

Steve released a derisive laugh. "Like that ever matters. I was labeled the villain on day one. Poor little Bianca. Everything I ever say about our breakup gets twisted around to make me look even worse. I just keep my mouth shut these days. Lesson learned."

Better writers than Toni had tried to give Steve's side of the story and he was correct—even when he wasn't portrayed as a complete asshole, he ended up looking like one.

"I could try to put a different slant on it in the book," she said. "Maybe we could include nice memories of Bianca with the band before your relationship got rocky." She'd seen photos of Bianca with the band when they'd first started out. If Steve was okay with it, Toni would love to include her as part of the band's beginnings.

"That relationship was always rocky, but we did have some good times in the beginning."

"Can I include her in the history of the band?"

"Depends on what you include," he said with a laugh.

"I'll run it by you and you can give me some insider information on her part."

"Maybe," he said, still looking unconvinced. She knew he'd need time to digest the possibility of portraying Bianca in a good light. They'd been battling each other so long, he probably had a hard time remembering the good times. And that was what Toni was after for the book. The good times.

Shifting gears, Toni asked, "So what about your second wife?"

Steve's face fell. "Where did you hear—" He shot to his feet and raced to the door. "I'm going to kill him. Dead."

Toni reacted on instinct, hurrying after him and catching his hand just before he grabbed the handle to slide the door open.

"I'm sorry I asked," she said. "I didn't realize it was a touchy subject."

"Not touchy," Steve said. "Secret. Logan swore on his life that he'd never tell anyone, so that means I get to kill him."

"Wait." It hadn't been Logan who'd told her.

Steve ignored her plea and slid the door open so hard it crashed into the frame with a loud *bang*. Like a freed beast, Steve sprang from the room with murder in his eyes.

Toni caught the astonished expression on Logan's face just before Steve jumped on him. She could add interviewer to her list of things she sucked at. Not only had she asked only one legitimate question during their short interview, she'd managed to send her interviewee into an uncontrollable rage in mere minutes.

As no one else on the bus seemed intent on saving Logan's life, Toni dashed down the aisle and tried to get a hand on the flailing drummer before he did permanent damage to her squirming boyfriend or justfriend or whatever he wanted to call himself.

CHAPTER 20

LOGAN WASN'T SURE why he was suddenly caught up in a brawl, but he wasn't about to sit there and take a punishing without retaliation. He took several punches to the ribs before he got in a single well-placed blow to Steve's shoulder.

"You're a dead man, Schmidt," Steve yelled.

Logan was sure he'd done something to deserve getting his ass kicked, but hell if he could think of anything.

"What did I do?"

All the air rushed from Logan's lungs as a body landed on Steve's back and flattened them both to the floor. He was astonished to see a mass of long brown hair writhing about over Steve's shoulder. Steve easily tossed Toni off his back by flipping to one side. While Logan took advantage of his opening and tried to scramble from beneath Steve, the drummer caught Logan's neck in the crook of his elbow and squeezed him into a headlock. Already winded, Logan latched onto Steve's forearm with both hands and tried to pry his arm loose so he could take a decent breath.

"Please don't hurt him," Toni cried, her hands next to his on Steve's arm.

Technically, he was already hurt, but he didn't feel that he was truly in danger. It wasn't as though he and Steve didn't regularly get into fights. True, they were usually both drunk, so the blows hurt less, but unlike Max and Dare, who preferred to talk through problems like a couple of wimps, he and Steve preferred to let off steam through their fists. Which was why everyone on the bus with the exception of Toni didn't intervene in Logan's impending murder.

"Why can't you ever keep your big mouth shut?" Steve growled.

Logan's grip loosened as his surroundings began to swim around him.

"I don't care if you're screwing her, she's a goddamned journalist. You have to watch what you say to her."

Logan racked his brain for something he'd told Toni that Steve wouldn't want her to know about. Everything in Steve's past was pretty much an open book to reporters already. Steve had one deep, dark secret, but Logan hadn't mentioned the guy's eighteen-hour marriage to Meredith.

"I didn't tell her—" Logan gasped through his crushed windpipe.

"I don't care if she doesn't know the details. She knew enough to ask about it, and that's too much."

"Let him go," Toni said, jerking wildly on one of Steve's wrists. They guy had impressive upper body strength, so Toni's attempts to save Logan's life were completely ineffectual.

Toni switched tactics to slapping the crap out of Steve's back.

"Ow!" he protested.

"I said let him go. He isn't the one who told me."

Logan's vision tunneled. He knew he was in danger of passing out, yet he was more worried about Toni's distress than his own.

"Knock it off," Steve said. He released his hold on Logan's neck so he could grab Toni's wrists.

Gasping for air, Logan climbed to his hands and knees, hoping Toni could hold her own, because he wasn't sure if he was much use to her in his current semi-conscious state. He tried to rise to his feet, but stumbled sideways against the sofa and ended up sitting in the middle of the floor, staring up at the ceiling because he was too exhausted to hold his head upright. Toni's concerned face was suddenly in his line of vision.

"Are you okay?" she asked, leaning close to peer into his eyes.

He lifted a finger—a signal that he needed a minute to respond—as he sucked air into his lungs and huffed it back out painfully.

He watched in astonishment as she sprang to her feet and began jabbing an angry finger repeatedly into Steve's chest as she told him off.

"You can't just jump on people like that! What are you, eight? Learn to control your temper! Fighting is never the answer. If you have a problem with something I've done, then you need to take it up with me like a mature adult. Not attack Logan when he least expects it."

"But—"

"You could have seriously injured him, choking him like that. I understand that you're mad, but how would you feel if you'd actually killed him?"

"He—"

"You'd never forgive yourself, now would you?"

Logan sniggered at the astonished look on Steve's face as he failed to get more than a word in.

"The two of you are going to apologize to each other and I'm going to apologize to both of you for being an inexperienced idiot who can't—" She took a deep shuddering breath. "Who can't even—" Her shoulders shook as her emotions finally got the better of her. "Even conduct a decent interview."

She burst into tears and raced back to the lounge area, sliding the door closed behind her with a loud bang.

"What just happened?" Steve said, rubbing the red spot in the center of his chest.

"Seems she told you off for acting like a child," Max said calmly. "Logan didn't say anything to her about Meredith."

"It was *you*?" Steve's eyes narrowed.

"I panicked when she started asking me personal questions and it slipped out."

"Poor Toni is obviously upset," Dare said with a devious smirk. "I guess it's time for my interview." He rose from his recliner and headed toward the back of the bus.

Oh shit. Logan knew how Dare comforted women. As soon as he could find the strength to climb to his feet, he'd do something about it.

INTERVIEW
WITH
DARREN
MILLS

WHEN THE DOOR SLID open, Toni turned and looked up from her tissue. She'd expected Logan to come reprimand her for being ridiculously unprofessional—she didn't deserve to be comforted after the foolish way she'd acted—but the man standing in the doorway was dark-haired and green-eyed, not golden-haired and blue-eyed. He was also the last person she'd expected to cuss her out and tell her to pack her bags immediately.

Dare Mills strode into the room and slid the door shut behind him. She supposed at least they'd have a little privacy when he fired her.

"Are you okay?" he asked.

She nodded, and his handsome face blurred out of focus as fresh tears flooded her eyes. On second thought, no, she was decidedly *not* okay. She shook her head, pursing her lips together to stifle the sob creeping up her throat.

"I must say, I never thought you had it in you." He chuckled and approached her slowly. "You don't get angry very often, do you?"

Actually, she rarely got mad. And whenever she did, she reacted to her own tirade by crying, which was flipping ridiculous.

She blew her nose and yanked another tissue out of the box to wipe at her eyes. "I'm so embarrassed." Mortified was a better word, but she'd truly be showing her geekiness if she started using that kind of vocabulary. She'd actually put her hands on another human being and then she'd started spouting words that under normal circumstances she'd think but never say aloud.

"Why? Steve deserved to be told off. And I think after you give what happened a little thought, you'll give Max the tongue-lashing he deserves as well. He should have never told you Steve's personal affairs."

She blinked at him, completely baffled. He'd come back here to praise her for behaving like a raving lunatic?

"Do you need a hug?" He opened his arms wide and flicked his wrists, directing her to the hard chest at his center.

She shook her head. Sniffed her nose and dabbed at her eyes. On second thought, yes, she definitely needed a hug. She nodded and took several steps in his direction. Closing the distance, he wrapped both arms around her and squeezed tightly. She relaxed against him, astonished by how quickly her cares melted away. She would have preferred Logan to be the one comforting her, but whenever she ended up in his embrace, sexual urges consumed her. Being hugged by Dare was different. It was almost like when she was a girl and her father had comforted her when the world had treated her unfairly. Except her father hadn't had such a firm muscular chest and didn't smell like a little slice of heaven. Being hugged by Dare was like being hugged by the gorgeous big brother she'd never had but had so longed for when the responsibility of taking care of the family had fallen on her after her father had passed away.

Dare rubbed her back, turning her muscles to butter. Toni appreciated that he kept his touch platonic and his embrace comforting. She'd done enough yelling for the day and if he tried anything, she'd be obligated to tell him off. She'd made a promise to Logan, and she didn't take such things lightly.

"Feel better?" Dare asked, leaning back to look at what must be a tear-streaked disaster, aka her face.

She nodded.

"You'd better not be touching her, Mills," Logan called hoarsely from somewhere in the bus.

"I don't think we need two fights in one day," Dare said. He released her and stepped away. "Guys like Logan don't understand how it's possible to touch a woman without trying to initiate sex."

"According to him, we're just friends," Toni grumbled.

Dare laughed. "Right. The two of you are much more than friends. Anyone can see that."

The corner of Toni's mouth curved upward. She thought so

too, but she wasn't going to press the issue with Logan just yet. She didn't want to send him running for the Canadian border to escape her.

Dare took a seat on the sectional and made himself comfortable. "I'm ready when you are."

"Ready for what?"

"My interview."

She scratched her jaw. Her confidence had been completely shattered by the fiasco of Steve's interview and the lack of cooperation during Max's. She doubted she was capable of attempting Dare's session today.

"I'm not sure I know what I'm doing," she admitted.

"I'm sure that you do. Sit down. Take a deep breath. And get to work."

If she hadn't just been wrapped in his comforting embrace, she would have hugged him for the vote of confidence.

She sat beside him on the sofa, pushed her glasses up her nose, and took a deep breath. She released it slowly and then reached for her legal pad, flipping to the second sheet of questions so that she wouldn't be distracted by her margin notes about Dare's deceased fiancée. Nope. She was not asking him that. There'd be only nice, *safe* questions asked in this interview.

"Okay," she said, taking another deep breath, hoping it would steady her shaking hands. "Every member of the band is listed in the songwriting credits for all of Exodus End's songs. Do you participate equally in writing music or do certain members contribute more than others?"

"That's a loaded question," Dare said.

She hadn't meant it to be. Though now that she'd read it aloud, it did sound kind of rude. The undercurrent of *who works hard and who skates along accepting undeserved credit* was definitely there. Surely Susan, with her years of superior interview experience, could have worded the question better. The trembling of Toni's hands intensified.

"I'm going to answer it anyway," Dare said. "But I'm not naming any names. We basically lock ourselves in a room for twelve hours a day for several weeks. We start out with brainstorming and our ideas are practically flying from our mouths and fingers and everybody shows enthusiasm for each other's thoughts. Then someone disagrees with someone else, we take sides, we argue, everyone decides they hate each other, sometimes we try to kill each other. One of us always threatens to leave the band—usually the same person. We don't see each other for days or weeks, depending on which of us stubborn assholes was the most insulted by the fighting. Eventually one of us either gets tired of the bullshit and forces apologies or the jerk who started the disagreement decides his butt hurt isn't worth losing everything over and he eats crow. We then lock ourselves into a room again and start over, this time with fewer stars in our eyes and more compromise in our spirit. And somehow songs come out of that chaos."

Toni wondered which one of them usually started the arguments, which one threatened to quit the band, and which one of them was likely to get them back together. She was almost positive that Dare was the one who made them compromise and get over their differences. Or maybe Max.

"Which one of you threatens to quit the band?" she couldn't help but ask.

Dare lifted a brow at her. "I said I wasn't naming names."

She lowered her gaze. There she went again, shoving her foot in her mouth. His answer had been vague, but a lot more descriptive than the answers she'd pried from Max and Steve.

"You really don't know?" Dare asked after a moment.

She had a suspicion. "Logan."

"When the going gets tough, Logan goes."

Why did that sound like a warning?

The door slid open. "Sorry to barge in," Logan said, rubbing his neck. "Just making sure I don't have to punch Dare in the nose again."

Dare's look of annoyance sent Logan back a step.

"Everything looks fine back here to me." Logan closed the door as he left them alone again.

"He's different with you, though," Dare said. "I never realized he was such a jealous son of a bitch."

Toni didn't particularly like Logan's behavior when his jealousy got the better of him, but the idea that he was so possessive of her made her heart smile. She couldn't deny it. Even if they were just friends.

She turned back to her questions, hoping the next one was better.

"You supposedly own a legendary Flying V guitar that you use to compose all your guitar solos. Is that true?"

"It isn't exactly legendary," he said with a chuckle. He nodded to the guitar on the wall. "Does it look legendary to you?"

She glanced over her shoulder at the guitar in question. "Well, it doesn't glow with a godly power or anything, but if it's really responsible for the amazing guitar work you create, then yeah, I'd say it's totally legendary."

"It's not even a quality guitar," Dare said. "By my current standards, it's a piece of shit. I'd never use it onstage or in the studio. But something about holding it takes me back to my roots. Back to when creating music was new and fun and magical instead of expected or required. Back when there were no expectations of quality. Back when I had no experience and very little raw talent. Back when everything I played came from the heart even if it sounded like shit. That's where I always want my music to come from. That's why I still use that cruddy guitar to compose."

"Oh," she said breathlessly, completely swept up in his words. In awe of him. This guy was the real deal. "Can I take a picture of you holding the Flying V for the book?" she asked a bit too enthusiastically. She was already picturing a video clip of it glowing on the wall and flying into his hands. A bit cheesy, perhaps, but she could have a lot of fun with it.

"I guess so."

"I would love to be a fly on the wall when you guys are writing a song. I'd be the most privileged bug on the planet."

"Maybe I can talk the guys into writing a song for your book while we're on tour. We've got the guitar, after all."

Every molecule in the room seemed to stop moving. She was so stunned by his suggestion, time had ceased to move forward.

"You okay?" he asked, his brow crumpled with concern.

"Are you serious? Oh my God, Dare, that would be amazing! I can't . . . I can't even . . ." She covered her thudding heart with one hand. "Oh!"

He smiled and reached over to pat her on the head. "That's the heart I'm talking about, when excitement for your work isn't fabricated. You're still young enough that it comes naturally. I hope the real world never wears you down."

She hadn't really experienced enough of the real world to know how she'd fare. So far, she wasn't doing particularly well in the career department. And her love life was a sham. But at least she was trying.

"So do you always compose here in this room?"

"We usually hole up at my place. But we could try to compose here for your book."

"So why do you bring the Flying V on tour?"

Dare laughed. "This is going to sound stupid . . ."

Toni shook her head, doubted that anything the man said could possibly sound stupid. If he said two plus two was five, she'd have started a campaign to spread the word.

"I like to bring her out on the road so she remembers why we're working so hard and what we're trying to accomplish."

Toni laughed. "You make it sound like it's a living being, not an inanimate guitar."

"Her name is Genevieve. And she never fails to come alive in my hands." He scratched his jaw, smiling broadly. "I told you it would sound stupid."

Toni shook her head. "I get it. Some people name their cars. Why not name an iconic guitar?"

"I also have a tattoo of good ol' Genevieve on my back."

"Okay, you've crossed a line. That's definitely stupid," she teased.

"Hey! I bet you have a tattoo of your precious camera on your ass cheek."

"You would be wrong," she said, her face flaming.

"Are you willing to prove it?"

Oh lord, Dare Mills was flirting with her. Completely harmless flirting, she was sure, but still, definite flirting. First Max and now Dare. Maybe guys had always flirted with her and she'd been too dumb to realize it.

"You could ask Logan," she said. "He'll vouch for me."

"*What?*" Dare covered his mouth, pretending utter shock. "Logan has seen your ass cheek?"

Toni drew her eyebrows together. "I think he has. I'm not sure. He spends most of our naked time staring at my boobs."

At Dare's unexpected bark of laughter, Toni nearly jumped out of her boots.

"I'm sure they're an eyeful." He lowered a pair of invisible shades to give them an appreciative look.

Toni swatted at him. "Stop. These are supposed to be serious, professional interviews."

"I thought you were looking for the real us."

Rattled, she lifted her notebook against her chest like a shield. "Right. That's the idea."

"Then you're going about it all wrong," he said. "Just talk to us. We don't bite."

She nodded, knowing he was giving her good advice, but also realizing she'd be as exposed as they were if she just talked to them. She wasn't sure she was prepared to open herself up to the scrutiny of four worldly men.

"Unless you really do have a tattoo on your ass," Dare said. "Then I will bite." He made a biting motion and produced a little growl.

Toni stood abruptly and headed for the nearest exit.

"Where are you going?" Dare asked.

"To the tattoo parlor. Where else?"

He was still laughing when she entered the bathroom and shut the door.

INTERVIEW
WITH
LOGAN
SCHMIDT

WHEN TONI RETURNED from the bathroom, she found Logan sitting with Dare in the lounge.

Logan noticed her standing in the doorway and smiled at her. "Is it my turn now?"

"Yes, Logan. You're next."

"We're already finished?" Dare asked, his green eyes wide with surprise.

"Our interview completely deteriorated. There's no way we'll ever get it back on track today." She looked at Logan, who was grinning rather smugly. "I hope you're more serious about this process than Dare was."

She'd wager the chances of that happening were less than her chances of winning Olympic gold in the decathlon.

"I'll try my best to behave." He plastered his most angelic look on his face and pressed his hands together in a prayer pose. With all those soft golden curls framing his face and those pale blue eyes of his, he actually looked sweet.

"Let me know how that goes," Dare said with a laugh. He rose from the sectional and headed toward the door. Toni caught his arm and pulled him outside the room so Logan wouldn't overhear.

"I've decided you're right about how to get the best answers for my questions. I'm going to ditch the formal interviews entirely and just talk to all of you."

"So you're not going to interview Logan? He's going to feel left out."

"I have other plans for Logan's interview. So if he asks if my questions were about your sex life, just play along, okay?"

Dare grinned and shook his head at her. "I think that man is a bad influence on you."

"And I will be forever grateful."

She released Dare's arm and patted his biceps before returning to the lounge and sliding the door shut. Logan sat with his left ankle resting on the opposite leg, hands linked around his bent knee. She took a moment to admire the cut of his shoulders and arms and chest, having a deeper appreciation for his musculature now that she'd seen how much effort went into looking as good as he did. His toe began to tap, as if he struggled to contain his seemingly boundless energy.

She crossed the room and sat beside him, picking up her legal pad to pretend she was reading her prepared questions as she messed with him.

"John Entwistle," he blurted.

Toni blinked at him in confusion. "Huh?"

"The musician alive or dead I'd want to spend the day with."

She sat up straighter, excited to discover some common ground between them. "Oh, I love the Who. My dad and I used to sing 'Love, Reign O'r Me' to my mom and dance her around the kitchen every morning before she went off to work. It never failed to make her laugh." She hadn't thought about that for years. The memory was equally warm and heart-rending. She wondered if her mom missed those silly moments with Daddy as much as Toni did.

"Your dad sounds like a lot of fun." Logan grinned.

"He was. He and my mom were so different yet so perfect for each other. He was so affectionate and tender and fun-loving. She's ambitious and innovative and beautiful."

"So you got the best of both of them," Logan said.

Toni rubbed at one eye beneath her glasses. "I can only aspire to be like either of them." She smacked Logan on the foot with her legal pad. "How could you?"

"What did I do? I'm being perfectly charming over here."

Honestly, he was, but how could she tease him with her pretend questions if he knew the real ones in advance? "You read through my questions, didn't you?"

"Just a couple. So now you're supposed to ask why I chose John Entwistle."

"It's obvious. He was an amazing bassist."

Logan nodded in agreement. "He was. But that's not the only reason why."

"Then why?"

"The night before the first the Who reunion tour concert, the man died with a stripper in his bed at the Hard Rock Hotel in Las Vegas. If that isn't the most rock star way to die, I don't know what is."

Toni shook her head at him in disbelief. "I do hope you're joking."

"Seriously. The dude was fifty-seven years old and still rocking the mattress with hot chicks."

Toni smacked his foot with her legal pad again. "That is so crass, Logan."

"Maybe, but it's still an awesome way to go."

"I thought he died of a cocaine-induced heart attack." When her father had learned of Entwistle's passing, he'd been devastated and even used the tragedy to press his *Just Say No* agenda on his impressionable daughter.

"Yeah, but he had a stripper in his bed. So after I fist bump him for not dying on a toilet—"

"*Logan!*"

"I'll spend the rest of the day staring at him in awe and begging him to show me his fingering."

"That's what she said," slipped out before Toni could help herself.

Logan burst out laughing and grabbed her, hauling her onto his lap. "I can't show you *his* fingering," he said, "but I can show you mine."

"Later," she said, her eyes drifting closed as he found the sensitive spot on her neck. Her body shuddered as waves of pleasure coursed down her spine. "We need to finish our interview first."

"The entire time you were back here alone with the other guys, I was going crazy for my turn to answer your questions."

"*That's* why you were going crazy?"

His soft chuckle stirred strands of hair against the suddenly sensitive skin of her throat. "You got me," he said. "I just wanted to be near you and not let anyone else enjoy what I have."

"Oh, so you have me, do you?" He totally did, but the more time she spent with him, the more she realized she wasn't the only one who was completely infatuated in this pairing. She had him as much as he had her. She loved the way that knowledge made her feel: desirable, resilient, capable, confident. She never would have guessed that falling in love would make her a stronger person. Now if she could just get the man to stop using the f-word when referring to her; they were so much more than friends. He had to realize that as much as she did.

"I hope so. One-sided love affairs suck."

"So this *is* love," she pressed, her heart thundering in her chest. She wanted him to admit he had deeper feelings for her. Needed him to admit it so that she felt confident enough to tell him how much she already cared about him. He'd want to hear that, wouldn't he?

She instantly found herself sitting on the sofa beside him when he shoved her off his lap. Her heart sank.

"Don't be naïve, Toni. We haven't known each other long enough to put a name on what this is. Why can't we just be friends for now?"

She turned her face from him, struggling to keep her tears in check so he wouldn't know how deeply his words affected her. She *was* naïve and stupid about love, but he didn't have to be such a dick about it.

"Let's get this interview over with," he said.

She wasn't in the mood to interview him now. What had begun as a playful interaction had turned sour. Why had she insisted on getting him to admit he loved her? It made him defensive and cranky. It made her feel rejected and unworthy. If he loved her, he'd tell her when he was ready. And if he never did . . . Her chest tightened, and one of the tears she'd been trying to hold back slid down her cheek. She couldn't bear the thought.

"Toni?"

She wiped her face on her upper arm, hoping he hadn't noticed she was so upset. Being with him might make her stronger, but thinking of losing him turned her into an invertebrate. She had to find a way to harden her heart. She didn't want to be one of those desperate creatures who needed a member of the opposite sex in order to feel worthwhile. She wanted the kind of love her parents had shared. Where each person was whole and strong on their own and yet being together made their natural awesomeness shine. That was what she wanted.

"Dare warned me this would happen," Logan said with a sigh.

"Dare warned you *what* would happen?" she snapped.

"You'd confuse our sexual relationship with a serious, romantic one."

"If you just kept our interactions sexual, I wouldn't be confused," she shouted, her hurt rapidly changing to anger. "But you don't. You act like you want to be around me constantly. You get jealous of other guys. You're attentive and say some truly loving things to me. I know you care about me."

"As a friend."

Toni's jaw hardened. How was it possible to find such an affectionate word so odious?

"I don't think I'm the one who's confused at all," she said. "I think you're the one who's mixed up."

"Me?" He lifted his hands defensively. "Babe, you have no idea how many women I've banged in my life."

"Just because you've banged dozens—"

"Hundreds."

"*Hundreds*?" Her stomach lurched.

"Maybe." He shrugged. "I lost count."

She scowled at him. "Just because you've banged *hundreds* of women—really, hundreds?" She shook her head, trying to comprehend his claim. He had to be exaggerating. "That doesn't mean you know the first thing about love."

"Next you're going to claim you know more about love than I do." He snorted derisively.

"I haven't ever been in love," she admitted. *Until I met you.* "But I've seen it. I saw it between my parents every day for the first fifteen years of my life. I know what it looks like."

"Lucky you."

He glanced down at his lap, and for the first time Toni realized that Logan had never told her about his family. She'd talked about hers—Logan had encouraged it and even seemed to crave her mundane stories. But the only thing she knew about his family situation was that his parents had divorced.

"Didn't you recognize the love between your parents?" she asked. "Before they split up, I mean."

"The *love* between my parents?" He chuckle was cynical and cold. "There was no love between my parents. They hated each other. The best decision they ever made was to get a divorce. I don't know why they even got married in the first place."

"I'm sorry."

"For what? It's not your fault they couldn't get along. The

blame for that lies on my bratty older brother." His lips twisted slightly, and she figured he was joking. About which part, she wasn't sure.

"What's your brother like?"

"I hate him, so it doesn't matter, does it?"

Toni couldn't imagine hating a sibling. Her sister meant everything to her, and she missed Birdie terribly.

"Why do you hate him?"

Logan lifted his gaze to meet hers. "Why do you care? Is all of this going to end up in your book? *Poor Logan has never been in love*, you'll write, and then you'll offer up some sob story about a broken home and an irreconcilable feud between brothers."

"I wouldn't do that." She didn't know whether she should be hurt or angry that he thought she would betray him.

"Go ahead and include it. I might get some sympathy pussy out of the ordeal."

Toni scowled. "You can be a real jerk when your feelings are hurt."

"But I don't have feelings. Haven't you figured that out yet?"

She shook her head at him. "I don't believe it for a second."

"All those loving things you claim I said? I only say things like that to get in your pants."

Toni's face went numb with shock. That couldn't be true, could it?

"I say things like that to every girl I meet."

"Hundreds of them," she said dully.

"Exactly."

She stared at him, noting the tension in his shoulders, the crease in his normally smooth forehead, and the way his eyes refused to meet hers.

"You're lying." She hoped.

"Why do you say that?"

"You can't even look at me, Logan." She touched his hand, surprised when instead of drawing away, he turned his hand over to clutch hers in an iron grip. "At least look at me while you break my heart."

"I don't want to break your heart, Toni." He lifted her hand and pressed it into the center of his chest. His heart thudded against the back of her hand. "Not when seeing you upset breaks mine."

And she wasn't supposed to take those words as him having

deep feelings for her? Maybe he simply wasn't ready to admit how he felt. Or maybe she *was* thinking wishfully.

"I know you don't like me to refer to you as a friend," he said.

She cringed automatically. Her dislike was that obvious, was it?

"Hear me out, Toni."

She nodded, resisting the urge to shield her delicate heart with her hand. As if that would help.

"All the relationships in my life have been fucked up. All of them except those with my friends. My friends have always been more like family to me than my actually family ever was. So when I call you friend, I don't want you to take it lightly."

"Oh." She didn't know what else to say. She hadn't realized he'd attached special meaning to the word. She'd assumed it was his way of forcing her to keep her distance, not his way of drawing her close.

"It's not a marriage proposal either," he added, giving her hand a squeeze.

She laughed hollowly, more from tension than any semblance of good humor. "I'm sorry for pressuring you."

"You are?" He lifted his eyebrows at her, meeting her eyes now, making her heart thud and her belly quiver with just a stare.

"Uh, well, I'm sorry you didn't react the way I'd hoped." She bit her lip, searching his face for answers she didn't find. "Are we still friends?"

"And lovers." He wiggled his eyebrows at her, and the tension melted from her muscles. She took a steadying breath. He hadn't dumped her. They were okay.

"So do you want to finish the interview," he asked with an ornery grin, "or learn to appreciate anal sex?"

Her buttocks clenched automatically, causing her spine to lengthen and her to sit ramrod straight. Ram rod? He would not be ramming that rod up in there if she had any say in the matter.

He snorted at what must have been her most horrified expression.

"Interview it is," he said, inclining his head in her direction.

Flustered, she touched her overly hot cheek with cool fingertips, tucked a poof of hair behind one ear, and then licked her lips. *Okay, let's see how he likes to be thrown off guard.*

Knowing him, he'd probably relish every moment.

She pretended to read from her legal pad. "Rumor has it that anatomically correct robot prototypes have been crafted in the images of each member of Exodus End," she said in her most professional voice. "Can you explain why there is *so* little going on in the pants of the Logan Schmidt model?"

He blinked and gaped at the wall.

"Uh, they ran out of android-making materials trying to generate a life-sized rendition of my love hammer," he said.

Toni managed not to snort at his ridiculous euphemism, but just barely. "That's not what I heard."

"What did you hear? If you've forgotten the size of my pool noodle, I'd be happy to offer it up for your journalistic inspection."

At this rate, she'd never keep her composure. But she was going to try.

She stared into his eyes and said, "I heard engineers feared that life as we know it would come to a standstill as all under-sexed women on the planet became addicted to your life-sized mechanical beaver cleaver—"

His bark of laughter startled her to silence. "Did you seriously just call it a beaver cleaver?"

"I'm sorry. Do you prefer yogurt cannon?" She tilted her head to peer at him over the top of the rim of her glasses. "Got it. Logan's . . . yogurt . . . cannon," she said as she wrote the words in the margin.

She waited until he stopped laughing before she continued.

"I also heard somewhere that you were the original lead singer for Exodus End; care to sing me a few lines?" She stared at him hopefully, her heart fluttering in her chest with romantic anticipation. She was dying to hear his singing voice.

"And who told you that? Was it Max? Because he seems to think understating his vocal talent earns him more compliments or something. I can't sing. Never could. I have the harmonics of a drunken crow."

"Prove it."

He squawked out a few lines of their first-ever hit, "Rebel in You," and he did indeed sound like a drunken crow. She was pretty sure he was singing horribly on purpose, but that didn't stop her from cringing and covering her ears with both hands.

"So you see," Logan said, "we needed Max whether I liked it or not."

She blinked at him. "You didn't want Max in the band?"

"I thought we were just fine with three members. I was

fortunately outvoted by the other two, and we sought an additional band member."

"*Fortunately* outvoted?"

"I was devastated at the time, but you've heard me sing. Do you think we would have been at all successful with me as a front man?"

She shrugged. There was no way to know for sure.

"There are those occasional instances in your life when you're glad you're proven wrong. I was wrong. We needed Max to make us a better band. But never tell him I said that." He winked at her, and she smiled before glancing down at her notes. It was time for her to get a little silly just for fun.

"Are you ready for more questions?"

He recrossed his legs so his ankle rested on the opposite knee and leaned back against the cushions to get comfortable. "Shoot."

"What's your favorite color?"

He lifted an eyebrow at her. "Seriously?"

She nodded, feigning extreme interest in his answer by holding her pen at the ready and staring at him as if on the edge of her seat.

"Pink," he said.

She dropped her pen. "Pink?"

"It's the color of your nipples."

"Are you thinking about my boobs again?"

"I'm always thinking about your boobs."

She slipped her hand under the sofa and pulled out what she expected to be her dropped pen, but what she'd grabbed was a lot longer, made of some flexible purple material, and slightly enlarged at one end.

"What *is* this?" She drew it toward her face for closer inspection.

Logan chuckled. "It's a magic wand. I'm pretty sure it's been in someone's ass, so you might not want to put it too close to your nose."

With a shriek, she tossed it. It skittered across the gleaming white coffee table and landed on the carpet on the opposite side.

"We'll add toys to your lessons at the hotel," Logan said, not looking the least bit concerned that she'd touched that thing. "We should be there in a couple hours."

That bit of knowledge made her squirm with desire and feel a bit queasy with nerves at the same time. She was pretty sure her lessons up to this point had been relatively tame, and she wasn't sure if she was ready to step it up to the next level. She wiped her hand on her skirt—as if that would sanitize her skin after touching a used ass wand.

"Was that yours?" she asked, eyeing the end of the "magic wand" just visible on the other side of the table.

"I plead the fifth." He grinned. "But if I'd known it was hiding under there, I'd have given you a demonstration of the magic it works when I had you bent over the sofa arm last night."

She crinkled her nose in disgust. "Eww. Even though you know where it's been?"

"I would have cleaned it first."

That didn't make her feel any better.

"Promise me that any toys you use on my body are new. There are some things I'm not willing to compromise on and *that* is one of them."

He was grinning entirely too wolfishly for her peace of mind.

"Logan!"

"I promise to use dozens of brand new toys on your body— singly and in combination."

"That's not what I said."

"I would never have touched you with someone else's toy, Toni. I just love how cute you look when you get all freaked out."

"Well, who wouldn't freak out about something like that? It's gross."

"Would you still think it's gross if I admitted that the ass tormented by that thing was mine?"

Had she been holding her pen, she would have dropped it. "You're messing with me again."

He lifted his eyebrows and shook his head. "I wouldn't mess with you about something as important as explosive orgasms."

Toni sat up straighter so she could take another look at the toy she'd tossed. "I could use toys on you too?"

"I'd prefer if we made it a requirement."

She turned her head to catch his gaze, not sure if he was trying to throw her off guard again. He was so good at duping her that she was starting to suspect him of it at all times.

"It sounds like playing with toys should be an imperative part of my lessons," she said.

"I agree."

"Can we get back to my questions now?"

"Hey, you're the one throwing magic wands around."

"What's your favorite food?"

He shook his head at her in disbelief. "Are these really the questions you want to ask?"

"The other band members answered them without belittling their importance."

"Tacos." He scratched his ear. "Fish tacos. Preferably clean shaven."

Another innuendo?

"What would it take to convince you to shave your muff?" he asked.

She glanced down at her lap. "A huge diamond," she teased.

"Done."

She'd already been convinced to shave her muff; she didn't need a diamond. "Are fish tacos really your favorite food?"

"Your fish taco is my favor—"

"Logan, is it really so hard for you to take my job seriously?"

"It is when you use words like *hard*."

She glared at him, and he sighed.

"I don't know what it is about you that keeps me in a constant state of arousal," he said. "Maybe after I fuck you twenty or thirty times over the next couple of days, I'll be able to remember what my favorite food is."

Twenty or thirty times? Was he insane?

He snapped his fingers unexpectedly. "Macaroni and cheese."

She'd had a hard enough time figuring out the fish taco reference—what could he possibly mean by macaroni and cheese? She was still puzzling over it when he tilted his head at her.

"You don't like macaroni and cheese?"

"I'm pretty sure the macaroni must be referring to your cock, but what's the cheese?"

Logan laughed so hard, she thought they might need to commandeer an ambulance. She hated that she was so naïve about all these sexual things. She was going to have to start studying the online Urban Dictionary like it was her Bible just so she could keep up with this guy.

"Macaroni and cheese really is my favorite food. It has nothing to do with my cock and whatever your cheese is."

"Oh."

He could have continued to tease her, but he touched her arm instead. "What's your favorite food?"

"Strawberry shortcake." She didn't even need to think about it.

"I should have known it would be something sweet."

Was he flattering her? Or was he being serious?

"How old were you when you lost your virginity?" she asked.

"You're putting that in your book?"

"Of course."

"Fifteen."

Her stomach dropped when she thought about him experiencing his first sexual encounter at the same age she'd been when her father died and she'd basically become a housewife to her mother and a mom to her sister.

"It wasn't very good," he added.

He patted her arm when she smiled him in relief.

"I'm lying," he said. "It was the best thing that had ever happened to me at the time. For a teenage boy, every waking *and* sleeping moment is spent thinking about sex." He rubbed his lips together and scowled at her. "Oh. That's why this feels familiar."

"Why *what* feels familiar?"

"Being with you. It's like I'm a horny, lovesick teenager all over again. The only difference is now I know what to do with you."

Of course she fixated on his using the word *lovesick*. Of course. She immediately chastised herself for being so fricking desperate for any mention of love when she knew damned well that he was referring to sex and only sex.

"That makes one of us," she said.

He frowned. "I don't make you feel like a horny, lovesick teenager?"

Yeah, he did. "I mean I don't know what to do with you."

"You're doing far better than you realize, babe. If you just want to lay there while I rut all over you, I'd be perfectly okay with that, you know?"

"Wouldn't that be boring?"

He laughed. "After a few years."

Now that she had him off guard—*maybe*—she could ask him a more important question. "So why do you hate your brother?"

"I don't really hate him. I just don't see him as part of my life anymore."

"Did he commit a horrible crime or something?" Toni's reporter senses were tingling. There was an important story here, she just knew it.

"He's not in jail, if that's what you're asking." Logan shrugged. "I've lost track of him, to be honest. We haven't spoken in over a year."

"What did he do?" Toni leaned close and squeezed his knee. "I'm dying to know."

"Nothing. During my parents' divorce they split everything fifty-fifty. Including their children. I lived with my father, and my brother with my mother. We were supposed to continue with weekly visitations, but my mom got remarried and moved to another state."

"So you never saw them after that?" Toni asked, sweeping a curl from his forehead so she could peer into his troubled gaze.

"I wouldn't say never. I did stay with them for a couple of weeks each summer, and I celebrated the occasional holiday with them, but it was obvious I'd been replaced."

"Replaced?"

"My mom's new husband had a son from his previous marriage. And while Daniel and I—Daniel's my brother—never got along and were always arguing and getting into scrapes, his new brother, Ray, quickly became his best friend. They did everything together. They never argued. Never fought. They just lived together as brothers. His stepbrother obviously meant more to him than his real brother did. I never felt like part of their little family when I visited. Not even with my mom. When she picked up and moved on from my dad, she moved on from me too."

Toni's lower lip trembled, and she sucked it into her mouth.

"Don't cry," Logan demanded.

She shook her head, knowing that if she spoke, she'd be bawling like a baby. Since she was too emotional to offer words of comfort, she hugged him fiercely. At first he merely tolerated her embrace, but after a moment his arms went around her and he hugged her back. She melted against him, breathing in his scent, absorbing his warmth, cherishing his strength and the glimpse of his weakness.

"At least you still had your dad," she whispered.

"Yeah," he said flatly. "Good ol' Dad."

Toni pulled away slightly so she could see Logan's expression. He smiled wryly.

"He didn't beat me or anything," he said, "so don't look so tragic. He made sure I was clothed and fed, that someone got me to ball practice and trumpet lessons, but he wasn't what one would call *affectionate*."

"And he never remarried?"

He shook his head. "Nope. He had a revolving door to his bedroom when he was married to my mother, and it got even more use after they split. I didn't realize what was going on until I was older."

Toni cringed. She had no idea what he was suggesting. "What do you mean his bedroom door revolved?"

He laughed and patted her head. "Because there were so many different women going through it."

"Oh. So the apple didn't fall far from the tree."

Logan gaped at her as if she'd slapped him.

"I'm not like him," he said, scooting back on the sectional so they were no longer touching.

She lifted an eyebrow at him. He didn't really expect her to believe that, did he?

He rubbed his jaw in one hand and squeezed his face—an attempt to keep himself from spouting more lies? His troubled blue eyes refused to meet her imploring gaze.

"It's different with me," he said finally.

"How so?"

"I don't have an impressionable child who has to witness it. I have never betrayed someone who loved me the way he betrayed my mother."

"That's true."

Since Logan had previously boasted about his own so-called revolving bedroom door, she hadn't realized her claim would upset him. But he still wouldn't meet her eyes. She fought her urge to comfort him as they sat in awkward silence, her watching him closely. Him staring at the wall, trying to burn a hole through it.

"How do you do that?" he asked, his gaze flicking to hers at long last.

She shook her head in confusion. "Do what?"

"Get a guy to spill his guts one minute and then reevaluate his entire outlook the next."

She shrugged. "Gifted, I guess."

"I guess." He shifted closer again so that their knees touched, and he gave her leg a playful nudge.

She was starting to think their little spats strengthened their growing relationship rather than hurt it. She'd never seen her parents argue. They must have had an occasional disagreement, but had shielded her from that reality. She wondered if only witnessing the happy times between her parents and none of the strife had somehow skewed her perception of a good relationship. Logan's ideas about romantic relationships had obviously been swayed by his father's philandering ways. She supposed they'd have to figure out the balance required for a healthy relationship on their own.

"So you played trumpet?" she asked.

He laughed and nodded. "I heard that it strengthens your lips and makes you an excellent kisser."

"Does it work?" She straightened, trying to look her most hopeful.

"You should know. You've tasted my strong lips more than once." He puckered his lips and made obnoxious kissing sounds. When he began to flick his tongue in and out of his mouth, she couldn't help but laugh.

"I don't have much to compare to," she admitted. "Timothy in sixth grade—very slobbery. Brent at a middle school dance—interrupted by a chaperone. That one drunk guy in college—so boozed up he made my lips numb. I did play spin the bottle with Julian and his friends a few months ago—those kisses were all, uh, brief." And platonic. "And then you. You're definitely winning, but . . ." She held her hands out and shook her head at him.

"Who's Julian?"

"A friend," she said, blushing as she remembered Julian had threatened to buy her a male prostitute in Vegas. Good thing she'd lost her virginity, even if he hadn't believed her text. She suddenly realized she hadn't seen her phone all day. Real life had rapidly become more interesting than a touch screen.

"I'd judge by your blush that Julian is more than a friend. Got a little crush?"

"Wouldn't matter if I did," she said. "He doesn't like girls."

Logan wiped pretend sweat from his brow. "Thought I might have a bit of competition for your affection. You know I don't deal well with that."

"Julian doesn't need to be dealt with," she assured him. "At least not as a romantic interest."

"Does he need to be dealt with for another reason?"

"Maybe. He's obsessed with the fact that I'm a virgin."

"Was a virgin," Logan reminded her.

"Right. Was a virgin. So he makes me get dressed up and

takes me out on the town to get me laid, and where do we always end up?"

"A bookstore?"

Ha! She would have actually enjoyed that more and would have had a better chance of getting laid there. "No. He takes me to gay bars. I'm not sure how that's supposed to help my love life. He's the one who ends up hooking up with a guy every time we go out."

"You're his wing girl."

"What?"

"No matter how hot you are, you have no chance of stealing his dates."

"Yeah, that sounds like Julian's logic. Do you know what he told me before I left?"

Logan shook his head.

"He said if I didn't lose my virginity before I returned home, he was taking me to Vegas and hiring a male prostitute to do the deed."

Logan snorted. "All he really needed to do was take you to any regular bar and pour a few drinks in you to loosen your inhibitions a little."

"I wasn't drunk when I fell into bed with you."

"True, but I'm especially irresistible."

She opened her mouth to deny his claim, but he smiled at her, a spark of mischief in his amazing blue eyes, and she couldn't bring herself to lie. He *was* especially irresistible. The danger existed in him knowing it.

"So you really don't have any idea how good a kisser I am?"

She shook her head. "I can only assume all decent kisses make a woman's knees weak and her tummy flutter and her . . . *pussy*, uh, ache." She still struggled with saying the word aloud.

"Is that what my kisses do to you, Toni?" He shifted closer, licking his lips slowly and tilting his head, staring her down like some sort of ravenous predator.

She swallowed hard and nodded. Hell, he didn't even have to kiss her to get that response. Just him looking at her the way he was at that exact moment was enough to melt her panties clean off her body.

His fingertips brushed her cheek, sparking nerve endings as if electricity flowed through his body. How else could she explain how easily his touch made her tingle from head to toe? Zapped her to life? Caused her heart to palpitate? Yep, the guy must be concealing some electric superpower beneath his rock star facade.

He pressed his lips to hers, caressing her sensitive skin until her mouth fell open and she couldn't resist tasting him with an explorative flick of her tongue. Her breath caught when his free hand moved to unfasten the snap and zipper of her long skirt. Before she could think to protest, she was naked from the waist down.

"Logan." She murmured what was supposed to be an objection, but it sounded more like an invitation. "Someone might—"

He silenced her with a deep kiss as he slid from the sofa to kneel between her legs. Cool air bathed her hot, aching flesh as he eased her thighs open. He tugged his mouth free of hers and gazed down at her fully exposed pussy.

"I thought I could wait until you shaved it for me, but I'm going to have to risk the hairball."

She flushed, sometimes wishing he worded things a bit more delicately, but as was typical for Logan, his actions made up for any crude utterance. He raked his fingers through the damp curls attempting quite unsuccessfully to shield her sex from his heated gaze. He used both hands to spread her swollen lips wide and then held them in place, his hands a triangle framing her sex. This served to hold her open and keep her pubic hair out of his way as he lowered his head and kissed her throbbing clit. The muscles of her thighs clenched automatically as pleasure surged through her center, but she kept her legs open for him. She didn't want him to stop. She never wanted him to stop.

He kissed and suckled and flicked her clit with his tongue until her juices were flowing freely. He shifted his mouth to her opening, doing things with his lips and tongue that made her mouth drop open with shock as the writhing, sucking, swirling motions sent new sensations of pleasure pulsing through her.

He pulled away after a moment and sucked a deep breath into his lungs. "I could eat this pussy all day," he said, his thumbs rubbing a spot between her opening and her *other* hole that made her squirm. "But this position is really hard on my neck."

She tried not to pout when she realized he was saying he was finished already.

"Do you think you could sit on my face instead?"

Her eyes widened with shock. "I'll smother you!" she blurted.

"You won't," he said. "I promise. It's actually easier on my neck that way. But if you're unwilling to switch positions, I'll suffer through it this way."

He leaned forward and gave her quivering pussy the kind of deep penetrating kiss her lips craved. Her hips began to rock involuntarily to the rhythm of his thrusting, swirling, flicking tongue. Oh dear God, she never wanted this to end. Her fingers released their iron grip on the sofa cushion and threaded into the thick curls of Logan's hair. She tugged upward, and he followed her suggestion, shifting his mouth to her clit. She felt a huff of hot air against her as he laughed softly.

"That's it, lamb, take what you want."

He flicked his tongue over her clit so fast, she was soon sputtering on the verge of climax. She suddenly wanted him inside her. His cock, yes, definitely, but his tongue would do. She shoved his head down, and he obliged her by licking her throbbing hole. The soft exploration of his tongue felt amazing, but her climax began to slowly fall from her reach and so she yanked him back up to her clit. He sucked and flicked, sucked and flicked, building her pleasure. Higher. Higher. She was going to shatter. Oh. Her pussy clenched in protest of its emptiness, and she shoved his head lower again so he'd tongue-fuck her.

She groaned when her body refused to cooperate and give her the release she so desperately needed. After a moment, Logan lifted his head to catch his breath. He twisted his head side to side and winced at an apparent crick in his neck.

"Can't get there?" he asked.

She shook her head. She kept coming close, but it was as if her pussy was jealous of her clit and refused to allow her to come while his mouth was occupied with her most sensitive nub of flesh.

"Maybe if you sat—"

"Yes," she said, no longer hesitant to try a different position. If she kept tugging on his hair like that, he'd probably be bald by the time she finished.

He stretched out on his back on the sofa and she looked to him for instruction. After a bit of awkward maneuvering, she found herself straddling his head. This doesn't look safe, she decided, but he grabbed her ass in both hands and pulled her pussy to his mouth and she was soon too delirious with pleasure to be concerned about his ability to breathe. She no longer had to direct his mouth by yanking his hair, she just had to tilt her hips and shift slightly forward or backward to get him to put his tongue and lips exactly where she needed them.

God, yes. That was perfect.

Her cries of excitement matched the building orgasm clenching deep inside. Her eyes opened wide when Logan's tongue slid back a few inches and flicked against her puckered back entrance. Waves of pleasure shot up into her ass, shocking her so deeply she shuddered, before she shifted her hips back and filled his mouth with her pussy again.

"Sorry," she gasped, not sure how she'd managed to give him a mouthful of ass—poor guy—but she soon discovered that it hadn't been her slip but his when he jerked her forward and tongued her there again—the firm tip just breaching the center of the tight ring of muscle. She didn't want to like it, but oh God, it felt so deliciously dirty! Gasping with a mixture of pleasure and mortification, she shifted her clit into his mouth, rocking with his rhythm, wondering if she dared coax him into licking her ass again.

He released his hold on her ass and a moment later, she heard his pants unzip. She turned her head to glance over her shoulder and watched him tug his cock free and begin to stroke its length with a tight fist.

"Oh," she gasped.

She wanted that, his stone-hard cock. She wanted it in her pussy. In her ass. Between her tits. In her hands. But mostly she wanted it in her mouth.

Without asking permission, she stood, turned to face the opposite direction, and sat on his face again. She waited until his tongue found her clit and then leaned over to suck the head of his cock into her mouth. She didn't concern herself with wondering if she was doing it right. By the way he tugged at his shaft and his belly quaked and he groaned against her pulsing clit, she was definitely making the right impression.

She was so focused on sucking him off that she forgot to shift her clit from his mouth at the brink of her orgasm.

Thighs shaking uncontrollably, her pussy clenched at nothing in hard spasms. She made a strange series of animal-like groans around his cock as her body shuddered and she attained that elusive orgasm at last. She slid a hand into his pants and cradled his balls in her palm. It was enough to send him over the edge. With a deep groan, his back arched and his salty cum filled her mouth. She swallowed him, sucking harder, wanting more. He filled her mouth with a second spurt and then went limp beneath her. She continued to suck him—gently now—bobbing her head slowly, delighting in the way it made him shudder and curse.

"Toni," he said breathlessly from beneath her slowly gyrating crotch.

She took pity on him and shifted positions so that she could lie beside him in the nook between his side and the sofa back to catch her breath.

"I think you were the one giving lessons there," he said. "Damn, woman. That was hot."

She nodded in agreement and flushed, suddenly embarrassed now that she was no longer fucking his face in delirious pleasure.

But maybe, just maybe, she wasn't so bad at this sex stuff after all.

CHAPTER 21

ONCE HE'D REGAINED his composure, Logan helped Toni into her panties. He was unable to stop himself from caressing her silky thighs before she hid them beneath her unflattering skirt, which in his opinion was the most fantastic skirt in existence. He was the only one who knew what delights the thick brown fabric concealed.

"Crap!" she said, reaching over to grab her audio recorder from the table. She cringed as she pressed the pause button.

"Was that thing recording the entire time?"

She nodded. "I forgot it even existed. You have a way of making me forget anything exists but you."

His heart fluttered, and a knot formed in his throat. He coughed, trying to dislodge the discomfort and hoping he wasn't coming down with a cold. The tour had just started and after another month in North America, they were heading to Europe, Asia, South America, Australia and even South Africa. He wanted to enjoy every minute of the tour, not spend his time blowing his nose and being the whiny pain in the ass he knew he was when he was sick.

"Don't worry," she said. "I'll erase it."

He snatched the device out of her hand and searched for the reverse button. After rewinding several minutes' worth of recording, he pressed play. The sexy sounds of Toni finding orgasm with his cock in her mouth greeted his eager ears. His dick twitched with renewed interest.

"Oh God, is that really what I sound like?" Toni asked, her pretty face screwed up with displeasure. "Delete it."

"Hell no, I'm not deleting it. I'm making it your ringtone."

Her mouth dropped open, but she quickly recovered her shock and dove for the device. He yanked it out of her reach just in time.

"Logan," she pleaded, her big brown eyes full of turmoil. "Please don't embarrass me."

"There's absolutely nothing to be embarrassed about."

He rewound the bit of audio and played it again. He produced a delighted full-body shudder at the sound of her getting off. "You have to promise to call me every five minutes so I can hear this over and over again."

"You are not making that my ringtone."

"Uh, yeah, I am."

"You can't," she said, fist planted on either hip. There was something sexy about her standing her ground, but that didn't mean he was going to back down.

"You bet your fine ass, I can."

She shook her head. "You don't even have my number."

Stunned that she was correct, his teasing grin faded. He didn't have his own girlfriend's—um,   new friend's—phone number? He'd completely neglected his phone—quite unusual for him— since he'd met Toni. The woman was a constant distraction.

"We're going to remedy that right now," he said. And he rushed into the corridor to retrieve his phone from under his pillow.

Knowing she would erase the cock-thickening sound of her sexy vocalizations at her first opportunity, Logan played it back and recorded the sounds onto his phone through the mic. It would lose some of the sound quality, but that was better than losing it entirely.

"What are you doing?" Dare asked. He was lying in his bunk, watching the TV built into the underside of Max's top bunk.

"Retaining evidence," Logan said with a wink.

He grabbed a cola out of the refrigerator and hurried back to the lounge, flipping through a series of text messages, Facebook notifications, and missed calls that didn't interest him in the least.

"I brought you something to wash the taste of my cum out of your mouth," he said, trying to embarrass Toni. She didn't so much as blush. She was too busy scowling down at her smartphone.

"What's wrong?"

He handed her the bottle of cola. She opened it and took a long swallow, but avoided his inquisitive gaze.

"Toni?"

She set her phone and the bottle aside so she could massage her temples. "It's nothing."

It obviously wasn't nothing. She was upset. "You can tell me."

"It's just the mean things my editor says to me. Rattles my confidence."

"Shouldn't your editor support you?"

Toni laughed hollowly. "Not when I took her dream assignment away from her."

Logan lifted her phone from the table and read the string of messages still displayed on her screen beneath the name Susan Brennan. Brennan? Why did that name sound familiar?

His jaw dropped several additional inches with each text message he read.

> Are you on your way home yet? I have my bag packed and ready to go. We both know you don't have what it takes.

> Good thing your mom owns the company. There's no way you would have been hired for the job if you had to prove your worth.

> Are you not answering my messages because you know I'm right or because you're too ashamed to admit you've already failed?

Logan couldn't believe anyone would be so mean to someone as sweet as his Toni.

"What a bitch!" he said.

He began typing a response.

> Listen, bitch, IDK who u think u r bu

Toni jerked her phone out of his hand and started backspacing to delete his message.

"Why are you deleting that?"

"You can't send her a text like that. She's my boss! I owe her my respect."

Logan covered his eyes with one hand. "Your respect? She obviously doesn't respect you. You don't owe her a goddamned thing."

"But she's right." Toni wrung her hands together in her lap. Her hair slid forward to hide her troubled expression. "I wouldn't have this job if my mom didn't own the company. I don't have any experience. I do suck at this."

He sat beside her and rubbed her back. "What are you talking about? You're doing a great job."

She shook her head. "I'm having too much fun to be doing a great job."

"Just because work is fun doesn't mean you're doing it wrong. Unless you think my entire band is a failure."

Her head snapped up. "Of course I don't think that!"

"And I don't think you're going to fail. I hate to brag, but I'm an excellent judge of talent, and you, Ms. Nichols, are talented. Just look at how fast you learned how to give a fantastic hummer."

"I'll add it to my resume," she said glumly.

He wasn't going to let this drop until she was happy and smiling again, so she might as well stop resisting his attempts at a pep talk.

"Do you know how hard it is to get my bandmates to talk about their personal lives?"

She opened her eyes wide and nodded.

"And yet you got each of them to talk to you about things they never discuss with members of the press."

"That's because they don't see me as a real journalist, so I'm obviously doing it wrong."

"Or you're doing it right and just don't realize it. Like when we have sex. You worry that you aren't doing it like everyone else does it, but when you forget to be anxious, you're amazing."

"I am?"

"Amazing."

She smiled, and he swore the roof of the bus opened up, letting in rays of sunshine to brighten his day.

"Not that you're an expert yet," he said. "I do still have a lot to teach you in the bedroom."

"You haven't taught me a thing in the bedroom yet."

He gaped at her. "What? I've taught you plenty. I mean, you went for that sixty-nine all on your own—very nice, by the way—but the other stuff—"

"Didn't happen in a bedroom. It happened in this lounge and a limo and your bunk . . ."

He chuckled. "I guess it is time to introduce you to a real bed."

"Tonight," she promised, giving him a chaste kiss on the lips. "But first I need to interview Reagan."

"Because you don't suck at this?" He wanted her to believe it. Wanted to hear her say it. Still wanted to text her bitch of an editor and put her in her place.

"Because if I don't keep trying, I'll never gain the experience I need to be successful."

Logan nodded and patted her knee. Her confidence was still shaky, but it would strengthen with time. He turned his head to yell down the corridor, "You're up, Reagan! Do you think you can unlock your lips from Trey's long enough to answer Toni's expert interview questions?"

"Not really," Reagan's voice carried into the room.

"Then Toni's going to make up a bunch of shit about you!" Logan yelled. "And I'm going to put ideas in her head."

"I'll be right there!"

Logan rose from the sofa and bent to press a kiss to Toni's forehead. "You've got this, lamb."

She smiled and nodded. She lifted her chin a notch, and his chest swelled with pride, which was the weirdest-fucking emotion he'd ever experienced in all his thirty-two years.

Reagan bounded into the room and tackle-hugged Toni on the sectional. "Are you really going to include me in the book?"

"Of course I am," Toni said. She patted Reagan's shoulder as she tried to sit upright. "You're part of Exodus End, aren't you?"

"Not really, but I do appreciate the gesture."

Logan rolled his eyes and shook his head. Did Reagan still feel excluded? He supposed he would have to fuck with her more so she felt like one of the guys. Or perhaps they should forbid her from riding on Sinners' tour bus. She spent more time with Trey's band than her own.

"If you two start making out, holler for me," Logan said as he stepped into the corridor to give the women privacy. "I wouldn't want to miss that."

Toni's eyes widened when Reagan shifted to straddle Toni's lap and gave his justfriend's boobs a squeeze.

"I always wanted a pair like these," Reagan said. "If I can't have my own, I might as well play with someone else's."

Logan reentered the lounge and made a beeline for the

sectional. "Yes, I'd love to watch. Thanks for asking."

"I promise not to molest your girlfriend," Reagan said, scrambling from Toni's lap and shoving Logan out of the room. Smiling brightly, she made a peace sign. Then she turned her symbol of good will against her face to flick her tongue between her index and middle finger and slid the door shut an inch from his nose.

Logan groaned and rested his forehead against the cool surface of the door. Surely Reagan had her hands full with two men. She couldn't possibly need to add a woman to her stable of full-time lovers, could she?

INTERVIEW
WITH
REAGAN
ELLIOT

"I JUST CAN'T RESIST fucking with that guy," Reagan said, breezing past Toni and flopping onto the sofa. She propped her bare feet on the coffee table and patted the cushion next to her.

The same cushion that Logan had been lying on when he'd come in Toni's mouth moments before. Toni reached for the cola Logan had so thoughtfully brought her and took another swig.

She was going to have to start staging her interviews in a different location. She couldn't stop the X-rated images from filtering through her thoughts.

"He is fun." Toni scooted closer to Reagan, her nearly empty beverage clasped between her hands. Maybe she'd have more luck keeping on track while interviewing a woman. She hadn't planned on doing any additional interviews, having decided Dare's advice to just talk to them was her best move, but now that she felt she needed to prove herself to Logan as well as her mother and Susan, Toni decided she should at least *attempt* all the preplanned formal interviews, even if they didn't amount to much.

"We can finally have that girl talk," Reagan said, grabbing the bottle out of Toni's hands and taking a drink.

Toni cringed, thinking that if Reagan knew where her mouth had just been, she would not want to share.

"What's that face?" Reagan said, lowering the bottle and eyeing her with suspicious gray-blue eyes.

Toni shook her head. "N-nothing."

"Did you just suck Logan's dick or something?"

Heat flooded Toni's face. "Maybe."

Reagan crinkled her nose and shoved the nearly empty bottle into Toni's chest. "And you let me drink after you?"

"I'm sorry."

Reagan shook her head and went still when her gaze landed on something on the floor. "And you just leave your sex toys lying around on the carpet?"

So much for her interview with Reagan staying on track. "I found that under the sofa when I was hunting for my pen."

"Sure you did."

Toni was so embarrassed that she didn't know whether to hide under the cushions or cry, so she laughed uneasily. "Honest. I didn't even know what that thing was until Logan explained it to me."

Reagan cocked her head at her, her dirty-blond bangs sliding over her face to cover one eye. "So are you two serious or just having a good time?"

Toni wasn't sure how to answer that. She wanted them to be serious, and he made her feel like he was serious about her, but she was pretty sure she was just clueless about these things and reading more into his actions and words than was really there.

Reagan touched the back of Toni's hand, and Toni looked up into a pair of concerned eyes. "Don't let him play you unless you're playing him right back."

"I don't know if he's playing me. And I wouldn't know how to play him if I had an instruction manual and a tutor. Not that I want to play him." She just wanted to love him. She shook her head and planted her face in her palms. It was much too soon for that. Even she realized that.

"Oh, honey, you didn't do something as stupid as fall in love with him, did you?"

Toni nodded miserably.

"Because falling for someone too quickly . . ."

Toni steeled her heart for the advice she knew would follow. She knew the coming words were true. She just didn't want the truth voiced aloud, because that would make it real and then she'd have to face it.

". . . is the most amazing experience ever!" Reagan said.

Thinking she needed to clean out her ears, Toni lifted her face from her hands and arched a brow at Reagan. "Huh?"

"Are you recording this?" Reagan nodded to the recorder on

the table.

Toni shook her head.

"This is just between you and me, okay? Don't go selling it to the tabloids or printing it in your book."

Toni nodded mutely.

"I fell in love with Trey so fast—like soooo fast it was ridiculous and I convinced myself it was hormones—because the guy is sex on a stick."

Toni nodded.

"But it's so much deeper than that. It was from the first moment we met. Sometimes you just click with someone"— Reagan snapped her fingers—"and you know on a biological and psychological level that this is the one. Or the two . . ." Reagan's gaze shifted to the wall and she cleared her throat. "So if you feel that instantaneous connection with Logan, don't immediately discredit it. Just because it's a fast-burning love doesn't mean it can't be a long-lasting love. You just have to keep fueling the fire. Right?"

Toni had no idea. "I guess."

"Right." Reagan slapped her on the arm.

"How do I go about fueling the fire, exactly?" Toni asked. Sex? The answer had to be sex. Maybe anal sex. She still wasn't keen on the idea, but if that was what it took to keep Logan's interest, she'd allow it.

"You have to make him feel like he's important to you."

Well, that would be easy enough. She could see herself overdoing it, though. "But then won't he think I'm being clingy? Or obsessed?"

"You don't have to be all up in his face about it."

Reagan's nose was suddenly an inch from Toni's as she peered into her eyes. Toni laughed at the irony. She'd never met anyone as in your face—both literally and figuratively—as Reagan Elliot.

"Even little things can make a big difference," Reagan said.

"But what if he doesn't feel as strongly about me as I do about him?"

"Just keep being marvelous, sweetie. He'll come around."

She sure hoped so.

"So are we going to do this interview or what?"

"Can I ask you something first? Completely off the record." Toni's curiosity had gotten the better of her. She couldn't keep this question to herself for another second.

"Sure."

"Are you cheating on Trey with your bodyguard?"

Reagan gaped at her. Toni couldn't tell if she was shocked because her secret had been discovered or because someone thought she was capable of being unfaithful.

"No," she said flatly.

Either Reagan was lying or Toni's power of observation was less honed than she realized.

"I'm sorry if I offended you."

"I dated Ethan before I met Trey."

"So I guess Ethan still has feelings for you. I've seen the way he looks at you." She'd also seen the way he looked at Trey, but she was obviously reading that incorrectly. Though she had been around enough gay guys to recognize attraction between two men and there was definitely attraction between those two men. Unless . . . "Wait," Toni said as something overtly sneaky occurred to her. "Are you a cover for a relationship between Trey and Ethan?" But that didn't explain all she'd seen either. The intimacy she'd witnessed between Trey and Reagan was obviously not fabricated.

"Wrong again." Reagan grinned. "Can you keep a secret?"

Toni's heart thudded, and she nodded eagerly.

"What am I saying? Of course, you can't keep a secret," Reagan said. "You're a fucking journalist."

"Except I'm not," Toni said. "At all."

"And that's why you're doing interviews and recording footage and sticking your nose in everyone's business."

Toni shouldn't have felt hurt that Reagan didn't trust her—she completely understood why Reagan would have reservations about sharing personal information—but she wanted Reagan to feel that she could confide in her and believe that Toni would keep her promises. Her integrity was worth more to her than a few lines in a tabloid or a few dollars for an incriminating picture.

"I don't mean to be intrusive," Toni said. "I'm just trying to get an inside look at the lives of the members of Exodus End and share that look with the world. I absolutely do not want anything in the book that could hurt any of you. I haven't known you all long, but I consider you my friends, and I would never betray a friend's trust."

Reagan eyed her warily and then sighed. "Normally if a member of the media spouted that kind of nonsense in my direction, I wouldn't hesitate to call them a liar—"

Toni cringed.

"—but for some reason, I don't think you're capable of being a vindictive bitch, so I'll tell you, and you can either affirm my faith in humanity or get the shit beat out of you for betraying my trust."

Toni swallowed hard. She wouldn't betray Reagan's trust, not because of Reagan's violent threats—fabricated as they seemed— but because to be counted among the back-stabbing bitches of the world would eat Toni alive from the inside out.

"Trey is my boyfriend," Reagan said.

Oddly, Toni was relieved that the truth wasn't any more scandalous than that.

"And he knows that Ethan is my lover," Reagan continued.

Okay, so maybe it was more scandalous.

"Because Ethan and Trey are lovers too."

Jaw meet floor.

Reagan let out a deep sigh.

"I don't know why, but it feels kind of good to tell you that," Reagan admitted while Toni tried to remember how to blink. "I wish the world was open to polyamorous relationships. It's becoming more open to homosexual ones, so maybe, given time . . ." Reagan tilted her head at Toni. "Are you going to pass out?"

Toni shook her head and took her first breath in over a minute. Questions began to race through her thoughts.

"So you have sex with Trey. And with Ethan. And they're both okay with that?" Toni asked. Why was her voice so squeaky? She sounded like a mouse huffing helium.

Reagan laughed and crossed her legs, looking surprisingly at ease. "Well, yeah, since most of the time they're both there."

More questions bombarded Toni's psyche. "And they do each other in front of you?"

Reagan laughed. "If I'm lucky."

The logistics were completely out of Toni's grasp. She had a hard enough time figuring out what to do with one cock; she'd have no idea how to keep two satisfied. But even more than the mind-bending sexual positions, Toni was struggling to grasp the emotional connection. If Logan had sex with some other woman— or man—she'd be heartbroken. She didn't know if she'd ever be able to move past infidelity, no matter how much she loved him. But not everyone had the same ideas of sex and love as she did, and she was okay with that. She didn't have to participate in a certain lifestyle to accept it. "So you're in love with Trey and Ethan's just there as a sex partner?"

"You know, it started out that way," Reagan said, chewing on the end of her finger thoughtfully. "But nope, we're all emotionally invested now."

"That's wild," Toni said for lack of anything more poignant to add.

"It just feels natural to us. But the rest of the world doesn't get it. They might never get it. So that's why I try to hide it."

Toni nodded. She didn't get it, so she was sure plenty of folks out there were unable to grasp the concept. She didn't hold their unique lifestyle against them—love was love—but she knew there were a lot of people in the world who *would* hold it against them. And try to destroy what they had. So Toni completely understood why Reagan was keeping the truth about her complicated love life a secret.

"I won't tell anyone," Toni said. Though she would like to discuss it with Logan, her sex instructor. Maybe he could explain some of the sexual parts of a polyamorous relationship to her. "Does Logan know?"

"Yeah. All the guys in Sinners know and all the guys in Exodus End know, but no one else."

"Not even Butch?"

"Of course Butch knows. He helps us hide it more than anyone. But no one else knows. Well, except Myrna and Jessica. Um, and Rebekah Sticks and Jace's fiancée, Aggie." Reagan cringed. "And a couple of the security team. Shit. I didn't realize how many people know about us. It's kind of scary, you know?"

Toni nodded. She didn't plan to talk about it in front of anyone—with the exception of Logan—but it was good to know who was privy to the information, just in case something slipped or the trio needed help covering their trail. Toni would do her best to help Reagan keep her secret.

"What does your family think about it?"

Reagan paled. "My family definitely doesn't know. And I hope they never will. My father would die. And he'd take me with him."

"He'd probably freak out at first, but I'm sure he just wants you to be happy."

Reagan shook her head. "Nope. He wants me to be like you when I grow up."

Toni tilted her head, wondering what she meant by that. "Like me?"

"A sweet and charming *good* girl."

Well, that didn't sound very fun. Toni scowled.

"Who has been irreparably damaged by a very, very bad boy." Reagan laughed. "Don't look so glum, sweetie. Same thing happened to me. I just happened to be fifteen at the time."

"I'm a late bloomer," Toni said and laughed.

"Those bad boys are an addictive adrenaline rush. Once you're hooked, you'll keep going back for more."

"Until it takes two to feed your addiction?"

Mouth open, Reagan blinked at her in astonishment. But before Toni could utter the quick apology on her tongue, Reagan burst out laughing.

"I never thought of it that way, but I think you might be right."

The door slid open. "That doesn't sound like making out to me," Logan said, peeking in at them from between the doorframe and the edge of the sliding door.

"Privacy!" Reagan tossed a pillow that hit him square in the face.

"We're stopping for sandwiches, and Butch told me to ask Toni what she wants."

Steve's head appeared over the top of Logan's head as he stood on tiptoe to peer in at them.

"He means Butch was headed back to ask Toni what she wants, but at the mention of her name, Logan tackled Butch to the floor and sprinted to the back of the bus because he's obsessed."

Logan frowned, turned to shove Steve off his back, and then smiled into the lounge again. "So what would you like?" he asked Toni, his gaze so intense she could almost feel it against her skin.

"Oh my God, he *is* obsessed!" Reagan shouted.

"Shut up! The woman has to eat."

"What do they have?" Toni asked, trying not to grin at the way Logan's bandmates were teasing him.

"Cold cut subs."

"Turkey on wheat with extra jalapeños."

"You won't want her to suck your dick tonight," Steve joked. "It'll burn so bad, you'll need a fire extinguisher."

Logan covered Steve's face with his splayed hand and shoved him out of view again.

"Oh." Toni nibbled on her lower lip. She hadn't considered what effect eating jalapeños would have on Logan's anatomy. "Hold the jalapeños."

Logan grinned and winked at her before turning away. "Guess who's getting his dick sucked?" he said to Steve as he slid the door shut. "Again."

Toni's face flamed much hotter than any jalapeño that had ever existed. "Are guys always that embarrassing?"

"Pretty much."

Toni lifted her recording device. "I'm going to turn this on now," she warned, "so anything you say is fair game for the book."

Reagan nodded, and Toni pressed the record button.

"How did you get picked to play guitar for Exodus End?"

"Their manager, Sam Baily, thought it would be good publicity to do a contest. So hundreds, maybe thousands, of hopeful guitarists sent in demos of their work. I actually entered on a dare. Anyway, the top five were selected by Sam—which I didn't realize until recently. Have you met Sam yet?"

Toni shook her head.

"That would explain why you're still here."

Before Toni could ask what Reagan meant by that, Reagan continued her story.

"The top five had to audition live for the band, except the guys couldn't see us. They had to base their pick solely on our sound."

"So I'm assuming you won?"

"Yeah. I couldn't believe it. And neither could Pyre Vamp, apparently." Reagan's lip curled and she lifted a hand to cover her throat.

"The guitarist for Hell's Crypt?"

"Yep, that's the guy."

"Didn't they unexpectedly pull out of the tour last month?" Toni had run across that tidbit when she'd been preparing for her trip. The details of Hell's Crypt leaving the tour had been vague.

"They sure did. Because of this." She traced a faded yellow mark on her neck.

"Is it that a bruise?" Toni had no idea how a bruise would lead to an up-and-coming band pulling out of a career-changing tour with Exodus End.

"It's almost gone now. You should have seen it a week ago."

Toni leaned in for a closer inspection. The fading mark

completely circled Reagan's neck.

"How didn't I notice that before?" Toni asked. It was faded, but hard to overlook.

"I've been putting makeup on it to cover it. Is it still noticeable?"

Toni nodded. "It looks like you tried to hang yourself."

"Dude tried to strangle me with a guitar string. Pyre did this."

"No shit?" Toni blurted. "You must have been terrified."

Reagan shrugged. "I was unconscious for most of it. Anyway, his band got fired from the tour, obviously—your lead guitarist tries to kill someone and that's bound to happen—so lucky for us Steve is close with the guys of Twisted Element. They've done an awesome job filling in with no time to prepare a show."

"I had no idea that's why they were on tour with you guys. How did I miss that story? I scoured the Internet for news about the band just days ago. I didn't read anything about this." Reagan wasn't a pathological liar, was she?

"Sam said it would be better if we kept the controversy under the rug."

"Seriously? That guy could have killed you."

"But you can put it in the book," Reagan said. "It won't come out until next year, right?"

"Right. Why is that important?"

"I won't be under Sam's ridiculous contract anymore. So I can't make a stink about this now without getting my ass sued, but you better believe I'm going to shout it from the rafters after that contract expires."

"What do the guys think about you being hushed?" Toni couldn't imagine they'd side with Sam, but she didn't know Sam or how tightly he ruled the bands he managed.

"They think it's better not to expose this incident to the press for my sake. I guess they think Pyre Vamp is in jail for thirty days, so he learned his lesson. When it comes to their image, it's like Sam has them brainwashed. I don't know why they listen to him."

"Maybe it's in *their* contract."

Reagan's eyes widened. "I didn't even think of that. You're probably right. You know, Sinners basically manage themselves. They have a manager, but he's very hands off, not like Sam at all. If I ever form my own band, that's the kind of manager I want. The mostly absent kind."

"But look at Exodus End's success. You don't get as big as

they do without a good team to back you."

"Maybe," Reagan said. "But at what cost?"

"Do you think Sam's control stifles their creativity?"

"I hope not. I haven't been with them long enough to know." Reagan pondered quietly for a moment and then patted Toni's knee. "We got way off track on your interview question. So yeah, contest. I won. I was so excited I signed a beast of a contract without reading it. But I'm touring with Exodus End, so I'll grin and bear it." Reagan grinned so broadly, Toni feared her face might crack in half. "You're a little too easy to talk to, you know? You're going to get me in trouble."

Toni tucked her hair behind her ears, smiling to herself. She was glad she was easy to talk to. That made her job so much easier. And maybe she was doing it right, even though it still didn't feel like she knew what the hell she was doing. She decided her toughest undertaking would be sifting through all the information she was collecting for material she could actually use in the book.

"Are you sure you want me to include the story about Pyre trying to strangle you?"

"Yeah. And be sure to say the reason he did it was because he lost the Exodus End Guitarist for a Year Contest. *To a girl.*"

"What a turd." Toni pursed her lips to refrain from calling him more derogatory names.

"I'm done thinking about him for today. Next question," Reagan prompted.

Toni glanced toward her legal pad of Susan-prepared questions and shook her head. "So," she asked, "what's the most difficult thing about being on the road with a bunch of guys?"

"Lack of bathroom space," she said without hesitation.

"Yeah, that does suck," Toni agreed with a nod.

"These guys have been so great about accepting me into their fold, so I really don't have anything to complain about. And this whole three days on the road followed by two nights in a cushy hotel is fabulous. I was on tour with Sinners for a few weeks, and those guys never take a day off while they're on tour. I don't know how they stay sane."

"You talk about Sinners a lot," Toni noted.

"You know, you should write a book about them when you're finished with Exodus End."

"I've thought about it," Toni admitted. But first she had to prove to herself and the rest of the world that she could do right by Exodus End.

The bus shuddered as it came to a stop.

"I think it's time to eat," Reagan said. "We didn't get very far in your interview."

Toni laughed and shook her head in disgrace. "Don't worry about it. Not getting far in my interviews is officially a trend at this point."

"Well then, let's go." Reagan sprang to her feet and tugged Toni off the sectional. "I need to wash the taste of Logan's dick-by-proxy out of my mouth."

Could she really taste that? How mortifying.

Toni grabbed her recorder from the table and tucked it into the pocket of her sweater. She never knew when someone was going to say something important.

CHAPTER 22

L OGAN SIDLED up to Butch and waited to be noticed.

"What's up?" Butch said, not even looking up from the page attached to his clipboard.

"I have a few things I need at the hotel tonight."

Butch could get them anything they wanted. At any time. He'd never let them down yet. One time Steve had tested the bounds of Butch's abilities by requesting a gold-plated toilet seat in his hotel room in Beijing. It had been installed before they arrived.

"Girls?" Butch asked. It was Logan's typical request.

"I have a girl," Logan reminded him.

Butch glanced toward the back of the bus where Toni was finishing up her turkey sandwich. *Without* jalapeños, Logan's dick happily reminded him.

"Yeah, but I figured you wanted more than one."

"If it's that particular one, one is enough."

Butch grinned to himself, looking way too self-satisfied for Logan's taste.

"I need sex toys," Logan blurted.

Butch didn't bat an eyelash. "Okay. What kind?"

"All kinds. All sizes. For both men and women."

"Got it," Butch said.

"Isn't weed legal for recreational use in Montana?"

Butch's mustache twitched. "Nope."

"Damn. Can you get me some anyway?"

"Logan," Butch began his long-winded rehearsed speech

about rock star vices.

"Fine," Logan said. "But when we get to Colorado this weekend . . ." He didn't want to get busted for illegal drugs and suffer the fury of Sam Baily's wrath, but if it was legal? Sign him up for some of that shit.

Butch nodded in defeat. He had a long standing rule about refusing to obtain illegal substances for anyone while they were on tour, but he couldn't use that as an excuse in this case. "Just don't bring it on the bus. We don't want to cross state lines with it."

Logan patted him on the back. "Thata boy."

"Anything else?"

Logan sneaked a glance at Toni, and his heart fluttered at the sight of her. "What do women like? As gifts, I mean."

"Besides sex toys and weed?"

Logan laughed and whacked Butch on the back again. "Yeah, besides sex toys and weed."

Butch ticked off items on his thick fingers. "Flowers, candy, jewelry, lingerie."

"Okay, get her some of that stuff. What else?"

"It would probably mean more to her if you picked out something specific to her."

Logan pursed his lips and twisted them to one side, trying to think of something special. He snapped his fingers when he remembered something uniquely Toni. "Socks," he said, pointing at Butch to emphasize his own brilliance.

Butch's eyes narrowed as he stared at Logan. "Socks?"

"Yeah, get her a bunch of socks."

"Okaaay," Butch drawled. "And I thought I'd never be asked for anything weirder than a gold-plated toilet seat."

"Do you think Toni would like one of those?" Logan teased. "Her ass *is* precious to me."

"Nah," Butch said, shaking his head. "I'm sure she'd think it odd." He lowered his voice and said under his breath, "Not as odd as socks."

"And I'll need a supply of all my usual junk food."

"You don't even have to ask. It's already in your room."

"And I have an unusual craving for strawberry shortcake."

"That is unusual," Butch said, grinning to himself as he jotted a note on his schedule. "Got it."

Logan was going to write Butch into his will.

"Are you still going white-water rafting tomorrow?" Butch

asked.

Logan scowled. He'd completely forgotten he'd scheduled a day trip with a couple of buddies he'd met while rafting the Mad Mile a few years before. Every time he came through Montana, the three of them headed down the Gallatin River. But not this time. He'd much rather spend all day in bed, though he planned to get little rest. "I'm going to have to cancel."

"I'll take care of it," Butch said, his grin broadening.

"Thanks for having my back, man," Logan said as he slugged him affectionately.

"Any time."

Butch pulled out his cellphone to work his usual magic, and Logan headed to the back of the bus to join the others. There were no available seats, so he stood behind Toni and stroked her hair. He didn't understand his inexplicable need to touch her at all times. It was as baffling to him as it apparently was to the three men gawking at him from around the semicircular booth. The only guy on the bus who seemed to understand his fixation was Trey Mills. Trey offered him a curt nod and knowing smile before wrapping an arm around Reagan's shoulders and tugging her closer to him in the booth. She giggled when Trey whispered in her ear. They both turned their heads to look to the back of the bus where the door to the lounge stood ajar. Before Logan could blink, the lovers had risen from the table, sprinted through the open door, and slid it shut with a definitive bang.

"And there he goes again," Dare said with resigned sigh.

"At least you aren't competing with Ethan today," Steve said. His gaze darted to Toni. "I mean, those two guys are great friends, you know?"

"Inseparable," Dare agreed.

"I know about their polyamorous relationship," Toni said, munching on a plain potato chip. "Reagan told me. So you don't have to worry about guarding what you say. Why isn't Ethan here with them?"

"I'm sure he wanted to be, but he's with the rest of the security team securing the hotel before we arrive," Max said.

"Are you guys really in that much danger?" Toni asked, pausing with her sandwich halfway to her mouth.

"There have been incidents," Max said, drawing his brows together.

"There are a lot of crazies out in the world," Logan said.

"And for some reason, we attract them."

Toni reached into her pocket and pulled out her recording device. She set it on the table in plain sight. A red light blinked steadily on its top. Logan wondered how long the thing had been recording.

"What kind of incidents?" Toni asked, her gaze on Max.

"He's usually bothered by beautiful women," Steve said. "I'm the one that crazy dudes want to pick fights with for no reason."

"Can't blame a guy for wanting to smack the smug off your face," Logan said.

"I'm not smug."

"So you've been in a lot of fights?" Toni asked.

"A few," Steve said vaguely, his gaze trained on the ceiling as he took a draw off his beer.

A few? The guy had been in more fights than Mike Tyson. And he rarely instigated them. Dudes really did pick fights with him for no reason.

Getting no further details from Steve, Toni turned her attention back to Max. "I assume women do some pretty desperate stunts to get you to take them to your bed."

"They try," Logan said.

"Max is very discriminating when it comes to bed partners," Dare said, nudging Max, who was seated beside him, with his elbow.

"I believe in quality over quantity," Max said, looking amused as he scratched his nose with the back of his hand.

"Unlike Logan," Steve claimed. "He'll fuck anyone."

So that was why guys picked fights with Steve.

"Including me," Toni said. Logan couldn't see her face and couldn't tell by her voice if she was upset or not. "Boy, he *must* have low standards."

"I didn't mean it that way," Steve said, reaching across the table to squeeze Toni's hand.

He was really asking for an ass-beating now. No one touched Toni but Logan.

"Get your hands off of her," Logan growled.

"Or you'll do what?" Steve asked.

"Introduce your face to the bottom of my shoe."

Dare sighed and shook his head. "We get it, Logan. She's yours. You don't have to lift your leg and piss on her."

Max chuckled. "I'm actually enjoying this. How often do we

get to tease Logan about his feelings for a woman?"

That's it, I'm going to have to kick all their asses. The queue for ass-whippings starts here.

Toni lifted a hand to cover his. He hadn't realized he was squeezing her shoulder so tightly until her gentle touch brought attention to it. He immediately loosened his hold and tried to smooth out any damage.

"He doesn't have feelings for me," Toni said. "We're justfriends."

She was so very wrong about that, but he was still too much of a chicken shit to correct her. Why were jumping out of airplanes and doing back flips on his dirt bike and playing concerts in front of a hundred thousand people easier than telling this sweet woman that he was over the moon for her? It made no fucking sense to him, but it was a fact. Sharing how he felt terrified him to the bone.

"Of course he doesn't," Steve said, laughing hysterically.

Several hours later, they left the tour bus parked in the lot behind the arena and a limousine shuttled the band members and their weekend luggage to the hotel—because limousines were far less noticeable than tour buses. Right. Logan convinced Toni to leave her cameras and recording devices locked under the bus, but she insisted on bringing her laptop in case she had time to make progress on her book. Logan, however, was determined that she wouldn't have a second to spare on work. Tonight and tomorrow were all about play.

"It doesn't feel right to make someone else do my laundry," Toni said on the elevator after Logan had collected his room keys from Butch.

She'd wanted to bring her dirty clothes so she could head off to a laundry and wash them. She wouldn't have time for that nonsense either.

"It's not a big deal. We pay someone to come clean up after us on every off day. It's their job. You wouldn't want to deny them their job, would you?"

"I suppose not, but I should at least pay them out of my own pocket."

Logan chuckled. Then he brushed her hair behind her ear with one hand. "I don't think they'll notice a few extra socks in the mix. Unless they drive themselves batty wondering why the mates to those socks have vanished."

"I hope they don't discard them. My sister would be so

upset."

"Your sister?"

She pushed her glasses up her nose with the back of her wrist. "It wouldn't interest you."

"When are you going to figure out that everything about you interests me?"

Her slight smile and the blush on her smooth cheeks made him want to kiss her.

"Birdie had a very hard time learning how to dress herself," Toni said. "One morning she came into my room before the sun had risen, so proud of herself for having picked out her clothes and put them on without help. Her striped shirt was on backwards and her floral print leggings were wrong side out and she had on two different socks."

The look of love on Toni's face as she talked about her younger sister made Logan's heart swell. He wondered if anyone would ever wear that expression while thinking of him.

"I was tired and not ready to get out of bed yet, so I told her she'd done a good job but her socks didn't match. I was hoping she'd let me sleep a while longer, to be honest. So off she went to find matching socks. But then she couldn't find the mates, and she was so upset. I helped her search and we eventually found them in my sock drawer. I put them on as a joke and it made her so happy that we were both mismatched, but matching, that it became a regular thing. Every time we go to a store we buy several pairs of socks and divvy them between us. That way we're always mismatched but matching. It makes Birdie giddy."

Logan kissed her forehead. "And here I thought you were just quirky."

She grinned up at him. "I'm plenty quirky," she said, "but mostly I'm a slave to the happiness of those I love."

She said the word *love* so freely, he had no doubt she felt it deeply. And he envied her for both abilities. The elevator doors opened on the top floor just in time to stop him from spouting some sentimental bullshit he was sure to regret saying later.

"This is a nice hotel," she said, studying the narrow corridor. "Which room is mine?"

"You're staying with me."

"Are you sure you don't mind?"

"You're kidding, right?"

She poked him in the gut. "Yep."

He released an exaggerated sigh. "I thought I was going to have to resort to jerking off."

"You can still do that," she said so quietly, he almost hadn't heard her.

"You'd like to watch, wouldn't you?"

She shrugged, but he remembered what had happened the last time he'd stroked his cock in her presence. She'd become a self-taught expert at sixty-nine.

"I know it turns you on." He slipped his key card into the slot on his door, glad the rest of the band had decided to stop at the restaurant for dinner before heading to their rooms. With the exception of a rather discreet member of their security team camped out next to the elevator, the corridor was empty. "What else turns you on, Toni?"

"I'm not sure," she said, scowling with introspection. "I do plan to find out tonight."

"And all day tomorrow."

"I doubt we'll need the extra day to figure it out. I'm not all that complicated."

"You're the most complicated woman I ever met," he said as he opened the door to their room.

She laughed when some of the balloons blocking their entrance floated out into the hall. "Is this the right room?"

Logan batted his way through the red balloons, sending them bouncing off each other and the ceiling and Toni. There were several vases of flowers, tiered trays of chocolates, a silver bucket with chilling champagne, and the biggest strawberry shortcake he'd ever seen sitting on a table. Several sacks, which Logan assumed contained the requested sex toys, were lined up against the far wall, and half a dozen sets of lingerie had been artfully arranged on the bed. The outfits ranged from a sweet but short white lace teddy to a flirty babydoll made of a pink gauzy material complete with fur trim to a leather corset and thigh-high boots. Butch had overdone it again.

"It's the right room," he said, a blush coursing up his neck. When he'd requested such items, he hadn't realized it would look like he was taking his brand new lover on a freaking honeymoon.

"What is all this?" She came into the room, glancing around wide-eyed, and set her messenger bag down by the door.

Embarrassed, he shrugged. There was no way in hell he was admitting that this was his idea. "I guess the guys thought it would be funny to tease me about our first night together in a hotel."

He turned his head to peer at her sidelong. Was she buying it? A balloon bounced off his face when she volleyed it in his direction with the palm of her hand. He sent a barrage of balloons back her way, but very few managed to touch her. The helium kept sending them toward the ceiling before they could connect. But she was laughing as she fended off his attack with a swatting hand, and his embarrassment over discovering he was a romantic sap was quickly replaced by a buoyancy in his heart. Must be the balloons. He grabbed one in his hand and Toni's arm in the other, tugging their bodies together with the balloon squashed between their bellies.

"What are you doing?" she asked, her face flushed with laughter as she stared up at him.

His arms circled her back and his hands slid down to her ass to tug her closer. "There are too many balloons in this room."

The balloon squeaked in protest as their bodies came closer together.

"Don't break—"

Pop!

They both jumped at the sound and then burst out laughing. He couldn't resist kissing her smiling lips. When he drew away, she cocked her head to the side and scrutinized his face.

"So how did the pranksters know I like strawberry shortcake?" she asked.

Just play dumb. "What strawberry shortcake?"

"That family-sized one over on the table. I can't wait to devour it."

Logan turned his head to pretend to notice the pizza-sized cake covered with strawberries and whipped cream for the first time. "That *is* huge. Strange coincidence that it happens to be your favorite."

"Uh-huh," she said, not sounding the least convinced. She pulled away and darted across the room. "So what's in the sacks?"

She'd probably believe his bandmates would tease them by filling their room with sex toys, so he didn't try to stop her.

Her brow crumpled as she pulled a package out of the first bag. "Socks?"

She held up a clearly marked package containing a dozen pairs of plain white tube socks.

"More socks?" She pulled out another pack of tube socks and another.

Logan snorted and burst out laughing. He hadn't been specific about the kind of socks.

"Why do you need so many socks? Are your feet cold?"

He shook his head. "Toss me a bag and I'll show you what they're for."

He ripped open the package she tossed to him and rolled up the sock, tucking the bulk of the sock into the open end so that it formed a soft ball. Standing next to the far side of bed, Toni watched him as he did the same on about half the socks in the pack, setting each ball in a neat pile on his side of the mattress between her new corset and lace teddy.

"That's a strange way to fold socks," she said, fingering the soft fur that edged a tiny pink thong.

He lifted one of the balls and tossed it up and down in one hand.

"Sock ball fight!" he announced before throwing the sock at her and catching her in the shoulder. He managed to pummel her with several sock balls from his pile before she dove behind the bed for cover. A moment later her head poked up over the mattress and she threw a recovered sock ball at him, missing him by a mile. He bounced a ball off her head before she disappeared below the edge of the mattress again.

"No fair!" she cried. "I don't have any ammo."

"You have five bags of ammo," he said, tossing another sock ball at her.

"No prepared ammo!"

He heard the sound of plastic tearing. A sock went sailing over the bed in his direction.

"Sock snake!" she yelled. "It's poisonous."

The poisonous sock snake landed on the bed near his hip. She peeked up over the bed to see if her projectile had hit its target. Logan seized the sock, pretending to fight off its venomous fangs. The harder she laughed, the more he escalated his theatrics. He flopped onto the bed on his back, struggling to keep the sock from tearing out his throat, until the vicious creature got the better of him and connected with his jugular. Sock still gripped in his hand, he threw his arms wide.

"He got me," he gasped and then went still.

"Oh no!" Toni cried. "I need to suck the poison out."

It took every ounce of Logan's will not to move as she jumped onto the bed with him and lowered her mouth to his throat. Her soft sucking kisses did all sorts of tingly things to the snake in his pants.

"I'm too late," she said brokenly, sniffing theatrically.

"Keep trying," he whispered out of the corner of his mouth.

Her soft kisses on his throat strengthened, drawing a shudder from him. He was now wishing the snake had bitten him a bit farther south.

"Oh God," he said, lifting the sock in the air. "The snake is attacking again."

Toni leaned away to watch him struggle with the sock once more.

"Not there!" he yelled as he aimed the sock for his crotch. "Anywhere but there!"

Toni grabbed the sock to help him fend off the attack. "I'll save you."

He expected her to pull the sock away, but she bumped it against the thickening ridge in his pants.

"Oh no," she said. "He got you again. I'd better suck that poison out too."

She jerked open his fly, and he laughed. "God, I love you," he said. And then he sucked in a deep breath.

Toni went still, and her eyes lifted to meet his.

"U-u-ukuleles. I love ukuleles," he said. "Highly underrated instrument."

"Uh-huh," she agreed. "Now, hush. It's going to take a long time to get all this poison out."

It didn't take all that long really. Her technique was perfect. The way her mouth sucked, lips rubbed, throat vibrated—perfect. Her hand tugging gently at the base of his shaft, long hair tickling his belly as her head moved—perfect. The sounds she made, the way she looked, her scent, her remembered taste—perfect. His sweet, sweet Toni—perfect.

I'm in big trouble here.

Logan's back arched as his pleasure intensified. He wasn't ready for the building pleasure to end, but she'd fully conquered his resistance and he couldn't help but let go.

"Toni?" he whispered hoarsely as he tapped the back of her head to let her know she was about to get a mouthful. His belly tautened as he found release, his bliss so intense he swore he saw stars behind his tightly clenched eyelids.

Toni tensed as he filled her mouth with cum, but she

swallowed every drop and then slowly pulled away, releasing her suction with a soft pop.

Winded, she lay down beside him, rested her head on his chest, and traced the outlines of a tattoo here, an abdominal muscle there.

"That's the second time you've tapped the back of my head when I've gone down on you," she said, tilting her head so she could look up at him. "Am I missing something?"

He grinned at her. Was it weird that he was *glad* she didn't know what it meant? "It's the universal signal for *I'm coming*, in case you don't want that stuff in your mouth."

"Oh," she said. "Am I supposed to swallow it? I meant to ask Reagan about proper protocol, but I forgot."

"It's up to you," he said. "It won't hurt my feelings if you pull off at the last minute or spit it out."

"If I pull off, will I get to watch it come out?"

"Do you want to watch my cum spurt?"

She grinned deviously and nodded. Her hand slid down his belly, and she touched his softening cock. "Right now," she said.

He laughed. "I'm not a teenager anymore, lamb. You'll have to give it at least twenty minutes." More like forty, but who was counting?

"Can I have some of that strawberry shortcake you ordered for me while we wait?"

"If you like." It had to taste better than his cum.

She sat up and poked his nose. "I knew it!"

"You knew what?"

"*You* did all this romantic stuff for me. The balloons. The cake. The socks. These totally inappropriate clothes. The flowers and chocolate. All of it."

Let's not forget the sex toys. Wherever those were.

He scowled and shook his head. "Did not!"

"Oh," she said, sliding from the bed. "Well, that's too bad. I was going to allow the sweetie who went to all this trouble to do anything he wanted to my naked body."

His cock twitched. "Anything?"

"Yep." She crossed the room and stuck her finger in the whipped cream topping on the shortcake. She sucked it off with the same skill she'd just showed his very appreciative dick. "Anything."

"Even anal?"

"*Any* thing. But since it wasn't you, I guess it doesn't matter."

He was torn between owning up to his ridiculous gifts and getting to do *anything* he wanted to the beautiful woman biting into a juicy strawberry with a look of bliss on her face.

"It was me," he said. "Well, I asked Butch to have this all brought to our room to surprise you. Apparently, I wasn't clear that the socks should be unique and colorful." And now that he knew that her sock collection was a product of many special moments between herself and her little sister, he was actually glad he'd botched that one.

"Thank you. This was all really thoughtful of you."

He sat up on the bed and rubbed a hand over his face. He actually didn't feel like a complete idiot for bringing a smile to her face. He actually felt happy that she was pleased.

"So now I can do anything I want to you?" he asked.

"Not anything," she said.

"Aw, man." He slapped his thigh.

"You have only yourself to blame. You should have told me the truth from the start."

"I was embarrassed," he admitted. "I don't normally do this kind of thing." And he wasn't sure what had compelled him to do it this time.

"It was very sweet of you."

"Exactly," he grumbled. He hauled himself off the bed and kicked his jeans off before sitting at the table where she was still picking at her strawberry treat with her fingers.

"New friend?" she asked, nodding toward the sock he still held in his hand. He'd completely forgotten it was there.

"Attack snake!" he shouted and touched her boob with his sock. "Oh no, she's been bitten. She's too young to die!"

He wrestled her sweater off over her head and sent her bra flying across the room in his haste to suck out the poison and save her precious life. She was laughing so hard by the time he freed her of her constrictive clothing, she couldn't catch her breath.

"This snakebite looks all swollen and red," he said, dipping his fingers in whipped topping. "Better put some salve on it."

He loved the way she shuddered as he drew his cream-dipped fingertips over her hardened nipple. Her giggles turned to sighs of pleasure as he lowered his head to lick and suckle the tip of her breast.

"Thank you for saving my life, sir," she murmured, threading her fingers through his hair.

"My pleasure." He tilted his head back to look up at her. There was a far juicier cream he wanted to sample at the moment. He slid a finger down her belly toward his preferred destination. "Will you shave for me?"

She rubbed her jaw, checking for beard growth. "I shaved just this morning."

"I'll even let you use my razor." She probably had no idea what he was sacrificing by offering his favorite blade. "You'll find it in the bathroom." That was where the team that delivered the band's day-off luggage and set up their hotel suites always put it for him.

"I'll try it," she said. "But I've never been good with sharp objects. Prepare a tourniquet."

He chuckled, not sure how he'd apply a tourniquet to her lady parts.

She kissed his forehead and scooted out of the chair to head for the bathroom. "I'll pretend I'm doing this for you, but I'm really doing it for me."

He was definitely going to make the effort worth her while. "And will you wear one of the sexy outfits I bought you?"

She came to a halt just outside the bathroom door and turned to stare at the disheveled pieces of lingerie on the bed. "Which one?"

"You choose."

Would she go for the sweet white lace negligee or the more daring black leather corset? He planned to see what she looked like in each of the pieces by the end of their stay.

She scooped all five of the getups into both arms and carried them toward the bathroom. "I'll try them on and see which one looks the least terrible on me."

Least terrible? She was joking, right? "You'll look hot as hell in all of them, I guarantee it."

Her self-deprecating smile let him know she didn't believe his words. Apparently he didn't compliment her enough. He wondered how obnoxious he'd have to get in order for her to feel as attractive as he found her.

She entered the bathroom, and there was a series of thuds as a collection of somethings tipped over in succession.

"Logan! What in the world are all these things? There's a rainbow of dicks in here!"

Ah. She'd found the sex toys.

CHAPTER
23

RESHLY SHAVEN and surprisingly without massive blood loss, Toni slipped into the pink thong with a soft tuft of fur at the front. She'd just shaved her fur, so why would she want to wear synthetic pink fur on a pair of panties that disappeared up her ass crack? She slipped the matching babydoll over her head and pulled it over her breasts. She gaped at herself in the mirror. Her nipples were clearly visible through the gauzy material, and there was no hiding the size of her boobs.

A knock at the door made her jump.

"What's taking you so long?" Logan asked. "I'm lonely out here."

Her hands automatically flew upward to cover her breasts. "Just trying things on."

"Can I see?"

Her gaze darted to the mirror. She wasn't sure if she wanted him to see.

"I'm not decent," she said, lowering her hands, which were trembling uncontrollably.

"That's the general idea," he said and opened the door.

She wasn't sure what to do with her hands, so she slapped them over her eyes. Because if she couldn't see herself, surely he couldn't see her either.

Logan produced a guttural purr that made Toni's tiny panties demonstrate their complete lack of absorbency. "You're the sexiest thing I've ever seen in my life," he said.

"Don't tease," she said, still covering her eyes with both hands.

"Oh, I plan to do plenty of teasing," he said.

Toni heard him moving around the bathroom, but couldn't figure out what he was doing. She slowly lowered her hands to find him scooping up dozens of sex toys. He left the room with overflowing arms only to return a moment later empty-handed.

"What are you going to do to me?" she whispered, her belly fluttering with a combination of nerves and anticipation.

He took her hand and tugged her toward the bedroom. "Lamb, the question you should be asking is *what* aren't *you going to do to me?*"

The first thing she noticed was that except for the stark-white fitted sheet, he'd stripped all the bedding from the bed. The second thing she saw was the pile of sex toys on a club chair he'd maneuvered to the bedside. The third was the belt lying on the mattress. She didn't understand the thrill of excitement that streaked through her at the sight of the simple strap of black leather.

"What's that for?" she asked as he tugged her ever closer to the bed by her wrist.

"The belt?"

She flushed and nodded, unable to meet his eyes.

"What do you think it's for?" he asked.

She could think of a number of purposes it could be used for, but only one she wanted it used for.

Her eyes flicked up to his before she lowered them again. "To tie me down?"

He hooked a finger under her chin and forced her to look up at him. "That's exactly what it's for." His thumb slowly traced her lower lip.

She had no way of knowing if tying her down had been his original intention or if he'd had other ideas for the belt or had just left it there by mistake, but she was glad he was agreeable to her suggestion.

"Lie down and let me look at you first."

She wasn't sure she liked that idea—he was sure to find every flaw of her imperfect flesh—but she couldn't deny him anything when he stared at her with that hopeful expression. She stepped back and turned to the bed, placing both hands and a knee on the mattress so she could crawl to the center.

"Stop right there," he said.

One foot still on the floor, she paused and peered over her shoulder at him.

"Take those panties off before you crawl up there."

She lowered her foot to the floor and reached for the thin straps on her hips. She started to pull the garment off as she normally would, but decided he probably wanted a little show. She spread her legs and leaned forward, slowly tugging the strings over her rounded ass, stopping just short of exposing her newly shaved pussy to his riveted gaze.

"Are you sure you want them off?" she asked, her voice low in her attempt to be seductive. "They're necessary to complete my outfit."

"I'm sure."

When she tugged the fabric free and cool air bathed her hot pussy, Logan sucked in a deep breath through his nose.

"Damn, you're beautiful."

"It feels so different now that it's shaved." She slid a hand over her smooth mound, her fingers gliding into her slit. Her panties were caught at the top of her thighs, and something about them being there keeping her legs from spreading farther apart, made her feel sexy. She stroked her outer lips in slow circles and then spread them to give Logan a peek at what was hidden between.

He groaned his approval of her sudden brazenness. The feeling of empowerment she got from his attention made her bold.

She closed her thighs slightly and pushed the panties down her legs until they dropped to the floor and she kicked them aside. She inexplicably wished she wore a pair of pink stilettoes. She doubted she'd be able to walk in them, but was sure they'd make her legs and ass look fantastic. But from the way Logan was staring, she decided her ass must look pretty good even without the aid of perception-bending shoes.

Toni crawled up on the bed, taking her time to get to the center so he could take his time ogling her. By the time she lay on her back in the center of the mattress, Logan had his dick in his hand.

"God, what you do to me, woman." He moved to the end of the bed, and her legs popped open as if the man were telekinetic and had willed them to spread for him. He crawled up between her legs, not stopping until he was suspended above her on his hands and knees. Her belly clenched when he lifted a hand to touch her nipple through the transparent material of her fur-trimmed babydoll.

"I think I get so caught up in your spectacular breasts that I underappreciate that gorgeous ass of yours," he said.

"It in no way compares to that gorgeous ass of yours," she said, giving his butt a playful swat.

He reached for the belt, and her belly quivered. He slid the leather through the buckle to form a loop and slipped it over her hand to encircle her wrist. When he jerked the strap tight against her skin, heat and moisture surged to her center and a gasp of excitement escaped her.

"This is turning you on," he said.

It was that obvious, was it? What had given her away? The pounding of her heart? The quickening of her breath? The way her nipples and pussy had instantly swelled and now tingled with arousal? He obviously couldn't feel what she was feeling, but he was absolutely correct—the feel of that tough leather against her delicate skin definitely turned her on.

He pulled her bound arm up above her head. Her heart thudded faster. Breath quickened until she was gasping. Logan scowled when his gaze lifted to a spot above her head.

"You know what sucks about hotel beds?"

She liked this bed pretty well, so she shook her head.

"They all have fabric headboards affixed to the wall. I guess it's good for protecting your skull while I'm pounding you so hard you're banging your head, but it's not good for tying a woman properly. I need a nice brass bed or a four-poster for that."

She pressed her lips together, hoping her disappointment didn't register on her face. It wasn't his fault they didn't have the proper setup. He'd tried to do what she wanted. "It's okay. You don't have to tie me down."

"But I want to fulfill your wildest fantasies."

She giggled. "I do have more than one."

He glanced at the chair full of toys. "Does one of them involve coming more times than you can count?"

A renewed thrill of excitement pulsed through her core. "It does now."

"We'll save your bondage fantasies for another lesson," he promised, stroking her hair from her face and kissing her tenderly.

"I'm going to hold you to that," she said with a soft chuckle.

"Today's lesson begins with vibration," he said matter-of-factly as he reached over the bed and lifted a small silver vibrator from the pile. He turned the base and it hummed to life.

"Are you sure these toys are new?" she asked. None of them were in their original packaging, and they'd apparently been fitted with batteries.

"I'm positive," he said. "Some poor crew member had the chore of unpacking and powering up these suckers before we arrived."

"So someone knows what we're doing in here?" she squeaked.

He chuckled. "Honey, everyone knows what we're doing in here."

The tip of the vibrator was cool as he slowly drew it over the hot flesh between her thighs. Its small smooth tip slipped easily inside her. He glided the vibe deeper and then shifted down the mattress so he could flick his tongue against her throbbing clit while he worked the vibrator inside her. She clung to the sheet with both hands to keep herself from launching off the bed as she quickly spiraled toward bliss. He slid the vibrator free of her body and massaged the tip against her already throbbing clit. The combination of his tongue flicks and the vibration sent her flying. She cried out, her eyes flying open in shock at how quickly she'd found her peak. At least she'd thought it had been her peak. Logan seemed determined to take her higher. As the waves of pleasure rippled through her clenching pussy, he dipped the tip of the vibrator inside her, working it against her spasms. When she was sure her pleasure couldn't be topped, he sucked her clit into his mouth.

"Logan!" she screamed as her climax intensified.

She tensed when the vibration slipped back a couple of inches and brushed her back entrance.

He wouldn't, she thought, just before he did.

She gasped as her ass tightened around the smooth, vibrating tip inside her.

"Logan?" She wasn't sure if she liked the sensation. Okay, she was totally sure that she liked it, but she wasn't sure why she liked it.

"Do you want me to take it out?" he asked.

She should want him to take it out. Shiny metal vibrators did not belong in her ass. "N-no."

He licked her quaking pussy as if to reward her admission.

"Do you want it deeper?"

She wasn't sure. It felt bizarre to be breached there, even if it was only inside her an inch or two. Bizarre, yet thrilling. "Maybe a little," she whispered.

He popped the vibrator free and then pressed it inside her ass again, taking it several inches deeper this time.

She groaned in bliss.

"I want to feel that," he said, kissing his way up her body.

She wasn't sure what he meant until he fumbled between their bodies and pressed his cock into her opening. He sucked in an excited breath. "Oh yeah," he murmured, "that's nice."

Nice? She moaned as he began to thrust, pulling out slowly and pausing just inside her, where he must have been able to feel the vibration against his cockhead, before ramming deep and withdrawing oh so slowly again. His arm shot out to the side and he grabbed a rubbery pink vibrator from the collection of devices on the chair.

"Here," he said. "Use this on your clit. I'm too far gone to multitask."

She didn't think she needed the added stimulation, but ever the good student, Toni did as her instructor demanded. He straightened his arms to give her enough room to massage her clit with her new best friend. She wasn't sure if she experienced multiple orgasms or just one long, ever-intensifying orgasm, but by the time Logan pulled out, tears were streaming down her face.

Toni lifted her head so she could watch him stroke his cock between her thighs. He erupted with a hoarse cry, his fluids jetting from his body in a high arc and splattering over her belly and shaved mound. His head dropped back, golden curls tumbling about his strong tanned shoulders as he gasped for air.

Still laboring for breath, he lifted his head and looked down at her. "That was very irresponsible of me. We really need to get you on some sort of birth control."

She flushed and avoided his gaze as she pulled the vibrator out of her ass. She probably should have mentioned that she'd been on the birth control shot for years—not because she was having sex, but because her menstrual periods had been dangerously heavy and her doctor had thought the shots would help lighten them.

"I'll call Butch for some Plan B."

He shifted to move from the bed, and Toni grabbed his wrist.

"That won't be necessary."

He looked at her like she was a raving lunatic. "I'm not ready to be a father."

"Me neither," she said. "I mean I'm not ready to be a mother. I'm already on birth control. I get the shot every three months." She'd never thought of it as birth control before, but she supposed it was now working double duty.

"And we've been using condoms why?"

"Because," she said, her heart aching. "Because you've been with a lot of women."

He laid a hand on her head. "And I've always been extra careful."

She lifted a skeptical brow at him, and he laughed.

"I guess that's hard to believe, considering I can't seem to keep my unprotected dick out of you, but it's a fact. I've never had this uncontrollable need to be skin on skin with a woman before. Being safe has always been more important than feeling good."

Her skeptical brow lifted a notch higher.

"I'm not just saying that to gain your cooperation, Toni. I mean it. And if you're worried that I've got some STD, you can check my physical report. We all get a full health screening before every tour. It's in our contract." He scowled. "There's a lot of weird shit in that contract."

"What else is in that contract?" she asked, her curiosity getting the better of her.

"Nope, we're not talking about that tonight."

"Why? Does the contract prevent you from discussing the contract?" *Wow, that must be some seriously iron-clad document.*

"No," he said. "It's your night off, and I still have a whole lot of lessons planned."

She smiled. She'd definitely rather enjoy his lessons than talk about contracts.

"And since we don't have to use condoms anymore . . ." He tilted his head toward her and waited for her to nod, which, after a few seconds of contemplation, she did. "Yes!" He made a victory fist and then used it to cover a weak cough. "The lessons are sure to become more spontaneous."

A group with laughing, boisterous voices traversed the hall just outside their suite. A loud knock on their door sent Toni scuttling after the nearest cover—a comforter wadded up in a corner of the room.

"Logan," Steve called through the crack in the door. His voice sounded slurred. "Loooogan. Need some help in there?"

"Knock it off," Max said. "You know he's with Toni tonight."

"You don't think he needs any help with her?" Steve said, his voice carrying through the door. "Loooogan, let me in. I've got a boner with your pretty friend's name on it."

"Go away," Logan called. "I'm balls deep in a piece of heaven right now and need no assistance."

Toni bent over and scooped up a stray sock ball to throw at him. Logan's claim would have been true ten minutes ago, but even then, it wasn't information Steve needed to know.

"If you change your mind, you know where to find me and my boner."

Logan pressed three fingertips to the center of his forehead and shook his head. "Sorry about that, lamb. He must be drunk."

"And horny."

"He's always horny. He's just more likely to share that information when he's drunk."

Toni stared at the door, thinking about what Steve had said. Did he really have a boner for her, or was he just messing with Logan?

"You aren't considering his proposition are you?" Logan asked.

She pulled her gaze from the door and fixed on him. "Of course not. I want only you. Not Steve. Not even the toys. Just you."

He stared at her for a long moment and then moved to the desk where several bouquets of flowers were arranged in vases. He picked up a room service menu.

"Are you hungry?" he asked. "I'm starving."

She was very aware that he didn't return her blurted sentiments, but what could she do? Just because she'd fallen head over heels for him immediately didn't mean he had contracted the same unfortunate condition.

"I could eat," she said. She tucked the comforter around her body. "But I think I'll start by doing some damage to that strawberry shortcake." The one he'd so thoughtfully ordered for her. For a guy not willing to admit he had feelings, he sure was playing all his cards at once.

Toni could honestly say it was the best night of her life. They talked and laughed, pigged out on room service, made love, watched eighties movies and quoted memorable lines, and played a game of truth or dare in which Logan wound up naked in the elevator and Toni revealed her most embarrassing moments. Still, though exhausted, Toni had a hard time falling asleep. She decided it wasn't because Logan snored every time he rolled onto his back, but because she was afraid she'd wake up the next morning and find everything had been a dream.

Not sure when she'd finally drifted off, she woke at first light and smiled to find Logan still beside her. She touched his beard-roughened face, traced his brow, and wrapped his golden curls around her fingertips until she was met by a disgruntled, blue-eyed stare.

"What are you doing awake so early?" he asked.

"Just thinking that if last night was that much fun, today is going to be beyond great."

"The only lessons I give before noon are for anal sex."

Her butt cheeks tightened automatically. Yes, she'd enjoyed having a slender vibe back there, a finger or two, and even the occasional flick of his tongue, but she didn't ever want to find out what it felt like to have his huge cock pounding the wrong hole.

"I'll let you sleep then."

He winked at her. "I'll wear you down eventually." He flipped onto his side and curled into his bunched pillow, while she spent the morning trying to convince herself that lots of prison inmates had anal sex. So how bad could it be?

May 5

Dear Journal,

Sorry I missed writing to you yesterday. I was really busy. First with interviews, then with Logan. I almost didn't write again today, but my head is so full of thoughts right now, I can't contain them. The same cannot be said for Logan. It's almost noon and he's still asleep. I didn't want to disturb him on his day off, but I was starting to get bored, so I decided to write.

Yesterday I did all my interviews with the band. Most of what they told me can't be used in the book. Figures, right? It's good that they trust me enough to tell me their secrets, but I do need material I can actually include. There's one secret incident that Reagan actually wants me to spill in the book. And I guess I don't blame her.

A couple of weeks ago someone tried to kidnap and kill her. And the public doesn't know about it. I can't believe it was covered up. I Googled the incident before we arrived at the hotel and the full story isn't online anywhere. There is a short report about Pyre Vamp assaulting someone and being arrested, but it doesn't say who he assaulted or what happened. I didn't think it was legal to cover up crimes and protect the culprit. And maybe it's not. So I'm going to write something about it in the book. Hopefully it'll make Reagan feel better. She seemed really upset that it's being kept a secret. But I think she'd be more upset if her other secret became public.

Reagan admitted to me that she's dating both Trey and Ethan—Ethan's her bodyguard, by the way. Even more shocking is that Trey and Ethan have sex with each other too. So they have a committed threesome. I don't get how that works exactly. I guess I'm dense. Logan said he's had threesomes before and even suggested that Steve would be a willing participant if I wanted to try it, but I don't think I'm brazen enough to be naked in front of two men. He also said something about him being with two women at once and while I might be okay with being intimate with another woman, I don't think I'd be able to stand watching her touch Logan. He's mine.

Or I want him to be. He guards his heart so fiercely, I'm afraid he'll never let me in.

He did open up to me a little during our interview. He told me about his estrangement with his brother. I can tell that he's hurt more than mad. Logan apparently feels that he was replaced in his brother's life by his stepbrother. I was surprised the two of them never made amends—*they're brothers*. I can't imagine letting anything come between Birdie and me. Unfortunately, I don't think Logan has ever told his brother how he feels. I guess that's to be expected. Logan has a very hard time admitting his feelings to me too. He probably never even told his mom how hurt he was to be excluded from her happy little family. I guess his relationship with his dad is pretty distant as well. It's no wonder he tries to keep me from getting too close. But too bad. I'm not backing away.

I talked to Birdie for a little bit this morning. She had to go to school, so we didn't get to talk long. I feel bad that I'm on this assignment and left her at home. I know I need to make a life for myself, but surely there's a way to include Birdie in it. I'll have to think about it. She seems to be doing okay with Mom, but I can tell she misses me. I miss her too.

So what else has happened since last I wrote?

Oh yeah—Steve's ex-wife. I read things about her when I was doing my research and he's right, he always comes across as the bad guy in their divorce. I never even questioned the tone of the information out there. Even when the truth is told, it can be worded in such a way that points a finger or exaggerates or understates or picks sides. I must be careful with my own phrasing in the book. The written word is arguably the most powerful tool on Earth. Too often it's used to cause harm. I can tell it bothers Steve to always be portrayed as the one at fault for the breakup. I don't think I'll pry about it. I don't want anyone to get hurt by something I write.

Dare said he might be able to talk the band into creating a song just for the book and letting me be a part of it. Wouldn't that be cool? He came up with the idea. And he told me all sorts of stuff about their creative process. Sounds stressful. I hope they don't throw things around the room. I'll have to wear a helmet.

I need to remember to make a copy of Susan's questions for Max. He didn't like being put on the spot during the interview. Actually, if the guys are willing to sit there and write out answers, I should probably do the same for them all. They've been so great to me, I'd hate to be a pest. But damn, Susan is a total bitch. If I could show I already had all of her stupid questions answered, maybe she'd quit pestering me. Or maybe if I answered her text messages and told her to fuck off and leave me alone, she'd go away.

Highly doubtful.

Okay, I think Logan has slept long enough. I wonder if he'll mind if I wake him up with a kiss.

On his cock. And let's find out how much he likes a vibrator up his ass.

Feeling-frisky,

Toni

CHAPTER
24

N EEDING SOMETHING TO DO with her hands besides put them all over Logan, Toni switched on her video recorder to capture footage inside and outside the limo. After their thirty-six hour marathon of sex, fun, and more sex had come to a climactic end that morning, Toni thought she'd be able to concentrate on her work today. But all the man had to do was sit beside her and she was wondering how long she'd have to wait before she could get him naked.

Unfortunately, getting naked wouldn't be happening soon. The line of Exodus End fans in front of the record store was five deep and wrapped around the block.

"Looks like we'll be here for a while," Logan said.

Darn. She hadn't known what to expect at a record store signing in Billings, Montana. She should have known that fans would drive for miles for the privilege of meeting the band.

The limo drove around to the back of the store and the band members were escorted inside by Exodus End's security team, which had arrived a few minutes before them. Once again Toni was allowed to follow them behind the scenes. They ended up in a storeroom where some woman fussed over Max's hair for ten minutes. Toni snapped a couple of pictures, not sure if she'd include a chapter on preparation for public appearances, but it was better to collect too much information than not enough.

Noting that her video camera was already out of storage, Toni put a new memory card and freshly recharged batteries into the device, which she could also use to take still shots. Someone stepped up behind her, and she knew by the way her body yearned for his that the person was Logan.

"I am so horny right now," he said into her ear. "And it's all your fault. I can't stop thinking about my cock in your mouth with that thing up my ass. You give the best wakeup calls."

She grinned to herself. She liked her newfound power. That *thing* had been a prostate stimulator, and she was now an expert at its usage. She could set the man off like a rocket in seconds. If they'd been alone, she might have discreetly rubbed up against him, but she was still too skittish to do something that bold in public.

Once the band members were seated at a long table near the back of the store, security opened the entry door and allowed ten people inside. Toni recorded one of them being patted down and having a metal detector run over his body. She'd wait until he finished talking to the band before she asked him to sign a release form. She decided to stick with this guy through his entire meeting. He was probably in his midthirties and was tattooed from head to toe. That didn't mean he didn't squeal like a schoolgirl when he got to shake Dare Mills's hand.

"You are a god, dude! A rock god," he professed.

"Nah. A disciple at best," Dare joked.

The tattooed man held his forearm out to Dare. "Sign right there under the band logo. I'm having it fucking inked there permanently."

While Dare carefully signed his name with a permanent marker under the gargoyle that loomed over the band's name, the man started telling him about all the Exodus End concerts he'd been to. "I saw you in Hamburg, Germany, a couple of years ago. There were a hundred thousand people there. They never have concerts that big in the U.S."

"I remember that show," Logan said. "It rained buckets. Everyone was drenched and muddy. Max got shocked by his microphone."

"He did?" the guy said, eyes wide. "I never knew that."

"Yeah, just a little jolt," Logan said, glancing at Max, who was too busy interacting with a female fan to know he was the topic of their conversation. "But the way he talks about it . . ."

"Dude!" the fan said to Logan, apparently just realizing who he was speaking to. "Duuuuuude! Will you sign my arm too? I'll get all your names tattooed on there. It will be fucking awesome."

He bellowed *awesome* like a demon-possessed death-metal singer. This guy was a riot. Toni simply had to interview him for the fan section of the book. She hoped he'd agree to answer a few questions.

Logan signed his name on the man's forearm and then turned his attention to the giggling young woman holding a life-sized poster of him.

"Will you sign this for me?" Giggle. "I'm going to be at the concert tonight." Giggle. "If you wanna hook up with me backstage, I'll rock your world." Giggle giggle.

Toni had no idea what Logan would have said if she hadn't been standing right there, but she was relieved when he said, "There's no after-party tonight, doll. We have to get on the road again as soon as the show ends."

"What if I follow the bus to your next show? Will there be an after-party there?"

Logan scratched his head. "I think our next party is in Salt Lake."

Giggle. "I'd follow you anywhere."

Toni scowled. She wondered if she had any chance at keeping this man's interest. Did she want to even try? He lifted his sexy eyes to meet her gaze and smiled suggestively. Her mismatched socks melted in her loafers. Oh yeah, she definitely wanted to try.

Through three hours of autographs and hugs, squeals and *duuuudes,* all the members of the band kept their cool and gave each fan a bit of personalized attention. When Butch announced it was time to go, there was a roar of outrage outside the store. People were still waiting, but the band had to get to the stadium to assist with sound check. Toni wondered how they had the energy for music with all this other stuff clogging up their schedules. Logan stretched his arms over his head, giving Toni a delicious view of his belly. She wondered if he'd like her to lick those abs of his.

Logan caught her drooling over his bare skin and offered her a little wink. Heat flooded her face, and she decided now was a good time to interview the record store employees. She needed to get her mind off Logan's fascinating body and back on the job she was there to do.

All the store clerks raved about the band. The co-owner, who happened to be the owner's wife, was particularly eager to share her enthusiasm.

"We usually only get unknown bands in here. Maybe twenty

people show up to their signings—usually the band members' moms and girlfriends. This is beyond awesome. I love how an act as huge as Exodus End is willing to take time for little record stores like us."

"It's because you have the best water," Steve said, tilting his nearly empty glass in her direction in an informal toast. He downed the rest of his water in one gulp and then signed the bass drum skin that some wanna-be drummer had just slid onto the table in front of him.

"You, dude, are the god of drummers," his fan proclaimed. "No one tears up a set of skins like Steve motherfucking Aimes."

Interesting middle name. Toni wondered if the guys ever tired of fans calling them gods. If she had a dollar for every time she'd heard them called gods today, she could retire to the Caribbean and spend her days on the beach sipping mai tais.

"We really need to leave, guys," Butch said, obsessively checking his watch now.

"Then we're taking the long walk around the building," Max said.

"Absolutely not!" Butch said.

Toni wasn't sure what was meant by "the long walk," but she followed the band as they stood, thanked the record store owners—smiling for pictures with them that were sure to grace the store's walls in gilded frames before nightfall—and then headed out the front doors, where the waiting crowd was still milling.

"We have another engagement," Max yelled over the screaming crowd. "We have to do the rest of this like sluts."

Steve tilted his head, his brow crinkled. "Fast and easy?"

"Exactly."

And thus began the assembly-line signing. The band started at one end of the crowd and signed anything shoved in their face— music scores, guitars, CDs, posters, boobs, T-shirts—if it had a surface, it got a signature. There wasn't time for much personal interaction, but none of the band members seemed to mind all the touchy-feely going on. Toni would have taken a swim in a vat of hand sanitizer after being grabbed by that many strangers.

The band reached the end of the line, lifted hands of farewell to the enthusiastic crowd, and dove into the limo like a synchronized swim team. Toni scrambled in after them, followed by Butch. The rest of their security team got into a minivan and they all headed off to sound check.

When they arrived, crew members were putting the final touches on the stage assembly. So much was happening all at once that Toni didn't know where to start with her data gathering, so she mostly gawked.

"Close your mouth or you'll attract flies," Steve said.

Her jaws snapped shut, and she shoved him.

"Where did Logan go?" Steve asked. "Didn't get to see much of him yesterday. I have to tell him about the twins I meet at the bar Monday night."

"*Female* twins?" She was teasing, but Steve scowled.

"Yes, female twins. I thought I made it clear that I'm one hundred percent heterosexual."

"I didn't mean to insinuate . . ." She cut off her apology and slapped him on the arm. "Don't be so sensitive. I was just joking."

"Oh." His gorgeous face lit up with a smile. "Good one, Toni." He returned her slap on the arm.

"What time do they start setting up the stage?" Toni asked. It was an amazing work of engineering. Assembling the hydraulics must take hours. Disassembling must take just as long. And then they had to load it, drive it to the next destination, and assemble it again. Toni suspected the road crew needed those days off even more than the band did.

"Hell if I care," Steve said. "Why don't you talk to Colby? She's the head engineer."

Toni's eyes widened. "You have engineers?" She wondered just how many hands it took to put this tour together.

"I wouldn't step onto that moving drum platform without them. So where's Logan?"

"I don't know. He said something about going to the dressing room."

"Thanks."

He turned to go, but Toni called after him. "When you find him, give him a kiss for me."

Steve stopped in his tracks and turned to scowl at her. It must have occurred to him that she was teasing again as a grin soon replaced his frown. "With extra tongue," he promised and strode toward the backstage area.

Toni went off in search of Colby the engineer. After asking around, she was directed under the partially assembled stage. She located the woman cussing up a storm under Logan's platform.

"These things aren't designed to carry that much extra

weight." *Bang! Bang! Bang!* A hammer ricocheted off a metal bar. "Next time one of them wants to bring a guest up on their goddamned platform, they'd better fucking ask me first." *Bang! Bang! Bang!* Colby shifted the hammer to her other hand and wiped the first hand on her grease-smeared coveralls. "Fucking thing!" *Bang!*

Toni cringed, realizing she was the extra weight the engineer was cursing about. Toni started to back away. She probably shouldn't bother the woman. Especially when she was busy repairing Logan's hydraulic lift.

"Did you need something?" Colby asked, apparently catching Toni's movement when she attempted to slink off.

"You're busy. I don't want to bother you."

"Bother away." *Bang!*

"Um, well, I'm writing an interactive biography on the band."

"So you're the one who bent the support bar." *Bang! Bang!*

Toni placed a hand on her belly. "I have been meaning to go on a diet."

Colby laughed. "It's already too late for that." *Bang!* Something snapped into place. "Got it!" She slid out from under the platform and wiped her face on her sleeve.

Toni gaped at her. Not only was the band's head stage engineer a woman, but she was ancient. Perhaps if Colby didn't curse like a drunken rock star, Toni wouldn't have been so stunned to find herself face to face with a woman old enough to be her grandmother.

"So you're writing about the band *and* . . . ?" Colby twirled one hand at Toni to encourage her to get on with it.

"And I want to include a chapter on stage setup."

"Why?"

"Because it's interesting and not many people get to see all the work that goes into the show before it even starts."

"Colby, are you ready to test it?" someone called under the stage.

"Give it a go!" she shouted. To Toni she asked, "So what do you want from me?"

"When you're not busy, I'd like to ask you some questions and record some footage of the stage being erected and torn down. Maybe do a time-lapse video." Toni nibbled on her lip, trying to come up with something that hadn't been done a thousand times before. "Maybe one of the crew could wear a head camera as he goes about his work. That would pick up some really neat footage."

Colby tilted her head and assessed her for a moment before shrugging. "Okay, I'll talk to the crew and see if any of them are willing to be your guinea pig, and then I'll let you know which day would work best for filming. They're going to want to put on their makeup."

Toni smiled. That had been easier than she'd anticipated. "Great!"

Metal groaned as Logan's lift shuddered and rose several inches. "No good!" Colby yelled, and the grinding sound stopped. "Stupid fucking thing."

"I won't take any more of your time," Toni said. "I hope you get the lift fixed." Mostly because the man she loved had to ride that thing to the stage later that night.

"Oh, I'll get it fixed." Colby dropped down to slide under the metal platform again. *Bang! Bang! Bang!*

Toni emerged from beneath the stage and blinked in the sudden bright light. Crew members were testing the functioning platforms by riding them up and lowering them back down. Or maybe they were just goofing off since they seemed to be having a lot of fun taking turns launching each other onto the stage.

"There you are," Logan said.

"Did Steve find you?"

"To brag about banging a pair of twins?" He grinned and nodded. "Yeah, he found me. What were you doing under the stage?"

"Talking to Colby about capturing footage of the crew at work."

Logan nodded toward the stage, where one crew member had just catapulted off Dare's lift with a loud *yeehaw*! "Are you sure that's work?"

"Just because work is fun doesn't mean you're doing it wrong," she repeated what he'd told her a few days before.

He laughed and wrapped an arm around her shoulders. "We're getting ready to do one of Mad Dog's famous sound checks. I thought you might want to get some work done and film it."

"*Famous* sound checks?" She winked at him. "They can't be too famous. I've never heard of them."

"They're legendary among soundboard operators. And they're also fun."

A legendary, fun sound check? Now this she had to see.

Toni immediately understood why Mad Dog had been given his nickname. With impressive jowls, small dark eyes, underbite and upturned nose, he looked like a bulldog. But not a *mad* dog—either angry *or* insane. He was incredibly nice to her as she stuck a camera in his face and asked how he'd met the band. But Toni supposed the nickname Friendly Dog wouldn't have given the desired impression.

"Can I try first this time?" asked a cute blonde with lavender streaks in her hair.

"I don't see why not," Mad Dog said.

"How many soundboard operators does Exodus End have?" Toni asked.

"I'm FOH." Mad Dog patted her hand and leaned close. "That stands for front of house," he said quietly. "And Trevor is our monitor engineer. He's up by the stage."

Toni turned to the other two people in the barrier fence situated in the center of the arena. In addition to the blonde, there was a young man in a wheelchair. "So you two are?"

"Sorry," the blonde said. "I should have introduced myself. I'm Rebekah Sticks, co-FOH for Sinners, and this is my big brother, Dave, who sometimes lets me touch his soundboard."

"I'm also FOH for Sinners," Dave said as he shook Toni's hand.

"Is it usual to have two FOH engineers?" Toni asked.

"Nope," Dave said, "but her husband's with the band, so they won't let me fire her."

Rebekah slapped her brother on the shoulder, and he winced.

Mad Dog spoke into his microphone, and his voice was projected through the arena. "Sound check one."

No less than fifteen men and a few women took the stage, each carrying a different electric guitar or bass. Toni spotted the familiar faces of the Exodus End guitarists, along with several Sinners' band members and half a dozen people she didn't recognize. Several loud *blangs* and *pings* blared from the speakers as the musicians arranged themselves on the stage. Some faced forward, but most formed mixed groups so they could chat with each other.

"What's going on?" Toni asked.

"Mad Dog likes to show off," Dave said.

"Hey," Mad Dog said, "when you've done eighteen billion

sound checks in your life, you have to do something to keep it entertaining."

"I'm going to get it this time," Rebekah said. She put on a set of headphones, flexed her fingers, and held them hovering over her soundboard sliders, buttons and switches as if she was about to play a rousing game of Whac-a-Mole.

Mad Dog's voice came over the sound system again. "Ex-End will play 'Bite.' Sinners will play 'Twisted.' The rest of you just make some noise."

"Twisted," Rebekah whispered under her breath. "Focus. Focus."

"And a one and a two and a three," Mad Dog said.

Everyone onstage started playing at the same time. Toni cringed at the wailing, screeching cacophony blaring from the speakers. Face screwed up in concentration, fingers trembling, Rebekah began to move sliders on the giant soundboard in front of her. The raucous sounds coming from the speakers began to alter. The obnoxious blanging noises disappeared first, and then several blended melodies increased in volume. Rebekah raised one slider, cringed, and then shoved it back down before raising the one next to it. A few more adjustments, and Toni was astonished to hear the unmistakable music of "Twisted" blaring from the speakers. The drum track was missing and there were no vocals, but rhythm, bass, and lead guitar were all clear as day. Rebekah did a little dance of victory. Toni looked up to the stage and found everyone onstage was still playing. Sinners' FOH had picked out the threads of her musicians based on sound alone.

Dave high-fived his sister. Toni would have high-fived her as well, but she was trying to hold her camera steady while she gawked at Rebekah in awe.

"Cut," Mad Dog said. "Not bad. I heard only one mistake that time."

He'd heard it?

Rebekah sighed. "Can't get anything past this one," she said as she pushed all the sliders to the top of the board.

"Do we have the mics ready?" Mad Dog said.

"Mic check."

"Mic check."

Mic check, mic check, mic check was repeated in different voices from various microphones all feeding into the same sound system.

"Vocalists take the stage," Mad Dog said. "And Steve, get

under there and give us a beat."

The drum kit was already assembled under the stage.

"It's hard because you don't know which piece of equipment is attached to each set of sliders," Rebekah said. "Mad Dog knows his soundboard so well, he can pick up on slight variations between the channels."

"You can do it too," Dave said.

"I'm getting there," Rebekah said, blowing out a long breath. She dropped down beside Toni on a folding chair, and they both watched Mad Dog do his thing.

This time when Mad Dog instructed everyone to begin, there were various voices and drums added to the mix. There was no need to pick out the drum track—as there was only one—but with a few flicks of the FOH's wrist, the sound of the drums came alive. After a couple dozen more motions from Mad Dog, Toni found herself listening to an Exodus End song. She could hear a bit of the other singers onstage—their voices carried through the air—but every sound coming from the sound system was pure Exodus End.

"And that, my friends, is how you mix a live show old school," Mad Dog said.

"Show off," Rebekah said with a giggle, but she hopped out of her chair to kiss the man on the top of his shiny bald head.

The meet and greet that evening was a subdued occasion compared to the one in Oregon. There were no protestors picketing the venue, and the security team had no problem keeping a handle on things. Toni chatted with several fans, noting that whenever the fan happened to be male, Logan mysteriously appeared at her side.

As the food was brought in for their evening meal, Reagan got in line behind Toni. "I haven't gotten to talk to you all day," she said. "How did things go with Logan yesterday?"

Toni flushed remembering all the naughty things he'd done to her body in the hotel. She was definitely missing their alone time today and couldn't wait until their next day off.

"We had a great time," Toni said.

"He's treating you right."

Toni nodded. "He's the best."

"Are you still planning on riding up on my platform tonight? I have the cutest outfit you can wear."

Toni cringed. Not about the outfit, about the platform.

"About that . . . Apparently my fat ass broke Logan's platform last night. They were under the stage trying to fix it earlier."

"Fat ass? Where?" Reagan slid her hand over Toni's rump to flatten her skirt. "Please. If your ass is fat, mine is a vat of lard."

Reagan stuck her butt out to prove that hers was bigger than Toni's.

"Damn, woman," Trey said from behind them. "Can I get through one meal without you giving me a hard-on?"

Reagan giggled. "I hope not."

A pair of strong arms circled Toni's body from behind. Logan's hands cupped her breasts and lifted them. "So I heard your enormous tits broke my hydraulic lift last night."

"Now *that* I believe," Reagan said.

Toni flushed as everyone within hearing laughed at her expense. She shoved Logan's hands from her boobs and turned sideways to discourage him from grabbing them in public.

Logan kissed her briefly. "Thanks for saving my spot."

"Back of the line, Schmidt!" Steve called from several feet behind them.

Toni grabbed Logan's arm to make sure he stayed beside her. She felt they hadn't spent any time together all day and if standing in the chow line was their best opportunity to see each other for a few minutes, so be it.

They did get to sit together through dinner, but Dare chatted with Trey, which meant Reagan talked Toni's ear off about customers she'd had when she worked as a barista, and Steve told Logan—yet again—about his latest adventure with some twins and a couple of other women named Candice and Tonya. Steve's mantra of "You missed out, dude!" was starting to play on Toni's last nerve. Even though she didn't talk to Logan much through their meal, his knee was pressed against hers beneath the table and he had a wonderful habit of touching her bare wrist whenever their hands weren't otherwise unoccupied. Strange how after all the intense sexual encounters they'd shared the days before, those little touches meant so much to her.

She was almost finished with her dinner when a strange rumbling seeped through the walls and into her bones. She cocked her head to one side, listening. "What *is* that? An earthquake?"

"The first opening band is starting the show," Logan said.

The rumble was greeted by enthusiastic cheers and screams, all muffled by the thick concrete walls of the corridor. "Oh!" she said. "Sinners?" No, that couldn't be since their rhythm guitarist was still at the table deep in conversation with his brother.

"Sinners is on third tonight. That would be Riott Actt."

She knew of them. She'd listened to some of their music when she'd been researching Exodus End and found out that they'd be one of the two opening bands on this tour. She'd also done research on Hell's Crypt, but that band hadn't lasted long in the lineup.

"Do you ever watch the opening bands?" she asked.

"All the time," he said with a smile. "I might be a rock star, but I'm still a metal fan. Do you wanna watch from backstage? It's a perk of the rock star gig; we always have a backstage pass."

She nodded eagerly. This was a neat little glimpse into Logan the metal fan. Logan the man. It was just the kind of thing she wanted to include in their book, the kind of detail that the fans wanted to see—a peek into Logan's reality. Toni reached into her pocket to set her camera on record. She'd captured a ton of footage that day, so she hoped there was enough memory left to record Logan enjoying Riott Actt. It certainly sounded like the audience in the stadium loved the band's set. She was sure the entire state of Montana was vibrating from the combined sounds of the band and the audience. Could that much noise trigger an actual earthquake? She wouldn't doubt it.

Making their excuses and leaving the remnants of their dinner behind, Logan took Toni's hand and led her through the backstage area. They passed many security guards, but no one stopped them or questioned them. They recognized Logan, and it was clear that she was with him. Walking with Logan was much different from her experiences of trying to make her way through the backstage area on her own, where she was stopped so frequently, she'd started showing her press pass to anyone with eyes.

Logan pushed open a set of swinging doors, and Toni was assaulted by sound. She winced. Logan squeezed her hand and led her around the side of the stage to a set of steps. He didn't even hesitate climbing them to stand in the wings and as he still had Toni's now sweaty hand trapped firmly in his, she had no choice but to follow him. The band was finishing up their first song. Their lead singer jumped from a riser to the stage on the final note, punctuating the sound with the thrust of his arm and the microphone in his fist.

Logan cheered with the rest of the crowd, but Toni was too

busy staring at him to give the band onstage its due. Logan had come alive. Switched on in a way she hadn't seen before. She'd watched plenty of footage of him onstage and witnessed secondhand what an outstanding performer he was, but being here with him in the flesh gave her an entirely new insight that no video could convey. So how could she show this side of him in the book? Could she capture the life in him, the vibrancy? She wasn't sure it was possible. The energy coming off him was almost tangible. His love for music, that was what she was seeing. No, what she was feeling. But how did she show the world how remarkable it was? How remarkable *he* was?

Matt Chesterfield was onstage chatting with the crowd in a heavy British accent. Toni tore her gaze from Logan to look at the vocalist.

"We're amped to have the opportunity to play for the amazing metal fans in the Billings area. How many of you came to the show just to see us tonight?"

There was a mild spattering of applause, mostly from a small sector in the pit near the front of the stage. The lead guitarist leaned toward his microphone and said, "Well, that's a bit disappointing. I don't think we've rocked their faces off enough yet."

Logan chuckled. "God, I remember being an opening act for a bigger band. You feel so fucking privileged to be allowed on the stage, to share the excitement of a famous band's fans, but you feel like such a douche bag for pretending anyone gives a shit that you're there."

Toni couldn't imagine Exodus End ever being in a position of smallness. It seemed to her that they'd always been marked for great things.

"Who's here to see Twisted Element?" the singer asked about the other opening band, which would play a set after theirs was over.

A bit more applause and cheers sputtered from the crowd.

"Steve got Twisted Element to join the tour. He's really good friends with their drummer," Logan told Toni.

Zach Mercer. She already knew about his friendship with Steve. "Is it common for members of different bands to be good friends?"

He gave her an odd look. "Well, yeah. We're all in this together, aren't we?"

"Aren't they your competition?"

He shook his head. "Our brothers. If we're going to keep rock alive, we have to work together, not against each other."

She smiled. That was a nice way of thinking about the music business. She wondered if the record label executives shared that point of view.

"Okay, I think I see some Sinners fans in the audience," Chesterfield said, shielding his eyes with one hand against his forehead as he scanned the crowd.

"Maybe a few," the lead guitarist's words were mostly drowned out by the screaming, stomping, whistling, and clapping going on in the stadium.

A chant of "Sinners, Sinners, Sinners" began to rise up through the ranks.

"Who else is playing tonight?" the vocalist asked. "I forget."

The audience erupted into chaos as they very loudly informed the world that Exodus End was playing.

The vocalist pointed to his ear. "What was that? Did you say Exodus End is playing here tonight?"

Toni had to cover her ears due to the volume of the crowd. When the roar died down a bit, she lowered her hands and fixated on the vocalist, hanging on his every word.

"Get the fuck out. Exodus End is going to be on *this* stage in less than two hours?" He jabbed a pointed finger toward the stage beneath his boots. "Are you fucking kidding me?"

Logan chuckled. "He's really getting them pumped up," he yelled over the noise of the cheering crowd. "I hope we live up to their expectations."

Toni glanced at him, beaming an exuberant smile in his direction. Of course they would live up to the fans' expectations; they'd exceed them. She didn't doubt it for a second. She wondered if they were ever swamped with self-doubt the way she was. Not likely.

Riott Actt finally began their second song and Toni tried to keep track of all that was occurring onstage. The flurry of activity was overwhelming. She didn't know whether to watch the pacing vocalist, the wailing guitarists, or the rhythmic stylings of the drummer and the bassist. She glanced at Logan for direction and tried mimicking his devil-horn-shaking, head-banging, body-thrashing celebration of the music, but ended up feeling like an awkward fool.

"I have got to get in on that circle pit," Logan said unexpectedly. He pecked her on the cheek and then vaulted himself over the stairs to the floor before hurdling the railing and several members of the audience and disappearing into the crowd. It took Toni at least half the song to comprehend what he'd done. She finally found the mental capacity to close her mouth. She stretched up on tiptoe and craned her neck, trying to see down into the audience and the writhing chaos occurring in a round area that at first appeared empty, but was actually the center of activity. Bodies bounced off each other around the periphery—shoving, stumbling, thudding, dancing, or maybe they were fighting. Hell, she couldn't tell. It looked just plain violent from her vantage. She caught sight of a blue T-shirt, a tangle of golden wavy hair, and hard-muscled arms covered with sleeves of familiar gray-shaded tattoos. When Logan slammed chest first into a member of the audience, she cringed and hid her eyes behind both hands. What was he thinking? What if he got hurt and found himself unable to perform? How could he want to be involved in something that had to be painful?

Even though she personally didn't want anything to do with the circle pit, Toni realized she should be getting pictures of Logan's interaction with the crowd for the book. She sidled along the edge of the stage, hoping to stay out of sight as she cautiously made her way to the front left corner of the high platform. She looked through her camera, trying to capture Logan as one of the crowd, but it was all a hopeless blur. She couldn't tell who was who. She noticed a riser at the very front of the stage but off to the far side and bathed in darkness. Riott Actt wasn't using that part of the stage at all. Maybe she could see better from there. She'd be a bit higher up, but farther from the mosh pit. But that was what a zoom lens was for. To get the best shot, she needed a high vantage point, not a close one.

Once she was standing on the platform, she zoomed in on the mass of writhing bodies below. Scanning the crowd, she eventually focused on the center of the mosh pit and took dozens of shots in rapid succession. She hoped she captured something usable. Watching through the viewfinder, she cringed each time someone got shoved a bit too hard, hit a few too many times. She didn't see the appeal of this ritual in the slightest. But then she didn't have mass quantities of testosterone pulsing through her veins.

"Hey," she heard someone yell from down below. "You can't

be up there."

She wasn't sure if the security guard was talking to her or not. Before she could figure that out, something hard and solid hit her in the stomach—an arm, she realized as the air wooshed out of her lungs—and then she was falling. Her arms pinwheeled before her, her hands trying to catch hold of something—anything—but all her desperately clawing fingers found was empty air.

CHAPTER 25

LOGAN WAS HAVING the time of his life releasing pent-up energy until the music stopped abruptly. The men in the mosh pit continued bounding off each other for several seconds before stopping to face the stage in confusion. Logan stared up at the band with the rest of the audience, wondering what had drawn their fun to a sudden halt. When he saw a familiar brown boot poking out from behind a riser on the stage and several concerned faces peering down at the figure attached to that boot, his heart skipped a beat.

"Toni!" he yelled, shoving his way through the crowd toward the stage.

He scarcely heard the whispers of his name in his wake. "Logan Schmidt. Isn't that Logan Schmidt? That *is* Logan." The whispers became yells, and then the crowd rushed in on him, surrounding him, trapping him in a press of bodies and enthusiasm. He was oblivious to the dozens of hands on him as he fought his way forward inch by inch. He focused on the neon yellow shirt of one of his security team and pushed and shoved his way through the crowd until he finally reached the metal barrier fence. The entire pit audience tried to follow him over the barricade; he'd apologize to the security crew later. Now he had to find out what had happened to Toni. Why was she lying on the floor? He'd thought she'd be safe on the stage—far safer than she'd have been in a mosh pit—but apparently he'd thought wrong.

He galloped up the steps and weaseled his way through the group of onlookers surrounding Toni on the stage. He breathed a sigh of relief to find her sitting up and smacking at a medic who was trying to shove an oxygen mask over her face. "I said . . . I'm fine. I . . . I don't . . . need . . . oxygen," she said between wheezing gasps for air.

"Did you have the wind knocked out of you or not?" the medic asked, following her twisting face with the mask in one hand and the stretchy strap in the other as he tried to affix it to his target.

"Yeah, but . . . I'll find . . . my wind . . . myself. Thanks."

"So you're refusing treatment?"

"Yes!"

The paramedic backed off, shaking his head at her stubbornness.

Logan squatted next to Toni and brushed her hair behind her ear. "What happened?" he asked.

"Where . . . are . . . my glasses?" she wheezed, shoving his hand aside and struggling to her feet.

She was still gasping, but apparently had no intention of waiting until she caught her breath before causing an additional scene.

"And my camera? If it's . . . broken, I swear I'll . . . I swear I'll . . . " Her bottom lip quivered as she glanced from one person to the next as if trying to figure out who they were. Maybe she had a concussion or something.

"Did you hit your head?" he asked.

"No!"

Logan wrapped an arm around her shoulders and slowly urged her from the stage. "Find her glasses and her camera," he said to a stagehand, who jumped at the opportunity to do his bidding.

"Well, that was a bit of excitement," the lead singer of Riott Actt was saying to the crowd. "But the show must go on."

Logan helped Toni down the stage steps. She was trembling so badly, she could scarcely stay on her feet. He would have scooped her into his arms and carried her, but somehow he figured that would upset her even more. He led her into a corridor—where it was a bit quieter—found an empty equipment case and promptly forced her to sit on it. Once seated, she slumped forward, elbows resting on her knees as she sucked in deep ragged breaths. He knew she was seconds from a monumental meltdown, and he was okay with that, but he didn't think *she'd* be okay with it. He squatted before her and tilted his head into her line of vision.

"Now tell me what happened," he said. "Are you hurt?"

"I've been better," she snapped and then she started gasping again. "I can't breathe . . . I need . . . inhaler."

"Why didn't you let that medic help you?"

"Shut . . . shut . . . shut," she said between gasps. "Shut up. Y-you."

Logan would have smiled at how cute she looked trying to be mad and catch her breath at the same time, but he was too concerned for her well-being to dwell on her appearance for more than a second. He waved down the nearest onlooker. "Go see if the medic has a rescue inhaler, but whatever you do, don't tell Toni she needs help."

Toni glared at him for a brief instant before doubling over and wheezing in misery.

Logan had no idea what to do for her, so he just crouched at her feet, patting her knee. Toni glared at the man who returned with a tank of oxygen hooked to a face mask.

"I said no"—wheeze—"oxygen."

"How about a nebulizer with albuterol?" the medic said. He seemed to be used to working with difficult patients.

She nodded and closed her eyes while the medic slipped the clear plastic mask over her nose and mouth. She sucked in a deep breath. And another. Tears leaked from beneath her tightly squeezed eyelids. Logan touched her hair, his heart twisting with a mixture of anxiety and anguish. Her wheezing lessened slightly, and she took another deep inhale, finally catching her breath. He wasn't sure what she was so upset about. Perhaps she was embarrassed. But he sensed there was something deeper going on in her head.

"Better?" he asked when her breathing normalized.

She opened her eyes and nodded. She then tilted her head back, panting at the ceiling as she fought the tears pooling in her eyes.

She pulled the oxygen mask off her face and tossed it at the paramedic.

"Thank you for helping her," Logan said. "I'm not sure why she's being so cranky. She's usually really nice."

"Leave me alone," she said.

"I could start an IV. Give her some meds to help her

breathing," the concerned paramedic offered.

"Go away!" Toni yelled. "I can breathe just fine now. Having the wind knocked out of me triggered an asthma attack, is all. I haven't had an asthma attack in over ten years."

Feeling completely useless, Logan shrugged at the paramedic. If she really needed the meds, he'd hold her down if necessary. "Will she be okay without the additional medication?"

"She should be." The young man grinned. "She seems to have her wits about her."

Logan didn't fully agree with the man's assessment. Her behavior was irrational. At least for her. Still, he couldn't call her out on refusing medical treatment. He'd once walked around for three weeks on a broken foot because he was sure he was fine after a rather tame wipeout on his dirt bike.

He sat beside her on the equipment case and took her hand. She squeezed with surprising strength, but refused to look at him as she used a soppy tissue to blot her eyes and nose.

"Toni? Tell me what's wrong."

She shook her head.

"Toni," he said cajolingly.

"I don't . . . I don't belong here," she said.

Logan laughed. That was all it was? Seriously? She felt out of place? "You're at a metal concert. The only requirement for fitting in with a bunch of metal heads is to not fit in."

She wiped at her tears with the heels of both hands. "Then I must be the most metal metal-head who ever lived."

"You did just do a stage dive onto a stage. We usually aim for the crowd. But hey, keep the audience on its toes, I always say. Do the unexpected. I don't know why I've never thought to get the wind knocked out of me onstage. Very metal."

She rolled her eyes at him and then produced a breathy laugh. "That really hurt."

"Your head or your pride?" He stroked her hair again, wanting to kiss her so badly he was practically salivating.

"My rear end."

"Oh," he said.

She rubbed a hand over her ass and winced. "I think I'm going to have a huge bruise."

"Well, there's only one thing to do in a situation like this," Logan said.

She frowned at him. "What's that?"

"Let me take a look."

"You just want to see my butt," she said wisely.

"Your butt?" he asked. "Oh no, I want to take a closer look at dat *fine* ass."

Her eyes widened at his use of ghetto speak. "You're weird."

He tapped her nose with his index finger. "I prefer to call it *obsessed*." He rose to stand before her, his best bored supermodel look in place. "Obsession by Logan Schmidt," he said, framing her face with his splayed hands. "Obsession," he repeated, like the distant echo heard in an arty commercial, at the same time framing her boobs with his hands. "Obsession." He framed her ass. "Obsession." He framed her crotch. "Obsession by Logan Schmidt."

She got caught in a fit of giggles that made her wheeze again. He immediately dropped his hands. He wasn't sure if the paramedic would survive another attempt to put a breathing mask over Toni's face.

"Are you always this silly?" she asked.

"I think the word you're looking for is *sexy*. And yes, *I'm sexy and you know it*," he sang, doing a dance that was part ride the pony, part running man, part stripper lap dance until Toni was laughing so hard he feared she'd stop breathing altogether.

"Stop, please," she gasped as he shook his ass for her and turned to grab her by the back of the head so he could dry hump her face stripper style. "I'm dying."

He loved to make people laugh—didn't care if it was at his own expense—and in all his years, he'd never made a woman laugh so hard she might actually die laughing. He took it as another sign that she was his perfect woman.

"Literally dying," she wheezed.

He stopped in midmotion and sat on the equipment case beside her to catch his breath and allow her to catch hers again. "So," he said, "how's your ass?"

She flushed. "Huh?"

"Does it still hurt?"

She shook her head. "No, but my stomach hurts from laughing so hard."

"It's a miracle," he said throwing up his hands like a TV evangelist. "You've been healed by the power of my sexy."

She giggled. "If that's what you want to call it. Aren't you embarrassed? People were staring at you."

"Fuck them. No one invited them to my party."

She opened her mouth, but just then the stagehand returned with Toni's camera in one hand and a wide-angle lens in the other. She groaned and accepted the two pieces, immediately trying to fit them together.

"Is it broken?" Logan asked.

"It's seen better days," she said as she forced the lens to turn in place and held the camera up to her eye. She groaned again. "The optics are out of alignment."

"Can it be fixed?"

"I don't think so. At least not by me." She squinted up at the stagehand. "Did you find my glasses by any chance?"

"She can't see a thing without her glasses," Logan said. That might explain why she'd been tickled rather than impressed by his sexy.

"No," the stagehand said, "and I looked everywhere. That's what took me so long. I found the camera right away, but no glasses. Sorry."

Toni cringed. "I really *can't* see a thing without my glasses."

"I'll go look," Logan said.

The stagehand insisted on helping him, so they left Toni alone and went back into the noisy arena to look for her glasses. Poor woman was having a rough day. He would be sure to make her feel extra nice later when they were alone. Well, as alone as they could be while riding on a tour bus with five or six other dudes. Every time he'd tried to get close to her today, either she was busy or someone was commandeering his attention. Was it strange that he'd missed her? He was certain it was.

Logan hunted the stage wing for any sign of Toni's glasses. The main problem was that it was dark and the flashes of light from the performance onstage kept momentarily blinding him. He was seeing so many spots, it was a wonder he ever found the elusive eyewear. But he did find them. With his foot. *Crunch!* He cringed as he lifted his shoe and spotted the familiar glasses. The lenses were intact, but the frame had been snapped in two at the center of the nosepiece.

"Oh no," he said and lifted the separate pieces up to his eyes. Maybe she wouldn't notice.

He waved off his useless assistant and returned to the corridor where he'd left Toni. Broken camera in her lap, she was staring down at it, her hand clenched in the thick material of her skirt and avoiding the curious gazes of anyone who glanced her way. He sat beside her and bumped her arm with his.

She looked up from her demolished camera and smiled hopefully at him. "Did you find them?"

He cringed and handed her the broken pair of glasses.

"What happened?" she said as she took them from his hand and tried fitting the two pieces together, as if the frame would meld back together if she lined it up just right.

"There was this icicle and it fell off the roof and it, and it, hit me in the eye. And it, broke your glasses." He made fake crying noises, not sure if she was familiar with the movie he was quasi-quoting.

"You'll shoot your eye out, kid," she said miserably.

Yep, she was familiar with the movie.

He rubbed her back, liking her a little more with each interaction they shared. "Do you have another pair?"

She nodded. "At home."

"I'm sure we'll have time to get you a new pair on our off day," he said, "until then, we'll probably just have to glue them together."

"I hope it holds," she said. "I can't—"

"See a thing without my glasses," he finished for her.

Logan grabbed a passerby and sent him on a mission for superglue.

"You never explained what happened to make you fall," Logan said. All he knew was that she'd been lying on the stage with the wind knocked out of her. He had no idea how she'd gotten that way.

"I was trying to get a good shot of you down in the crowd, so I climbed up on a riser and some security guard tackled me to the ground."

Fists clenched, Logan jumped to his feet. "Someone fucking *tackled* you?"

She nodded. "I should have gotten permission to climb up there. I'm sure they thought I was a deranged lunatic and a danger to the band."

"Tell me who did it. After I beat the shit out of him, I'll make sure he's fired."

Toni grabbed Logan's wrist and pulled him toward the equipment case, encouraging him to sit beside her again.

"Don't be ridiculous," she said. "He was only doing his job."

"And you were only doing yours," Logan pointed out. He was still as far from calm as he could be. No one put his hands on Toni.

"Lesson learned," she said. "I won't be doing that again."

Logan wasn't sure how he was going to keep her safe so she could have the run of the place while she collected footage for her book, but he would find a way.

The glue retriever returned with a roll of white tape. "No one had any superglue. Will this work?"

Toni groaned and shook her head. "Seriously? Please tell me you're joking."

"Why would I be joking?" The guy handed her the roll of white tape and hurried away.

"Tape won't work?"

She sighed and had Logan hold the pieces of her glasses together while she wrapped tape around the nosepiece.

When she was finished, she put her glasses on and turned to him. "Revenge of the nerds. Heh heh heh," she said, doing an excellent impression of Lewis from the movie.

He burst out laughing and grabbed her in a tight hug. "God, I love you," he bellowed, and then he went still when he realized what he'd said. "I mean as a friend," he quickly amended, though he knew *friend* didn't measure the depth of his feelings for her.

She pushed him away and stood. "I need to go to the bus. I have another camera in my bag. I'll run and get it before the show starts."

"I'll come with you," he said.

She had her back to him, so he couldn't see her expression, but she shook her head. "I'll go on my own. You should probably do your job and return to the meet and greet."

"It's over." And if he got Toni alone on the bus for a few minutes, maybe they'd have time to explore the more lustful feelings of their developing *friendship*.

"Please don't follow me," she said and hurried off.

He stared after her in puzzlement until she disappeared around a corner. Was she still upset? He was sure she had plenty to be upset about after being tackled to the stage by an idiot—and he would find out who had assaulted her. He might not punch the guy, but Logan would be sure the man was reprimanded or, if the douche bag wasn't apologetic enough for Logan's tastes, fired.

No one hurt someone he cared about and got away with it.

Sinners had already taken the stage when Logan's worry finally got the better of him and he went to check on Toni. It shouldn't take over an hour just to collect a camera from the bus. He found her in the lounge with her laptop open. Her nose was red, and her eyes glassy, but she didn't appear to have slipped into a concussion-induced coma.

"What are you doing?" he asked, entering the room and sitting beside her on the sofa. "I was worried."

"I'm okay." She didn't even take her eyes from her computer screen to look at him. "Really."

"You've been crying again." He nodded toward the pile of wadded tissues on the coffee table.

"I stopped."

"Will you tell me why?"

When she didn't respond, he closed the lid of her laptop on her hands.

"I'm trying to work," she said.

"Did I do something wrong?"

She pursed her lips together and shook her head. Alarmed by the tears suddenly flooding her eyes, Logan slid a hand along the top of her back, not sure if he should hug her or what.

"You're perfectly wonderful to me." She yanked a tissue out of the nearby box and dabbed at her eyes. "Sorry."

"Will you please tell me what's wrong? Are you in pain?"

"Yes and no," she said. "When that medic tried to force that oxygen mask over my face, I kept seeing my father the day he died. They tried everything to resuscitate him, but that oxygen mask didn't do him a bit of good. The paramedics didn't do him a bit of good. *I* didn't do him a bit of good."

"I didn't realize that's why you didn't want assistance."

"How could you?"

He stroked her hair from her face, and she lifted her head, eyes streaming. When she sucked in her lips to stifle a sob, he scooped her onto his lap and pressed her face into the crook of his neck. He couldn't stand to see the pain in her expression.

"Thinking about Dad made me really miss my sister. I just needed to hear her cheery voice, so I called home." She laughed hollowly. "That was a mistake."

Toni had told him about her little sister's heart condition and her weak immune system. Was that the real reason she was so upset. "Is your sister okay?"

"She's fine. I asked my mom if she could drop my spare set of glasses in the mail."

"Good idea."

"Not really. She decided she'd deliver them in person. She'll be at our hotel on Saturday."

The bottom dropped out of Logan's stomach. "She's coming to Denver?"

"And she's bringing my sister."

"Oh." Logan tried to pull his shit together before she caught on to his distress. "I look forward to meeting them." Sure, having to entertain uninvited guests would cut into the time they'd planned to fuck like maniacs, but he knew Toni's family meant a lot to her. And he really was curious about them. Even though he normally had a rule about meeting mothers.

"And worse, my editor's coming too." Toni's body trembled uncontrollably until he tightened his embrace and she snuggled closer.

"That bitch Susan?" Maybe he'd have the opportunity to tell her off in person.

Toni nodded. "You know she wants this job for herself," Toni said. "She doesn't think I'm capable of doing it properly. And as much goofing off as I've been doing thus far, I don't have much to show her to prove that I'm capable of producing professional results." Toni sat back on his knees and met his gaze. "Mom says if I can't demonstrate I'm making good progress on this assignment, Susan will take my place in Denver and I have to go home."

Like hell!

"You haven't even been working at it for a week," Logan said. "I'm sure you have tons of material for the book already."

"But it's not organized. At all. I've got notes on napkins. And release forms shoved into my messenger bag. Half of my photos are on the video card in my broken camera. My boobs are blocking the periphery of some of my backstage footage."

"And you have sex sounds on your interview recording."

She flushed and threw her hands in the air. "Exactly!"

"I'll help you organize it," he said. "We'll put together a presentation that will wow the socks off your mom. And Susan can go to hell."

"You'll help me?"

"Of course."

She beamed at him and wrapped him in an enthusiastic hug.

"Thank you!"

He wasn't sure why her happiness and thankfulness filled him with overwhelming joy. But he wasn't going to dwell on it, simply enjoy the sensation. Smiling down into her lovely face, he cupped the back of her head and claimed her lips in a deeply satisfying kiss.

When he pulled away, she blinked up at him. "Why are you helping me?" she asked, squinting her eyes at him suspiciously.

"Because I don't want you to leave." It was probably the most open and honest thing he'd ever said to her, and she rewarded him with a dazzling smile.

"Oh," she said. "I thought maybe you were going to use your generosity to coerce me into having anal sex."

He lifted his brows at her, wondering why he hadn't thought of that. "Would it have worked?"

"Maybe." She grinned. "But it's too late for that now. I know the truth. You want me to stay."

Of course he did. How could he not? She was unequivocally marvelous.

"Logan! Are you on the bus?" Butch called from up the corridor.

"Yeah!"

"Curtain call, buddy. I hope you've finished with her."

He hoped he never finished with her.

"We're just talking!" Toni called.

"Then hurry up," Butch yelled. "You're late."

"Are you coming to the show?" Logan asked as he helped her slide from his lap.

"I'd like to," she said, "but I need to try to salvage the data off my memory card."

"You can do that tomorrow."

"Please don't force me to go out in public with taped glasses."

She gazed up at him with imploring brown eyes, and he melted on the spot.

"You look cute." She always looked cute.

She gave him a look that called bullshit.

"Logan! What's taking you so long?" Butch bellowed.

"You'd better be at my next show," he said, backing out of the room.

"Find some superglue to fix these glasses, and I promise I won't miss it."

He smiled at her. She gave him so much and asked for so

little. Something bounced off the back of his head, and he turned to find Butch glaring at him from the aisle. "Get a move on. She isn't going anywhere."

Not if he could help it.

Logan raced out of the bus with Butch on his heels. "I need superglue," Logan said as they dashed toward the arena.

"By now, I know better than to ask you why."

Backstage, someone handed Logan his bass guitar and sound equipment, and then shoved him toward the access door beneath the stage. He hurried to his platform, finding his place just as Steve's drum kit began to rise. Logan rushed to put his instrument in place while a technician switched on his amplifier. His heart thudded with panic when he missed the first note of the song, but he caught up on the second chord and braced himself as the platform beneath him shuddered and began to lift him toward the stage. It moved even slower than usual, rising until it reached the enclosed area of his chute. The platform produced an earsplitting shriek and then stopped with a thud. Logan kept playing as the rest of the band entered the stage, and he wondered if his platform was ever going to start moving again. He was trapped in the chute, the stage several feet above his head and the open side of the chute that allowed him to get on his platform inaccessible from this height. He kept his eyes trained upward to the open space above him so that panicky feeling of being trapped in a small enclosure didn't get the better of him.

Well wasn't this just great?

He wondered if anyone had even noticed that he was stuck. He was just the bassist after all. Max's head appeared far above. He pointed down at Logan as he sang the chorus of "Ovation" and Logan played the bass line as though he weren't trapped in a hole.

Reagan checked on him next and finding that he wasn't dead, hopped away to keep her newfound fans entertained. The song ended, and Logan reached up to see if he could touch the edge of the stage above. It was much too far for him to climb out. Maybe if he wedged his back against the metal wall, he could press his feet against the opposite wall and inch his way out of this hell.

"What are you doing, Schmidt?" Max asked, peering down at him from the stage above.

"I'm stuck." Logan jumped and tried to get a hand on the edge of the stage to pull himself out of his pit, but he missed his mark by at least a foot. "A little help here, guys."

Max and Dare were too busy laughing to offer him a hand and Reagan did nothing but stand at the edge of his hole and shake her head at him.

Toni should have followed him onstage tonight after all. Surely she'd want to include this fiasco in her book.

May 6

Dear Journal,

Busy, busy day. We started with an album signing, and then everyone participated in a crazy sound check that was a lot of fun. I'm sure the stuff with Mad Dog and Rebekah is going to turn out awesome in the book. I interviewed a few fans backstage and got footage of Logan enjoying a mosh pit before I was tackled to the stage. I hurt my pride more than my ass, but unfortunately my glasses ended up broken. Somehow Logan found some superglue and fixed them for me. He's such a sweetie. Don't tell him I said that. Apparently he got stuck in his stage chute and they had to use a ladder to rescue him. Poor baby. He brushed it off as funny, but I'm sure it was scary.

So can you believe this? Mom is bringing Birdie and Susan to Denver in two days. Between now and then I have to get some really good, usable material about each of the band members and start organizing my data. I have a lot of work to do in a short amount of time, so I probably won't write much over the next few days.

Oh, Logan's done with his shower. Time for bed. Don't wait up.

Overwhelmed-but-determined,

Toni

May 7

Dear Journal,

I didn't get much sleep last night. And not because I was working. Logan surprised me with a sex pop quiz, and I had to demonstrate all the things he's taught me so far. By the time I was finished with him, he said I definitely earned my A. So I was a bit tired all day.

We're in Salt Lake City now. The band had a signing at a guitar store today. Sinners, Riott Actt, and Twisted Element were all there too. A lot of people brought their guitars to be signed by a favorite band member or sometimes the whole band or sometimes every musician present. Some fans forked out hundreds of dollars to buy guitars at the store to have signed. I didn't know each band member has licensed instruments on sale to the public. The guys designed the shapes and colors of the guitars themselves. More stuff for the book! The event was great fun, as usual. I really enjoyed watching Dare and Trey interact. They're so close. Almost as close as Birdie and I. I used to think that was common, but I'm starting to see the bond we share is truly special.

And I guess I'll get to see her in Denver day after tomorrow. I'm looking forward to seeing her, but not Mom so much. When she told me she was coming, I was so pissed that I—Well, I didn't really do anything. But next time I see her . . . Right. I probably won't do anything then either. Or maybe I will. I'm just not sure what yet. And poor Birdie. Mom knows she hates flying, so why is she subjecting her to it? I texted her and told her she didn't have to come, that I can email her sample pages of the book if she needs evidence that I'm working. She said it was too late, she'd already bought the tickets. And Susan is coming too. Ugh! I'm not sure if I'll be able to tolerate her abuse. I don't have to take her shit, right? Right. Still, I'd rather get her off my case in a nonconfrontational manner. She scares the piss out of me.

Logan's at the after-party right now. I watched him play live tonight. God, he's amazing. He was so sexy, I jumped his bones as soon as he came off the stage. I hoped he would skip the party and stay on the bus with me, but he wanted to go celebrate. I don't know where the man gets all his energy. I'm not upset that he goes partying with Steve and the rest of the guys after their shows, just baffled by how they manage to keep going. I suppose at some point I'll have to find the energy to attend another one of those things for the book. I didn't stay long enough at the first one to get the full experience.

Tomorrow we drive to Denver. The guys have agreed to write out the answers to all of Susan's questions. Except Logan. Logan said he wouldn't answer any of them unless I was naked and I asked in a sexy voice. He's such a tease!

Still waiting for him to admit he has feelings for me, but I'm content with things the way they are for now.

I won't always be this patient. I need to hear him admit he loves me almost as much as I need to tell him how I feel.

I'm going to bed now. I need to get up early and practice my seductive interviewer voice.

May 8

Dear Journal,

So the wonderful man who is currently snoring across the room helped me put together a portfolio. So far I have several pages for each band member and a backstage section and one for live in concert. I also have a folder full of clips and photos that I can use later. We had to sort out the good from the bad, such as me ass-planting on the stage—I didn't realize I'd taken a picture on the way down. Haha! And all of the incriminating stuff they don't want in the book? I've hidden that away. There's a lot of it. There's actually more of that kind of material than stuff I can use. But that's okay; no one has to know but me. Susan can gloat that it seems like I haven't gotten much work done this week. I don't care. If the finished product is garbage—and I guarantee it won't be—then she can complain. Until then she can shut the fuck up.

Wow. Not sure where all this anger is coming from. I guess the high from smoking pot wears off quickly. Logan talked me into smoking a little. I don't think I'll do it again. It wasn't as fun as I thought it would be. But food does taste really good. All I wanted to do was eat and lounge around. It was a good way to unwind after finishing the portfolio. And the sex afterwards was as good as always, but Logan fell asleep right after. He's usually good to a go a few times before he crashes. I think he does need these off days to unwind.

The guys were great about answering Susan's questions. They passed my laptop around and filled in the blanks as we drove from Salt Lake to Denver. I honestly can't believe how good they are to me. I thought they'd treat me cordially at best or disdainfully at worst, but they make me feel like I'm a part of their group. Reagan says we're going to go clothes shopping when we're in New Orleans next week. I wonder if that's her way of politely saying my wardrobe sucks.

Well, I'd better head to bed. Not sure if I'll be able to sleep. I'm still a little worried that Mom will say I haven't done enough work and let Susan take my place. I'm not sure how I'll handle that situation. I'm not ready to leave yet. Those feelings have a lot to do with the job, but much more to do with Logan. Eventually this job will end and then what? Do we go our separate ways?

I don't want to think about it today.

And unlike Scarlett O'Hara, I don't want to think about it tomorrow either.

Good night. Wish me luck!

Toni

CHAPTER
26

TONI ANSWERED her phone, glad it was her mother's name on caller ID and not Susan. She had her presentation ready to go, but she was not ready to face the woman.

"We're down in the lobby," Mom said. "Why don't you come meet us for breakfast?"

"Yeah, okay. I'll be down in a few minutes."

Logan rubbed at the tension knot between her shoulders. "Your editor?"

Toni shook her head. "My mother. She wants me to come down for breakfast."

"Am I invited?" Logan asked.

Toni smiled. "Do you want to be invited?"

"I'm not sure. Is she going to rip my balls off, toss them on the floor, and stomp on them?"

Toni covered his crotch with a hand. "I'll protect you from her wrath."

He laughed and kissed her cheek. "Just let me get my shoes."

When they reached the hotel lobby a few minutes later, Toni didn't have to bother searching the expansive area for her party. Birdie's loud mantra of "Toni, Toni, Toni!" immediately alerted her to her mother and sister's location.

She took a few steps in that direction, very conscious of the fact that her hand, which Logan was gripping rather tightly, was suddenly damp. She wasn't sure if it was her nervousness or Logan's resulting in a sweaty palm, but she didn't have long to ponder it as Birdie dashed across the lobby and threw her arms around her waist, squeezing her breathless.

"Oh, Toni! I miss you. I miss you so much."

"I miss you too, Buttercup," Toni said, releasing Logan's hand so she could give her sister a proper hug. Birdie tilted her face up to grin that winning smile of hers at Toni. Toni couldn't help but smile back and give one of her light brown pigtails an affectionate tug. Birdie had a smudge of what was probably chocolate at the corner of her mouth, which Toni took to cleaning with her spit-moistened thumb. Birdie didn't protest. She was used to Toni cleaning her face with spit. And tissues. And hems of T-shirts. The occasional dish towel.

Mom followed at a more socially appropriate pace. In heels and an expensive navy-blue pantsuit, she looked as well put together as she always did. Her silver hair was cut in a smart bob, and even in her midfifties, she was still turning heads.

When she reached the small group, she touched Toni's shoulder and leaned in to kiss her cheek. Her gaze, however, was trained on the gorgeous man standing just behind Toni.

"You look familiar," Mom said to Logan.

"He's a rock star," Birdie said helpfully. "But not the pretty one."

Toni chuckled. When Toni had explained to Birdie why she was leaving for a while, she'd given Birdie a picture of Exodus End to familiarize her with the reason she was going. Birdie had immediately taken to Steve, who had long hair and thus was *pretty*.

"You don't think I'm pretty?" Logan fluttered his eyelashes at her.

Birdie tucked in her chin and appraised him closely. "No. You're a boy."

"Steve is a boy too," Toni said.

Birdie scowled as she tried to assimilate this information into her ideas of boys and girls.

"Don't worry about it," Logan said. "I mistake him for a girl all the time."

Birdie beamed at him and took his hand in both of hers, instantly finding a new friend. "You are so funny."

"So which one are you?" Mom asked.

Logan gave one of Birdie's pigtails a tug—which made her giggle—and then lifted his gaze to Mom's curious stare.

"I'm just the bassist," Logan said with a heartthrob of a grin.

"This is Logan Schmidt," Toni said. "This is my mother, Eloise Nichols, and my little sister, Bernadette."

"Birdie!" Birdie corrected, staring up at Logan worshipfully. "I can't say Birdadent right."

"Nice to meet you, Mrs. Nichols," Logan said, lifting his left hand for a shake since Birdie was gripping his right. "And Birdadent." He tugged her pigtail again.

Watching him interact with Birdie had Toni melting into a puddle of sentimental goo. So many people tried to ignore her because they were uncomfortable with her condition, but he'd already won Birdie's heart. And her big sister's too.

"You said it wrong," Birdie said.

"That's a hard name to say," Logan said. "I think Birdie suits you better anyway. Can you whistle like a bird?"

Logan whistled a tune. And Birdie rounded her mouth and blew soundless air.

"Let's go find a seat in the dining room," Mom said. They turned in the direction of delicious breakfast smells—bacon, sausage, biscuits, and cinnamon.

Logan and Birdie ambled ahead, Logan offering instructions on whistling, Birdie too happy for his attention to get frustrated that it didn't come easy for her.

"Are you seeing that man?" Mom asked, nodding in Logan's direction.

"Sort of," Toni said, realizing too late that she wasn't prepared to answer questions about her undefined relationship with Logan.

"Does he have a degree?"

"You mean, like, college?"

"That's exactly what I, *like*, mean."

Toni resisted the urge to cringe. She'd been hanging around normal people too long. Her use of language had already slipped and her mother—being the CEO of a publishing company and having a Ph.D. in literature and a bachelor's degree in English— had always been a stickler for the use of proper grammar. *Like* was like her least favorite modifier ever.

"He doesn't really need a degree, does he? He's a rock star."

"What can you two possibly have in common?"

Good question.

"You'll become bored with him quickly."

He was more likely to become bored with her, Toni mused.

"We're having fun together. I thought you wanted me to get out and experience life," Toni reminded her.

"Perhaps I was a bit hasty. I'm having an awful time balancing the corporation and the household and meeting Birdie's needs. Unlike your father, I never was good at the domestic stuff."

"What are you getting at?"

"I want you to come home. Birdie needs you."

Toni gaped at her. So that was why her mother had brought Birdie with her? So she could guilt her into coming home early no matter how well she'd progressed with the book?

"You need to figure out how to care for Birdie, Mom. She's your daughter."

"I'm trying. She's just . . ."

She gazed across the nearly empty dining room at her younger daughter, who had her nose pressed against the sneeze guard of the buffet as she eyed the available dishes. Logan stood nearby, keeping an eye on her and shooting Toni questioning looks.

"She's a handful, Toni."

"Is this supposed to be news to me? I practically raised her myself."

"I understand why you want to get away from her—"

"I don't want to get away from her," Toni interrupted. "I just want you to take responsibility for her for a change."

"Toni, can I have pancakes?" Birdie yelled.

"Go sit at the table, Buttercup," Toni called, not wanting her to overhear the conversation she was having with their mother. "Logan will help you pick out something to drink."

Toni was sorry to put Logan on the spot like that, but he didn't seem to mind as he ushered Birdie to the table and then, with a napkin over his forearm, bowed to her like a *garçon* offering champagne.

"Maybe she can stay with you," her mother said.

"On a tour bus?" Was her mother insane? She had to realize what went on in those tour bus lounges. "Besides, she has summer school," Toni said.

"A lot of good an education is going to do her. She's perpetually five."

School had done wonders for Birdie—especially her language skills—but this wasn't really about Birdie. It was about her mother.

"A lot of good an education is going to do *me* as your lifelong housekeeper and nanny." Toni had never spoken to her mother so brusquely in her life. She stalked off before her obviously stunned mother could close her gaping mouth.

"You are so funny!" Birdie said to Logan as Toni flopped down in the chair next to her. The table was square, which meant she didn't have to decide if she should sit next to Birdie or Logan—she could sit between them. But that also meant her mother sat across from her, so she'd be forced to look at her while she ate.

"Your glasses," Mom said. She set the case down next to Toni's plate.

Toni replaced her glued pair with the ones in the case. These weren't her favorite frames, but at least they weren't broken.

"I really wish you would get Lasik," her mother said. "You have such a pretty face. It's a shame to cover it behind those glasses. Don't you think so, Logan?"

Logan jerked slightly. Why had Mom put him on the spot?

"She's stunning with or without glasses," Logan said. "But I think she should stick with whatever makes her comfortable."

Birdie giggled and covered her mouth with her hand, blushing ferociously.

"I think he likes you, Toni," Birdie said with another bashful giggle.

"Of course I like her," Logan said.

Why else would he be willing to subject himself to breakfast with her family?

"We've become fast friends," he added.

Toni frowned at the napkin folded on her plate. Fast, maybe, but still just friends. Wonderful.

Their waitress appeared and Mom started her typical order of poached egg, no salt; whole grain toast, no butter; fresh fruit; and sliced tomatoes.

"I want pancakes," Birdie said.

"You don't need all that sugar," Mom said. "You can have oatmeal."

Birdie scrunched up her nose.

"How about we get the buffet?" Toni suggested, knowing Birdie would rather not eat than have oatmeal. They had fought this battle a thousand times in the past.

"That's what I'm having," Logan said.

"Coffee?" their server asked.

"Decaf," Mom said.

"Can I have some?" Birdie asked.

"No. You can have milk."

"Chocolate milk?"

"You don't need—"

"The occasional treat won't hurt her," Toni butted in.

"She will have plain, skim milk," Mom said.

Birdie made a face of disgust. "Yuck."

"And what will you have to drink?" the waitress asked Logan with a flirty smile.

"I think I'm going to need a fifth of whiskey."

"Jack Daniels okay?" the waitress asked, writing on her order pad.

Logan glanced sidelong at Toni. She knew he was joking—trying to reduce the tension at the table—but apparently no one else realized it.

"Change that to orange juice," he said.

"With vodka?" The waitress glanced up from her notepad.

"Just orange juice."

"It's okay. Butch said I should get you anything you want, sir. I won't judge." She smiled at him.

"Musicians don't really drink hard liquor with their breakfast," he said.

She opened her mouth to argue, but Logan interrupted.

"*I* don't drink hard liquor with my breakfast. I was joking about the whiskey."

The waitress shrugged and turned to go, but Logan caught her sleeve. "You didn't ask Toni what she's having."

"Oh, I'm sorry. I must have overlooked you."

Story of her life.

"Chai latte," Toni said.

"Got it. Just help yourselves to the buffet." She touched Mom's shoulder. "And I'll have your special order out as soon as possible, ma'am."

The three of them left Mom sitting at the table conducting business on her smart phone.

"So the editor chick didn't come after all?" Logan asked in a low voice while Birdie tried to add individual grapes to her plate with a spoon. "We could have used last night for fun instead of work."

"She's here; I'm sure I'll get to deal with her after breakfast." Scowling, Toni heaped several more sausage links onto her plate.

"Do you know why my mother came?"

"To bring your glasses?"

"No, she's trying to guilt me into coming home early. She doesn't want to deal with Birdie on her own," Toni hissed. It felt good to confide these things to a live person. Perhaps she didn't need her journal anymore.

Logan turned his head to scratch his beard scruff on his shoulder so he could peek at Mom. "She seems perfectly in control."

"Exactly. Dad used to even her out and make her relax, but since he died, she's become so engrossed with her work, she won't even take the time to raise her own daughter."

"Sounds like she's still mourning."

His simple statement punched Toni in the gut and stole her breath. Maybe it hadn't been ambition that had driven her mom to choose work over family. Maybe it had been grief.

"Do you think I should go home?" she asked.

"No," he said, placing a biscuit on his plate with a pair of tongs and then adding one to Toni's plate as well. "And I don't say that for selfish reasons. Though I would if it came to that. I think she needs to face the reality of raising a daughter without your father instead of dumping the responsibility on you."

"But I feel so guilty."

"That's because you're a sweetheart."

"Is Toni *your* sweetheart?" Birdie asked, her three hard-won grapes rolling around on her plate. Toni could have helped her fill her plate, but she wouldn't unless asked. A lot of everyday tasks were challenging for Birdie, but she accepted her difficulties and took them in stride. She'd rather struggle a little than depend on others to do everything for her. It had taken Toni a while to figure out why Birdie would get so mad when Toni took over every task in order to complete them more efficiently. Birdie just wanted to do things herself no matter how time consuming or frustrating.

"Yep," Logan said. "Toni is everyone's sweetheart."

Birdie scowled. "Are you a slut, Toni?"

Toni gaped at her. "Where did you hear that word?"

"At school. Jill has a lot of sweethearts. Ashley said it's because she's a slut."

Ah, the joys of an all-inclusive classroom.

"That's not a nice word to call someone," Toni said. "I don't want you to use it again."

Birdie's near-constant smile faded. "It's a bad word?"

"A very bad word."

"Toni only has one sweetheart," Logan said.

"Is it Spiderman?"

Toni snorted. Where had she come up with that? "No, not Spiderman."

"Better not be." Logan scowled. "Slinging his sticky webs all over the city. It's not decent, I say."

Birdie giggled and tilted her head, a bashful blush on her round cheeks. "I joking. I know Logan is Toni's sweetheart."

Toni was glad someone was sure about that.

After they'd filled their plates, they returned to the table.

"You're not really going to eat all of that, are you?" Mom asked, shaking her head at Toni's overflowing plate.

Toni was admittedly a stress eater and yes, she was going to eat every bite of her high-fat, high-starch, high-protein breakfast.

"I'm hungry," Toni said.

Mom eyed Toni's waistline, which had never been as trim as her own, but Toni wasn't yet ripping the seams out of her skirt. She speared one of her sausage links and bit into it angrily. Stress eating at its finest.

"I really don't think you need that much food," Mom persisted.

"Are you insinuating that she's fat?" Logan asked.

"She will be if she eats like that."

"I'm fat," Birdie said, hanging her head.

"You're beautiful," Logan said, "just like your big sister." He tugged on one of Birdie's pigtails, and she grinned.

If the man didn't stop making Birdie light up like warm summer sunshine, Toni was going to tackle-hug him out of his chair right in front of everyone.

Logan tilted his head toward their mother. "And it's plain to see where both of you got your good looks."

Most mothers would have taken that as a compliment, but not her mom. Oh no. Comparing her to her frumpy older daughter and her special needs younger daughter was obviously an insult. Toni blew out a breath and dug into her biscuits and gravy. At this rate, she'd be heading to the buffet for seconds.

"After breakfast, Susan will be meeting us in the conference room down the hall," Mom said. "I invited her to breakfast, but she said she wasn't hungry."

Toni tried not to frown at the news. But her presentation was ready, so hopefully this impromptu and completely ridiculous meeting would be over quickly. If all Mom had wanted was to make her feel guilty over Birdie, why had she insisted on bringing Susan along? Toni was pretty sure that Susan was her plan B, in case her guilt trip of a plan A failed to entice Toni to go home.

"What are you doing this afternoon?" Logan asked.

Toni glanced at him. Weren't they going to spend the afternoon in bed? She was ready for another marathon session of lessons. They scarcely had time for sex on concert days.

"We need to be at the airport around five," Mom said. "We have an evening flight."

They weren't even staying one night? Toni was starting think her Mom had completely lost it.

"Toni and I are heading to the track in a couple hours. If you want to come—"

"What track?" Toni asked, picturing herself running along behind him, panting from exertion. Running was not her idea of a good time.

"Motocross. They have a fantastic track set up just outside the city. Every time the band tours here, I burn energy on a bike."

She wasn't sure if she'd enjoy watching him zoom around in a circle on a dirt bike, but she did want to spend time with him and participate in his interests as much as possible.

"I want to go!" Birdie said. "I can ride a bike."

"He means a motorcycle," Toni said.

"He said bike."

"Sorry, I should have clarified," Logan said. He pulled out his phone and started flipping through his photos. "I'll show you what I mean."

He passed his phone to Toni, and she was stunned by how hot he looked in a form-fitting racing suit with knee and elbow pads. In the photo, Logan was leaning against a red mud-flecked dirt bike, holding his helmet against his hip. Did the man always look devastatingly gorgeous? She was going with a definite yes on that.

"Let me see!" Birdie yelled, startling Toni out of her musing.

"Bernadette, keep your voice down at the table," Mom scolded.

Toni handed Logan's phone to Birdie, who sat on her opposite side. "Oh, that's a big bike," she whispered. She touched the phone's screen and scowled. "Who is this girl?" she asked.

Logan's eyes widened and he jumped up so fast, his thighs hit the underside of the table, rattling dishes. "You weren't supposed to see that," he said as he grabbed the phone out of Birdie's hand.

"She had no shirt on," Birdie informed the table, looking with wide eyes from Toni to her mother. "I saw her boobies!"

Mom laughed, for whatever reason finding *this*—of all things—hilarious.

"That was taken months ago," Logan said, inching down in his seat as if trying to slide under the table.

"Why are you looking at her boobies for, Logan?" Birdie asked.

"I'm not."

His face was beet red, and Toni enjoyed watching him squirm. She was sure he'd seen thousands of boobies in his life, and she doubted he'd regretted viewing a single one until called on it by a nine-year-old with Down's syndrome.

"Did you look at Toni's boobies too? She has great big ones!"

Logan glanced at Toni out the corner of his eye before snorting on a laugh. "I didn't notice."

"Bernadette, this is not an appropriate conversation to have at the breakfast table," Mom said, though she was still grinning ear to ear.

Birdie ducked her head in shame. "Sorry."

Toni touched the back of Birdie's head. "Eat your breakfast."

They somehow got through the meal with their relationship intact. Logan had to listen to a long-winded, one-sided conversation about raising chickens, but at least Birdie was no longer asking questions about boobies. Thank God.

After breakfast, Mom pointed out the conference room where they would meet shortly. Toni and Logan headed upstairs to collect the messenger bag where she'd stashed her laptop.

"Sorry you had to deal with that," Toni said to him.

"I didn't mind," he assured her, drawing her against him for a much too short kiss. "It's kind of nice to recognize the dysfunction in other people's families."

Her mouth dropped open in mock outrage, and she smacked his ass. "Are you insulting my family?"

"Birdie is a sweetheart."

"And now you're trying to change the subject?"

"Yep." He kissed the tip of her nose. "I need to go hunt

down Butch and have him arrange a morning at the track. Will you be okay alone with your mother and the dragon lady?"

His concern touched her far more than it should. "I'll be fine."

"After this day is over, I think a full body massage will be in order."

She sighed in bliss, already imagining the feel of his hands on her tense muscles. "That sounds wonderful."

"I can't wait. I have to warn you, though—I'll probably fall asleep."

She lifted a brow at him. "How can you fall asleep while giving a massage?"

"Giving one? I'll be on the receiving end."

He danced sideways as she reached out to swat his butt again.

"Tease!" she accused.

"Is that a challenge?"

She wasn't sure how she felt about his raised eyebrows and crooked grin. What did he mean by *challenge*? How could being teased by him be a challenge? She didn't have time to ponder or question; she had a presentation to give.

"Text me when you're finished," he said. "Or if you need rescuing."

"I'll be fine," she said, more for personal assurance than for his benefit.

"I know you will. I have faith in your abilities."

She hadn't had anyone say something like that to her since her father had passed away. She wasn't sure how sincerely Logan meant his words, but they gave her the fortitude to straighten her spine and head to the conference room with a confident smile on her face.

Her smile faltered when she entered the room and saw her mother and Susan with their heads together, talking in low tones, looking like they were plotting the crime of the century. At the far end of the room, Birdie was drawing rainbows on the dry erase board, her tongue protruding from between her lips as she concentrated on the curved lines.

Toni bumped into a chair, which drew everyone's attention.

"There you are," Mom said. "We were starting to think you'd gotten lost."

". . . in your rock star's bed." Susan grinned.

She wished. "Sorry to keep you waiting."

Toni pulled out her laptop and booted it up. She connected it to her small portable projector and lowered a screen from the ceiling. Birdie frowned at her as the screen slid down in front of the dry erase board before edging behind it to continue drawing rainbows.

"Birdie, come out of there. I need to use the screen."

"I'm bored," Birdie said, and Toni could hear the pout in her tone. "I wanna draw."

"I have paper and pens in my bag. Draw on that until I'm done."

Generally cooperative, Birdie did what she was told. Toni handed her bag to Birdie, and Birdie sat cross-legged in the corner, digging through the bag hunting for treasure.

"Why are you setting up for a presentation?" Susan asked. The derisive tone of her voice wasn't lost on Toni.

"I wanted to show you what I've been working on so you have a better idea how the book is coming along."

"That's not why we're here," Susan said.

Toni scrunched her brows together. She was at a complete loss.

"Then why are you here?"

"Your mother and I have been talking about the direction of the book," Susan said. "We think it will sell more copies if—"

"Let's see what Toni's been working on first," Mom interrupted.

Toni offered her mom a relieved smile and opened the first mocked-up page she'd created the night before. It was a table of contents.

"I'm sure some of these topics will change as I continue on tour with the band. The longer I'm with them, the more ideas I get. I'll start with their history, the formation of the band in their own words. Dare saves band memorabilia. He said I can use reproductions in the book if I can secure the rights from the copyright holders."

"Sounds expensive," Mom said.

"According to him, it shouldn't cost us anything. We'll have to credit the photos to the photographer, but most of the photos were taken by friends and family. He doubts they'll be interested in money."

"Everyone is interested in money," Susan said.

"A lot of people are just happy to help the people they love,"

Toni said, trying not to glare at the woman.

"Yeah. Until money's involved."

It must be hard to go through life so bitter and jaded, Toni thought, but she moved on with her presentation. "There will also be sections on what goes on backstage."

"Now we're talking," Susan said.

Toni ignored her and continued down what she'd worked out so far for the table of contents. "The crew. The fans. Promotional events. The tour bus. The private jet—which I haven't seen yet. A huge section on concerts and a chapter on each band member. Each of those will vary depending on the band member. For instance, Logan is an open book and has tons of hobbies outside of music, so his chapter will look a lot different from Max's because Max is very private and more focused on the fans. I'm really excited about the section on what it's like to create and record new songs as a member of Exodus End. Dare says they'll consider creating a song exclusive to the book. And let me track the entire process from brainstorming to writing to recording."

"That sounds exciting," Mom said, her eyes wide with wonder.

"That sounds dull," Susan said as she pretended to stifle a yawn. "Where's the real dirt on these guys? That's what will sell books."

"There's no dirt," Toni said. That was exactly what she didn't want in this book. No dirt. Nothing that could potentially hurt a member of the band.

"There has to be dirt," Susan said. "You're around them twenty-four seven. You have to be privy to things more exciting than what they had for breakfast."

"You'd be surprised how much preparation goes into getting them breakfast. Their tour runs like clockwork."

"Which is boring," Susan said. "This is all very boring."

"I think the fans will love it," Mom said.

"Oh, yeah, they'll eat this shit up," Susan said. "But we discussed this, Eloise. Remember? The fans are a niche market. And you want to sell this book to millions of people. To do that, you need dirt."

"Exodus End has millions of fans," Toni said. "It may be a niche market, but it's a huge niche."

Susan and her mother stared at each other for a long moment, as if communicating by telepathy.

"Before I saw this, I was convinced the book needed dirt to sell, but I think Toni is on to something here," Mom said.

"I think you're making a mistake," Susan said. "Let me take over. I'll create a book that will sell like wildfire."

"This isn't only about sales," Toni said. "If we do a good job with this book, other bands will come to us to have their biographies written. If we publish a bunch of scandal, it might make us money now, but our chance at future projects will be obliterated. No one will trust us."

"Publicity is publicity," Susan said. "Even if it's bad publicity. Actually, bad publicity gets more attention than good publicity. What are you more likely to recall: Steve Aimes cheating on his wife or Steve Aimes sending shoes to poor kids in Africa?"

"Steve sent shoes to poor kids in Africa?" Toni mused.

"See what I mean!" Susan said.

"Toni," Birdie interrupted, tugging on Toni's sleeve.

"Just a minute, Buttercup," Toni said absently before continuing to plead her case. "Maybe this book isn't about publicity."

"Of course this book is about publicity," Susan said. "That's the only thing their manager wants out of it. He wants it to draw more attention to the band. And how better to do that than to get people's attention with *dirt*?"

"Just because someone reads the book to get this so-called *dirt* you're so fixated on, that doesn't make it more likely that they'll buy Exodus End's music or go to their concerts, does it?" Toni had never argued with a nonfamily member before. She wasn't sure why it was so much easier to stick up for her new friends than it was to stick up for herself, but she wasn't backing down on this. She wasn't writing the book to sell it to a bunch of nosy people who would snigger and ridicule the band members for their mistakes. She was writing this book to glorify a group of men— and one woman—who deserved to be recognized for their greatness.

"Toni!" Birdie said, yanking on Toni's sleeve anxiously.

"I said just a minute, Birdie," she snapped, prying fingers from her sleeve. "Can't you entertain yourself for a few minutes?"

"She's bleeding," Mom said, jumping to her feet.

Toni looked down at Birdie, who had blood trickling out of one nostril, over her lip, and down her chin. "Oh God," Toni said, forcing Birdie to tilt her head forward and catching the blood in her hand so it didn't get all over the boldly patterned carpet. "What happened?"

"I don't know," Birdie said. "I just sneezed and blood came out."

"Just a nose bleed," Toni said. "Don't panic." She looked at her mom. "Is there a bathroom nearby?"

"Just down the hall," Mom said. "Do you want me to take her?"

"I want Toni to do it!" Birdie wailed.

Mom bit her lip and nodded her go-ahead. Toni wondered if the reason Mom struggled to care for Birdie was partially her fault. Toni was always the one to jump in and fix Birdie's tragedies. This situation was no different.

"I'll be back in a few minutes," Toni promised.

"Can we look at the rest of your mocked-up manuscript pages while you're gone?" Mom asked.

Toni was rather proud of those few pages, especially since Logan had approved of them.

"Sure. They're in the folder labeled *manuscript pages*," she said before steering Birdie out of the conference room and hunting down the nearest restroom.

"I think Mom liked your hard work," Birdie said as Toni packed her nostril with toilet tissue to stem the flow of blood.

Toni smiled. "I think so too." It felt great to have won her mom over to her side. And she was pretty sure Mom liked her ideas because they were sound, not because her flesh and blood had come up with them.

"That other lady is not nice to you." Birdie gave her a comforting pat on the arm.

"I noticed." Toni doubted anything would convince Susan that Toni knew what she was doing. She hoped that Mom didn't head back to Seattle and immediately cave to the outspoken editor's wishes. She liked to think that her mom was made of stronger stuff than that, but Susan was as persistent as she was opinionated.

"Are you coming home with us?" Birdie asked, her inquisitive brown eyes enlarged by her thick glasses.

A pang of guilt twisted Toni's heart. She stroked Birdie's cool cheek. "I still have work to do."

"Mom said if I rode on the plane like a big girl, you'd come home."

So that was how Mom had gotten Birdie on the plane. "I'll come home in a few more weeks."

"It's too long."

"I know it feels like a long time—"

Birdie shoved her away and stomped out of the bathroom. By the time Toni returned to the conference room, Birdie was already sitting cross-legged in the corner and writing bold angry words across a page. Probably things like *Toni is a jerk* and *I wish Susan was my sister*.

"I think we've seen all we need to see," Mom said from the end of the conference table. The sample page Toni had made about band promotion was displayed on the screen at the front of the room. Susan was conspicuously absent. Thank God. "Continue with your vision for the book."

Toni's shoulders sagged in relief. "Is Susan in agreement?" She wasn't sure why she cared. The woman's opinions never meshed with Toni's.

"Not exactly," Mom said, "but let me worry about Susan. I'm impressed with how much you've accomplished already."

"You are?" Mom didn't hand out compliments regularly. Toni couldn't help but smile.

"I am," she said. Turning, she called out, "Birdie, how's your nose?"

"It's fine!" Birdie yelled. "Leave me alone."

"She's mad," Toni said as she moved to the table to shut down her laptop and disconnect the projector, allowing it to cool down so she could stow it away again.

"Why is she mad?"

"Someone told her that if she rode on the plane, I'd come home."

Mom bit her lip and rubbed at an eyebrow with one finger. "I did tell her that. I figured you'd be more useful at home than here. I was wrong. We'll figure something out to make this work."

"Are you coming with us to the track?" Logan would be almost as happy as she was that she was staying and completing the project as she envisioned it.

Mom laughed. "To watch your boyfriend play with his bike?" She shook her head. "I think I'll pass. I can get some work done before we have to catch our plane."

"Is it okay with you that Birdie comes with us?"

"Of course."

"Birdie," Toni called to her sister, who was sulking in the corner, "are you too mad at me to go watch Logan ride his dirt bike?"

"Yes!" Birdie said.

"Logan will be sad. He wanted you to see him do a trick. I thought you were his friend."

It was probably wrong of her to manipulate her sister, but Birdie would get over her anger quickly if she was having fun. And who could be around Logan for more than ten seconds without having fun?

"I'll go," Birdie said. "But I'm not sitting by you."

"Don't be cross with Toni," Mom said as she rose from her chair. "I'm the one who told you she was coming home."

"I'm not sitting by you either!"

"This should make our flight home interesting," Mom said under her breath as she walked toward the door. "Make sure you're back here before three."

Toni nodded and sent a text to Logan.

> Meeting is over. Went well. I'm bringing my equipment and my sister to our room. You might want to hide the toys.

His reply came a few seconds later.

> OK. Where am I supposed to hide them all?

> IDK! Use your imagination.

> I'll meet you in the hallway. Just knock.

He was right; it probably wasn't the best idea to allow Birdie into their suite. No telling what she might see. Still upset that she'd been lied to, Birdie followed begrudgingly. Her attitude changed entirely when Toni knocked on the suite door and Logan appeared with two long-stemmed white roses.

"For the pretty ladies," he said.

He offered a flower to Birdie first, who lifted the blossom to her nose and sniffed. Toni was too busy ogling the gorgeous spectacle of Logan's ass in his thin red race pants to give a fig about a flower.

"Thank you!" Birdie said. "It doesn't smell good."

"It stinks?" Logan asked, smelling the rose he was still holding.

"No." Birdie laughed. "I mean you can't smell it."

"Well, that's disappointing," Logan said, tossing his rose on the floor.

"But I love it!" Birdie rescued the discarded flower from the hall carpet as Toni nudged her way into the suite and dropped off her bags.

While Logan occupied Birdie in "safe" territory, Toni grabbed a couple of sweatshirts. She had no idea what the weather would be like in Denver in May.

By the time they were settled in the waiting limousine outside the hotel's front lobby, Birdie was too distracted with awe to hold on to her anger toward Toni. Birdie fiddled with the television and other various buttons, while Logan and Toni snuggled close together in the seat.

"Is it stupid that I missed you?" he murmured close to her ear.

She probably should force some distance between them when a young witness was in their midst—those pants of his left very little to the imagination and she knew what kind of effect she had on the man. But she found herself squirming to get closer and burying her face in his neck.

"Not stupid, flattering," she assured him.

"Tell me about the meeting," he said, and then whispered to her out of Birdie's earshot, "to distract me from my desire to devour you."

"My little sister is watching," she reminded him.

"Which is the only reason I haven't made you naked."

If Birdie hadn't been present, Toni was quite sure she'd be enjoying one of his fabulous lessons.

"Uh, the meeting," she said. She placed a hand on his chest to steady herself, not finding the rapid beat of his heart steadying in the least. "Right."

She told him what had happened—trying not to overstate what a bitch Susan had been to her—and he listened. Somewhere in the middle of her recap, she realized that she liked having him as a friend. And that if this relationship between them didn't work out, she'd lose so much more than a fantastic lover. She'd lose a confidant, her champion, her partner. When had she started thinking of him like that? Probably in the wee hours of that morning when he'd been squinting blurry-eyed at video footage and searching for the perfect thirty-second segment from their record store signing.

"I'm glad you get to stay," Logan said.

Looking up into his tender blue eyes, she was sure she'd have stayed with him for as long as possible even if her mother had given the job to Susan.

"I'm not," Birdie said crossly. "I want Toni to come home."

"Birdie . . ." Toni began.

"Aren't you proud of your sister?" Logan asked Birdie. "She's been working hard to make me look good."

"That *is* a hard job," Toni teased.

He poked her in the belly, but didn't reply to her barb. "And no one believed she could do it. Not your Mom. Not Susan. Not the guys in the band."

"Susan is mean!" Birdie said.

"But your big sister did an excellent job, and now everyone realizes how amazing she is. That's good, isn't it? She couldn't do that if she was at home."

Birdie nodded. "I proud of her, but I miss her so much." She dropped her head forward and plucked at the petals on one of her roses.

"And I'd miss her if she went home with you," Logan said.

Birdie lifted her head, her eyes alight with the excitement of discovering a perfect solution to everyone's problems. "Then you come home with her!"

Logan laughed. "Maybe I'll visit someday."

Was he serious? Toni couldn't imagine him trapped in their quiet house in the wilderness. The man needed people and excitement. Neither was in abundance on a farm situated miles outside of the small town of Enumclaw, Washington.

"He has to perform in his concerts," Toni said.

"You'll come when you're finished?" Birdie asked, giving her unscented rose another sniff. The blossom was already starting to droop.

"Yeah," Logan said.

"And that's when Toni will come home too?"

"Actually, I'll be home months before then. Logan's traveling to far-away countries this summer. Without me."

Logan squeezed her shoulder. Maybe the idea unsettled him as much as it did her.

"But aren't you getting married?" Birdie asked.

Logan laughed. "Uh, no."

"Why not?"

The man was already jittery about commitment; Toni didn't want uncomfortable questions to send him running into the wilderness of the Rocky Mountains, never to be seen or heard from again.

"We just met, Birdie," Toni said. "Marriage isn't something two people should take lightly."

"Or even consider," Logan said under his breath.

"If you kiss her, you have to marry her," Birdie said.

Logan laughed again and rubbed at one eye with his fingertips. "I must have a lot of wives I don't know about."

Birdie looked utterly bewildered. Toni supposed it was time to have *the* talk with her. Or maybe Mom would do the honors, because Toni wasn't exactly an expert on romantic relationships. Not yet.

As for marriage, Toni wasn't ready for that level of commitment either, but someday . . . Did Logan mean he'd never consider marriage? She apparently needed to have an awkward talk with him too.

The limo drew to a halt and they stepped out into a cloud of dust. The hum of the dirt bikes on the track sounded like a horde of gigantic angry bees. Logan directed Toni and Birdie to a small set of stands where they could watch the action.

"I guess I should ask if you want to ride or just watch," Logan said.

"Just watch," Toni said.

She hadn't been sure what to expect, but now that she could see the track, she saw riders zooming up and down dirt hills, skidding around sharp turns, and launching themselves high into the air before landing with solid thuds.

"How 'bout you just watch too?" she said to Logan. She cringed when she saw a rider wipe out and skid sideways through the dirt. As soon as he came to a stop, he jumped to his feet, picked up his bike, and kick-started the engine before zooming off again, dirt spraying out behind his spinning back tire.

"You're kidding, right?" Logan asked.

She wasn't, but she nodded and grabbed the front of his jacket to pull him close for a kiss, clinging to his lips as if it was the last time she'd see him alive. He patted her butt when they drew away.

"I'll wave to you," he said and with a quick wink, he walked away, leaving Toni to clutch her sweatshirt with apprehension.

Birdie stood at the fence that separated spectators from the track. She had her hands over her ears, but was watching the dirt bikes zoom past in wide-eyed, slack-jawed wonder.

"Come up top so you can see both sides of the track," Toni called, slipping the sweatshirt over her head and her arms into the sleeves. Now that Logan had gone, she was chilly. Birdie paid her no mind. Likely she hadn't heard Toni over the squalls of the engines when she had her ears covered.

Toni touched Birdie's back, and Birdie looked up, eyes wide. "They're fast!"

"Are you cold? I brought you a sweatshirt."

Birdie uncovered her ears long enough to put on the sweatshirt, but she covered them again as they climbed the metal stairs of the bleachers. About halfway up, Toni barked her shin on the edge of a bench, which sent her hobbling in pain. She should probably wrap herself in bubble wrap before she ventured out in public.

"Special treat today, folks," an announcer said over the speakers. "Logan Schmidt is on the track."

There was a smattering of enthusiastic applause and cheers from the small crowd that had congregated in the stands.

Toni spun around so quickly, she almost tumbled down the steps. Birdie grabbed her and pulled her down on the nearest bench. Yeah, they were probably high enough. The higher she climbed, the more likely she was to die from a fall.

Birdie clapped excitedly and pointed as Logan, dressed in red from boots to helmet, sped onto the track. He zipped past other riders as if they were standing still.

"He's going too fast," Toni said, her heart thudding in the vicinity of her throat.

When he reached the top of the first hill, his bike leaped so high into the air, she thought for sure he was going to sail right over the fence. But he landed on the top of the next hill as though his wheels had never left the ground. Toni's stomach plummeted when on his next jump he released one handlebar to offer her the wave he promised. Birdie waved back excitedly, but Toni couldn't pry her fingers from the metal seat she was clinging to with all her strength.

Logan sped around the track faster—how was that possible?—and this time when he hit the highest hill, he did a back flip in midair. The crowd went wild. Birdie jumped to her feet. Toni's vision tunneled and her head swam. When he landed safely on his back tire and gunned the engine to ride out the rotation in a wheelie Toni sagged in relief only to tense again when he popped over the next hill and flew sideways, his bike parallel to the ground.

"He's good!" Birdie clapped excitedly on Logan's next jump.

He was good—no, better than good. He was *amazing*. But dear God, he was going to kill himself! Or kill *her* from heart failure.

By the time he'd skidded, jumped, flipped, and sped around the track half a dozen times, Toni began to relax and then got caught up in the excitement of watching him control the bike as though it were an extension of his body. The strength and athleticism he displayed was truly inspiring, but it was his daring that had her switching from terror to arousal. The man was risking his life for a thrill, and Toni suddenly wanted to tackle him off that noisy motorcycle and ride him for hours.

It was almost an hour later before he finally zoomed off the track. Toni took Birdie's hand and together they left the stands to find him. He was easy to spot in his bright red race pants and jersey, even though he was completely surrounded by women. And a few men. But Toni only noticed the women. Jeez, not only did they flock to rock star Logan, they also flocked to freestyle motocross Logan.

"Is Logan a slut?" Birdie asked.

Good question.

"He has a lot of sweethearts."

He certainly did.

Toni squeezed Birdie's hand. "You aren't supposed to use that word, remember?"

Logan leaned in close to a woman to hear what she was saying over the noise of the track and then laughed, that charming smile of his turning heads.

"Is there a *good* word for someone with a lot of sweethearts?" Birdie asked.

Asshole came to mind. Toni knew it wasn't Logan's fault that he was gorgeous and talented and fun and outgoing, but she wished she was the only woman who noticed.

"Toni? Is there a good word?"

"Um." Toni racked her brain for a child-friendly synonym for manwhore. "Popular?"

"Logan sure is pop-a-lure. Did he see all these girls' boobies?" Birdie looked up at her, her inquisitive eyes enormous behind her thick glasses.

"I don't think so." But she couldn't say for sure. Toni stood on tiptoe and tried waving to catch his attention.

Logan smiled when he spotted them standing at the edge of the gathered crowd. He easily meandered his way to her side.

"There are my girls." He moved to stand between them and settled one arm around Toni's waist and his other across Birdie's shoulders.

"You already have enough girls," Birdie said.

"A man can never have too many girls."

Toni's scowl didn't lessen even when he kissed her temple.

"Are you ready to head back to the hotel?" he asked in her ear.

She'd been ready to jump his bones, but now she was plain grumpy.

"You were jumping so high!" Birdie said. "And then you did a flip and flew like Superman with your feet out. Was it fun?"

"Very fun." Logan tugged at one of Birdie's pigtails.

"Can I try it?"

Logan glanced at Toni, and she gave him a *definitely not* shake of her head.

"Maybe when you're older," he said. "These bikes are for grownups."

"Do they have loud bikes for kids?"

Logan looked to Toni for assistance, but she was still irritated about his entourage of dirt-bike groupies, so she let him struggle for his own answer.

"I almost forgot," he said, unzipping a pocket in his race pants and pulling out a small brown paper bag. "I got something for you and your sister at the gift shop."

Birdie was immediately distracted. "What is it?"

"I'll give it to you in the car."

"Let's go, Toni!" Birdie grabbed Toni's hand and jerked her in the direction of the entrance. She'd apparently already given up on the idea of a kid-sized loud bike.

Birdie bounced up and down in the limo as she waited for Logan and Toni to settle in the seat. "What is it? What is it?"

"It's nothing huge," Logan said.

He reached into the sack and pulled out a pair of gaudy orange and purple race socks. He pulled them apart and handed one to Birdie. "One for you." And then he put the mate on Toni's lap. "And one for you." He retrieved a second pair of socks—baby blue and lime green—and divvied them up between the sisters.

"New socks!" Birdie yelled as if she'd just gotten her own rainbow-farting pony. "Oh, thank you, Logan!"

He grunted in surprise when he got the Birdie tackle-hug treatment and only hesitated a second before hugging her back. "You're most welcome."

Toni suddenly wanted to jump his bones again.

Birdie sat back and yanked off her shoes, tugging off her old socks and replacing them with the new. Touched by Logan's thoughtfulness, Toni had to use one of her new socks to dab away a stray tear before she followed Birdie's lead and changed into them. They wriggled their matching mismatched socks at him and he laughed, that charming smile of his turning heads again—Toni's head.

Yep. Bones. Jumped. Now.

Toni was ecstatic to find Mom waiting in the hotel lobby with Susan. Not because she actually wanted to see either of them, but because she needed to hand off her sister so she could get her hands on her man as soon as possible.

"Thanks for visiting." She gave her mom the quickest of hugs. "Be a good girl for mama." She kissed Birdie on the cheek. "Later," she said to Susan and started to back away.

"I don't want to go on the plane," Birdie wailed.

"You don't?" Logan asked.

Birdie shook her head vigorously. "No. I hate them."

"I love planes," Logan said.

Birdie looked up at him adoringly. "You do?"

"Yeah. They go even faster and higher than dirt bikes. You can fly through the sky like Superman." He demonstrated his flying skills—extending his arms and making *zoom* noises.

Birdie pursed her lips together, obviously struggling with a huge dilemma: fear of flying versus impressing her new friend. The new friend won. The two of them zoomed around the group several times. Susan looked rather annoyed by their childishness, but Mom was smiling. She squeezed Logan's arm when the two pretend airplanes came to a stop. "Thank you," she said to him.

He grinned. "No problem."

"Hello, Logan," Susan butted in, her tone dripping with something nasty. Disdain?

Logan turned his head to look at her and scowled. "Do I know you?"

"I don't know," she said, with a sly smile. "Do you?"

"This is Susan," Toni said, not really wanting to introduce them. She wanted to get away, get him alone, and get busy.

"It was good to meet you all," Logan said when he apparently understood Toni's persistent tug on his elbow as *it's time to go*. He gave Susan one last look, patted Birdie on the head, and turned to follow Toni.

"There's something familiar about that Susan woman," he said as they stepped onto the elevator.

"Please don't tell me you've slept with her," Toni pleaded. There wasn't enough bleach in the world to clean that skank off his dick.

"No. I recognize every woman I've ever slept with. I might not remember their names . . ." He turned his head toward her. "What was your name again?"

She slugged him in the ribs.

"No." He shook his head, still scowling. "I know I never slept with her, but I think I've seen her somewhere."

"She used to be a journalist," Toni said. "Maybe she interviewed you." *Please let that be all there was between them.*

He released a sigh and nodded. "Yeah, that must be it." He turned toward her and smiled. "So why were you in such a hurry to ditch your adorable little sister?"

"Well," she said, "there was this hot guy doing all sorts of dangerous stunts on a dirt bike and I thought to myself, damn, I need to get me some of that." She turned toward him and slid a hand down his belly, stopping just short of touching what she really wanted. "And after he got me excited with his daring, acrobatic feats, I found him surrounded by all sorts of women, which made me wonder if I even stood a chance with him."

"You do," he murmured before directing her hand several inches lower.

"And then he bought a little girl some socks which made her incredibly happy."

"He sounds pretty lame. I ain't gonna lie."

She smiled at him, her heart throbbing with the love trying to burst from her chest.

"You're wrong. He's amazing."

"So you still want him? Even after he unapologetically tried to buy a child's affection with *socks*?"

She shook her head, lost in his gorgeous blue eyes. "I want him because of it." She slid her hand the final few inches and cupped his cock.

He sucked in an excited breath. "So I heard that this hot guy of yours had a naughty surprise installed in his hotel room while he was at the track."

Toni pressed her breasts into his chest, gently stroking his hardening cock through his thin race pants. "What kind of naughty surprise?"

The elevator dinged as they arrived on their floor, and the doors slid open. Steve stepped onto the elevator but took a startled step backward when he noticed them in the corner.

"Am I interrupting something?" he asked.

"I'm not sure," Logan said. "Were you about to hike up your skirt so I could fuck you right here in this elevator?" he asked Toni.

Her eyes widened, and her face flamed. Feeling him up through his pants was probably as bold as she was willing to get in a public elevator.

"No?" he asked with a teasing laugh.

She shook her head.

"Maybe if you tried taking instead of asking," Steve suggested.

"There will be plenty of taking," Logan said. He tugged her out of the corner by both arms and stopped the elevator door from closing with one well-placed heel before directing her into the hall. "Just not somewhere she feels uncomfortable."

Steve made whipping sounds until the elevator door closed and cut him off.

"What was that sound supposed to mean?" Toni asked, following Logan without the slightest resistance.

"That I'm pussy whipped."

"I don't think you are." He was just considerate to her. He still had a life of his own. He didn't jump all over himself to do everything she asked.

Logan chuckled. "That's because you didn't know me before I met you."

"Obviously."

"As long as it's your pussy doing the whipping, I'm perfectly okay with it."

Standing at their suite door as he fumbled with his key card, she thrust her pelvis toward him and mimicked Steve's whipping sounds. "Get in me," she said in an eerie voice. She wasn't sure how a pussy would sound if it could talk. "Now. *Wa-psshhh!*"

He laughed and opened the door. "Yes, ma'am."

Giggling, she brushed past him but came to a sudden halt when she saw the naughty surprise he'd mentioned on the elevator. A brass headboard had been affixed to the bed just in front of the standard hotel wall-mounted one. Just looking at it made her tremble with need.

"Now we'll find out who's really in control here," he said in her ear. "Strip."

He didn't have to tell her twice. Somehow keeping her glasses on her face, her sweatshirt went flying in one direction and her T-shirt in another. She wriggled out of her bra while kicking off her shoes, and removed her skirt, panties, and socks with one sweep of her hands. Naked, she practically skipped to the bed with an enormous smile on her face.

When he didn't follow her immediately, she asked, "Did you mean for me to strip seductively?"

"A little late for that, isn't it?"

"I can get dressed and start over."

He shook his head. "You'll make it up to me."

For some reason his words sounded like a threat.

When he came toward her with a black leather belt, she shrank into the mattress. This would be a game, right? He wouldn't actually hurt her, would he?

"Offer me your wrists," he said.

His voice was so commanding and his gaze so intense that her arms shot upward as if controlled by his puppet strings. He cinched the belt around her wrists and then pulled her arms over her head. She hadn't gotten a good look at the belt, but she assumed it wasn't an ordinary one. It had formed a loop, but there wasn't a belt buckle digging into her flesh. Logan leaned over her to knot the belt around the brass bars above her head. He then grabbed her around the waist and pulled her down the mattress until her arms were fully extended. Toni tugged at her bonds, not sure if she could escape them, and when they held, a thrill of excitement snaked through her.

He stared into her eyes as his hand slowly slid up her body.

He cupped her breast, giving it a harsh squeeze that forced a gasp from her lungs.

"I can do anything I want to you, and you won't be able to stop me," he said.

He stroked her nipple with gentle fingertips until it hardened, begging for additional stimulation.

"I can lick every inch of your body."

"Yes."

"Fuck you until you beg me to stop."

"Yes."

"Come all over your face."

"Yes."

"Take your ass nice and slow."

She shook her head. "I don't want—"

He grabbed her face harshly. "It doesn't matter what you want. You're at my mercy."

Her heart thudded out of control. He wouldn't take advantage, would he?

Two fingers slid into her pussy, and he rubbed at her clit with his thumb.

"I'll give you pleasure when I think you deserve it." A third finger slid into her ass and she tensed. "And I'll take whatever I want from you."

"Logan!"

"Your body belongs to me. You're mine. You can't deny me anything."

She couldn't look away from his intense gaze. "Yes."

He blinked at her. "Seriously, Toni? You like this kind of manipulative bullshit?"

She flushed and turned her head to break eye contact. "N-not all the time. But sometimes it's exciting to be at someone else's mercy. If you trust them not to push you beyond your boundaries. Though one of your fingers happens to be pressing my boundaries right now."

He wriggled the finger in her ass, and she gasped. "This boundary-pressing finger right here?"

"That's the one."

"If this is your thing—"

"Not every time," she said defensively.

"I'll do my best to get you off this way. But it makes me feel like a jerk."

"The more of a jerk you are, the harder I'll come," she promised.

He seemed determined to prove her wrong as he fingered her until she almost came and then licked her until she almost came and then fucked her until she was begging to come. He shuddered as he thrust into her deep enough to almost bump his pelvis against her throbbing clit. She'd never get off with him holding back like that. And he had to realize it.

His shuddering intensified and a broken gasp escaped him.

Wait just a goddamned minute here.

"Are you coming?" she asked, completely stunned that he'd do so without taking her along with him.

"Oh yeah. R-r-really h-hard."

"Logan!"

He collapsed on top of her, squashing her into the mattress and breathing heavily into her ear.

"I could get used to putting my needs first," he said, pulling out and sitting next to her on the edge of the bed.

She was so horny and unfulfilled, she could cry. "Please don't leave me like this."

"I'm going to take a shower."

"Logan, please."

"Please, what?"

"Please make me come."

"Maybe later." He stood from the bed and stretched his arms over his head.

The headboard rattled as she jerked at her bonds. "Bastard," she hissed.

He leaned over her, his mouth close to her ear. "While you're lying there with your legs spread wide and your pussy aching and my cum trickling down your ass, I want you to think about all the things you want to do to me when I untie you."

She narrowed her eyes at him. "Such as stab you?"

He slid a finger into her cleft, rubbing the sensitive nub of flesh he'd ignored until now. "If you try, I'm sure you'll come up with something a bit more creative."

Seconds shy of sending her flying at last, he lifted his finger to his mouth and licked its shiny tip in a way that made her ache. He turned away and headed to the bathroom. The shower kicked on a moment later, and Toni groaned. She hoped that the shower invigorated him, because when he came back and untied her, she was going to fuck him senseless.

CHAPTER 27

LOGAN STEPPED up behind Toni and filled his hands with her full breasts. The tips instantly stiffened against his fingertips. "Good morning," he murmured against her temple. "Did you sleep well?"

"Have you seen my journal?" she asked.

Her first response wasn't *Take me back to bed right now, my irresistible stud?* He apparently needed to work on his delivery.

"What journal?" he asked, sliding his hands down the smooth skin of her torso.

He was sure they'd both still be in dreamland if Butch hadn't started banging on the door before the sun had even risen. The band had an early promotional commitment this morning. Logan had forgotten about it or he probably would have saved Toni's lessons on incorporating food in sex for another night. But after he'd untied her, she'd retaliated by getting herself off and leaving him so turned on he thought his dick would explode. He'd had to think of some excuse to get them rejoined at the groin, and they both had a love for food.

"The little book I put into my bag yesterday. It's not there." She turned her head to look at him, concern clouding her pretty brown eyes. "It has a pink leather cover and is about so big." She made a rectangular shape with her fingers about the size of a four by six snapshot photo.

"Did you have it out when we were working on your presentation? Maybe it's with your notes and stuff."

She shook her head. "It's not for the book. My journal is full of my private thoughts."

"Are they thoughts about my privates?" He prodded her in the rear with his achingly hard cock in case she'd forgotten which privates he was referring to.

She laughed softly. "A few," she said. "I really need to find it. It's important."

"I'm sure it's around here somewhere," he said. "Let's check the bed first."

He tried easing her back to the bed, but she pulled away.

"It's not in the bed, Logan. Help me find it."

They tore the room apart and after getting dressed, Toni went down to the conference room to see if it had fallen out of her bag during her presentation. He found her at the front desk asking if anyone had turned it in to lost and found. Toni's shoulders sagged when the clerk shook her head.

"Don't worry about it," Logan said "If it doesn't turn up, then someone will get an interesting read about my privates."

"But I wrote secrets in there. Not just secrets about me. Or you. About everyone in the band."

"Maybe it's in the limo."

Unfortunately they'd already missed their window of opportunity to grab a quickie in their hotel bed, but maybe he could distract her from her worries in the limo. When they climbed inside the waiting car, half the band was already inside.

Fuck. These guys again.

"Did you even comb your hair?" Max asked Logan.

Logan tried smoothing his unruly curls. "No."

"We have a television appearance in an hour, and you look like your head lost a fight with a wolverine."

"So I'll skip it. No one gives two shits about the bassist anyway."

"You aren't skipping it," Max said.

"We didn't even have time for breakfast." He glanced at Steve for backup, but Steve's head was leaning back against the seat, and he was undoubtedly asleep behind his sunglasses.

"Won't be the first time or the last," Max said.

Toni tried to calm Logan's curls with her fingertips and a bit of spit. Logan was tired of all these stupid promotional events. They interfered with his sleep. With his hobbies. With the time he could spend with Toni. He longed for the days when all he had to do was stay sober enough to find the stage and the rest of his time was his own.

"Are you dropping me off at the arena? Or do I need to find a cab?" Toni asked.

"You aren't following us to the TV station?" Max asked. "We don't do many morning shows. This will probably be your only opportunity to catch any behind-the-scenes footage."

"I'm with Colby and the crew today. They start assembling that stage early. And all my equipment is on the bus anyway."

"Let's hope they have my platform fixed," Logan grumbled. "I don't know why we need all the fanfare anyway."

"You know the fans expect us to top the previous year's stage setup every concert season," Max said.

"And when did we start doing what's expected of us?"

"About ten years ago when we hit the top of the record charts for the first time. Why are you so pissy this morning?" Max asked.

Logan scrubbed his face with both hands. "I'm just tired."

"We've barely gotten started on this tour," Max said. "If you think you're tired now, wait until we take on the rest of the world and the jet lag kicks in."

"We should fire Sam and go indie," Steve said.

So he wasn't asleep.

"Don't be ridiculous," Max said. "We don't do many morning events. Fucking suck it up."

"Going indie sounds great to me," Logan said. "Is Sam still shopping the rights to our next album?" He didn't remember signing a new contract after they'd fulfilled their previous one with the release of their last album.

"He's holding out for more cash," Steve said.

"Where the hell is Dare?" Max asked.

"Do you think he'll side with you?" Steve asked. "I'm sure he's tired of all this bullshit too."

"You're not really considering going indie, are you?" Toni asked.

"Yes," said Steve.

"No," said Max.

"Maybe," said Logan.

The door opened, and Dare tumbled in. He was barefoot and shirtless. Butch followed him into the car, carrying Dare's boots and T-shirt.

"Where's Reagan?" Butch asked, his eyes searching each face

in the car as if he'd somehow overlooked her.

"Haven't seen her," Max said.

"Dammit!" Butch tossed Dare's clothes at him before jumping out of the car again.

"Fuck, it's early," Dare grumbled as he tugged his T-shirt on over his head.

As soon as he pulled the fabric down to cover his belly, Dare leaned over and put his head on Toni's lap, snuggling into her like she was his favorite pillow. Logan might have slugged him, but he was too tired for that level of activity, and if he'd have thought of it first, he'd have done the exact same thing.

Toni glanced nervously at Logan, but he offered her a reassuring smile. He trusted her not to break his heart, trusted his bandmates not to steal her away from him. The only one he didn't trust with her was himself. Soon the North American leg of their tour would be over and she'd go back to her little chicken farm in Washington and they'd have to say goodbye.

A churning lump settled in the pit of his stomach, a sensation he quickly dismissed as hunger.

"How does Dare feel about going indie?" Toni asked.

Dare's eyes eased open, and he zeroed in on Steve. "This again? Give it a rest, will you?"

"So this isn't the first time you've discussed it?" Toni asked, her fingers twitching. Logan guessed she was itching to write down their entire conversation.

At times, Logan wished her reporter side had an off switch.

"It's Steve's favorite topic of conversation," Max said.

"I just have a different definition of success than the rest of you," Steve said. "I don't need the limousines and the fancy house and the five-star hotel suites and the piles of cash."

"But you do need the gorgeous babes," Logan said with a grin.

"Of course I need the gorgeous babes," Steve said, "but as far as everything else goes, I just need to make music and earn enough to get by. The rest of this is just . . . *stuff*. Unnecessary fucking stuff."

"I'm so tired, he's making sense," Dare mumbled. He covered a yawn, and then a second, with the back of his hand.

The car door opened, and Reagan stumbled in wearing a bathrobe, a pair of combat boots, and a sleepy expression. "This shit is for the birds," she declared before sitting next to Max and glowering at Butch, who tossed her overnight bag into the car and climbed inside, slamming the door behind him.

"We're going to be late," Butch said as the limo took off.

"Six a.m. is never late," Steve said, "unless you haven't made it to bed yet. Which I haven't." His fingertips disappeared under his sunglasses to rub at both eyes.

"How am I supposed to get dressed in the car?" Reagan said, tilting her head at Butch and giving him a glare that would freeze molten lava.

"Figure it out," he barked.

"I'll help you," Toni said. She scooted out from beneath Dare's head to stumble to the other side of the moving limo.

Toni held Reagan's robe like a makeshift curtain while Reagan tossed on clothes in the corner behind it. Once dressed, their sassy guitarist fixed an icy stare on Butch as she flopped into the seat, shoved her feet back into her boots, and jerked the laces tight.

None of this was Butch's fault. He didn't arrange their schedule. He was just in charge of making sure they stuck to it. Poor bastard.

At the TV station, they climbed out one at a time. Logan lingered so he could be with Toni for as long as possible. The limo was taking her to the arena so she could start her day and then would return to pick up the band after their television appearance.

He kissed her, his heart panging unpleasantly, as if he were saying goodbye to her forever instead of for a few hours. He much too attached to her, he decided. Much, much, much too attached.

"You be careful around all that heavy equipment," he said, kissing her again.

"I will. Don't worry about me."

How could he not worry about her? She collected more bruises by walking across an empty room than he did wiping out on his dirt bike.

"Don't be too charming on television," she said. "I don't want the whole world to covet what's mine."

He stumbled out of the car, her words tumbling around in his head like socks in a dryer. To covet what was *hers*? Did she really think he was hers? He'd have to set her straight when he had time. Still, even if she was mistaken, he wasn't sure why her show of possessiveness made him happy. Such things weren't supposed to make him happy. They were supposed to scare him away.

The limo drove off and he made sure it made it safely into the flow of traffic before jogging to catch up with the guys.

"I hope Kirk runs you all through the ringer after this," Butch grumbled. "Fucking whiny little bitches."

Ugh, they had to go to the gym today? After a trip to the store, Logan had hoped he could climb into his bunk and sleep until noon. Well, if he couldn't find time to go to the store himself, he knew someone who could.

"Hey, Butch?" Logan touched Butch's arm as he caught up with him.

"What?" he snapped.

"Can you do me a favor?"

"Am I allowed to say no?"

It seemed his bandmates weren't the only ones being fucking whiny little bitches this morning. "Toni keeps a diary and she needs a new one," Logan said. "Do you think you could send someone out to buy her one?"

"It's for Toni?"

Logan nodded.

Butch sighed and lifted his pen to write a note on his clipboard. "What kind?"

May 10

Dear New Journal,

Welcome to my world. You were a gift from Logan, so even though I'd decided I wasn't going to bother keeping a diary anymore, I pretty much have to fill your pages, don't I? He says the reason I lost my previous journal was because it wasn't blue to match his eyes. So because you're blue and will always remind me of him, he insists I'll never lose you. The ego on that guy!

But he always makes me laugh. And I do love him. More than he'll ever know. But maybe I shouldn't write that here. He might read it.

I watched the stage being set up today, and everyone in the crew volunteered to wear Logan's head camera to capture a first-person view of their job, so we sent some poor lackey out to buy five more. I haven't had a chance to review that footage yet—I hope it turned out. I also set up my big video camera to record the stage being set up from the center of the arena. It's really cool when watched on fast forward. It should definitely make it into the book.

I promised myself I wouldn't write anything scandalous in this diary, in case I misplaced it, but holy hairy balls, Batman, this morning on the way to their television interview, the band was talking about going indie. While Max seemed completely against it, the rest of them didn't think it was a bad idea. This kind of decision would change everything for them. I'm not sure if it's a good idea, but I have faith that whatever they decide, they'll be successful.

And Steve's words got me wondering about my personal definition of success. The more I think about it, the more I keep changing my mind. So maybe success is an ever-moving target. Does that make sense? Once you've found success, then what? You find new success, right? A different kind of success or a higher level of success. I don't know. I haven't found success yet. I'll let you know when I do.

Logan is making come-to-bed noises, so I have to go now. I hope my ramblings don't bore you to tears.

Toni

May 11

Dear Journal,

It's really late. Logan somehow talked me into going to the after-party with him tonight. I had more fun than I thought I would, mostly because Reagan wouldn't let me sit down. And after she'd poured a few drinks down my throat, she got me dancing and I couldn't stop. I'm sure I looked like an awkward fool, but it was fun. Until I got sick.

She held my hair while I threw up in the bathroom—what a great friend—and now my head hurts so bad I can't sleep.

Would I do it again?

Sure!

The band had a mall appearance today. It was in a novelty shop, so they spent most of their time signing T-shirts. Apparently signing T-shirts is an art. Or a science. I'm not sure which. You'd think it would be easier to sign a shirt when it's stretched out on a hard surface, but nope, it's easier to sign them when they're wadded up in a soft ball. Who knew?

The things I learn on this job.

Ugh, I swear this bus is riding on a roller coaster track tonight.

We're on our way to New Orleans now, and we'll be staying there on our day off. Reagan wants to go clothes shopping. I'd rather eat beignets and listen to jazz. Logan says he'll bring me back during Mardi Gras. With tits like mine, I'll be buried in beads.

And while that's what he said, I bet he'd freak out if I actually flashed them. He has a fascination with my boobs. I'm not sure it's healthy.

Tomorrow we're going to work on the exclusive song for the book. Or at least they're going to try to come up with something. Sam said it isn't a contract breach, so yay! I'm really excited about it.

Ugh, being excited makes my stomach queasy.
Why is the floor spinning?
I'm never drinking again.

CHAPTER 28

LOGAN TOOK a seat beside Steve's bare feet on the sectional and waited for Toni to finish hooking up every piece of equipment she'd brought with her and even a few she'd borrowed. He knew she was tremendously excited to capture the band creating a song, but he knew from past experience that these things never, ever went well. He was positive she was going to end up disappointed. The only good thing about that was that she'd probably need him to console her. But he'd rather this session go well because he knew it meant a lot to her. He was determined to be on his best behavior.

"I think that's everything," she said and turned to look at them expectantly.

Was she expecting genius to flow from them all on cue and converge into a perfect melody? Yeah, right.

Dare stood and lifted good ol' Genevieve off her pegs on the wall. He blew a puff of dust from her fretboard and sat down on the coffee table to tune her.

"You're blocking the shot," Toni whispered. "Do you want me to move the camera?"

Dare glanced over his shoulder at the video camera trained at his back. "I'll move," he said.

"But you usually sit in the middle of the room," Max said.

"Then I'll pull the camera over here," Toni said. When she had a new shot lined up, she stared at them expectantly again. Logan was pretty sure he wasn't the only one feeling awkward.

"Um," Max said, "so I guess we should decide what kind of song to compose. I was thinking something acoustic. We haven't done an acoustic track and since—"

"Fuck that," Steve interrupted. "Why am *I* being excluded?"

"You aren't being excluded," Max said, raising a placating hand.

"Oh yeah?" Steve said. "How many drum tracks will you require to accompany your *acoustic* song?"

"Acoustic songs don't have drum tracks," Logan said.

"Exactly," Steve said. "So that means I'mmmm . . . ?"

"Excluded?" Logan supplied.

Steve slapped his thigh. "Exactly."

"We could add a drum line to an acoustic song," Max said. "You could play snare."

"Technically, drums are acoustic," Dare said. "Acoustic just means without amplifiers."

"Why are you defending him?" Steve said. "You hate playing acoustic guitar."

"I wouldn't say I hate it," Dare said. "I just prefer electric."

"So we're scratching the acoustic idea," Steve said, crossing his arms over his chest.

"You just don't want to do it because it was my idea." Max was starting to shout already.

"No," Steve yelled back. "I don't want to do it because it's a *stupid* idea!"

Logan would normally have chosen a side by now, but he didn't want to escalate the problem. Toni was counting on them.

"Guys!" Reagan yelled over all of them. "Calm down."

Max rose to his feet and waved an arm in Steve's direction. "I'm not going to calm down until he admits that he'll think any idea I have is stupid—"

"I freely admit any idea you have *is* stupid," Steve said.

"I wasn't finished," Max said in a clipped tone. "He will *think* any idea I have is stupid because it wasn't his idea."

"I definitely admit that too," Steve said. "We need a song with a huge drum solo. Currently all we have is guitar solo, guitar solo, guitar solo."

"What about a bass solo?" Logan suggested.

"No one wants to hear a bass solo," Steve said.

"No one wants to hear a fucking drum solo either!" Logan said.

"We have to have a guitar solo," Dare said.

"Why?" Steve said. "Because we always have a guitar solo? You're all so predictable. Why can't we do something different for a change? It's not like this song is going on an album. It's just for this stupid book."

Logan glanced at Toni. He wasn't sure if her shell-shocked expression was due to Steve undermining her work or because, as usual, the arguing between them was already intensifying. He hit Steve to show his support for his woman. "Toni's book is not stupid."

"Guys, guys," Reagan said. "Maybe we should start with lyrics and—"

"Start with lyrics?" Max asked. "We never start with lyrics."

"How is she supposed to know that?" Dare snapped, shoving Max in the chest. "She's never had the pleasure of being involved in this fucking bullshit."

"Okay, not with lyrics then," Reagan said calmly. "How do you usually start?"

"Exactly like this," Logan said. He was sure Toni wasn't getting what she expected for her book, but she was getting an authentic experience. "These assholes can't agree on anything."

"We can all agree that you contribute nothing, so you might as well leave," Steve said.

"I contribute!" Logan shouted, anger making his skin hot and his heart race.

"What do you contribute? D chord, D chord, D chord, D chord," Steve said, keeping the beat to his improvised bass line with shakes of his head.

"Shut up," Logan growled. "I sometimes play E."

"We usually start with a guitar riff," Dare said to Reagan. He looked to their original rhythm guitarist. "Max?"

Max looked at the electric guitar he'd brought in and hooked to one of the practice amps. He swallowed hard, rubbing his wrist brace, and then switched his attention to the acoustic guitar in the corner. "I still think acoustic—"

"No," Steve interrupted.

"Bull headed," Max grumbled under his breath, but he rose from his spot on the sectional to yank his favorite blue guitar off its stand—it was the only guitar he hadn't allowed Reagan to borrow when she'd joined the tour. He took his time adjusting the tuning while the rest of them twiddled their thumbs or exchanged glares.

Max took off his wrist brace and carefully laid it on the coffee table. He flexed his fingers several times and then shook blood into the underused hand. "This one has been keeping me awake at night," he said. He played several notes of a raunchy riff, shook his head, slid his hand along his fret board to a lower octave and started over. Smiling, he nodded and bobbed his head slightly to the rhythm as he came to the end of the string of notes and returned to the beginning.

Logan sat up straighter, listening to the natural rhythm of the piece and mentally adding his lower bass tones to the midrange.

"Oh, I love it," Reagan squeaked.

"So you hear this kind of stuff in your head?" Toni asked. She was staring at Max with the kind of awe she usually reserved for Logan.

"Only when it's quiet and I'm trying to sleep," Max said with a wry grin.

His smile turned into a grimace, and he jerked his hand off the fret board, cradling it against his chest with his right hand. He massaged his left wrist and shook it out before returning his fucked-up hand to his guitar and playing the riff again. Dare's rapid string of notes blaring from his amplifier made everyone jump. He shook his head and tried a completely different string of notes, shrugged and started over, now alternating E-minor triplets with a four-note pattern.

Wow, they were actually getting things done. Logan was proud of his band for holding their shit together for a change. Well, for the most part. Heads hadn't started rolling yet.

Logan stood and went after the bass guitar he'd hooked up on the far side of the lounge. Dudes were going to flip when they heard the awesome bass line running through his head. Before he could even lift the strap over his head, Max's riff ended abruptly, and he jerked the plug out of the end of his guitar.

"Fuck this!" he yelled, slinging the free end of the cord on the ground.

"If your wrist is bothering you, I can play the riff." Reagan extended her hands toward the now-silent guitar.

"I'm done for today," Max said. He slid the door open so hard it slammed against the frame with an earsplitting *crack*.

"We should have gone with acoustic," Dare said.

"What difference would that make?" Steve asked. "Don't you

have to strum harder when you play acoustic?"

"Strumming isn't his problem," Dare said, setting his guitar aside. "It's fingering frets rapidly."

As was done in *all* Exodus End songs. Even the ballads. Max was probably thinking if they took a huge departure from their norm and slowed things down—*a lot*—he could play.

So it made perfect sense to Logan why Max would rather play acoustic. "If you'd let him play what he wanted, he could have used a few connected chords. Not had to move his fingers much."

"So we switch him to bass," Steve said, shrugging. "That solves everything. Max can play. We don't have to put up with you anymore."

"Seriously?" Logan shook his head at Steve.

Steve jumped up from his seat on the arm of the sectional and whacked Logan on the back. "No, not seriously. Learn to take a joke, man."

"It's easier to take jokes when they're actually funny," Dare said as he set his guitar back on its stand.

Toni collected Max's wrist brace from the table and quietly left the room. Knowing her, she had tears swimming in her eyes and was offering Max a tender hug before she helped him put it back on. A week ago, Logan probably would have flown into a jealous rage and intervened, but now he realized she had a heart big enough for everyone around her, with plenty of room to spare for him.

May 12

Dear Journal,

Well, the song-writing session didn't go as planned. Max wanted to do an acoustic ballad, which pissed off Steve because there are no drums in acoustic ballads. They usually get along so well, but were all arguing within seconds. I was stunned by how quickly the session deteriorated. Eventually Max caved and shared an amazing riff that's been floating around in his head. I don't need to tell you how amazing that is, do I? And then Dare joined in with this solo he pulled out of nowhere. I think Logan was about to add his bass line—and God, I wanted to hear it so bad—when Max's wrist started bothering him. He left the session angry, but he wasn't really angry, he was hurting. I don't think he's ready to let go of playing guitar and I don't think his bandmates have any idea how much he's lost by handing his guitar over to Reagan. Even temporarily.

I did get some footage. And I can piece together the good parts. This creative genius business is kind of scary, but I know the fans will love to see them writing a new song. I sure did! Well, except the arguing stuff. I'll just cut out that part. Steve is such an instigator.

We should be at the hotel soon. I'm so looking forward to spending the night alone with Logan. He says there's a hot tub in our suite. So you know what that means? Hot tub sex lessons for me tonight. Score!

I better call Birdie before we get to the hotel, or I'll end up being too distracted by Logan to remember to call her. Maybe Mom will let her use her cellphone so we can face chat. I miss my buttercup's smiling face.

In-awe-of-the-talent-around-me,

Toni

CHAPTER
29

"**G**ET DRESSED," LOGAN SAID, kissing Toni's shoulder as he rose from the bed. "We're going out."

"Out? Where?"

"It's a surprise." He wasn't sure if she'd like the surprise, but there was only one way to find out.

A few hours later they were flying over their drop zone. He'd checked their gear several times, but he checked it again. He'd never taken a woman tandem skydiving and though he wanted to share the exhilaration of hurtling toward the earth with this particular woman, her safety was at the forefront of his mind.

"I am not jumping out of a perfectly good airplane," Toni said.

She'd also said she wasn't getting on an airplane the size of a sparrow, but he'd managed to convince her.

"You'll be strapped to my chest. And perfectly safe." He hadn't done many tandem dives, but as a licensed instructor, he was allowed to do them and take his inexperienced girlfriend along with him. "Just enjoy it."

"What if the chute doesn't open or, or, or I pee my pants?"

He cupped her cheek and kissed her. "Don't you trust me?"

"Yes," she said without hesitation.

He tucked a stray lock of hair into her bright red helmet. "Then stop worrying. You'll be fine."

He claimed her mouth in a deep lingering kiss, only drawing away when the pilot called out, "It's time."

"Time?" Toni squeaked.

Logan shifted behind her and attached the carabiners that linked her harness to his. He could feel the tremble of her body—knew she was terrified—but he wanted to share this with her. He loved skydiving and hoped it was something they could do together for fun. If she tried it and hated it, he wouldn't pressure her to do it again. He wanted to find something he liked to do that she enjoyed as well. He'd already decided to buy her a dirt bike for her birthday, and he couldn't wait to teach her to ride it.

He slid open the door on the side of the plane, and Toni leaned slightly forward to peer down at the ground far below. Thick areas of trees dotted the lush green landscape and twisted streams wound around the hills, all dumping into the wide green river that resembled polished jade from this height.

"Nope. Not gonna happen," Toni yelled over the roar of the engine. She shook her head so hard, he feared her neck would snap. "No way in hell, Logan. Nope. Nope. Nope."

"Is your camera on?"

She nodded, touching the camera on the side of her helmet.

Without warning he wrapped his arm around her waist and lifted her toes from the floor before diving sideways out of the plane and taking her with him.

The first moment of free fall always stole his breath, but then the wind caught. Flying and falling at the same time. Adrenaline surging. Heart pounding. And then the overwhelming feeling of being alive hit him. It was that feeling that kept him coming back for more.

"Oh my God!" Toni yelled. "Oh my God!"

"Did you pee your pants?" he teased.

"I'm not sure. But this is amazing!"

His heart soared. She, she was amazing.

"God, I love you," he said, wrapping his arms around her and squeezing her from behind.

"What?" she yelled. The wind rushing past their ears as they plummeted howled and made hearing difficult.

"I said, I love you!" he shouted.

She stiffened in his arms. "Don't say it if you don't mean it."

"I do mean it. I love you, Antonia whatever-your-middle-name-is Nichols!"

"I love you too!"

Her confession should have terrified him far more than the

ground rushing toward them, but it didn't. It thrilled him beyond any free fall he'd ever experienced. Maybe love was the adrenaline rush that had been missing from his life all these years.

"But I'm very mad that you told me now!" she yelled.

Surprised, he craned his neck to try to see her face, but it was useless in their his-front-to-her-back position. "You are?"

He thought she'd *want* to hear him say it.

"Yeah," she said. "I can't kiss you. You have no idea how much I need to kiss you right now."

He did have an idea, actually. "Next time we'll jump separately, so we can kiss all the way down."

"Deal!" A few seconds later her hands clutched at the flapping fabric of his sleeves. "Logan?"

"Yeah, baby?"

"Aren't we getting rather close to the ground?"

They were. He yanked his ripcord, and there was, as always, that brief instant of terror when he wondered if the chute would come out. If it would open. If it would catch. There was something addictive about that feeling too, knowing he might be meeting his maker soon. The wind caught their chute, and their bodies jerked as their acceleration slowed abruptly.

Toni commented on the scenery as they soared back to earth. But Logan's mind was racing.

What had he done? He'd told her that he loved her. Was he insane? They weren't ready for this step. Hell, he wasn't sure he'd ever be ready for this step, but he definitely wasn't prepared to love her after less than two weeks together. He had to be completely nuts. Or he'd been caught up in the excitement of the free fall. That was all.

They touched down smoothly, their yellow-and-blue-striped parachute drifting past them and settling on the grass. His hands were shaking as he unfastened her harness from his.

"Did you enjoy skydiving?" he asked.

"I loved it!" As soon as the last clip came free, she turned and threw herself into his arms. "That was so much fun. I'm so glad you forced me to jump."

"I'm stoked that you want to go again."

"Did you mean what you said?" she asked.

The smile dropped off his face. "Uh." He shrugged, his heart trying to thud itself through his ribs. "I guess."

He turned away and started pulling the chute toward himself.

Toni grabbed his arm and spun him around to face her. "Say it to my face," she demanded. "Tell me while you're looking at me, while I can see into you and you can see into me."

His breath caught. Surely it wouldn't take the courage afforded by a skydiving adrenaline rush every time he told her he loved her.

"I . . ." He took a deep breath, forcing himself not to close his eyes to her. Not to close his heart. "I love you, Toni."

Her smile could have lit the heavens. "I love you too."

May 13

He finally said it. He loves me.
Skydiving is awesome.
Sex after skydiving? I have no words.

Toni

May 14

Dear Journal,

The concert in New Orleans was really fun tonight. I got into the audience to record footage. I'm pretty sure my toes will never be the same after being stomped on dozens of times, but I think I finally get it, why every Exodus End show sells out. It's because when you're in that audience looking up at them, in total awe of their talent, you don't feel like you're just watching. You feel like you're a part of them.

I'm so in love with their bassist.

In love with the band.

In love with this job.

I hope it never has to end.

Toni

May 15

Dear Journal,

It occurred to me today that I haven't heard from Susan since that meeting in Denver. I guess that means she's given up on taking my job. Not that I'd ever move aside for her—this is where I belong.

Tonight I'm putting head cams on all the band members so we can get a first-person perspective of what it's like onstage. I'm really glad we bought extra cameras for the crew. This is going to be amazing!

Logan and the band are currently at some bar grand opening in downtown Dallas. Apparently it's a big deal. I probably should have gone, but I'm burned out on promotional events and I know they are too. I'll go to the after-party tonight, though. I have some new clothes to show off. Not sure how Reagan talked me into that leather corset, but it's really cute. Jace Seymour's girlfriend— Aggie— embroidered strawberries all over it. I'm going to wear a jacket with it because my boobs are so out there in that thing, but it's definitely the most daring article of clothing I've ever worn in public.

I'm off to do some work now while I have a rare moment to myself. I have a ton of footage to sort through and will be collecting even more tonight.

Overworked-and-loving-it,

Toni

CHAPTER 30

THE LOUNGE DOOR SLID open, and Toni dropped her phone. She fell to her knees on the carpet, hunting for it.

"What's going on in here?" Logan asked, grinning at her.

"Just face chatting with my sister." She'd been caught acting silly, and her face flamed with embarrassment.

"Oh. It sounded like you were watching *The Princess Bride*." He entered the room uninvited and settled on the sofa.

"Not watching it. Reading it. It's Birdie's favorite book." Actually, as far as her sister was concerned, it was the *only* book. And since the road trip from Dallas to Albuquerque was so freaking long, Toni had plenty of time to read it to her.

"There's a book?"

Toni laughed and picked up her phone, dusting off a few crumbs.

Birdie smiled when her face came back into view. "I thought you was lost."

"It was a book before it was a movie," Toni said to Logan. "Don't you read?"

"All the time. Menus. Road signs. Text messages."

Toni picked up the used book she'd purchased at a truck stop and shook it at him. "I meant books."

"Is that Logan?" Birdie asked.

"Yep. He didn't knock, did he?" Toni turned her phone so that Logan came into view in the corner of the screen.

Birdie beamed. "Hi, Logan! Mom let me use her phone. Now

Toni can read to me and I can see her."

"Awesome. She can read to me too."

"No, she cannot," Toni said, her cheeks blazing again. There was no way she was letting Logan see her acting like a complete fool on purpose. He got to see her acting like one accidentally far too often as it was.

"Please, Toni," Birdie said.

"Please, Toni," Logan mimicked as he slid a hand up her thigh out of view of the camera. She caught his hand before it disappeared under the leg of her sleep shorts.

"Sit over there." Toni shoved him so he'd move out of reach. She didn't want to become an inferno of insatiable need in front of her little sister. After she hung up? Well, that was another matter entirely.

"Only if you promise to read to me."

Mr. Grabby Hands reached for her boob, and she smacked his hands away.

"Fine!" Toni said. "But you can't laugh at me."

"Can I laugh *with* you?"

"Birdie, it's time for bed," Mom said from out of sight on the other end of the line.

"Not yet," Birdie complained. "Toni is still reading to me."

"Five minutes."

"Hurry, Toni!"

Toni wasn't sure if she could do this in front of Logan. She took a deep breath and said in her best Cheech Marin impression, "My name is *Meee*-ster Featherface. You keeled my *cheeek*-ken, prepare to die."

A strange snorting sound came from Logan's general direction as he tried to swallow a laugh. No good. He cackled with glee until Toni gave him her death stare, and he stiffened, releasing an occasional snort as he tried to contain his mirth.

"I don't think that's how it goes," he said. "I've seen the movie dozens of times."

"The book is better," Birdie said wisely.

"I don't recall a chicken or a Mr. Featherface," Logan said.

"Mr. Featherface is our rooster," Birdie said.

"You have a rooster?"

Toni nodded. "They're kind of necessary on a chicken farm."

"I still can't picture you as a chicken farmer," Logan said, shaking his head at her. "Do you wear overalls?"

She laughed. "On occasion. Actually, Birdie is in charge of the chickens. Isn't that right, Buttercup?"

"Yep!" The chirp came loudly out of the phone's speaker.

"So your rooster plays the part of Inigo?" Logan asked.

"Yep. I'm Princess Buttercup and my dog Jonesy is Prince Hump-and-stink," Birdie said. "And Toni is Tozinni."

Logan lifted his brows at her. "Tozinni?"

"Vizzini, the mad Sicilian," she clarified. "There aren't many female characters in the book."

"Do the funnest part, Tozinni!"

Oh, what the hell. If Logan could handle her many quirks, surely he could tolerate her reinventing parts of a book to keep herself entertained as she reread it for the billionth time.

"Do you know that sound, Highness?" Toni asked with a lisp that rivaled Daffy Duck's. "It's the shrieking peels."

"Shrieking banana peels!" Birdie yelled. "They're going to attack the princess. Oh help. Help meeeeee!"

"Inconceivable," Logan said, shaking his head grimly.

Birdie giggled, and Toni couldn't help but laugh with her.

"Your five minutes are up," Mom said, taking the phone from Birdie.

"But, Mom . . ."

"I'll call you tomorrow afternoon, Buttercup," Toni said.

"We're going to the dunes tomorrow," Logan reminded her.

Toni wasn't sure if she'd like racing dune buggies through the desert, but Logan was keen on getting her involved in all his insane hobbies.

"Make that tomorrow night," Toni amended, smiling when Birdie's face came back on screen.

"I miss you so much," Birdie said, her eyes watery with tears.

Toni blinked back a few tears of her own. "I miss you too. Good night, Buttercup."

"Good night, Princess," Logan said. Toni turned the screen in his direction so Birdie could catch his wave.

"Will you be Westley next time?" Birdie asked him. "Please!"

Logan bowed his head graciously. "As you wish."

Birdie was still grinning when Mom disconnected the call.

"Thanks for humoring her," Toni said, setting the phone aside. "She'll love you forever."

"It's hard not to love her in return."

Toni smiled. "I know exactly what you mean."

"And it's impossible not to love you."

Toni's heart thudded as their eyes met. "I know exactly what you mean," she whispered.

Logan grinned. "I like this newfound confidence in you."

"Huh?" It eventually dawned on her that he thought she meant it was impossible not to love *her*. She still had a hard time accepting that he did, so she wasn't yet capable of bragging about it. "I meant it's impossible not to love *you*."

He shrugged, looking devilishly irresistible as usual. "Improbable, maybe, but not inconceivable," he said with a pronounced lisp.

She smacked him in the face with a pillow, and he tackled her to the sofa. He kissed her, chasing all teasing thoughts from her mind and replacing them with X-rated versions. He shifted his hips between her legs, and she could feel him hardening and lengthening through his jeans and her shorts. He pulled her glasses off and set them on the coffee table. He was close enough that his gorgeous face appeared perfectly clear, and for once she was glad for her myopia. It gave her an excuse to make him stay so close she could feel his warm breath against her sensitive lips.

"What are you going to teach me today, sensei?" she asked, as always, ready for a new adventure with her talented instructor.

He threaded his fingers through her hair and stared deeply into her eyes. "I think it's time you graduated. With honors."

She grinned. "Mega cum alotta?"

"That sounds appropriate," he said tersely.

"Or *in*appropriate," she teased, but he wasn't teasing her back.

Her grin faded. He looked far too serious for Logan. She touched his face, and he closed his eyes, pressing his cheek into her palm.

"Is something wrong?"

He shook his head and opened his eyes. She'd never tire of staring into those expressive, soulful blue beauties.

"You're planning to stick around for a while, aren't you?" he asked.

"Forever, if you'll let me."

He nibbled on her lower lip, sending sparks of pleasure down her throat. Her nipples tightened, suddenly craving his attention.

"Toni, you can't be my sex student forever," he said.

"I can't? Why not?" This sounded like being dumped. Was she about to be dumped? She could not handle being dumped.

"Because we're in a relationship now."

She loved that he said it. Loved even more that she knew it to be true. "So?"

"Sometimes I just need to fuck you without a lesson plan." His fingers tightened in her hair, tugging in a way that she probably shouldn't find exciting and pleasurable, but did. She couldn't ignore the way the ache in her scalp made her pussy throb.

"Like now?" she asked.

"No, right now I need to be tender and you need to stop asking so many questions."

"But what if I don't know what to do?"

"You'll know."

He ground his still-clothed erection into her clit and then shifted his hips so that his cock was massaging her opening through their clothes. She groaned, surprised by how much she wanted him already. How much she always wanted him. She wondered how couples ever left their beds. Would the passion between them always blaze this brightly? God, she hoped so.

She opened her mouth to ask him what he wanted her to do, but snapped it closed again when she remembered he no longer wanted to instruct her. At least not formally. Did he want her to initiate their lovemaking? Or was he just going to drive her nuts by rubbing himself against her so that she was undeniably aware of what she was currently missing thanks to his jeans and her sleep shorts?

She tugged at his shirt impatiently—wanting him naked, wanting to feel the warm skin of his belly against hers and the hairs on his chest to tease her nipples. She wanted him inside her, filling her with slow deep thrusts, staring into her eyes, stroking her hair, stealing deep lingering kisses. Was it strange that with all the adventurous positions they'd tried, missionary was her favorite? She found staring into his eyes beguilingly intimate and while it might not be the best position for her to get off quickly, it was definitely the best position to fulfill her.

Logan stripped his shirt off over his head and tossed it aside. She filled her hands with hot, smooth flesh—his back, shoulders, arms, and chest. She couldn't get enough of him. Doubted she'd ever get enough. Her hands moved down his chest, and he shifted so she could fumble with his fly. When his cock sprang free—hard, long, and thick in her hand—she was too impatient to remove her clothes. Pushing her sleep shorts and panties to one side, she guided him into her waiting body, gasping as they became one.

His strokes were slow and deep and drove her crazy as her panties dug into her clit every time their bodies came together.

"Why is it always so good with you?" he asked.

She had no answer for him. She had no means of comparison.

"Is it because I've taught you how to please me?" He brushed the hair from her face, staring deep into her eyes as he took her. Slow and deep. Slow and deep. "Is it because I know no man but me has ever been with you like this?" His hand slid under her top to caress her breast, bringing her to new heights when his fingertips found its sensitive tip. "Or is it because I love you?"

"That," she said.

He bent his head and kissed her gently, grinding his hips to take her deeper. "I think it's all those things," he whispered against her lips. "Promise you won't go after the tour ends. Stay with me."

She couldn't exactly promise that. She wasn't sure what would happen after her assignment ended. She did know she didn't have a passport, so she couldn't leave the country. How long did it take to get a passport? "I'll try."

He buried his face in her neck, his thrusts slow and gentle. "I need you with me."

Her fingers moved to tangle with his hair. "And I need to be with you. We'll make this work, Logan."

He lifted his head to look down at her. "But how?"

"How does a woman get a brainy guy to stop thinking while he's fucking her?"

He chuckled and kissed her. "She gets on top."

Well, that solved one of their problems.

CHAPTER 31

WHILE THE BAND WAITED for curtain call in Albuquerque, Toni switched on one of the videos she'd recorded a few days before and leaned back into the sofa. The entire band had gathered in the dressing room so they could watch their footage. All five of them had been gracious enough to wear rather unflattering headbands with cameras attached to the sides of their heads so she could get video of their individual perspectives while they performed.

"Okay, wait," Reagan said, leaning close to the laptop screen and squinting at a leather-encased ass. "Whose camera is this?"

Dare laughed. "Considering that all we've seen so far is Max's ass, I'd say it's yours."

"I didn't know you stared at my ass onstage," Max said, wiggling his eyebrows suggestively. "Is there something you'd like to share with the group?"

"I don't stare at your ass!" Reagan insisted.

"It's not Reagan's feed," Toni said. She'd checked the label several times to be sure. She snorted and covered her mouth with the back of her hand.

"Then whose is it?" Max asked, looking rather green around the gills all of a sudden.

"It's Logan's." Toni burst out laughing.

"What the fuck, dude?" Max roared. "Why were you staring at my ass?"

"I wasn't!"

"I think his camera was on crooked," Toni said.

"Likely story," Max grumbled.

They all turned their heads and squeezed their eyes shut as the camera focused directly on a spotlight overhead.

"Turn it off," Steve said. "I want to see mine. It has to be better than this."

"I just need a minute of good footage for each of you," Toni said. "I'm sure there's something usable on here."

She fast-forwarded through half a minute of blinding-lights footage and then they were back to staring at Max's ass.

"Turn it off!" Max insisted.

Toni replaced the SD card labeled *Logan* with the one labeled *Steve*. The recording of Steve rising from the stage was kind of cool, with his drum kit in the foreground and the arena coming into view behind it. But when he started to play, it was another story entirely.

"Pass the Dramamine!" Reagan shouted, sticking out a hand to block her view of the screen. Drums and sticks seemed to be flying at them in all directions as Steve banged his head to the beat while he played.

"Dear lord, Steve, do you ever hold still?" Dare asked. He swallowed hard and crinkled up his face in disgust.

"Some of us work hard for a living," Steve said.

"Maybe we should try putting your camera on a stand behind you," Toni said. "That way we can see you in action without giving ourselves whiplash."

"That could work," Logan said. "And you can put my camera on my bass stock so it's not cockeyed and making it seem like I'm staring at Max's ass."

"You *were* staring at it," Reagan said with a laugh. "And we have photographic evidence."

Logan reached over and grabbed her knee, squeezing until she was bucking and laughing uncontrollably.

"Why don't we see what Reagan's got?" Steve suggested. "Since she's so insistent on mocking the rest of us."

"We don't really need to watch two feeds of Max's ass." Toni winked at the man attached to that ass.

"Hey," Reagan said, "there isn't anything better to look at from the back of the stage."

"Oh really?" Logan said, twisting his head to try to look at his own ass. "I'm pretty sure I've got it going on in the ass department."

"If that's what you need to believe to help your self-esteem," Reagan said.

Logan grabbed her knee again, squeezing repeatedly until she bucked her giggling self off the sofa. "Boy crazy," Logan said. "Not that we're surprised."

"So we want to see Reagan's next?" Toni asked.

"Hey, guys, sorry to interrupt," Butch said from the dressing room door. "Can I see you on the bus for a minute?"

"All of us?" Dare asked.

"Uh." Butch's gaze fell on Toni. "Just the band." He considered Logan for a second. "And not Logan."

"Not Logan?" Max asked.

"It will take just a few minutes," Butch said. He backed out of the doorway and disappeared around the corner.

Toni and Logan, exchanging puzzled looks, watched the others leave the room.

"Why didn't he want to see you with the rest of them?" Toni asked.

Logan shrugged. "They're probably planning a surprise party for my birthday or something."

"Isn't your birthday at the end of October?"

"Yeah, well maybe it's a *big* surprise."

He didn't seem too concerned about being excluded, so Toni shrugged the oddity off.

"Do you think we should put cameras on all the instruments to get shots of your fingers moving?" Toni asked. "That might be interesting for the book."

"Dare's fingers, maybe, but mine just kind of go back and forth like . . ." He demonstrated playing two chords over and over again.

"So we'll get shots of the audience with your bass cam." She grinned at him. "If you can keep it off Max's ass for a few minutes."

He poked her in the ribs and she jerked sideways.

"You know what you should do?" he asked. "Get audience members to wear the head cams in a mosh pit. Since you're too scared to crowd surf."

She was definitely too scared to crowd surf.

Toni gave him a tight squeeze. "You're brilliant! Yes, I should totally include that."

"You're the brilliant one," he said. "You came up with the

camera idea in the first place."

She laughed and kissed him on the chin. "And I never would have thought of it if you hadn't made me watch your cliff-diving and bungee-jumping experiences."

"Not sure how covering your eyes in horror is considered *watching*." He smirked at her.

"See, if I can't watch, there's no way I'd be able to do it myself."

"Just like you couldn't skydive?"

"You threw me out of that plane, Logan Schmidt."

"So I guess I'll have to throw you off a bridge sometime."

"You have to get me *on* the bridge first."

Logan glanced around the room, looking a bit lost without his bandmates surrounding him. "Do you want to watch Sinners tonight?"

Toni clapped her hands together excitedly. "I would love to." She hadn't had the opportunity to watch Sinners perform a show yet. She'd been too busy collecting material for her book, and the hour before Exodus End performed always seemed to be the most hectic of her day.

"We'd better hurry. I think they're starting soon."

Logan led her through several corridors and into the arena. A few stagehands lit their own paths with flashlights, but otherwise it was dark behind the stage. Before Logan and Toni reached the wings, the lights flashed on and the unmistakable wail of Brian "Master" Sinclair's guitar started the intro of their first song. Toni dashed up the stage steps, not wanting to miss anything. The rest of the band joined the guitar, and then Sed Lionheart screamed out his trademark battle cry.

Toni cheered with the rest of the crowd, her heart thudding with excitement. Several lines into the first verse, Sed's voice cracked and he lowered his mic midverse. The rest of the band fell silent, first the guitars, then the bass and drums. His bandmates looked to Sed for direction.

"You okay?" Trey asked into his microphone.

Sed nodded. "From the top."

His eyes sparkled brightly in the stage lights, but he quickly squeezed them shut.

"What's going on?" Toni asked Logan, who shook his head and shrugged.

The song started over again. Lead guitar followed by rhythm, bass, and drums. Sed's battle cry. This time Sed didn't even make it through the first line before he lowered his mic and turned his back to the crowd. He rubbed his eyes with one hand and took several deep breaths. His three guitarists quickly surrounded him, talking to him out of range of the mic, patting him comfortingly on the back or arm. Nodding and gesturing, they seemed to come to some consensus, and Sed turned back to the agitated crowd.

"I'm sorry," he said to his audience. "I thought I could do this tonight. I thought performing would make it easier, take my mind off things." He swallowed hard and pressed his lips together, obviously fighting tears. After a moment, he continued, "I received a call from my sister just before the show. This afternoon, my father passed away unexpectedly."

The bottom fell out of Toni's chest, and her heart sank with it. She pressed her fingertips against her lips to stop their trembling. She knew exactly what he was going through and wondered if he'd appreciate any words of comfort from her—not that words were any comfort when a beloved parent passed away—but she wanted to reach out to him in some way.

"So I need a minute to pull my shit together so I can sing." He laughed hollowly and swiped a stray tear from his cheek. "Knew I should have taken up drums."

"Nope," Logan said as he rushed onstage. He covered Sed's mic with one hand and leaned in close to speak to Sed.

Toni strained her ears for threads of their conversation, but the murmur of the crowd prevented her from hearing anything. There were vehement head shakes on Sed's part followed by him tilting his head to listen to whatever Logan was saying. After a moment, Sed smiled at Logan, nodded, and gave him a hearty pat on the back.

Sed lifted his microphone and said to the crowd, "I'm going to leave you in good hands here."

He handed the mic to Logan and jogged offstage. His fiancée, Jessica, who had been waiting at the edge of the stage, wrapped him in her arms. He leaned into her for support, seeming to breathe in her strength, and then took her hand and left via the steps.

Confused, as was everyone else, apparently, Toni turned her attention back to the stage.

"We're all family here," Logan said. "The bands, the crew, all you sick motherfuckers in the audience." This prompted loud cheering from crowd. "We're family. So when one of our own is struggling, we stand up to help. Everyone in this arena knows Sedric Lionheart needs to be with his other family—his blood—tonight. Everyone knows that except Sed. He said he doesn't want to disappoint the fans. Said he wasn't leaving until after Sinners performed tonight. He figures you'll be upset with him if you don't get to see his band play. So I promised him you'd be able to see them even if he left."

Audience members, band members, and crew exchanged confused looks. Toni looked over her shoulder to see if Sed had returned. There was no sign of the hunky vocalist anywhere backstage.

"I apologize in advance for any damage to your hearing," Logan said, "but this is the only way I could convince the stubborn bastard to go take care of himself and his family."

"What are you talking about?" Trey asked through his microphone.

Logan grinned and lifted a hand toward the rafters. "Tonight, ladies and gentlemen, we're doing Sinners karaoke, and I'm up first. Hopefully we can convince some of the *real* vocalists hiding out backstage to sing a few Sinners songs too."

Toni was astonished by how quickly the crowd got behind Logan's idea. She supposed they really were there to have some fun—she knew for a fact that Logan was fun from head to toe—and this karaoke idea was a lot better of a solution than not getting to see Sinners at all. Of course the fans couldn't be upset about Sed leaving—the man had just lost his father. Toni knew that pain, and she was certain everyone in the audience had lost someone important to them at some point in their lives.

"Prepare your ears," Logan said, sticking his finger in one of his to demonstrate. She'd heard the man sing and couldn't help but think he was doing them a favor by warning them.

"You are crazy," Trey said, shaking a finger at Logan but also grinning from ear to ear.

Logan spread his arms wide as if to say *tell me something I don't already know.*

For the third time, Sinners began the intro to "Gates of Hell," but this time Logan let loose the battle cry, one that made chills race down Toni's spine. When he started to sing, she couldn't believe her ears. Was he lip-syncing? He sounded amazing and though he didn't have quite the same grit to his voice that Sed

Lionheart did, he sounded enough like him that no one seemed to care they were listening to the bassist of Exodus End belt out a Sinners song. It was during the guitar solo, when Logan began to overexaggerate his lead-singer theatrics, that Toni realized she didn't have her camera with her. This was perfect material for the biography.

Slapping herself on the forehead, she groaned aloud and made a mad dash back to the dressing room. Would she ever learn? Now she was going to miss some of Logan's amazing karaoke performance because she kept forgetting that the members of Exodus End were *always* interesting. And that their bassist, in particular, was pretty fucking spectacular.

She'd just stepped into the room when a pair of hands shoved her in the chest and sent her stumbling backwards into a wall.

"How could you?" Reagan screamed at her. "I trusted you. I stood up for you. How could you do this to me?"

Toni gaped at her, completely taken aback by Reagan's fury. "What?"

Toni searched the room, looking for a bit of backup or at least a clue as to what was going on, and discovered Reagan's wasn't the only furious face glaring at her. Everyone in the room looked pissed off and their ire was directed at Toni.

"I don't understand what's going on," she said, gaze darting from scowling Max to jaw-set Steve to arms-crossed Dare. Butch actually cracked his knuckles—was he preparing to strangle her?

What the hell was happening?

"You sold our secrets to the tabloids," Reagan said, shoving a copy of the *American Inquirer* under her nose.

Headlines read "Exodus End's Newest Member Prefers Taking Members in Twos" and "Worth Dying For? Maximillian Richardson Knocked-up His Lead Guitarist's Fiancée Resulting in Her Tragic Suicide" and "Exodus End's Bassist Hates His Own Brother! Find Out Why Inside." Before she could read the other headlines, Reagan tore the paper in half and tossed it on the floor.

"What do you have to say for yourself?"

Toni swallowed the bile burning up her throat. How had those stories even been released?

"Those are terrible, awful, but I didn't . . . I *wouldn't.*" The knot in her throat strangled her words.

Her journal. *Shit!* Apparently someone had found it and used it for personal gain.

"Don't you dare fucking lie about it," Reagan yelled. "Don't you fucking lie."

"I would never—"

Toni's eyes filled with tears and she shook her head. How could they think she'd do such a thing? She'd been stupid, yes, writing those things in her journal and then misplacing it, but she would *never* hurt anyone she cared about.

"Get your shit off the bus," Steve said, "and get the fuck out of here. We never want to see you again."

"Butch," Max said.

It was all he needed to say. Butch marched forward, grabbed Toni by the arm, and forced her out of the room. Toni yanked at her arm, but it did no good. Not only did Butch have five times her strength, but he'd obviously escorted unsavory individuals out of buildings in the past.

"Butch, you have to listen to me," she pleaded. "I didn't sell any information to the tabloids. I swear."

"You could at least have the decency to admit you're a traitor."

Traitor? This couldn't be happening.

"Logan will vouch for me. Go get Logan."

"What he says doesn't matter. The majority has spoken, and the band wants you off the bus and out of their lives."

As she collected her belongings, Toni dawdled on the bus in the hope that Logan would show up in time so at the very least she could tell him the truth. He would believe her. He *had* to believe her. Humiliation filled her with an aching heat as Butch watched her pack her stuff to make sure she didn't take anything that didn't belong to her. So not only did he believe she'd betrayed the band and released insider information, but he also thought she was capable of stealing.

"The crew is wearing some of my cameras," she said. "I'll go collect them."

"You're not going back into the arena," Butch said. "We'll mail them to you."

Mail them? Jeez, did he think she would wrap herself around Logan's leg and refuse to release him? Yeah, she'd totally do that.

By the time she'd collected everything, some of her hurt had been replaced with indignation.

"I didn't release any of the band's secrets. What kind of people don't even let a person defend herself before passing judgment?" she growled at Butch as he nudged her toward the exit.

"People who've been screwed over by conniving reporters a million times in the past," Butch said. "Get a move on."

"I need to talk to Logan first."

"He'll call you *if* he wants to talk to you," Butch said. "If I were you, I wouldn't sit by the phone."

"Butch," she said, trying to keep the tremor out of her voice, knowing it was no use. "You know I wouldn't do anything to hurt those guys. I care about them too much. I did write those things in my journal, but—"

"You might as well shut up. I'm done listening to you."

He escorted/carried her off the bus and then pushed her toward the barrier in the parking lot that kept undesirables away from the musicians. She dug her heels into the asphalt. How was she supposed to see Logan and explain to him that she hadn't betrayed him or his friends if she was forced outside the barrier?

"Don't make me carry you," Butch said. "Retain a little of your dignity."

She'd trade dignity for the chance to tell the truth any day.

"What can I do to convince you that I'm innocent?"

He looked down at her, took her in from head to toe, and crossed his arms. "Not a damned thing."

In the end, she refused to give up and Butch had to carry her across the lot. One of the roadies followed with her luggage and tossed it none too gently over the barrier fence. Butch set her struggling body down on the opposite side of the metal bars and spoke to one of the security guards, making sure she could hear him.

"Keep a close eye on her and do not let her near the buses. If she puts a toe on this side of that barrier, you call me to deal with her, and I'll call the police to have her arrested."

Arrested? For what? She hadn't done anything.

Why wouldn't Butch believe her? Why wouldn't anyone listen?

"Please let me talk to Logan," she pleaded. "The world won't end if I lose this job, but if I lose him—" Her voice cracked and all the tension and anxiety, the hurt and humiliation, the fear and devastation streaked down her cheeks in a torrent of tears. She didn't even care that everyone was staring at her complete meltdown.

"Keep an eye on her," Butch said to the guard again, and then he whirled around and strode back toward the arena.

She tried to climb over the barrier, but the guard proved worthy of his title.

"Come on, lady, be smart about this. Do you want to go to jail?"

She honestly didn't care if she went to jail, but if she ended up behind bars, she wouldn't get to talk to Logan. She called his phone and left a short message. She knew he didn't have his phone on him since she'd found it between the sofa cushions when she'd been packing her belongings, but she couldn't just stand there idly and not try to contact him. He was probably still onstage having the time of his life, wondering where she'd gone. Or maybe his band had already informed him that she'd supposedly done exactly what she'd promised she'd never do. She prayed he'd give her a chance to explain and not simply take their word for what had happened.

And what *had* happened? Someone had obviously gotten hold of her journal, but who? Had a hotel maid taken it from her bag? Had she dropped it and a stranger picked it up? Had Susan stolen it during her presentation?

"Susan," Toni said, her eyes narrowing. Her editor had wanted dirt on the band members. And boy, had she gotten it. Feeling defeated, Toni rubbed her forehead to try to ease the pounding in her skull. "How could I have been so stupid?"

She hadn't personally released the information to the tabloids, but she was responsible for someone gaining access to it. She hadn't protected those she cared about. If she hadn't written those things down in the first place . . . If she'd been more careful with her journal . . . If she'd just stuck to the prescribed interview questions . . . If she didn't trust people so easily. If, if, if.

She leaned against a rough stone wall and waited not so patiently for the band to come out after the show. The guard seemed to realize she'd been defeated, so he wasn't watching her closely as he flirted with a pretty blonde trying to get in to see the bands. Toni hoped to use his lack of attention to her advantage when an opening presented itself.

It seemed to take an eternity for the band to emerge from the back exit. They were uncommonly grim as they strode toward the waiting bus. Reagan, especially, looked pale and forlorn. Logan brought up the rear, walking several paces behind the rest of them with his head down, as if he was the one who'd betrayed them. She wondered if they'd yelled at him because of what she'd supposedly done.

The security guard was too busy gawking at rock stars to notice Toni shift from the wall to the barrier fence. Abandoning her gear and luggage, she hiked up her skirt and climbed the cool metal railing. She dashed toward the bus. Logan drew to a halt as Toni streaked toward him. He turned in her direction. The look of betrayal on his handsome face made her stumble, but no, she couldn't fall. Not now. She had to reach him. Had to explain. *Oh God, don't look at me like that, Logan.* She feared he wouldn't listen to her or believe her even if she did plead her case.

An arm around her midsection stopped her abruptly, and her feet came off the ground as she was pulled against a large hard body from behind. She struggled, kicking her feet and shoving down on the arm around her waist with both of her hands.

"Let me go!" she demanded.

"Not a chance," the guard said. He grunted when her heel connected with his shin.

"Logan!" She struggled harder. "Logan, you have to listen to me. I didn't do it. I swear."

Logan shook his head at her, turned away, and continued toward the bus.

"Logan!"

He didn't so much as look at her as she screamed for him. Yet her struggling had finally weakened the guard enough that she slipped from his grasp. Unprepared for freedom, she stumbled forward, catching her fall on her palms, before regaining her footing and racing toward the bus.

"Logan, please hear me out," she yelled as he stepped onto the bus. He was too far ahead. She wasn't going to reach him in time, and he refused to look at her, to give her a chance to explain. He was pulling away from her and taking her shattered heart with him.

The door shut behind him, and she slammed into it with both hands. Pain shot through her asphalt-scraped palms, but she didn't care. Didn't care about anything but reaching him. She didn't know if he'd be able to hear her through the closed door, but she had to try.

"Logan, you know I'd never do anything to hurt you or anyone in the band. Remember when I couldn't find my journal? Someone stole it or found it. I don't know. But that's where the information came from. I didn't give it away. I didn't sell it. You know I wouldn't do that. I love you!" Tears overflowed as she pounded on the door. "Please, Logan, listen to me."

The bus shuddered as it rolled forward. She walked beside it, banging on the door with one hand. And then she was running, trying to keep up. She stumbled through the parking lot, but it was no use. He was gone. Without even speaking to her. Gone.

She didn't struggle when someone grabbed her and held her still. It was over. Her dreams. Her relationship with Logan. Her life. Over.

Her legs gave out, and she crumpled to the ground, sobbing for all she'd lost against the unforgiving asphalt beneath her quaking body.

CHAPTER
32

L OGAN LEANED his forehead against the inside of the bus door and swallowed against the lump of despair strangling him. He couldn't hear Toni's words as she tried to yell through the reinforced steel, but he could hear the desperation in her tone. How could she have betrayed them all this way? Had she played him a fool the entire time, like some sort of spy who used sex to get a man to spill his deepest secrets? No, she was too honest. Too sweet. Too gentle to do anything so underhanded.

But the evidence was on the page. Toni was the only person outside of the band who knew all the stories that had been printed. It couldn't be a coincidence that they'd all been released in the same tabloid at the same time. What he didn't understand was why she'd do it. She never seemed desperate for cash. Was she trying to earn enough money to get out from under her mother's thumb?

"She should be glad Butch was the one who kicked her ass off the bus," Reagan railed. "I probably would have killed her."

"You might as well settle down," Max said. "What's done is done."

"Does anyone know a good attorney? I'm going to sue her for libel."

Logan understood that Reagan was upset. Her story was the only one that was current. Everyone else's was something they'd had years to process. But she was overreacting. Did she really expect to keep her relationship with Trey Mills and Ethan Conner a secret forever?

"You can't sue for libel unless malicious *lies* are printed," Logan said, shoving off the door and climbing the steps. "Everything in that article was true."

"I can't believe you're defending her!" Reagan yelled. "She ratted you out too."

"I'm not defending her, just saving you time. You'd never win a libel case. You can ask Jessica Chase if you don't believe me. She's a lawyer, you know."

"You don't want to take this to court," Dare said. "If you think this little article has exposed your relationship with my brother, imagine the stink a full-blown trial would create."

Reagan crossed her arms over her chest and flopped into a chair. "What am I going to do?"

"Own up to your relationship," Dare said. "You're not doing yourself any favors by trying to hide it."

"People won't understand. They'll think I'm some sort of deviant just because I'm in love with two men."

"I agree with Dare," Steve said. "People blow secrets all out of proportion, and then after the truth comes out, the gossip quickly dies down."

"I can't out our relationship. My father will kill me."

"And if he reads the tabloids?" Dare asked.

"I'll just deny everything."

Dare shook his head. Logan sat beside him on the sofa, his stomach roiling with so much turmoil, he feared he'd be sick.

"Did Toni say *why* she did it?" Logan asked. He still couldn't wrap his head around the idea that she'd sold their souls to the tabloids. It simply didn't seem like something she would do. Maybe if he knew why she'd stooped to such a low level, he could find a reason to forgive her. Because damn it all, he couldn't imagine spending the next five minutes, much less the rest of his life, without her.

"Of course she didn't say why," Reagan snapped. "The lying little bitch denied everything."

"She denied it?"

Logan had initially felt too betrayed to even want to hear Toni's side of the story, but now that the dust had settled, he was wishing he'd taken a moment to hear her out. She'd obviously been upset outside the stadium. He'd assumed it was because she'd been caught and subsequently fired.

"Yeah, she was going on about some journal she'd

misplaced," Steve said, flicking his wrist dismissively.

"Her journal?" Logan's breath caught. She'd talked about losing her personal journal over a week before. He'd even gotten her a new one to replace it. "She was upset when it went missing. Shit, she didn't sell any of us out. Someone took or found her journal and *they* sold us out." A weight lifted from his heavy heart as he realized he hadn't misjudged her character. Toni was the woman he'd fallen in love with, not some poser just trying to get the inside scoop on the band.

He had to call her. He slid his hand into the pocket where he usually kept his cellphone, only to find it missing. He checked his other pocket. Not there either. Shit! Of all the times to be without his phone.

"Has anyone seen my phone?" he asked, rising from the sofa to head for his bunk. Maybe he'd left it there when he'd changed before the concert.

"You are not calling her." Reagan stepped into his path and placed both hands on his chest.

"Yeah, I am. I can't even imagine how hurt and confused and upset she is right now." He needed to tell her everything was going to be all right. That he still loved her. That they had to work things out because she was a necessity to his very existence.

"How hurt and upset *she* is? She betrayed you Logan," Reagan said. "She betrayed all of us. You've known her a couple of weeks. How long have you known the members of your band?"

"Bros before hos," Steve joked, throwing up a pair of devil horns.

Logan scowled. "Toni is not a ho. She's the love of my life. And I'm not going to lose her over some stupid tabloid bullshit." He grabbed Reagan by both arms and shook her, hoping to drive his point home. "This is the price you pay for fame, Reagan. Your private life is no longer private. The sooner you get used to it, the better off you'll be. I know you're pissed off, but let it go and move on. Your life isn't over because the world now knows you fuck two gay guys. They might think you're a slut, but so what? There are far worse things you could be."

Reagan's jaw dropped. Logan released her and scarcely felt her half-assed slap to his face. He turned back to his bunk. "Where's my goddamned phone!" he yelled, ripping the bedding from his mattress and shaking it before throwing it on the floor. The phone wasn't under his pillow or beneath the mattress. He dug through the drawer under his bed, thinking maybe it had fallen in with his clean clothes.

"Dude, you need to calm down," Steve said.

"I'm not going to fucking calm down. What I *need* is my goddamned phone."

"Maybe it's in the back," Max suggested, grabbing Logan's bedding off the floor and shoving it back into the empty bunk.

And then Logan heard Toni's ringtone—Kelis's "Milkshake"—playing from the lounge. She was calling him! He sprinted down the corridor, expecting to see his phone resting on the coffee table, but it wasn't there. And neither were Toni's familiar belongings. He didn't have time to dwell on the emptiness that barren sight opened in his chest; he had a phone to find. He followed the sound toward the far end of the sectional, eyes closed and head cocked to one side as he listened for direction. The phone stopped ringing, and his heart sank. No matter. It was somewhere in this room. Sofa cushions and pillows went flying in all directions. He shoved his hand into the crack between the sectional's back and seat, finding a few coins, a cheese curl older than Keith Richards, and a few things he didn't want to identify, but no phone. He dropped onto his belly and peered under the sectional, hoping it hadn't slipped too far under there. He'd never get it out.

Face pressed to the carpet, he yelled, "Someone call my phone."

"Should we put him out of his misery?" Steve asked from the doorway.

"I don't know," Max said. "It's pretty funny, if you ask me."

"What's funny?" Logan sat up and pushed his wayward curls out of his face to glare at his *comedian* bandmates who had congregated in the doorway. All except Reagan. After what he'd said to her, Reagan would likely never speak to him again, but he had more pressing matters to deal with.

"What's funny? How about the way you're tearing apart the couch and flopping around on the floor in a panic when your phone is sitting peacefully in the charger." Dare pointed at the charger on the end table.

"Who the hell put it in there?" But he knew. Toni had been looking out for him. Anticipating his needs and doing those little things that showed she cared without prompting or asking for anything in return. He grabbed the edge of the bare sectional in one hand and the coffee table in the other and hauled himself to his feet.

"I do think he's actually in love with her," Steve said, scratching his jaw.

"Why else would he make such an ass out of himself?" Max said.

Dare tugged the two men out of the doorway and started to slide the door shut. Just before it closed, he poked his head into the room and said, "Don't fuck this up. Sometimes you don't get a second chance at happiness."

Logan waved him away as he returned Toni's missed call. The door banged shut just as he lifted the phone to his ear.

"Logan?"

She answered on the first ring. Her voice wavered on his name, and she sucked in a deep shaky breath. He could tell she was crying, and the thought of her turmoil jabbed him in the gut.

"Please, you have to believe me," she sobbed. "I didn't—"

"Shh, sweetheart, I know you wouldn't sell our secrets to the tabloids."

"You know?"

"Yeah, so don't cry. We'll get this all straightened out."

"If you knew, then why wouldn't you even look at me after the show? I thought you hated me."

"I could never hate you." It was true. Even if she *had* been a conniving bitch and sold their stories to the tabloids, he would have eventually forgiven her. But thank God he didn't have to. "At that particular moment, I was convinced you'd betrayed us, but after a few minutes of thought, I realized you wouldn't do that to the band."

"Fuck the band. I would never do that to *you*."

Logan's brow furrowed. "So you did sell them out?" What was she saying?

"Of course not. But if they hated me, I would eventually move on. I wouldn't be able to live with myself if I ever hurt you."

"I'm not sure Reagan will forgive you, but if the guys aren't already over it, they will be in a few days. This isn't the first time our shit has been smeared all over the tabloid toilet. We're used to it."

Toni snorted on a laugh, and Logan's throat tightened. Who would have ever thought that such a tiny sound would bring him overwhelming joy. Toni was no longer crying, no longer heartbroken. His world could start turning again.

"Do you want us to turn the bus around and come get you?" he asked.

"He better not be making up with her!" Reagan yelled from the corridor.

"Will you calm down?" Max's muffled voice advised.

"No, I will not calm down! Get your fucking hands off of me."

There was a repetitive slapping sound. "Ow!" Max complained. "Some help here, guys?"

"Reagan is still pretty upset," Logan said to Toni. *Understatement of the century.* "But maybe she'd be willing to ride with Sinners."

"No, go on without me," Toni said. "I have enough to get started on the book, and you know Reagan struggles to be a part of the band. You should support her. I'll keep my distance until she calms down."

Why would Reagan be struggling with being a part of the band? They'd accepted her from day one. And there was no way he was supporting Reagan when she blamed Toni for her problems. Toni was innocent. "How can I support her? She's accusing the wrong person."

"I don't mean that," Toni said. "Support her through the impending media shitstorm. You know it's just started. They won't leave her alone now that the story is out. All the other stuff they stole from my journal is old news, but Reagan's relationship is a current event. It's going to get ugly, Logan."

Logan scratched his head and scowled. He hadn't thought about that. Of course Toni, who always empathized with everyone, would think to worry about Reagan's future struggles.

"So you don't want to be with me for the rest of the tour?" he asked. He needed to see her. He was glad they were talking like rational adults—who'd have guessed he'd ever be so mature about such a situation—but he needed to see her, to touch her. He needed the physical reassurance that she loved him. To see it in her eyes. Feel it in her touch. Words weren't enough.

"Of course I want to be with you. But even more than that, I want to confront the bitch who did this and out her for the thieving, back-stabbing, heartless cunt that she is."

Logan's jaw dropped. He'd never heard Toni say negative things about anyone before. Apparently her hurt had turned to anger.

"So you know who did it?" Logan asked.

"I'm pretty sure I do. Remember Susan, the editor who works for my mom's company? The entire meeting in Denver, all she could focus on was the dirt she wanted on you guys. I never saw my journal again after that day. I think she took it when I was with Birdie in the bathroom."

"You're going home," he said, a strange tug pulling at his chest. He rubbed at the spot. He suddenly realized that they hadn't been apart for more than a few hours since they'd met. If this was what it felt like to be without her—this ache, this yearning—he wasn't going to last a day on his own.

"For a few days at least. I'm not going to let her get away with this."

That was too long to be without Toni. But she needed to take care of business, and he had to be supportive, even if it was from a fucking distance.

"I'll miss you," she said to fill the silence.

"I already miss you."

"Be there for Reagan," she reminded him.

"I'd rather be there for you."

"I'll be fine," she assured him. "I'm stronger than I look."

That was a fact he couldn't argue against. "If you need anything, call me. I'll come running."

"I love you."

Those three little words still made his heart fill to bursting. "I love you too. Let me know when you get home so I don't worry."

Toni chuckled. "You've changed, Logan."

"Why do you say that?"

"When was the last time you worried about anyone but yourself?"

"Hmm." He scratched his chin. "I guess never. It's a damn hindrance, to tell you the truth."

"Sorry—*not* sorry—to cramp your style, Mr. Rock Star. I'll call you."

He wasn't ready to hang up when they said their goodbyes, but she had places to be and evidently he needed to support Reagan. He slid the door open, found himself caught in Reagan's glare of intense loathing, and shut it again. She needed a bit more time to herself, he decided. And he needed to sleep. Alone. He returned the cushions to the sofa and flopped down on his back, staring at the ceiling, already bored out of his mind. With a sigh, he picked up his phone and downloaded a movie to help him pass the time. It had been a while since he'd seen *The Princess Bride*.

CHAPTER
33

TONI RUBBED at her eyes with one hand and yawned as she fished around inside the flower pot on the back porch for the spare key. She hadn't caught much sleep on her red-eye home, and then driving a rental car home through fifty miles of dense fog had drained her remaining energy. She needed to find her bed for a few hours' sleep before she drove to Nichols Publishing and planted the sole of her boot firmly in Susan Brennan's conniving face.

It had been after midnight when she'd boarded the plane. She'd been certain the household would already be asleep, so she hadn't called home to warn anyone of her impending arrival. She'd decided Julian wouldn't appreciate her calling him at six in the morning for a ride either, so she'd opted for a rental car. She unlocked the back door and was immediately engulfed by the delicious smells of freshly griddled pancakes and bacon.

"Oh!" her grandmother said from behind the island stove top. She had a spatula raised in defense and her free hand over her heart. "You startled me."

"What are you doing here?" Toni asked, dropping her bags by the back door and rushing across the enormous farm-style kitchen to squeeze the stuffing out of Grandma Joanna.

"I'd ask you the same. Your mother said you were off getting into trouble with some rock band." She patted Toni on the rear end with her spatula before using it to flip pancakes.

"I was *working* with a rock band," Toni said. "But I sort of got fired."

"Whatever for?"

"It's a long story, and I'm too tired to tell it now. How long are you visiting? We need to catch up."

"I'm here to stay."

Toni's chewed on the tip of her finger. Grandma Joanna was her paternal grandmother. They hadn't seen much of her since Dad had passed away. For almost a decade she'd been traveling the country in her motor home with her two Pomeranians.

"Toni!" Birdie squealed from the kitchen doorway that led to the hallway. "You're home!"

She dashed into the room, trailed by two orange fluff balls and her ever faithful border collie, Jonesy. All three dogs wagged their tails at top speed.

"Just for a few days, Buttercup."

Birdie pouted and then glanced toward the door expectantly. "Is Logan here too?"

"No, he has a performance tonight."

"Who's Logan?" Grandma Joanna asked with a sly grin.

"That's Toni's sweetheart," Birdie said matter-of-factly.

"It's about time she got one of those," Grandma said as she scooped several pancakes onto a waiting stack. "Are you ready for breakfast?"

"Mmm, mmm. Pancakes!" Birdie said, dancing on her tiptoes and licking her lips as she eyed the stack.

Toni had been planning to go directly to bed, but her stomach growled loudly and changed her mind. It would be rude not to join them for breakfast. Mostly because her grandmother's homemade pancakes were to die for.

"Should we call Mom down?" Toni asked as she carried butter and syrup to the breakfast table in the corner nook of the kitchen. Birdie followed with plates and silverware.

"She left for work about an hour ago," Grandma said with wave of her spatula. "Some catastrophe at the office."

Toni wondered if the catastrophe centered around a certain editor who deserved a boot to the face. And one to the ass. Scowling, Toni went to the refrigerator for milk. She wasn't feeling so tired all of a sudden. Perhaps it was best to confront Susan before she had a decent night's sleep. Toni might find herself in a rational state of mind if she rested, and rational was not what she was going for.

She listened with half an ear as Birdie enthused about school and her chickens and as Grandma talked about her last trip to Wisconsin and the antics of her Pomeranians, but Toni didn't feel like sharing tales of her own adventures. She was still rattled by everything that had happened the night before. She'd picked up a copy of the tabloid at the airport, but had been too disgusted to read it. She was sure every word written had painted her lover and her friends in a terrible light. As Toni sat there stewing, her anger and indignation began to boil over.

Someone grasped her arm to gain her attention. "So why did you get fired?" Grandma asked. "From what little your mother said, it sounded like you were doing a fine job."

Toni lowered her eyes. "It was a misunderstanding. I'd like to claim the entire fiasco isn't my fault, but it is. I wrote some incriminating things about the members of the band in a journal— with no intention of publishing a word of them—but the diary ended up in the wrong hands and all the secrets were published in a tabloid." She glanced at Birdie, who was suddenly sliding under the table. Getting bored, most likely. "You better go feed your chickens before school."

"Toni?" Behind her thick glasses, Birdie's eyes filled with tears. "Are you in trouble?"

Toni scooted closer to her on the nook bench and gave her a hug. "No, Buttercup. Everything is fine."

Birdie clung to her, sniffing tears. "I want you to come home, but I don't want you in trouble."

"I'm not in trouble. I promise." Toni reached for a napkin and dabbed at Birdie's eyes. "Don't cry." In the emotionally unstable place that Toni currently found herself, she was almost in tears herself. She kissed Birdie's forehead and nudged her out of the booth. "I'm sure your chickens are hungry."

"I'll hurry," Birdie said. She rushed out the back door, her entourage of dogs on her heels.

Toni turned to Grandma, who was smiling at her. "I never saw two sisters as close as you two. Of course, you practically raised her yourself, so I'm not surprised."

Toni munched on her last piece of bacon. "How did Mom rope you into taking over the house?"

"She didn't have to rope, just ask. I think I'm done with traveling. Seen everything I care to see. I'm ready to be with family, and with Charlie and Phillip gone, you girls are all I have left."

Toni reached across the table and squeezed Grandma's hand. She'd lost her husband fairly young, and the loss of her only son had all but destroyed her.

"I'm glad you're here," Toni said.

"Now you can follow your dreams without worrying about Birdie," Grandma said, patting their joined hands.

Toni hadn't thought of it that way, but Grandma was right. Toni would worry far less with Birdie in Grandma's expert care. But it didn't matter. Her dreams were probably over. No band would ever trust her with their personal lives. Not after what had happened to Exodus End.

But maybe she could redeem herself by writing their book. By making it perfect and showing the world what wonderful people they really were.

"I'm going to the office now," she said. All the computer programs she needed to craft her masterpiece were there. And so was the bitch who'd caused all her problems.

"You need to get some sleep. You look exhausted."

She was exhausted. But she was too amped up to sleep. She had important business to attend to.

And she didn't mind looking a bit wild and scary when she faced Susan.

An hour later, Toni dropped off her gear next to her desk before storming down the hall to Susan's office. Toni had gone over everything she'd wanted to say to Susan a thousand times in her head, but she wasn't sure if she'd be able to hold it together enough to express her words rationally. She didn't even bother knocking, just flung the door open so hard it slammed into the wall.

In unison, Julian and Susan looked up from the tabloid paper spread across the desk.

"Toni!" Julian said. "What are you doing here?"

Every carefully chosen word flew straight out of Toni's head. "You're *reading* it with her?" she snarled, Julian's betrayal slashing across her heart.

"Wow, Toni," Susan said. "I never thought you'd actually have the balls to publish something like this. Bravo to you, kiddo!"

"You're congratulating *me* for something you did?"

Susan scrunched her brows together. "Huh?"

Either Susan was innocent or she was a fantastic actress. Toni was counting on the actress thing.

"You stole my journal and used it to write this garbage! The band fired me because of what you did!" Toni splayed her hand in the center of the tabloid paper and clenched her fist, crumpling the pages into a messy ball.

"No idea what you're talking about, but do you really think I'd still be editing other people's crap at this shithole job if I'd sold this kind of gold to the tabloids?" Susan rolled her eyes. "You really are a naïve idiot."

Toni narrowed her eyes. "Pack your shit and leave. You're fired."

Susan's jaw dropped, but she quickly replaced her look of astonishment with a smirk. "You can't fire me."

"I just did. Get lost."

Julian circled the desk and caught Toni by the arms. "I've never seen you like this," he said, staring deeply into Toni's eyes. "When's the last time you slept?"

"I slept on the plane," she said. *For like twenty minutes.* "It doesn't matter. I'm not going to let Susan talk down to me anymore. I don't care if it was someone else who screwed me over." Toni had been so sure it had been Susan, she was still halfway convinced she'd been the one. "I don't want her here. She's not even very good at her job."

Susan huffed in disdain.

"She's rude and unprofessional," Toni said, looking Susan square in the eye while she said it. "Nichols Publishing doesn't need an employee like her, so she's fired." She turned her face toward Julian and cocked her head at him. "Are you going to give me any more lip, Mr. Reynolds?"

Julian laughed and hugged her, of all things. "I like this new you, Miss Toni. I knew you had a sturdy backbone somewhere in that stacked little body of yours."

"I'm not leaving," Susan said. "You have no authority in this company."

"My mother has been trying to make me a partner for years," Toni said, and though she wasn't necessarily ready to take that step, Susan had no way of knowing that. "Trust me, you're fired."

Toni slid out of Julian's grasp and headed for the door. She needed to talk to her mother—the real boss of this establishment—as soon as possible.

"I didn't take your journal," Susan called after her.

"Fired. Do I need to spell it for you? It starts with an *F* and ends with a *U*," Toni said as she stormed out of Susan's office with Julian on her heels.

"Remind me to never get on your bad side," Julian said.

"Susan's been rude to me since day one."

"Only because you never stood up for yourself."

Toni scowled at him. "That's no excuse to be an asshole."

"Most assholes don't need an excuse. So how are things going with your new boyfriend? I saw your story about him. Makes him sound like a whiner."

"Not my story," she reminded him.

"But he *is* your boyfriend?" Julian wiggled his eyebrows at her.

"Yes, I told you he was in response to those badgering texts you sent."

Julian pouted. "You never did send me proof."

"I'm not sending you a naked picture of my boyfriend, Julian!"

"Then I don't believe you." Such the little manipulator.

"Believe whatever you want. I'm lucky he didn't dump me after what Susan did."

"I'm still not clear what she did that has you so pissed off."

"She stole my journal and published secrets I'd written in it."

"Are you sure?"

"Yes!" Though her certainty was diminishing by the second.

"How would she know to steal your journal? Or even how to get her hands on it?"

"How the hell should I know?" she screeched.

Julian leaned away from her, apparently deciding she was too scary to keep pestering.

She stopped at Julian's desk, which was situated in front of her mother's closed office door and waited for him to buzz her via his intercom.

"Your mother's in a meeting downtown," Julian said. "She won't be back for at least an hour."

She tossed her hands in the air. "Why didn't you tell me that before I walked all the way down here?"

"Because I was starting to believe you two switched bodies or something. I've seen that fire in her hundreds of times, but I've never seen it in you before."

"You should be glad you've never made me that angry." Toni rubbed her forehead, fatigue setting in now that her so-called fire had burned itself to embers. "I guess I'll work on the book until she gets back. Will you call me in my office when she returns?"

"Of course."

Toni turned to head back toward her office, and Julian fell into step with her again. "So is their drummer, Steve Aimes, really gay? Because I would very much like you to introduce me to him."

"Nope, he's not," Toni said. "You shouldn't believe everything you read in the tabloids, Julian. Or *anything* you read in the tabloids."

"Damn. I have such a boner for that guy. Are you sure I'm not his type?"

"I'm positive. He's the biggest womanizer of the band," Toni said. "Well, he is now that Logan is mine."

"Prime man meat there as well, Miss Toni. Excellent score."

"Um, *thanks*?" She wasn't sure how to respond to that compliment. Because yes, Logan was gorgeous, and that had probably been why she'd succumbed to his charms so quickly, but now that she knew him on a deeper level, he was so much more than a handsome face and a big dick. "I have to work now," she said as Julian followed her into her office, apparently still wanting to talk about men.

"So those other two guys, Trey Mills and the bodyguard . . . Any chance I could enjoy some threesome action with the two of them?"

Toni grabbed Julian by the arm and shoved him into the hallway. "Is dick all you ever think about?"

"Yes," he said as Toni closed the door soundly in his face.

She raked her fingers through her hair, snagging them on tangles. Her mind was spinning at a million miles per hour. If it hadn't been Susan who'd stolen her journal, then who could it have been? Maybe it had just been a random hotel maid or other stranger reading all her personal thoughts. Sharing them with the world. She glanced at the clock, surprised to find it wasn't even nine yet. It was still a little early for Logan to be awake, but she needed someone to talk to. Someone she knew she could trust. Someone who was there to listen. Someone who gave her sound advice. Or not so sound. She wasn't sure when Logan had become her best friend—or when the word *friend* had stopped making her cringe—but she was lucky to have him in her life.

She pressed his icon on her contact list, noting that he'd changed his picture to a dick pic.

Really, Logan? Was he afraid she'd forget what it looked like?

"Hello?" a woman answered.

Toni pulled her phone away from her face and checked to make sure she'd dialed the correct number.

Noting that it was definitely Logan's dick she'd pressed, she asked, "Can I speak to Logan?"

"He's in the shower."

"Who are you?" Toni asked, her face inexplicably numb.

"I'm just his entertainment."

Entertainment? What exactly did she mean by that and why the hell was she answering Logan's phone?

"I'll tell him you called," the beautiful-sounding woman said. "Who is this?"

"It's Toni. His *girlfriend*."

The woman laughed. "He didn't tell me he had a girlfriend. I'll have to get after him for hiding that from me. But I will tell him you called, Tonya."

"Toni," she corrected automatically.

Toni was too stunned to voice the hundreds of questions swirling around in her head. Before she could gather her wits, the woman hung up.

She'd been gone for less than twenty-four hours and Logan was already fooling around with another woman? Apparently Toni was the fool for believing she meant something to him.

She took several deep breaths, fighting the ache in her eyes, her throat, and her chest. She wanted to give Logan the benefit of the doubt, but she'd seen too much over the past two and a half weeks. She knew how persistent those damned groupies could be. But if he couldn't be faithful to her for even twenty-four goddamned hours, then she didn't need him. Fuck him and his flattering words, his expert touch, his easy smile, and his irresistible charm. Fuck him.

Well, that was what her brain said, but her heart was too crushed to do anything but yearn for him. The fickle, weak organ wanted him to tell her that she was mistaken. Needed him to tell her that no woman could ever replace her in his heart or in his bed. She really was a fool.

She rose from her chair and began to unpack her gear. Work would help her keep her mind off what an incredible asshole she'd allowed herself to fall in love with. She'd start with the section on Max or maybe Dare, because she was pretty sure anything she wrote about the band's bass player at that particular moment would be unbecoming to his character.

A couple of hours later, she'd found her zone. Her fatigue and hurt were forgotten as words and images, audio and video clips, all came together on the page. She'd designed the software interface herself, and it was pretty intuitive—similar to making web pages. She just had to drag and drop the sections she wanted into a template form and then add her text and supporting files.

When her cellphone rang and the ringtone Logan had chosen for himself—Right Said Fred's "I'm Too Sexy"—interrupted her train of thought, she paused with hands hovering over her keyboard. Part of her wanted to answer and forget about work, but the pissed-off part of her moved her hand to her phone's screen and rejected the call. It had taken him almost two hours to call her back. She knew how much trouble the man could get into in that length of time. Especially when he had a willing woman in his bed. She bit her lip, blinking back a sudden rush of tears. She wasn't ready to face their inevitable breakup just yet. She'd been through too much in the past day to add another heartache to her agenda.

Less than a minute later, Right Said Fred was proclaiming himself too sexy for her party again. She took a deep breath, rejected Logan's call, and shut off her phone, hiding it in her desk drawer so she wouldn't be tempted to call him back or read any text messages or listen to voicemail. She needed to have her head together before she talked to him. She didn't want to be his doormat and if she talked to him while in her current frame of mind, she knew she'd prostrate herself at his feet and gladly allow him to walk all over her.

She found it far easier to bury herself in her work than to face reality and mourn the loss of the man she loved. Perhaps she was more like her mother than she cared to admit.

She'd just found her zone again when there was a knock on her door. Some stupid part of her brain wanted it to be Logan. But that was impossible. Even if he had dropped everything and rushed to beg her forgiveness and make amends, he didn't know she was at work and even if he'd commandeered a jet fighter, there was no way he could have flown halfway across the United States in an hour. Unless Butch had invented a teleporting device at Logan's request, the person currently interrupting her work wasn't him.

Toni cleared her throat and croaked, "Come in."

She was not fit for human company at the moment. When her mother opened the door and poked her head into the room, Toni groaned inwardly.

"Are you busy?" Mom asked.

Yes, she was fucking busy. Didn't she look busy? Nothing made Toni crankier than being hungry, except being tired. She was currently starving and exhausted. *Enter at your own risk, lady.*

"I could use a little break," Toni said.

Mom shuffled into the room and closed the door, placing a hand against it and taking a deep breath before turning to face Toni. Mom dropped her shoulders in defeat and lifted a trembling hand to her lips. Toni was too stunned by her mother's uncharacteristic show of weakness that she couldn't do anything but gape at her.

"I'm not sure how to tell you this," she said. "I was downtown talking to my financial advisor."

Toni scrunched her brow. And Mom was telling her this why? Toni had nothing to do with the business's finances. That was what accountants were for.

"Is there a problem?"

Mom moved to a chair and collapsed into it. "Some of our big projects didn't pan out the way we thought they would. Sales didn't even cover the advances or that huge chunk of money I paid for the rights to publish the book you're working on." She shook her head. "I should have negotiated better. I didn't have that kind of money lying around, so I borrowed most of it and . . ." She shrugged as if she couldn't bring herself to say the words that came next.

"The business is going under," Toni said flatly. The reality of it punched her in the gut.

"Not necessarily," she said. "I still have one ace in the hole."

"We can put the Exodus End book out early. I've been working on it most of the day, and it's already coming together. I know it will be a best-seller. Exodus End's fans will be rabid for it."

"That might get us out of the hole *next* year, when cash starts flowing in, but that's not what I was referring to."

Toni tried to think back to their staff meetings and which books were being released in the coming season. Besides an interactive cookbook that gave video instructions with each recipe, she couldn't think of any projects that were big enough to cover the million dollars they'd shelled out for the privilege of publishing Exodus End's biography. "Then what?"

"We'll have to sell the farm. There's a developer—"

"No!" Toni shot to her feet, sending her office chair rolling back to collide with the wall behind her. "You absolutely cannot sell Daddy's farm."

"I didn't want to buy it in the first place. That was your father's dream, not mine. He's been gone for almost a decade. It's time we moved on."

"What about Birdie?" Toni would be saddened if they sold the farm, but her little sister would be lost without the routine and comfort the familiar brought to her life.

"What about her?"

"She doesn't deal with change, Mom. You know that."

"That's because you've sheltered her, just as your father sheltered you. Life is cruel and chaotic. The only consistency in life is that things change. There's no permanence in anything. It's better that she learns that now."

"Don't you want her to be happy?"

"Of course I do. But when's the last time anyone considered *my* happiness? I've been doing that insane commute for fifteen years because I wanted your father to be happy and then I wanted you to be happy. When do I get my turn?"

"M-maybe I can buy the farm. You can move to the city and have the money from the sale to keep the business afloat, and Birdie and I and Grandma Jo—"

". . . can live happily ever after? Oh, grow up, Antonia. There are no happily ever afters."

"There are!"

There had to be. Maybe it wasn't one event or one person that gave someone happiness for the span of a lifetime, but rather a string of events and people. Maybe she had to work for her happily ever after and find happiness in each day, each moment, but that kind of bliss *was* possible. She knew it was possible. And something told her keeping the farm was part of her happily ever after.

"I'm selling the farm," Mom said quietly. "I already contacted an agent. Are you going to tell Birdie or do you want me to do it?"

Toni didn't want anyone to tell Birdie, because she would find a way to keep the farm. "I'll tell her," she said. That might buy her enough time to figure something out so no one would have to break her sister's fragile heart.

"Thank you," Mom said with a deep sigh. "She'll take it better from you."

Mom stood and headed for the door, and Toni remembered the reason she'd wanted to talk to her mother in the first place.

"I fired Susan," Toni said.

"Yeah, she told me. I assured her that her job was secure."

Toni's jaw dropped. "You can't be serious. Do you have any idea how she talks to me?" Even if Susan hadn't been the one who'd stolen her journal—and Toni still felt in her heart that she was involved—the bitch still deserved to be fired for being rude.

"We need her connections now more than ever."

"What connections?" Toni sputtered. Toni had finally worked up the courage to stand up to Susan and her mother overturns her decision just like that? Why had she even bothered?

"None that concern you. Now go home and get some sleep. You look like hell."

Like she'd ever be able to sleep with all the crap going on in her life. But she packed up her laptop and storage devices and headed for home. She didn't want to be in the same building as Susan or her mother at the moment, and she could work remotely. She'd done it for years. And maybe now was the time to take her creative expertise and strike out on her own. Go indie. Like Exodus End was considering.

It didn't occur to her until she was halfway home that her mother hadn't been even slightly surprised to see her in the office or even questioned why she'd been so upset with Susan in the first place.

CHAPTER 34

LOGAN RUBBED his hair vigorously with a towel. It took forever for his curls to dry, and he had a breakfast date with a very special woman he hadn't seen in at least a year. He supposed his usual just-rolled-out-of-bed look would have to do. He'd taken the time to shave, at least. Standing naked beside the bed, he searched his limited wardrobe for something to wear. Should he choose jeans and a T-shirt or maybe go with a T-shirt and jeans? He sighed and yanked on a T-shirt that *didn't* have pictures of various cats, each depicting a way he liked pussy—wet was his personal favorite. A guitar T-shirt from Max's Save the Wails charity campaign wasn't offensive, was it? He wasn't sure why he cared so much about what he wore. The woman had to know what to expect when she'd shown up at his hotel suite unannounced. Once fully clothed, Logan left the bedroom and paused to stare at the beautiful blonde waiting for him on the sofa. All sorts of emotions bubbled to the surface. He wasn't sure where to begin in sorting them out. Anger, regret, longing. Love. He couldn't deny that one.

"Are you ready to go?" she asked.

His stomach twisting with nerves, he smoothed his unruly curls and nodded. "Yeah."

He grabbed his phone, noting that there were no missed calls. He supposed Toni was still sleeping after her long night of travel. He shoved the device, along with his hotel suite key card and wallet, into various pockets and then opened the door, even remembering his manners to hold it ajar for his unexpected guest.

His mother breezed out into the corridor, and he breathed in the honeysuckle scent of her perfume. The remembered fragrance ratcheted up his emotions another notch. He still couldn't believe she was here. Sure, she lived in Phoenix, but she'd never before sought him out when he was in town touring with the band. In fact, she never sought him out period.

"You sure took your time in the shower," she commented on their way to the elevator at the end of the hall.

He'd been trying to pull himself together. He'd partially succeeded. He was pretty sure he could talk without stuttering now.

"I usually sleep in. Needed that shower to wake up."

The elevator dinged and opened its doors as soon as he pushed the down button. He waited for her to enter the car before joining her.

"All that partying must be exhausting," Mom said with a terse grin.

Dig number one. Not that he'd expected anything different from her usual disdain. Actually, that was a lie. He had thought things would be different for some stupid reason. When she'd appeared out of nowhere at his hotel room door and asked him to join her and Daniel for breakfast at a nostalgic diner across town, he'd thought maybe they were turning a page. That maybe he'd feel that sense of belonging he felt when he was with his band or with Toni, but nope, the woman was practically a stranger to him, no matter how much he wanted her love and acceptance.

"Yeah, it's definitely the partying and not the constant travel that wears me out," he said, slamming his finger into the button labeled Parking Garage.

"Daniel's already at the diner holding a table for us, so we can't dawdle. I hope you don't mind the rush."

Rushing to sit at a breakfast table with his absent mother and his apathetic brother? Why would he mind that? He couldn't think of ten thousand places he'd rather be. Or maybe he could. And yet when he'd opened his hotel door to her anxious face that morning, he'd been so happy to see her, he'd nearly pissed himself.

"So what made you decide to come see me?" He wasn't sure he wanted to know the truth behind her visit. He hoped she just wanted to see him because she loved him, but he doubted that was the case. She'd probably seen the tabloid article about his loveless childhood—he still couldn't believe how much that article had exaggerated his misery—and was hoping to make amends. He supposed it wasn't the end of the world that people thought he was a whiner if it prompted his mom's sudden interest in him.

"You brother put me up to this," she said, lowering her gaze. "He didn't feel comfortable seeking you out on his own."

Logan cocked an eyebrow at her. Why the hell would Daniel feel uncomfortable about having breakfast with him? They shared the same parents. For a good portion of their childhood, they'd even shared the same bedroom. Unless Daniel thought he had completely destroyed Logan's life. If Daniel believed that overblown tabloid article, he probably thought Logan cried himself to sleep each night, longing for familial affection.

"My childhood wasn't as bad as that article made it out to be," Logan said.

Mom's brows drew together. "What article would that be?"

"You're not here because of the article?" Logan said as they stepped off the elevator in the parking garage.

"Apparently not." Mom shook her head. "I have no idea what you're talking about."

"Forget I mentioned it," Logan said, surprised by how much tension seeped from his muscles when he realized Mom and Daniel wanted to spend time with him not out of guilt, but genuine interest. He couldn't help but smile at the insight.

Mom grinned at him as she opened the door of her late-model sedan. "Well, *there's* that knockout smile of yours. You do look like your father."

And maybe that was why his mom had all but deserted him as a child. His father wasn't the kind of man who should have ever married and had kids. Logan wondered if he'd taken after the guy in more than looks.

As they drove across town, Mom pointed out new shops and restaurants that had replaced the ones he'd known in his youth. The diner where their short-lived happy family had breakfasted every Saturday had somehow managed to survive in a world full of fast food and coffee house chains. The remembered bell over the door jangled nostalgically as they entered. The décor had been updated from red vinyl to green vinyl, but most everything looked just as Logan remembered it: except his brother. Daniel was sitting in a corner booth shredding a paper napkin. Pasty-faced and gaunt, he'd aged at least ten years since Logan had last seen him. And was that a bald spot shining on top of Daniel's head? Damn, he looked old. Daniel started when Mom slid into the booth beside him and kissed his cheek. He dropped what was left of the napkin and lifted his gaze to Logan, who was still too stunned by his brother's appearance to sit across from them.

"Daniel?" Logan questioned, not sure he would have recognized him on the street. "Is everything okay?"

Daniel licked his lips and nodded toward the seat across from him. "I wasn't sure you'd come."

Logan slid into the booth and stared quizzically at the brother who was more a stranger to him now than ever. "Why wouldn't I?"

"I didn't tell him anything," Mom said. She gave Daniel's hand an encouraging squeeze.

Before Logan could ask what the hell was going on, a grandmotherly waitress made an appearance. "Well, aren't you the best-looking thing that's ever been in this place?"

Logan was so busy puzzling over why he'd been asked to meet with his brother that he failed to recognize he'd been complimented until his mother spoke up.

"Oh, I don't know. Daniel here might win a few votes in that competition." Mom squeezed Daniel's hand again.

"Of course he would," the waitress said in a mollifying tone. "What can I get y'all?"

"Coffee," Logan said automatically. "Why exactly did you want to meet me here?" he asked his brother, who didn't answer because he was rattling off a list of instructions for his elaborate order.

Logan opened his mouth to repeat his question, but was interrupted when his mom decided to ask questions about every item on the menu. Already exhausted from their limited interaction, Logan rubbed at one eye wearily and wondered why Toni hadn't called him yet.

Finally deciding she'd just have the special, Mom folded her menu and handed it to the waitress.

"Are you sure all you want is coffee?" the waitress asked Logan.

Maybe if he ate something, he could gather his suddenly scattered wits. "What's good here?"

"I'd say *you* served up with a side of bacon, Hotcakes, but that would probably get me in trouble." The rather elderly waitress winked at him.

Logan chuckled. "I'm not sure I'm on the menu. I remember this place used to serve the best homemade biscuits with butter and honey. Do you still have those?"

"You've been here before?" The waitress's brown eyes twinkled with mischief. "I'm sure I would have remembered you."

"It's been many years," he said. Around twenty or so. "But I still remember those biscuits."

"I hope they're as good as you remember," she said as she wrote down his order, took the untouched menu from the table in front of him, and sashayed away with more swagger than most women half her age.

"I think you have an admirer," Mom said with a giggle.

"I'm sure he's used to it," Daniel said.

Did a man ever get used to women old enough to be his grandmother hitting on him? Logan thought not. But he honestly didn't mind her misguided affection. It was far better than being ignored and forgotten.

"Again," Logan said, "why did you want to meet me here?"

Daniel dropped his gaze to the table. "I was hoping you could help me out."

"I'd be happy to," Logan said without hesitation. "Now are you going to tell me what I'm supposed to be helping you out with?"

"I'm in a bit of a bind," Daniel said. "Financially."

Daniel's eyes, the same familiar blue shade Logan saw in the mirror each day, darted upward and then dropped to stare at the table.

"So you lured me here to ask for a loan," Logan said, all hope for a joyous family reconciliation fizzling out of him. He was sure it wasn't easy for Daniel to ask him for money. His brother must be fairly desperate to sink to that level.

"A loan?" Mom squeezed Daniel's hand again. "He's your brother, Logan. I know you have more money than you know what to do with."

"How do you know that?" Logan asked. "Maybe I spent it all on drugs and women."

Daniel jerked his hand from his mother's grasp and shoved her out of the booth so he could stand. "I knew this was a bad idea. He doesn't care about my problems."

"Sit down," Logan demanded. "I didn't say no, did I?"

Daniel offered him a suspicious look, but he sat. Mom sidled back in next to him and patted him consolingly on the back.

"Are you ill?" Logan asked. "Do you need money for medical treatment?" He looked like shit.

Daniel hesitated and then shook his head.

"Drugs? Gambling? Booze?"

Daniel glanced at Mom and then shook his head again. "Bad investments," he said.

"Someone played you for a sucker and took all your money," Logan guessed.

Daniel took a deep breath and nodded, refusing to meet Logan's eyes. "I didn't have all that much money to begin with."

The waitress arrived with their beverages. Logan thanked her as he took a hesitant sip of what turned out to be molten-hot coffee. She offered him a toothy smile as she sauntered away again.

"So what happened?" Logan asked. He wasn't against helping his brother without strings—he really did have more money than he knew what to do with—but he wanted details before he started tossing cash around.

"I was trying to get into real estate. Buying houses cheap, flipping them, and selling them for a profit."

"He loves to watch those shows on cable," Mom said.

Daniel rolled his eyes at her and turned his attention back to Logan. "Let's just say I'm not good at picking out profitable flip houses and leave it at that."

"He's also not good at plumbing," Mom added.

"You flood one basement and you never hear the end of it," Daniel grumbled.

"What's the damage?" Logan asked, taking another sip of his coffee and finding it now safe for consumption.

"A hundred should cover it."

Logan sputtered. "*Grand?*"

"No, a hundred dollars, Logan," Daniel said and shook his head at Logan's apparent idiocy. "Yes, a hundred grand. How much do you think houses cost?"

"Why don't you just sell it to recoup your investment?" Logan asked.

"I just need the money, okay?"

"The house isn't worth what he paid for it, much less what he still owes the contractors," Mom said.

"Why should I bail you out? I haven't seen you for over a year. We barely speak to each other, yet I'm supposed to hand over a substantial sum of money simply because you fucked up."

"Logan," Mom said. She reached across the table to touch his hand for the first time since they'd sat down. "He's your brother. He needs you."

And Logan had needed him once too. But not any longer. "I honestly thought you'd looked me up because you'd read that article printed in the tabloids and realized how terrible you both were to me when I was a kid."

"No one was terrible to you," Mom said. "Heck, Logan, we hardly got to see you."

"Exactly!"

"You hated visiting us," Daniel said.

"Because you all made me feel like I didn't belong."

"That's ridiculous," Mom said. "You were always welcome in our home."

"*Your* home. It was never my home."

The three of them stared at the table, the tension so taut Logan expected at least of one them to snap like an overtightened guitar string.

"Are you going to give me the money or not?" Daniel asked.

He didn't know. He was feeling a bit vulnerable and a lot put on the spot. He wished Toni were with him for moral support and to help him consider his options logically so he wouldn't simply run on blind emotion. "I might consider loaning it to you . . ."

Daniel shook his head, looking like a cornered rat—desperate, scared, and more than a little scummy. "You always were a selfish brat." He shifted sideways in the booth. "Let me out, Mom. I need to go to the bathroom."

Mom looked from one of her sons to the other as if she'd just discovered they were both adopted and her memories of their births had been implanted by futuristic scientists.

"Mom," Daniel prompted.

She slid from the bench to let him out and surprised Logan by slipping into the spot next to him. Daniel headed for the bathroom, and Mom took Logan's hand, squeezing it reassuringly.

"I had no idea you felt excluded from the family, Logan. I thought you didn't *want* to come visit us. I figured you felt you needed to be loyal to your dad and that's why you were so miserable whenever we saw you."

Logan snorted on a laugh. "You give me far too much credit; my emotions have never been that complicated. I was jealous as hell of Ray. He was closer to Daniel than I ever was."

Her arm went around his back. "You wouldn't think that if you had to live with those two," she said and offered him a smile. "Why didn't you ever tell me how you felt, sweetheart? I missed you so much." She brushed a curl from his forehead, the simple gesture clogging his throat with emotion. "I hated your father for being a cheating bastard, but I hated him even more for keeping you away from me."

"He didn't do it intentionally," Logan said. He knew he was partially to blame for keeping his true feelings bottled up inside himself for so many years.

"I wouldn't be so sure," she said. "Now, about Daniel . . ."

"He can have the money."

"I don't want you to just give him the money, Logan. You make him pay you back."

Logan traced the rim of his coffee cup with one finger. "Oh? What made you change your mind?"

She rubbed a hand over one eye. "I'm scared he's going to do something crazy," she whispered, "and I didn't want to set him off by not siding with him."

Logan scratched his forehead. "But it's okay if I set him off?"

"He expects you to be tough on him, Logan. Just don't be too tough, okay? He idolizes you."

Sure. That's why he never called.

"So what am I supposed to do, Mom? Stretch out his payments for decades and don't charge him any interest?" Logan asked.

"If you're okay with that." She smiled at him hopefully.

Logan nodded. "I'm okay with that." Hell, his current feelings of happy contentment were well worth a hundred grand to him. But if Logan started giving Daniel free rides now, he was sure to come back for more.

"So what's this about a tabloid?" Mom asked, reaching across the table to draw her untouched cup of coffee toward herself.

Logan shrugged. "Don't worry about it. Someone got a hold of personal information about the guys in the band and smeared our names all over the tabloids. All the hoopla will pass in a few weeks." And by then hopefully Toni would be back on tour with them. He already missed her terribly. "I know it's rude, but do you mind if I make a quick phone call? I'm starting to worry about my girlfriend. She should have called by now."

Logan wasn't sure if it was the idea that he had a girlfriend or that he was capable of worrying about someone besides himself that had his mother staring at him in wide-eyed shock. She waved a hand to indicate she didn't mind his rudeness, and he pulled out his phone.

Logan was smiling, anticipating hearing her voice, when after a few rings his call went to her voicemail. Strange. Was she rejecting his calls? Why would she do that?

"You have a girlfriend?" Mom asked.

"Well, I *did*. But I think she just rejected my call."

"Is her ringtone 'Milkshake' by any chance?"

Logan went still, and then turned his head to offer his fidgeting mother an inquisitive stare. "Yeah. How do you know that?"

"I kind of answered your phone while you were in the shower. And I might have said something she probably took the wrong way."

He dialed Toni again, and this time the phone barely rang once before he was sent to voicemail again.

Logan growled in frustration and slammed his phone on the table. "What did you say to her, Mom?"

"I didn't realize you were serious about her. What kind of man sets 'Milkshake' as his girlfriend's ringtone?"

"The kind of man you gave birth to." And Toni wouldn't let him use the sound of her climaxing with his cock in her mouth, so this had been their compromise. He dialed Toni for the third time. This time he didn't even hear a ring; his call went directly to voicemail. Which meant that either her battery was dead or she'd shut off her phone to avoid talking to him. He had a sick feeling in the pit of his stomach that it was the latter. He knew he should have gone after her the night before. "Toni," he said to her voicemail. He hated leaving messages, so he kept it as brief as possible. "Please call me as soon as you can. It's important."

He hung up and scrubbed his eyes with both hands before trying to smear the gloom from his expression by drawing his hands down his face. "Please tell me what you said to her, Mom. She's very sensitive."

"She asked me who I was," his mother said. "And all I said was I was your entertainment. I figured she was one of your fangirls and I was doing you a favor by suggesting you were with someone."

"You told her you were my *entertainment*?" Well, Toni would definitely take that the wrong way. Hell, was there even a right way to take such a claim?

"She went completely silent for a minute or two. I thought she hung up."

"She's obviously upset," he said. "She won't even answer my calls."

"Let her cool off and try back later," Mom said, patting Logan's knee under the table. "I see our breakfast coming this way."

He didn't feel much like eating. Not even the plate of fluffy biscuits set before him. Daniel returned just as the waitress set his meal in his empty spot. He flopped down into the bench like a petulant toddler.

"Logan has decided to loan you the money," Mom said, "but not charge you any interest. Isn't that nice of him?"

"Oh, yeah, that's swell," Daniel said, his tone thick with sarcasm. "I hope he agreed to give me fifty years to pay it off."

"Is that acceptable?" Mom lifted her eyebrows at Logan.

"Works for me," Logan said. "I'll have my accountant send you a check and whatever documents are required. I figure a year's grace period ought to give you time to get your feet beneath you before you have to start paying me back."

Daniel sagged into his seat. "That's fair," he said. He began digging into his breakfast like a man who hadn't eaten for days. And maybe he hadn't. Logan was relieved to see a bit of color return to his brother's cheeks. And he was oddly satisfied knowing he'd been able to help him out.

Normally Logan would have enjoyed his nostalgic biscuits drizzled with honey and the congenial chit-chat he shared with his family, but the idea of Toni thinking he was being entertained by another woman had him entirely distracted.

Holding his phone beneath the table, he started sending her a string of text messages. Maybe she was too upset to talk but would still read his texts.

> Toni, the woman who answered my phone this morning was my mother.

> She was just joking with you.

> She didn't know you were my girlfriend.

He might as well stop typing his guts out to her. The messages weren't going through as delivered anyway.

"Are you feeling okay?" his mom asked, even checking his forehead for fever.

"Just worried about Toni. Can you take me back to the hotel? Maybe she'll answer if I call her from a landline."

"I'm sorry I messed things up for you," Mom said.

"I'm sure it'll work out. She's a reasonable person. I just really need to talk to her and explain things."

"Of course."

When they pulled up to the hotel lobby about twenty minutes later, Mom grabbed Logan's arm to keep him in the car a moment longer.

"I don't want to hear any excuses out of you when I invite you to our Labor Day barbecue this year. You're coming."

"I'll have to check my schedule. If I remember correctly, we'll be touring in Indonesia in September."

"You can't keep blowing me off. I need to see you more often," she insisted.

He smiled. He never thought he'd hear her say that and believe that she meant it. "Definitely."

"And I need to meet this girl who has you out of your head."

Logan laughed at his transparency. "Definitely." He leaned over and kissed his mother's cheek and hugged her the best he could given the hindrance of her seat belt.

"Please offer Toni my apologies for upsetting her."

Staring into his eyes, Mom pet his curls as if he were her favorite lap dog. He didn't mind in the least.

"You'll have to do that yourself when you meet her."

If Mom ever got to meet her. First he had to set things straight and if Toni didn't answer her phone or read his texts, he was going to have to hunt the woman down and reassure her—and himself—that everything was all right between them.

On the elevator, he checked his phone, praying he'd somehow missed a text or an email or a call. Nothing.

The elevator stopped on the third floor and the door slid open. Logan had never been more happy to see Butch in his entire life, and the man had gotten him out of some real jams in the past.

"Butch! Are you busy?"

"Never too busy for you." He grinned crookedly beneath his mustache. Logan wondered how quickly the band would fall apart if this man ever left them to their own devices.

"I need to use the jet after the show tonight," Logan said.

"Let me guess," Butch said with a wry grin. "You want to go to Seattle. And you want a car waiting with gifts of chocolates and flowers and sex toys and socks."

Logan laughed, not even caring that he was so easy to read. "Actually, I thought I might head to the Caribbean for some parasailing, but I guess I'll go with your plan."

"You're damn right you'll go with my plan. Do you know how hard it was for me to force that little sweetheart to leave? It broke my heart to make her cry. And then to find out that whole mess wasn't her fault?" Butch shook his head. "If you don't go get her, I will." He grinned again. "And I'll buy her a whole busload of socks if that's what it'll take to have her forgive me."

"I could go now," Logan said.

"You'll never make it back in time for the concert tonight."

He had half a mind to say fuck the concert. He had more important things to do.

The elevator doors opened on the top floor, and they stepped out into the corridor.

"She won't answer her cellphone," Logan said to Butch. "Can we get her home number? Office number? Send a carrier pigeon? Something?"

"Carrier pigeons are extinct," Butch said. "But I'll get a

message to her somehow. What do you want it to say?"

Heat flooded Logan's face. Was he actually blushing? Lord. "Uh. I love her. It was my Mom who answered my phone this morning. I'm not cheating on her."

Butch's eyes nearly bugged out of his head. "She thinks you're cheating on her?"

Logan sighed and nodded.

"No wonder she won't answer her phone. I thought she must still be upset about being accused of selling you all out to the tabloids."

"I told you I straightened that out last night. This is a whole new fuck-up."

Butch chuckled. "I guess I'll add a florist and chocolatier to my speed dial. I have a feeling I'm going to need their numbers often."

Butch was probably right, but Logan shook his head at the dig.

"I'm still going to try to get a hold of her, but yeah, I need everything ready to go so I can head to Seattle directly after the concert."

Butch shrugged. "No problem. It's not like I have anything better to do."

Logan was certain Butch had thousands of better things to do, but the man was Logan's hero and had yet to let him down. "Thanks for having my back, dude."

"One of these days I'm going to call in all my favors. And then you won't be thanking me."

Logan doubted that. If Butch helped him get Toni back, Logan would owe the man his every happiness.

And he'd pay in any currency Butch demanded.

CHAPTER 35

TONI WAS about five miles from home when she realized she'd left her cellphone in her desk drawer at the office. She was truly having a shit-tacular day. Driving up the long drive to the A-frame wood cabin she'd called home for the past fifteen years made her heart ache. How could Mom even consider selling the place? Toni simply could not let it go. And Toni wouldn't let her father go either. It wasn't time to move on. It would never be time to move on. There was plenty of room in her heart for both the living and the dead. Especially now that the mistreated organ had a gaping hole recently carved into it by a certain cheating son of a bitch.

The sun was already setting behind the pine trees, casting long spear-like shadows on the walls of her home. Gravel crunched beneath her feet as she made her way up the driveway, and she reveled in the little nuances of the place that she usually took for granted. The scent of the pine forest, crisp and clean. The soft clucking of the hens settling into their nests for the night. The picturesque sight of the snow-tipped hunk of craggy granite in the distance. And the feeling, the comforting feeling of home. No place on Earth could compare. She had to figure out a way to keep this place. For Birdie's sake, yes, but also for her own.

Toni climbed the steps to the deck that surrounded the entire house and let herself into the mudroom. She figured she could fall asleep standing up until the mouth-watering scents of garlic, oregano, and basil filled her nose. Her grandmother must have spent the entire day cooking. Toni closed the door behind her and dumped her messenger bag and laptop case on the floor with a weary sigh.

"Eloise?" Grandma called from the connecting kitchen.

"No, it's Toni," she said.

"About time you came home. These delivery guys are about to drive me nuts. Ringing the doorbell every hour on the hour like clockwork."

"Delivery guys?"

Toni came around the corner into the kitchen and stopped dead in her tracks, her eyes widening and mouth dropping open with shock. Vases of flowers were perched on every available surface. The fragrant and colorful blooms ranged from a simple dozen red roses to several arrangements of mixed flowers to a bouquet of brilliant pink and white stargazer lilies that was as wide as the table that bore its weight.

"What in the world?" Toni said.

"You better call that young man and forgive him for whatever he's done. I don't think the next batch will fit through the door," Grandma said. "And don't get me started on those damned balloons."

"Balloons?"

"I told Birdie to take them to your room. It isn't safe to have them floating about in the kitchen while I'm cooking."

Over the sound of water boiling on the stove, Toni could hear Birdie giggling and the playful yap of one of Grandma's Pomeranians.

"Are these all from Logan?" Toni wondered aloud. She reached for the card on the closest bouquet.

Grinning at Toni, Grandma tapped the vase closest to her. "Unless you have more than one man who is crazy in love with you, I'd guess so."

The card read:

Please call me, Toni.
The woman who answered my
phone this morning was my
mother.
Logan

"His *mother*?"

Toni snatched the card from the next bouquet.

She went around the room, reading one card after another.

> Toni, I swear didn't cheat on you..
> I would never do that to you..
> Please call. I need to hear your voice.
>   Love, Logan

The next one seemed a little angry.

> What do I have to do to get you to
> answer your damned phone, Toni?
> Answer it! Now.
> Stop fucking ignoring me.

Then pleading.

> Please call me, Toni. Text me. Email
> me. Something. Please.
> Even if it's to yell at me.
> I can't take your silence.

Desperate.

> I'll do anything to win you back,
> lamb.
> Just tell me what to do.

Insulting.

> You are the most stubborn woman I've
> ever met.
> Will you just talk to me?

Threatening?

> I'm going to track you down and kiss
> you until you see reason. We are meant
> to be together. Don't you get that?

> I love you, Toni.

> Just . . . I love you.

> That has to be enough.
> I love you.
> Desperately. Unconditionally.
> Forever.

Resigned.

> Well, this obviously isn't working. I
> give up.

Clutching his little notes to her chest, she allowed tears to stream down her cheeks. Tears of happiness—he hadn't cheated on her. Tears of exhilaration—he truly loved her. Tears of empathy—the poor guy had been completely miserable all day. Her cellphone was still over an hour away in Seattle, and unfortunately she didn't have his number memorized. How could she reach him?

"Well?" Grandma asked.

Blurry-eyed, Toni spun around, still clutching Logan's notes. "He loves me."

Grandma smiled. "In that desperate I'll-die-if-I-can't-touch-you kind of way or the more settled I-can't-notice-anything-but-your-absence-when-you're-gone kind of way?"

"Both, I think."

"Lucky you. So you're going to forgive him and make amends?"

Toni choked on a laugh. "He didn't do anything wrong to begin with. It was just a misunderstanding. But yes, I'd forgive him. I'd probably forgive him anything. Just don't tell him that."

Grandma patted Toni's shoulder. "I guess you'd better call him and let him off the hook. Unless you think you need more flowers." She glanced around the room at the abundance of blooms.

"I have more than enough flowers, but I left my phone at the office." Toni gnawed on her lip, trying to decide on her best plan of action.

"Is your mother still there? Maybe she can bring it home with her."

"Good idea!" She was still upset with her mother, but Toni was desperate enough to ask her for a favor.

"You just caught me on my way out," Mom said via her office line. "I'll bring it with me."

"Thanks."

"But wouldn't it make more sense if I looked his number up in your contacts and read it to you? Just give me your pass code."

Toni almost jumped on that idea, but remembered that Logan had recently changed his icon to an X-rated close-up of his cock, and she didn't want her mother to get an eyeful of that.

"Uh . . ." She nibbled a fingernail. "No, that's okay. Just bring it home. I don't need it that desperately." She cringed at her total lie.

"By the way, I've set up some home viewings for tomorrow," Mom said, turning Toni's moment of jubilation to bitterness. "I'd like you and Birdie to come with me to look at condos."

Condos? Oh God, no.

"I might be busy," Toni said. Actually, she would make it a priority to be too busy to view condos, no matter if she ended up hurrying off to Logan or not.

Toni frowned as she turned to help Grandma put the finishing touches on dinner.

"She's not bringing it?" Grandma asked.

"She is," Toni said.

"Then why so glum?"

Toni glanced toward the stairs, no wanting Birdie to overhear. She was surprised her little sister hadn't come down to greet her. Toni supposed playing with dogs and helium balloons was far more interesting than she was.

"Mom is going to sell the farm," Toni said in a hushed tone.

Grandma's eyebrows shot up and she dropped her wooden spoon in the sauce, splattering red flecks on the stove. "Oh no, she's not!"

"She needs the money to keep the business afloat. And, well, she never really liked it out here in the sticks."

"If she's selling, I'm buying. This is the only place I still feel connected to Phillip. And I've been so happy here with Birdie this past week. I thought I'd finally found a place to call home."

"I thought you liked roaming the country with your dogs in your little RV."

"I did," Grandma said. "But I'm over all that. You and Birdie are the only family I have left. I don't want to waste another moment being alone."

Toni hugged her. "I'm so glad you've decided to stay, but even if we pool our money together, I don't think we can afford to buy this place. It's prime acreage."

"I have money saved up, and selling the RV will bring in a little more."

"Daddy left me some money. I'm all in. I just don't think it'll be enough. I'm sure we're talking a few million dollars, Grandma." Toni didn't have even close to that much money and was pretty sure her grandmother wasn't drowning in cash either.

"You could always let your boyfriend continue to think he's in trouble and open your own flower shop." Grandma leaned away and stared into Toni's eyes, patting her cheek affectionately.

Toni laughed. "That might work." She was joking of course, but there had to be a way to keep their home. She just needed time to think of a plan.

"Toni!" Birdie yelled from the kitchen doorway. "I didn't know you was home! Come see all the balloons. Logan gave them to you. Your whole room is full of balloons. Red ones!"

"It's time to eat dinner, Buttercup," Toni said. "Grandma made your favorite."

"Sketties!"

Grandma kissed Birdie's forehead when she came within reach, and Birdie smiled brightly. It melted Toni's heart to see such affection between them.

"Grandma says we should get a baby goat!" Birdie said.

Grandma cringed at being outed.

"That would be fun," Toni said. "But are you prepared to take care of it? It would be your responsibility."

"Oh yes!" Birdie carefully placed a napkin next to each plate on the table. "I saw a gray baby goat on Ameridas Funnest Home Videos. I want a gray one." She continued to jabber about gray baby goats for several minutes. "Can we go upstairs to show you the balloons now?"

"How about after we eat?" Toni had nothing better to do while she waited the hour it would take her mom to get home with her phone.

"Balloons, balloons, balloons, balloons," Birdie intoned as she placed silverware on the table. "Toni has balloons. Balloons. Balloons. Balloons."

"Why don't you go see your balloons so she'll stop fixating?" Grandma suggested. "I can finish up here."

So Grandma already understood how Birdie tended to fixate on one detail with infallible concentration. Toni wished Grandma had come to stay with them ages ago. Then Toni might have been able to build a more far-reaching life for herself without the constant guilt.

"All right," Toni said. "I'll go see the balloons."

"Yay!" Birdie grabbed her hand and yanked her toward the stairs.

The entire vaulted ceiling of Toni's large bedroom was completely concealed by red balloons. Just the sight made her smile. Remembering the last time she'd been given red balloons made her ache with longing for the man behind the gesture. The two Pomeranians jumping in the air trying to grab the dangling strings made her laugh. Her laughter died when she noticed a familiar, presumed-lost journal lying on her bed. How in the hell had her diary gotten here?

Toni darted across the room and lifted the pink journal from her pale green coverlet. Thumbing through the pages, there was no doubt it was the same journal she'd been writing in while on tour with Exodus End. The final entry was dated May 8 and the remaining pages were blank.

"I tried to read your book, Toni, but it was too much squiggles. I can't tell what it says. So I gave it back."

Toni turned to stare at her sister in disbelief. *Birdie* had taken her journal? If that was true, how had the tabloid gotten hold of the band's personal information?

"Where did you get this, Birdie?"

"I found it in your bag at Denver and I hide it in my pocket. Are you mad I taked it?"

"You shouldn't take things without asking first."

Birdie frowned. "I sorry. I thought it was a princess story 'cause it's pink."

"I'm not mad. Just ask next time you want to borrow something, okay?"

"Okay."

Toni tried to remember when Birdie had been with her bag in Denver. In the conference room while she'd given her presentation, maybe? That had to be the case.

"Did anyone else read my book, Birdie?"

"No," she said, tilting her head and shrugging. "Not even me. Toni, you have *bad* handwriting."

Toni couldn't help but laugh. Her handwriting *was* atrocious. But if Birdie had her journal and no one else had seen it, how had all those stories about Exodus End been leaked?

"Are you sure no one else saw my book, Birdie?"

"I sure. I kept it safe in my secret spot. Can we eat sketties now?"

"Of course."

Scowling with puzzlement, Toni trailed after Birdie to the kitchen.

"You've stopped smiling already," Grandma remarked to Toni as they sat down to eat. "You'll get things straightened out with Logan."

"I hope so," she said, but that wasn't what had her picking at her food. She supposed she would have to read the damned tabloid for clues. The only explanation she could come up with was that someone had somehow found the journal in Birdie's secret spot under her bed. But the only person who could have found it was her mother and Toni could not—*would* not—believe that her own mother would stoop to that level.

Mom didn't show up all through dinner or during Birdie's bedtime routine. Toni was starting to worry that something had happened to her. It wasn't unusual for her workaholic mother to come home late at night, but Mom knew Toni was awaiting the delivery of her phone. Unable to take the wait any longer, she gave in and called her.

When Mom answered, Toni said, "Why aren't you home yet? I've been imagining you dead in a gutter."

"I'm on my way," she said, her voice distant since she spoke through her car's speakerphone function. "Another half hour or so."

"Did you remember my phone?"

"Yep."

"Mom, have you seen my journal?" Toni's stomach twisted with anxiety as she waited for her response. She knew how desperate her mother was for cash, but surely she wouldn't sell information to the tabloids.

"Which journal?"

"Pink faux leather cover. Small enough to fit in a pocket." And with privileged information written inside.

"No idea what you're talking about. Maybe Birdie has seen it."

Toni let out a deep breath as relief spread through her body. "I'll ask her. See you in a bit."

Grandma had already retired to the guest suite, so Toni

retrieved the copy of the tabloid she'd bought at the airport. At the time she hadn't been sure why she was encouraging the further publication of trash by giving them her money, but now she was glad she'd bought a copy.

Dread weighed heavy on the back of her neck as she sat at her desk, opened the paper, and scanned the first article. There was no doubt that the stories could have been fabricated based on the snippets in her journal, but there was far more information in the articles than she'd written. She'd hardly even mentioned the false rumors of Steve having a homosexual relationship with Zach Mercer, and yet the author of the article had run with that. Another article was about Steve and his ex-wife. A third about Steve's mystery second wife. Wait? Had she even written about Steve's second wife in her diary? She didn't remember doing so. Another article about Steve fooling around with various women.

Why was there such a huge section devoted to Steve?

Toni flipped to the next article. Logan's troubles with his brother were completely blown out of proportion, making it sound as if he cried nonstop into his pillow over his lost childhood. And poor Reagan. No wonder she'd been so upset. Not only had the article author revealed the nature of her relationship with Trey Mills and Ethan Conner, but he or she had completely trashed Reagan's character and her "novice guitar playing." It was even suggested that the only reason Reagan had gotten her shot in the limelight was because she was screwing every member of the band, going so far as to imply marathon orgies.

The tragedy that bonded yet still stood between Max and Dare had been twisted into a story of back-stabbing cruelty when in truth it had been young, misguided love.

The group had been thoroughly and savagely trashed.

And then when Toni saw the picture she'd taken of Logan and Steve that first night—with the caption *Seems there's more than friendship between this pair. How many men does Steve Aimes keep in his closet?*—she knew without a doubt that the information in the articles hadn't come from her handwritten journal. It had come from the files stored on her laptop.

"Shit."

Toni removed her glasses and buried her face in her hands, racking her brain for times her laptop had been insecure. She'd left it on the bus when she'd followed the band members around. She supposed someone could have snuck onto the bus and downloaded information from her hard drive, but that seemed unlikely. Especially since her computer was password protected and the bus was never left unsecured. She'd taken her laptop to the hotel with her when Logan had helped her with her presentation, but the only time it had been unattended was when they'd gone to the motocross track.

Toni's heart slammed into her ribcage and her head shot upright as a clear scene of her unattended laptop flashed through her head. When she'd taken Birdie to the restroom to see to her bloodied nose during her presentation, her laptop had been open and running in the conference room with her mother and Susan. Toni had even encouraged the two women to look through her files while she'd tended to Birdie. During those few minutes, Susan had unexpectedly disappeared and her mother had decided that Toni was capable of completing the book.

"Fucking hell!"

And Toni had thought their change of heart had been due to her brilliant presentation.

"That back-stabbing, lying, double-crossing, motherfucking *cunt*!" Toni raged, hoping that the insult was reserved for Susan, but in her gut knowing that the woman hadn't worked alone.

She flipped through the articles again, this time paying more attention to the images. Perhaps she couldn't sue them for printing privileged information, but she might be able to sue for printing her photos. She recognized a few she'd taken, but most of them weren't hers. A photo of Steve's wedding party caught her eye. She smiled at how young and handsome he looked in a tux. He couldn't have been much more than twenty in the picture. She was a bit surprised to see Zach Mercer as his best man. How long had Steve known the guy? He'd been married before Exodus End had formed. Steve's wife looked stunning and radiantly happy. Her maid of honor looked pissed off and shockingly familiar.

"Susan?" Toni blurted.

The woman in the picture was at least fifteen years younger and about fifty pounds heavier, but there was no mistaking her cynical stare.

"What the fuck?"

Susan must be involved somehow, but had she acted alone or was Mom in cahoots with her? Toni prayed that Susan had taken her files when Mom had stepped out of the conference room to answer a call or something. Surely her mother wouldn't break her own daughter's trust and potentially ruin her entire career on purpose. Who did that?

Gravel crunched in the driveway when a pair of headlights turned onto the property. Toni slapped her glasses back on her face and crumpled the tabloid in an angry fist. She was going to get to the bottom of this right now.

Mom was just coming into the kitchen when Toni charged into the room.

Looking weary, Mom smiled and held out Toni's cellphone to her. "Here it is. Calm down. Sheesh!"

Toni was so pissed off, she couldn't form words. She stood there shaking for a long moment before yanking her phone out of Mom's hand.

"What's with all the flowers?" Mom asked as she made her way toward the refrigerator.

"How could you?" Toni croaked.

"What?" She turned a questioning gaze on Toni.

"At least tell me it was Susan's idea." Toni knew she wasn't making sense, but she couldn't pull her thoughts together with all the negative emotions swirling through her.

"What are you talking about, Antonia?"

"This!" Toni shoved the tabloid in her mother's direction. "You stole the information off my computer and sold it to the tabloids."

"Technically, the information belongs to your employer since you're a work-for-hire writer."

Mom was so calm about her betrayal, that Toni gaped in utter disbelief.

"So you *did* steal information from me?" Toni's voice cracked beneath the strain of her fury. "You sold those horrible stories about my friends to the tabloids?" *Please let this be a nightmare and let me wake up safe and warm in Logan's arms.*

"Friends? Oh please, Toni. You don't honestly believe those people care about you, do you? How quick were they to lay the blame at your feet and have you thrown from their lives? The paper hadn't been out for even a day before they sent you packing."

"They are my friends," Toni said. "You hurt them. And me. Was it worth it?"

Mom shrugged. "Not really. The paper didn't pay us nearly as much as we were expecting. My accounts are still in the red. Susan far overestimated how much money those kinds of stories would bring. Hell, only one of the tabloids she contacted would touch them. Something about Exodus End's manager having Satan's attorney in his pocket." Mom turned back to the refrigerator.

Toni clenched her hands into fists so she didn't strangle the woman who'd given birth to her. "You're so . . . You're so . . ." There wasn't a word to describe how she felt about her mother at the moment. "So . . ."

"I'm so what?" Mom said, her voice flat. Cold. "If you're going to insult me, use your words, Antonia."

"Self-centered. Self-absorbed. Egocentric." Not strong enough. "You're fucking narcissistic, is what you are! Do you care about anyone but yourself?"

Mom slammed a container of leftover spaghetti on the counter. "I did once. I cared for someone with everything that I am. But your father took my heart with him when he died on me. And it hurt so bad that I don't even want it back. He can have it."

She wiped the back of her hand over her cheek, dashing away tears Toni had never seen her shed. Not even at Daddy's funeral.

"There are still two very big parts of him left on this planet, Mom. Birdie and me. Is it really so hard for you to see that?"

"I can't let myself love like that again," she whispered. "The loss is too great."

"Is that why you push Birdie away? You're afraid of losing her?"

Mom kept her back to Toni, hiding her thoughts. Her feelings. But her white-knuckled grip on the edge of the counter told Toni she was listening.

"She's a blessing, Mom. She's not perfect. None of us are. But she's a loving, sweet blessing. A gift from Daddy. She deserves to be treasured."

"I know that. Of course I know that. But do you have any idea what it feels like to be told—before she's even born, while she's still protected inside you—that you're going to outlive your child? Told, before she's even taken her first breath, that your baby girl will die young? Asked if you'd rather abort her than live with her disabilities?" Mom sniffed loudly and reached for a dish towel to wipe at her face. "I do. I know exactly what that feels like, Antonia."

"You can't focus on losing her. She's here. She's yours. Love her while you have her."

"I want to," she said. "But when will I have time for her? Keeping Nichols Publishing afloat takes all my time."

"And your integrity," Toni said. She hadn't forgotten about her mother's betrayal or how she'd been willing to destroy Toni's credibility—her chance for the career she wanted to pursue—for a few bucks. And yet her forgiving nature wouldn't allow her to stay angry for long with someone she loved. Susan, on the other hand . . . That bitch had to go.

"I apologize for breaking your trust," Mom said, her grip on the counter slackening. "I knew you wouldn't give us dirt on those rock stars of yours."

Rock stars of *hers*?

"I thought it would be easier on you if we circumvented you entirely."

Toni snorted. "So you stole information from my laptop for *my* benefit? Come on, Mom, how stupid do you think I am?"

"Yes, for your benefit. Why do you think I work so hard? Why do you think I'm willing to do anything to keep this company afloat?"

Because the woman got off on it? Why else?

"For you, Toni. I built this company for you."

"But I don't want it," Toni said.

Mom's shoulders slumped. "It destroys me to hear you say that. Of course, you want it. You *have* to want it."

"Honestly, Mom, I don't. I'd much rather spend time with you. I'd much rather Birdie get to know her mom than to have all the benefits of your hard work handed to me. I can carve my own niche into this world, you know."

Mom turned and looked at her. She stared so hard, Toni began to fidget. "You can't mean that, Toni. *Christ!* What have I been killing myself for all these years?"

Toni shrugged. "Beats me."

Mom's shoulders shook as she snorted, and then her entire body quaked as she laughed. Laughed so hard she couldn't find air. Laughed until Toni couldn't help but join her. Until they collided in a tight embrace tempered by the release of tension and all the affection that had been lacking between them for too many years.

When their laughter turned to intermittent chuckles and eventually uneven breathing, Mom pulled away to search Toni's eyes. Toni couldn't remember the last time she'd seen her mom look so happy. So relaxed and, and free.

"I hope I didn't mess up your relationship with that rock band too much," Mom said. "You really do have a gift for gaining an insider perspective."

"Logan says they'll be fine. Except Reagan. I'm not sure she'll ever get over it. Her reputation has been all but destroyed."

Mom cupped either side of Toni's head and pressed their foreheads together. "So you write the best damn book you can, fix the woman's reputation, hit the best-seller list, and save the company from financial ruin."

Toni laughed. "Well, I will write the best damn book I can. The rest is out of my hands."

"My husband raised you right." Mom kissed the tip of Toni's nose and released her. "It's getting late. I suppose you still have time to call that boyfriend of yours. You are still involved with him, I take it?"

"Logan!" Toni cried. She'd been so wrapped up in her dealings with her mom that she'd forgotten to call him.

She read through his string of text messages. They were almost identical to the cards he'd sent with the flowers. She didn't bother to listen to his voice messages before calling him. Her call was forwarded directly to his voicemail. She checked the clock to see if he was still onstage, but as it was almost one a.m. in Phoenix, he should be on the tour bus and on his way to the next venue.

"Logan," she spoke to his voicemail. "I'm sorry I took so long to get back to you. I didn't get any of your messages until late and then I didn't have my phone with me, so I couldn't call you back until now. I really need to memorize your number." She laughed at how frustratingly inconvenient convenience could be. "Call me when you get this. I don't care how late it is, I promise I'll answer. I believe you when you say you didn't cheat, but we still have a lot to talk about. I've had quite a day." That was an understatement. "I love you. Hope to hear from you soon."

She disconnected and turned to find herself alone. Mom had apparently decided she needed privacy while she made amends with Logan. Toni trudged upstairs to her room, turned her ringer up to maximum volume, and plugged her phone into the charger. She refused to miss his call. But as she lay in bed staring up at the balloons floating overhead with no word from him, she couldn't help but wonder if he'd given up on her.

CHAPTER
36

A T SOME POINT, TONI MUST HAVE DOZED off, because an unfamiliar, low-pitched rumble pulled her from a fitful sleep. Headlights reflected off her ceiling as someone turned into the driveway. Lost and turning around, she decided, until the engine died and the lights were extinguished. She lifted her phone and glanced at the time. It was three thirty in the morning. And she'd somehow missed an hour-old text from Logan.

OMW

As far as she knew, that acronym was short for *on my way*, but that made absolutely no sense. He was on his way to where?

Her phone rang, startling her so badly that she tossed it onto the floor as if it had sprouted fangs and tried to strike her dead. She rolled out of bed and onto the hardwood with an *oomph* before crawling after the flashing device that was blaring "I'm-Too-Sexy."

"Logan!" she answered, her heart still tripping over itself from being scared out of her wits. Or maybe the battered organ was just happy he'd finally called.

"Which room is yours?"

"What?"

"You're home, aren't you?" he asked with a panicked edge to his voice. "At your mother's house?"

"Yeah."

"Which room is yours?" he asked again.

"I don't understand."

"How can I crawl into bed with you and kiss you awake if I don't know which room is yours? I don't want to accidentally scare the living daylights out of the wrong person."

"You're here?" Toni scrambled off the floor and flew across the room to her floor-to-ceiling windows. She peered down the driveway at an unfamiliar muscle car and the unmistakable, shadowy shape of the man she loved standing beneath a sky dotted with billions of stars.

"When I couldn't reach you, I panicked. So I did what any nonsensical man in love would do. I hopped on a private jet, borrowed a friend's car, and hunted you down."

"You're crazy," she said with a laugh. And thank God for that.

"When it comes to you, I don't know how to be sane."

She unlocked the glass door that led from her room to the enormous deck that encircled the second story of the cabin. Barefoot, she crossed the cool wood planks and leaned over the railing.

"Look up," she said and when he did, she waved down at him.

"Ah, my Juliet," he murmured in her ear.

"Oh. Is *that* her name?" she teased. "Juliet."

"Antonia. Her name is Antonia," he said before he disconnected the call.

She gasped as he began to scale the lower deck. Standing on the railing, he sprang upward, missing the beam below her by inches.

"What are you doing?" she whispered harshly into the darkness below.

"What does it look like I'm doing?"

She couldn't see his face in the shadows, but she heard his grunt of exertion when he jumped again, this time getting one hand on the deck near her toes. He dangled there for a moment before losing his grip and dropping back out of sight.

"Logan!" Why did he have to be such a daredevil?

"I'm all right," he said. "I caught my fall with my face. Can you throw me a rope or something?"

"You're going to kill yourself. I'll come down."

She didn't wait for his agreement, but scurried back into her room and bounded down the stairs two at a time. Still in her short, silky nightgown, she dashed through the kitchen and mudroom before unlocking the back door. She gasped in surprise as the door flew inward and she was tugged against him. One of Logan's hands pressed into her back to hold their bodies together, the other tangled in her hair, pulling her mouth to his as he kissed her.

"Don't ever leave me again," he said against her lips.

She shook her head slightly, not wanting to interrupt his deep, demanding kiss. He was the one to eventually pull away. His breathing was harsh and ragged as he cradled her head to his chest, his heart thudding against her ear in a rapid staccato.

"Are you okay?" she asked.

"I'm better than I've been all day, but I won't be truly okay until I have you naked and I'm buried balls deep inside you."

Toni shifted out of his grasp and slipped the slender straps of her nightie down her shoulders and arms. One tug pulled the garment from her breasts, and the scrap of satin fluttered down to pool at her feet. She lowered her panties next, kicking them aside impatiently, and stood before him naked. Naked and unashamed. On her mother's back porch.

"You're halfway there," she murmured.

"Here?" Even as he was questioning her, his hand moved to cup her breast, his thumb brushing over her taut nipple.

"If you want. Or maybe you'd be willing to teach me how to have sex in a car." She nodded toward the vehicle he'd left parked in the driveway.

"Maybe," he said calmly.

Toni squeaked in surprise when he scooped her into his arms and carried her across the porch and down the steps to the car. He set her bare ass on the cool hood of the vehicle, and she jumped when the temperature registered. Logan spread her legs and stepped forward, rubbing the rough fabric of his bulging jeans against the heated, sensitive flesh between her thighs. He kissed her again, stealing her breath, stealing every logical thought. She reached for his fly, wanting him—needing him—closer. Inside her. He caught her hands and held them against hard steel as he kissed his way down her chest, her belly. The tip of his tongue flicked against her throbbing clit so gently that she scarcely felt it. He continued with the same maddening, barely touching flicks of his tongue—teasing her there, faster, oh yes, faster—until she was moaning and squirming and tugging against the hold he had on her wrists. She somehow managed to keep her legs wide open for him, trusting that he'd eventually give her the mind-shattering orgasm she craved.

Her pussy quivered with need—aching and swollen, drenched, tingling. Hot. Christ, she was on fire. Logan completely ignored her need to be possessed, still barely flicking his tongue against her sensitive clit until she couldn't take it anymore.

"You're driving me crazy," she said. "You have to fuck me."

"I have to?"

She didn't find his amused tone the least bit funny. "God, yes. You have to."

"Not yet."

He continued to tease her with those feather-light tongue flicks. She hadn't thought it was possible to be more aroused than she already was, but she was oh so wrong. He took her higher, higher, until she was far beyond her normal breaking point.

"If you want to come, think naughty thoughts," he said.

Toni moaned, enslaved by the slight change in stimulation brought by his breath against her heated flesh.

"You told me not to think during sex," she reminded him. It had been hard to turn off her thoughts at first, but now she did it automatically. She didn't want to think. She wanted to feel. Feel him.

"Think of how your pussy feels when it's stuffed with my cock."

Yes, that was exactly what she wanted to feel. His words inspired vivid memories of his cock inside her. She cried out as her pussy clenched hard on nothing. She filled her aching emptiness with thoughts. The way he looked when he came. The sound of his voice when he whispered her name, when he told her he loved her. The feel of his skin beneath her palms and lips, against her belly and her breasts. Between her thighs. The way his scent lingered on her body even when he was absent. How he consumed her inside and out when he made love to her. She visualized his cock sliding in and out of her, his tongue against her nipple, his finger slipping into her ass.

She wasn't sure if it was her thoughts or the persistent flick of Logan's tongue that finally sent her over the edge, but over she went. He shifted upward, captured her screams of bliss in his mouth, pressed her quaking body against his warm chest, and slowly filled her clenching pussy with his thick, rigid cock. He thrust into her slowly, claiming her deeply. Gently. When what she wanted him to do was fuck her hard and fast.

She should have known he knew what she really needed. His tender possession chased her intense orgasm with a sweet, languid pleasure that brought tears to her eyes. When her body settled into his peaceful rhythm, he pressed his face into her neck and whispered, "That's how you have sex *on* a car. Are you ready to try it in a car?"

"I will try it in a car. I will try beneath the stars."

"Will you try it here or there?"

"I will try it anywhere."

He chuckled and kissed her collarbone. "I do love you, woman. We're always on the same wavelength."

"I will try it on a plane," she continued her X-rated version of a Dr. Seuss rhyme. "I will do it in the rain."

"Will you try it on a boat? Will you try it with a goat?"

Toni stiffened and pulled away to stare at him in horror.

"Not on a boat. Not with a goat," he said, shaking his head.

"*Yes*, on a boat," she said. "And maybe on a Thanksgiving Day float. But definitely *not* with a goat."

"Let's try in the car first. Your skin is chilled."

She wouldn't have noticed the chill at all if he hadn't been caressing her bare flesh with warm hands.

He opened the car door, shucked his clothes, and left them in the driveway.

"Whose car is this?" Toni asked as she stood in the sharp gravel waiting for him to shove the driver's seat all the way back and climb inside.

"Ever heard of the band Secondary Launch?" Logan sat in the leather driver's seat and patted his thighs to encourage her to climb on.

"Of course."

"It's Justin Paige's car."

Toni knew him to be the band's vocalist.

"He owed Butch a favor."

"Everyone owes Butch a favor."

"I owe him a million." Logan somehow managed to close the door, and Toni tried to find a comfortable way to ride his cock in the confined space.

He shifted her into a more comfortable position. No, less comfortable, actually.

"Ouch! There's a gearshift in my ass."

"Oh, sure, you barely know this car, and yet you're already

giving it privileges you won't give me."

She slapped him halfheartedly. "Not inside my ass. It poked me in the hip."

"You got me all excited for nothing. Back seat?" Logan suggested.

She nodded, and he reclined the seat completely so she could climb over him into the roomier back of the car. He caught her by the hips as she attempted to crawl over his head. She gasped when his tongue lapped at the hole he was so fixated on. She was more than ready to try anal, but it was so much fun to keep him begging for it.

"I can't believe you'll let me lick it but you won't let me fuck it."

"I'm saving my anal virginity for marriage," she said as she tugged free of his grasp and flopped into the back seat.

"You're going to make me marry you before you give up the goods?"

She was totally bluffing, but she said, "Yep."

He climbed over the reclined front seat and joined her in back. "I think you underestimate how much I want to stick my dick in your ass."

"I underestimate?"

"Yeah, I'd totally marry you for the privilege of claiming your anal virginity." He sat behind the passenger seat and reached for her.

She shook her head at him and, facing the rear of the car, straddled his hips. "Don't say it unless you mean it."

She reached between them and took his cock in her hand, rubbing the head against her clit, dragging it through her wet seam and pressing it into her opening. She lifted her hips and dropped them slightly, taking just his cockhead inside her and allowing it to pop free each time she rose.

"Deeper," he pleaded after several moments of the same treatment.

"This is payback for licking my clit so softly I could barely feel it."

"You didn't enjoy my sweet torture?"

"Loved every minute of it. You aren't enjoying mine?"

"You know I love your evil side."

Her evil side soon caved to the need to feel him deep inside. He showed her several positions, and she even discovered one of her own with her feet planted against the back seat and her back crammed against the passenger seat. The position provided phenomenal leverage for riding him hard, and he found her clit fully exposed so he could massage it with his thumb. The car was definitely rocking when she cried out with release. His body stiffened as he followed her over the edge, and she pulled off of him at the last instant, grabbing his cock with both hands and pumping his load out to spatter over her lower belly. She wished there was more light in the car; she loved watching him spurt. Loved the desperate, gasping sound he made when he came. Loved how he shuddered when she shifted his cock back inside her after he'd spent himself.

She relaxed against his chest and snuggled her face into his neck. "I have a bunch of stuff I need to talk to you about," she said, "but it just doesn't seem all that important anymore."

"I have a few things to tell you as well," he said, "but I think I'd rather sit quietly, just like this, and fall asleep with you in my arms."

"We really are always on the same wavelength," she whispered just before she fell into a blissful slumber.

She was woken hours later by a persistent knock on the windshield.

CHAPTER 37

LOGAN SQUEEZED his eyelids closed and then pried them open, squinting against the light of the rising sun. He couldn't feel his legs, and he was pretty sure his bare ass was permanently melded to the leather seat beneath him, but waking up with Toni in his arms was worth any discomfort.

"Are these yours?" said a muffled voice from just outside the car door.

The elderly woman—who had to be at least seventy—was waving Toni's panties at the window. The woman knocked on the glass, and Toni jerked awake. She groaned and smacked Logan in the chest with a graceless arm as if he were the reason for her rude and likely uncomfortable awakening.

"Don't look now," he said, "but I think we've been spotted."

Toni rubbed her face, and smacked her lips, scowling groggily as she squinted at him. She smiled when she recognized his face and snuggled against him, her breasts pressing delightfully into his chest.

The woman knocked on the window again. "Toni! I found your panties on the porch."

Toni's body jerked, and she slowly turned her head to peer at the woman outside the car. "Good morning, Grandma," she said in a squeaky voice.

Great. What a wonderful first impression he was making on another of Toni's relatives.

"Do you want them?" Grandma waved the garment at her.

"Yes, please." Toni leaned back, one arm across her bare breasts as she attempted to roll down the automatic window and keep Logan's lap covered with hers. As the car wasn't running, the button didn't respond to her persistent fingertip.

"Can you get me a robe?" Toni asked.

"Is that your boyfriend?" her grandmother yelled at the glass.

"Nope. I always meet strangers in the driveway for sex in unfamiliar cars."

Logan's jaw dropped, but her grandma just laughed. "I'll leave these here," she said and tucked Toni's panties under the windshield wiper. "And go get a robe."

"And some shoes, please!"

Her grandma nodded, offered a coy wink to Logan, who wasn't sure if he should be mortified or amused, and then headed toward the house.

"I'm glad it was Grandma who discovered us and not Birdie or my mom," Toni said.

"You're glad?"

"Relatively speaking," she said as she slid off his lap. She winced when she attempted to straighten one leg. "Let's agree to never fall asleep in that position again."

"Deal." He cringed as he peeled his ass off leather. "If Justin finds out what's been on his back seat, I'm afraid he's going to have to burn his car."

Toni laughed and leaned over the front seat in her journey to recover her panties. Logan groaned at the glorious sight her bare ass presented to him as she scrambled to get behind the wheel. The car started with a loud *vroom*, idling with the low ferocity only an eight-cylinder could produce.

"And if he finds out what's been on his front seat," Logan said, "he's going to get a boner every time he drives."

Toni snorted. "I highly doubt that." She rolled down the window and rescued her panties from beneath the windshield wiper, then squirmed into them. With one arm over her boobs, she eased the door open and grabbed some of Logan's clothes from the ground outside, tossing them into the back before closing the door. Visibly shivering, she fiddled with the heater while he acrobatically donned his underwear, jeans, and one shoe.

"Did you find my shirt?" he asked, grateful that his junk was covered. But her grandmother was headed back in their direction, and he still wasn't what he'd consider respectable.

"I couldn't reach it. If I could, I'd be wearing it. I'm f-freezing." Her teeth chattered as she shuddered.

He leaned over the seat and kissed her chilled shoulder. "I can't believe you aren't upset about this."

"I'm too happy that you're here to care. I'm just glad Birdie didn't catch us. Her questions would have been endless."

Still holding her boobs with one arm, Toni rolled down the window when her grandmother reached the side of the car. Toni took the proffered fluffy pink robe and slid her arms into the sleeves. Next she wriggled her feet into a pair of slippers.

Her grandmother leaned into the car and extended her hand to Logan, who took it uncertainly.

"I'm Joanna. You must be the guy with all the flowers."

Logan felt a blush rush up his neck to his cheeks. "Yeah. That would be me trying to get your granddaughter's attention."

"I'd say it worked." Joanna chuckled and released his hand.

"I'm Logan, by the way."

"Nice to meet you, Logan. Come on inside for breakfast," she said. She picked up Logan's shirt from the ground and instead of handing it to him, she carried it with her into the house.

"She took my shirt," Logan said.

"Can't blame her," Toni said. "You look scrumptious in nothing but those jeans."

Toni rolled up the window and shut off the car before climbing out into the chilly, damp air. She flipped the seat forward to let him out, and he hopped around in the gravel on one foot as he rescued his other shoe from beneath the car.

Once he had it on, he drew Toni against him and ran his hands over her terry-cloth-encased ass to pull her closer. He leaned in for a kiss, but she turned her head.

"You do not want to kiss me right now," she said. "My breath is toxic."

"I do want to kiss you right now," he said, capturing her jaw in his hand and turning her face toward his. "I want to kiss you every morning."

She buried her fingers in his hair and smiled up at him. "Okay, but no tongue until I brush my teeth."

"A little tongue," he bartered. He closed the distance between their mouths, stroking her upper lip with the tip of his tongue as he drew away.

Staring up at him with wide eyes, she took a step back. And

then another.

"Oh my God!" she cried. "My breath really is toxic. Your face is melting off!"

She dashed up the steps, and laughing, Logan chased after her. In the kitchen, her mother's harsh stare drew him to a halt. His smile faltered.

"Logan is here!" Birdie yelled, running in his direction with three dogs on her heels. She looked him up and down, her eyes overlarge and inquisitive behind her thick glasses. "Where is your shirt? Are you going swimming?"

Logan covered his chest with one arm, similarly to the way Toni had concealed her breasts in the car. "Someone took it."

Joanna grinned as she handed his shirt to him. "Someone misplaced it," she corrected before she returned to the stove to stir a pan of scrambled eggs.

Logan gratefully tugged his shirt on over his head, and he swore he heard more than one disappointed sigh in the room.

"I'm going up to shower," Toni said. "Keep Logan company while I'm gone."

And then she left him there. With her family. He would have tried to join her in the shower if three pairs of eyes weren't watching his every move.

"Do you need help with anything?" he asked Toni's grandmother, glancing toward the stairs in hopes that Toni had just secured the world record for fastest shower ever.

"You're a guest," Joanna said. "Have a seat."

He'd much rather have had some mundane task such as buttering toast to keep him occupied, but he sat on a stool at the kitchen island and fought the urge to pull out his cellphone to pass the time and avoid awkward questions.

"Not there, silly," Birdie said. She took his hand and urged him from his perch, leading him to a square blue-gray breakfast table in a corner nook. "We eat over here."

"As you wish," he said with a cordial nod, and Birdie giggled in delight.

He watched her collect plates and set one in each spot while Joanna manned the stove. Eloise hadn't moved since he entered the room. She was watching him so closely that he considered hiding under the table. After several uncomfortable moments, he met her gaze and held it, which apparently was her cue to sit at the table beside him.

"I'm not sure what Antonia told you about the incident with the tabloid," Eloise said.

"Just that she wasn't the one who sold our stories."

"It wasn't her," Eloise said, licking her lips. "I didn't act alone, but ultimately, I am responsible."

"You!" Logan blinked at her, unable to fathom what she'd just told him.

"I wish I hadn't done it. I don't want this incident to damage Antonia's future career prospects or her um, *friendship . . .*" Eloise tilted her head toward him as if waiting for him to qualify what she was saying. He shrugged and shook his head, not sure what she was going for. "Or damage her friendship with you."

Oh, she was baiting him for relationship information. "I wouldn't be here if it had damaged our friendship," Logan said. "I knew she wasn't capable of hurting people she cares about. She isn't like that."

Eloise closed her eyes and nodded. "I always worry that she's too soft, too good, too gentle for her own benefit and that the world will chew her up and spit her out. But maybe instead of her changing to try to appease cruel reality, the rest of the world would do better to become more like her."

Yes, exactly. He was surprised he and her mother saw eye to eye on something like that.

"I've got her back," Logan said.

"Do you think it would be best to break our publishing contract with your band—"

"No!" He hadn't meant to shout, but if there wasn't a contract, there would be no reason—besides him—for Toni to return to her place on tour.

"—and let Toni pursue the book's publication independently?" Eloise finished.

Logan rubbed the back of his neck. He had no clue what would be best for the book or the band or Toni in that regard. All he cared about was that she would be at his side.

"I don't know," Logan said. "Why don't you ask Toni? Or Sam. He's the one who thought your publishing house was best for the job. There has to be a reason for that."

"It's because Toni does excellent work," Eloise said with a smile. "I don't give her enough credit. I've been trying to get everything in order so I can retire and hand the reins over to her-"

"You're retiring?" Joanna said, dropping a bowl of biscuits on the table with a thud. A few popped out of their container and rolled toward the floor. Luckily Logan had fast reflexes.

"That's the plan. I was going to wait a few years, but something Toni said last night convinced me that it's time to sell the company and pursue other ambitions." She glanced over at Birdie, who was pouring orange juice into five small glasses with strict concentration and aided, apparently, by her protruding tongue. "Toni doesn't want to run the company. She wants to continue to create. It's what she loves. What she's good at. I don't want to be responsible for squelching that spark in her. I want her to be happy."

Logan hadn't been sure he liked Eloise until that moment. A few minutes earlier, he was sure he didn't like her. But anyone who wanted to ensure Toni's happiness was a champion in his book.

"So maybe *you* could ask her what she wants me to do about the book," Eloise said to Logan. "I think she'll be open with you. I'm not sure she trusts me much right now."

Logan shrugged. He didn't really want to be sucked into Toni's family problems, but he did want her to follow her dreams. Especially if they included him.

"Birdie?" Joanna said from the stove.

Logan leaned around Eloise to see what the sweet child was up to. She was standing at the counter, a puzzled expression on her typically smiling face.

"Birdie?" Joanna said again, louder this time.

The pitcher of juice dropped from Birdie's hand as she clutched her chest. Orange liquid spread across the tile at her feet. "Somefing . . . Somefing's not right, Mommy," she said, just before she crumpled to the ground.

CHAPTER 38

TONI HOPED her family hadn't managed to scare Logan away in the twenty minutes she'd taken to shower. She traipsed down the steps, tugging a handful of red balloons behind her, hoping they'd bring a smile to his face, just as they'd brought one to hers. In her other hand she carried a copy of the tabloid paper. She wanted to know if Logan recognized Susan in Steve's wedding photo. Toni still didn't know how the woman was connected to the band or why she seemed bent on hurting them all, and Steve in particular. Toni was pretty sure Reagan and the rest of them had been caught in the crossfire. Or maybe Susan got off on destroying lives. She'd certainly tried to ruin Toni's.

When she rounded the corner to the kitchen, all the joy she'd felt at reconciling with Logan was ripped from her in an instant. Her feet rooted to the floor. She couldn't move, couldn't breathe. The words coming from Logan's mouth as he knelt over Birdie's crumpled body and held his ear close to her mouth sounded distant, as though Toni was watching the nightmare in her kitchen from a different dimension.

"She's breathing," he said, "but I can scarcely feel her heartbeat."

"Joanna, call 9-1-1. Have them send an ambulance," Mom said. She dropped to her knees next to Birdie and pressed her ear to Birdie's chest. "She was born with a heart defect. They did surgery soon after she was born, but she hasn't had many problems since."

"Should we start CPR?" Logan asked while Toni stood frozen in the doorway.

This was not happening. Not happening. Not happening. She couldn't lose Birdie. Couldn't lose her. No.

"Her heart's beating," Mom said. "Doesn't sound regular to me. Go get Toni. She's taken CPR classes; she'll know what to do."

But she didn't know. She didn't know anything.

Logan jumped to his feet and noticed Toni standing in the doorway, clinging to the ribbons of half a dozen balloons.

"Toni?"

She sucked in a panicked breath. This was just like Dad. She was too late. Daddy was gone. He'd been gone before she'd arrived. She'd been too late to help him. Too late to save him.

Staring wide-eyed at Logan, she shook her head repeatedly. "Not Birdie."

"Toni! Snap out of it," Logan demanded. "What should we do?"

The ribbons slipped from her grasp, and the balloons rose to the ceiling, bouncing off the rafters with soft thuds.

"Ambulance is on its way," Grandma said. "They said if her heart has stopped, we should start CPR."

"I'm starting chest compressions," Mom said, linking her hands in a fist.

"Wait," Toni said. "You said she was breathing."

Logan nodded. "She is."

"Then she doesn't need CPR. It could do more harm than good." Toni rushed to her sister's side and dropped to her knees. She could see Birdie's chest rising and falling. She placed her hand over Birdie's chest and she could feel her heart beating, but the organ was stumbling over itself irregularly. Something wasn't right, but this wasn't like what happened with Daddy at all. Birdie wasn't gone.

"Birdie," Toni called in a soothing voice, rubbing the center of Birdie's chest gently. "Birdie, open your eyes."

Birdie's face twitched as if she were trying to open her eyes but couldn't quite get a grasp on consciousness.

Logan knelt at Birdie's head and stroked stray strands of hair from her forehead. "Hey there, princess, you'd better listen to your sister. She's worried about you. Open your eyes."

"Toni?" Birdie said, and she reached for the nearest hand, which happened to be Mom's.

Toni sucked in a gasping breath of relief. "Yes, Buttercup, I'm here."

"Oh, thank God," Mom said. She lifted Birdie's hand to her lips, kissing each of her stubby little fingers, her palm, her wrist.

"Is she okay?" Grandma Joanna asked, her knee brushing Toni's shoulder as she leaned over to look down. "She's coming around," Grandma said to the 9-1-1 operator she still had on the phone.

Birdie's eyes blinked open, and she stared up at Logan, who must have appeared upside down to her. She then turned her head slightly to look at Toni. "Did Logan come to take you away again?"

Toni closed her eyes to keep her tears from falling and shook her head. "No, baby. He's just visiting."

She couldn't bring herself to look at him. If hearing those words hurt him even half as much as it hurt her to say them, she expected to find him lying gutted on the floor. But as much as she loved him, she couldn't leave Birdie. Not now. Maybe not ever. He had to understand why.

"How are you feeling, Buttercup?" Toni pried her eyes open, but couldn't see through the blur of her tears.

"I feel tired," she said. "Why are you crying?"

"I'm just so happy you're okay." And still so sick with worry she felt like she was going to throw up. What was taking the ambulance so long?

"Why are you crying, Mommy?"

"Because I thought I'd missed my chance to be a good mommy to you."

Birdie smiled at her. "But you're already the best mommy."

Mom shook her head. "No. No, I'm not. But I promise I'm going to be." She sniffed loudly and clutched Birdie's hand to her chest. "I promise."

Birdie tilted her head back and looked at Logan. "Why are you crying, Logan?"

"Onions," he said, lifting the hem of his shirt to wipe his eyes. "I hate those things."

Toni leaned her forehead against his shoulder to hide a smile and somehow ended up in his arms. She hadn't realized how much she needed a comforting hug until she was smashed against his hard chest.

"She'll be okay," he whispered.

And she believed him. Birdie would be fine. But would Toni

be okay when he had to go back on tour and she had to figure out how to get by without him?

"Toni?" Birdie said. "Can I get off the floor now?"

Toni released her hold on Logan and settled her fingertips against Birdie's cheek.

"You need to lie still until the ambulance gets here. The doctors need to check you out."

"I don't wanna ride in the ambalance."

"*I* want to ride in the ambulance," Logan said. "They're so cool, all the other cars have to move over and let them go first. Even big trucks have to get out of their way."

"They do?" Birdie stared up at him with utter adoration. And yeah, Toni knew the feeling.

"Yep."

"Then you can ride it."

"Ladies and princesses first," he said.

Birdie beamed at him. Mom touched his shoulder and mouthed *thank you*. Logan winked at her.

When the ambulance wailed into their drive, Grandma rushed out to meet them. Toni stepped aside to give the paramedics room to work, but Mom sat beside Birdie on the floor the entire time.

"Her ECG indicates a heart block," a paramedic told Mom. "There should be an extra bump here and not all these squiggles there."

Mom paled, and Toni leaned against Logan for support.

"So it *is* her heart," Mom said.

"Easily treatable," he said. "But you don't want to delay."

"The heart doctors at Children's Hospital are going to fix your ticker," the other paramedic said to Birdie. "And then you'll feel good as new."

"I'm already good as new," Birdie insisted.

"Do you want someone to ride with you in the ambulance?" the medic asked.

"Yes." Birdie's eyes immediately went to Toni, who was still leaning against Logan. He had his arm around her shoulders and his jaw pressed against the side of her head. Toni started to draw away from him, anticipating her sister's request, but Birdie's gaze darted to Mom. "I want Mommy to come with me."

Mom blinked at her, looking as stunned as Toni felt.

"You're sure?" Mom asked.

Birdie nodded and didn't protest once as she was put on a

gurney and loaded into the ambulance.

"We'll follow and meet you there," Logan said to Mom. Toni tried waving at Birdie through the open ambulance door, but she was talking to the paramedic about the squiggles on her ECG. The second paramedic shut the door and rushed around to the driver's seat. They sped off with lights flashing, but left the siren off. It was a small bit of comfort that the sirens had been deemed unnecessary.

"You okay?" Logan asked as Toni stood watching until the ambulance pulled onto the main road.

"I'm worried sick, but the paramedics seemed to think Birdie would be okay."

"I meant about her requesting your mom to accompany her."

Toni shrugged as if to say she didn't care, but she did care. She wanted Birdie and Mom to be closer, and this was a good sign that their relationship was strengthening. So why had it hurt so much when Birdie had chosen Mom to ride with her in the ambulance?

"Let's get going," she said.

Grandma secured the dogs, Toni grabbed her purse, Logan made a quick stop in the bathroom, and the three of them headed toward Seattle in the borrowed muscle car. Toni couldn't bring herself to talk much during the hour-long trip and doubted Logan would ever know how much comfort he brought her by holding her hand whenever he wasn't shifting gears.

At the hospital, they found Birdie had already been admitted and had seen a cardiologist. "They're going to put a place maker in me right here." Birdie rubbed a spot near her left shoulder.

"*Pacemaker*," Mom corrected. "They're trying to get her surgery scheduled for next week. She'll only have to stay one night."

"What caused her problem all of a sudden?" Toni asked, sitting on the edge of Birdie's bed and stroking her hair.

"They want to do more tests, but the doctor said it's probably scar tissue from the surgery she had as a baby. Since she's growing, it's now blocking the electrical signals in her heart. At least that's what they think is going on. Whatever the cause, she definitely needs a pacemaker."

"So I guess you won't be coming with me to New York," Logan said.

"I'm not sure the band even wants me to come back on tour."

But no, she wasn't going off to have a great time with Logan and the band while her little sister was undergoing surgery. Birdie was only nine. She had to be terrified.

"I had a band meeting with myself and you're welcome to come back with us. When you're ready, of course. No pressure."

"I don't want you to stay, Toni," Birdie said. "I want you to go with Logan. Logan makes you happy."

"Buttercup, being with you makes me happy too."

"I already made you happy for a long time. It's Logan's turn now. Mommy will take care of me. And Granny Jo too."

"You can fly back for her surgery next week," Grandma Joanna said.

Toni was completely torn. She didn't think she could concentrate on working on the book when Birdie was facing heart surgery.

"I be fine, Toni. Really."

"I know you will, Buttercup, but what about the chickens? You won't be able to carry their food until you heal."

"If I can build a multimillion-dollar company, I'm sure I can figure out how to feed a few chickens," Mom said.

Mom had left out the part about running that multimillion-dollar company into the ground. The chickens might not stand a chance.

"I'm here to help too," Grandma reminded her. "You can have your own life, Toni, and still be there for Birdie."

"And I do have a private jet at my disposal if you need to return in a hurry," Logan said. "At least until we start touring Europe next month. You are coming with us, right?"

"I don't even have a passport." Why did she feel like everyone was trying to get rid of her? Or maybe they really did have her happiness in mind.

"You can get it before we leave if you put a rush order on it," Logan said. "I'm sure Butch could line one up for you."

Butch could probably line up a whole new identity for her if she needed one. "I don't know."

She wanted to be with Logan, wanted to finish the book, wanted to hang out with the band—assuming Reagan didn't try to kill her—but what if she was gone and something dreadful happened to Birdie? Something even worse than her collapsing and discovering she needed a pacemaker implanted.

"Please go, Toni," Birdie said. "I want to be an aunt. So you need to have a baby. I like babies."

Logan's comforting arm dropped from Toni's shoulders, and he swiveled his head to gawk at her. He probably thought Toni had put that crazy idea in Birdie's head, but Toni had no idea where this was coming from. She did know she didn't want to upset Birdie in her weakened state, so she'd try a little mollification first. Then she'd move on to a blatant "no way in hell" if necessary.

"I don't think it's a good time for me to have a baby, Birdie," Toni said.

"When is a good time? Tomorrow?"

Toni chuckled. "No, not tomorrow either."

"But you love Logan, right?"

"With all my heart."

"And you said when a man and woman love each other, then they can have a baby."

Logan began to inch away.

Toni cringed. "I did say that. But it takes nine months to have a baby."

Birdie's eyes bulged. "That's a long time, Toni!"

"So you'll have to wait. A long, long time." Way longer than nine months, but Toni would like to make Birdie an aunt someday. And she was almost giddy thinking about how adorable Logan's babies would be.

"You can make me a calendar and I can mark the days with an X."

"If I'm blessed with a baby in the future, I'll make you a calendar," Toni said, "but sometimes babies arrive early and sometimes they show up late."

"That's weird," Birdie said.

"Are you actually considering this?" Logan sputtered.

"Not anytime soon." She closed the distance between them, took his hand, and leaned her head against his shoulder. She gazed up at him adoringly, as if he could make all her dreams come true if he granted her wish for a child of her own. In actuality, she was just fucking with him to see how he'd react. "But I do eventually want children. Don't you?"

Three additional sets of feminine eyes turned on him, imploring him for an answer. "Maybe," he said. "I don't know. I sure wouldn't make a very good dad."

Toni squeezed his hand. "I've seen how you are with Birdie. You'd be a great father. But don't worry, I'm not in any hurry, and if you don't want kids, I can find someone else to have babies with."

Logan glanced around at Toni's menagerie of relatives and then took her by the elbow and promptly escorted her out of the room and into the hallway.

"What the hell was that supposed to mean?" he said in an angry whisper. "Are you considering a future that doesn't include me?"

Toni opened her mouth to tell him she'd been joking, but he didn't let her get a word in.

"How can you even consider having babies with some other man? Don't you know that means you'll have to have sex with someone else?"

Toni chuckled. "Relax, Logan. I don't want another man's babies. I don't want any babies right now. But someday I'd like to have half a dozen curly-haired, blue-eyed baby Logans and Loganettes." She anticipated him turning away and running for freedom since they hadn't talked about their distant future. But he didn't run. He didn't even take a step back. He cupped her face between shaking hands and held her gaze for an intense moment.

"You want to have my babies?" he croaked.

"Someday," she said, wrapping her arms around his back and tugging him closer. "But not any time soon. I've heard the little buggers really interrupt a couple's sex life, and I still have a lot to learn."

He laughed. "Are you sure you don't want to try out some other guy before you pledge forever to me?"

"Do you want me to try out another guy?"

"Fuck no," he said. "I'd have to kill him and then where would we be? Occasional conjugal visits while I serve time."

She grinned and shook her head at him, knowing he was pulling her leg. "I don't want another guy. I've already had the best, why settle for the rest?"

Logan chuckled and squeezed her close. "That rhymes."

"Maybe I should try getting into the music business," she said. "I could write lyrics for your new album."

"Uh, let's not and say you did."

She huffed at him. "Are you trying to stifle my creative genius?"

"I'd rather encourage it. You're coming back on tour with me, right? You have to finish your book. Your mom and grandma will take good care of Birdie. If you need to get home, we'll get you home. I don't know why you're hesitating—don't you want to stay with me?"

"I do," she admitted, but there was one more thing holding her back. "But I'm not sure the band wants me there." There, she'd said it. How could she spend weeks in close quarters with four people who hated her guts?

"I don't give a fuck what they want. *I* want you there. I'll do whatever it takes to keep you with me. We belong together. Always."

She stood on tiptoe and captured his lips for a kiss. "Don't say it if you don't mean it."

"I mean it."

He deepened their kiss, heightening her arousal, filling her thoughts with nothing but him.

Always.

CHAPTER
39

A S TONI STEPPED onto Exodus End's tour bus, her stomach took residence in her calf-hugging boots. She clutched the strap of her messenger bag and tried to swallow her queasiness. Would these guys ever accept her apology and let her close to them again? Or would she be forced to leave? The wall of muscle and mean that suddenly appeared in her path did nothing to put her at ease.

"No fans on the bus," Butch said, his mustache twitching with disapproval.

"Then I guess I'd better leave," she said.

"Is that Toni?" Max said from the back of the bus.

"Logan actually did something right for a change," Steve said with a laugh.

"Toni's back!" Reagan cried, nearly knocking Butch on his ass as she shoved him aside to grab Toni in a rib-crushing hug. "I'm so sorry I yelled at you. And that I pushed you. And I thought you were responsible. I should have known you weren't a backstabbing whorebag. We're going to get back at those bitches, aren't we?"

Well, considering one of those bitches was her mother, probably not.

"Welcome home," Dare said, his green-eyed gaze warm and inviting. Toni knew he reserved that look for people he trusted.

"It's good to be back," she said with a happy smile.

"What? No one cares that I'm back too?" Logan said, shifting sideways so Toni wasn't blocking their view of him.

"Not really," Reagan teased, but the guys smacked him around a little to let him know he'd been missed.

With the man she loved at her side and a bright future before her, Toni no longer had to reach for her stars. They were right there beside her.

June 2

Dear Journal,

It's been a while since I wrote. I've been super busy. Today is the last day of Exodus End's North American tour. We're heading to the UK in two weeks for the Download Festival. I can't wait to get that first stamp in my brand new passport. The band has the next two weeks off while their equipment ships overseas. Of course, I had to record footage of them loading the semis on the freighter, so Logan and I are currently down at the docks. Yes, it was cool to see the cranes lifting those big containers, knowing the tour was packed inside. Yes, this is all going into the book. I don't know if I'll ever completely finish gathering data for this book. I'll probably need to break it into two volumes. Or maybe three.

Logan and I plan to spend the next few days in Key West—he insists I'll love parasailing and sex in the ocean (sharks, anyone?)—before we head to his place in Southern California. Apparently he has a dirt bike track on his property, and he wants to teach me to ride. Not sure how I feel about that one, but he already ordered a bike for me, so I have to at least try it out. We're going to California because I'm his date for Sed Lionheart's wedding next weekend. Jessica will be such a beautiful bride—even if she has packed on a few pounds (don't tell her I noticed)—and I'll get to see Sinners in tuxedos! It should be a blast. Then Logan and I are heading north to spend the rest of our vacation time with my family.

Birdie can't wait to show Logan her new horse. Mom is probably rethinking her decision to read her *Black Beauty* now! She says Birdie has even more energy since her pacemaker was implanted. I can't imagine how that's possible. I miss her to pieces, but since we've been using Skype to talk almost every night, at least I get to see her smiling face on a regular basis.

Things with Logan are wonderful. He's shoved me out of my

comfort zone so many times, I'm not sure I even have a comfort zone anymore. I'll just hang on for the ride and see where he takes me. The rest of the guys in the band are doing well. I'm worried about Reagan, though. She hasn't been herself since that first tabloid article was published. Reporters hound her and Trey constantly. Trey's good about brushing them off, but they're really wearing Reagan down. I wish she'd stop reading those damned articles. Each time a new one comes out, she sinks a little lower. Steve still wants to confront Susan about starting this shitstorm. Unfortunately, the bitch disappeared as soon as Mom announced she was planning to sell the company. I still don't get why Susan thought she could follow Exodus End on tour to get dirt on them. Did she really think Steve wouldn't recognize her? She lost a lot of weight since he knew her, but she was his sister-in-law for five years; he's not that clueless. Hopefully she'll turn up one day. I'd really like to hear Steve cut her down to size. And if Reagan ever runs into her, I don't think Susan will survive the confrontation.

I have to go now. Logan is waving me toward the sailboat he just rented. Sex on a boat—just a typical day in the life of Logan Schmidt. But for me, it's another adventure of a lifetime.

I'm-in-love-with-a-rock-star,

AUTHOR'S NOTE

I hope you enjoyed the first book in the Exodus End series. There were many times that I believed I would never finish *Insider*. About a quarter of the way through the book, I got a horrible case of writers' block and for months I couldn't write anything. Being stuck is a horrible feeling, so to get past my block I started working on the Sole Regret series and put *Insider* on the back burner.

In hindsight, I blame Shade (aka Jacob Silverton) for getting me off track. If he wouldn't have sent those black roses to Reagan stating he was fed up with his lead guitarist, I never would have started wondering about a vocalist named Shade (of all things), his tragic lead guitarist, and the band that has to put up with both of them. That's when I became fixated on Sole Regret and took a detour, letting Exodus End's story churn in my subconscious while I concentrated on writing other books. That worked great. At first. Words were flowing again. All the band members of Sole Regret were being noisy and demanding their stories be told. I was so relieved to be writing. And then one day, I decided I missed the guys of Sinners and wanted to write about their weddings.

I never expected writing *Sinners at the Altar* would be such an emotional process. When I finish writing a novel, I grieve. It's like letting go of a pair of close friends. And finishing the Sinners *series* was like losing a dozen friends all at once. I know that's why I got stuck on *Insider* so soon after the final Sinners book was released. I was afraid to get attached to the characters and it was at the quarter mark that I felt myself growing attached to them. I thought writing the Sinners' wedding stories would remind me that the characters weren't gone. They were living their happily-ever-afters off-screen. But instead of the pick me up I anticipated, writing their weddings made me grieve them all over again.

Unfortunately, finishing *Sinners at the Altar* made it hard for me to go back to Sole Regret. Damn it! It wasn't because I had lost interest in them. I became afraid of how I'd feel after I finished their series, which is a more lengthy series—probably because I dread it ending. After I wrote *Tease Me*—Sole Regret #7 (a book twice as long as intended)—I finally convinced myself that I couldn't put off *Insider* any longer. I had to finish the book even if it killed me. So thinking what I'd written must suck big wind, I went back and read what I'd started two years before and... I loved it! I couldn't figure out why I'd stopped writing *Insider* in the first place. So while it took me two years to write the first forty-thousand words of this book, it only took four months to write the additional one-hundred-twenty-thousand. Actually if not for the two year hiatus in the middle, the book took about six months to write—which is about average for me. It's that damned long hiatus in the middle that needs to never darken my doorstep again.

I'm still writing Sole Regret books. Still writing Sinners shorts. And will continue to write the rest of the Exodus End series. I do hope I never have to contend with that writers' block bullshit again. I now know what to expect when I finish the Sole Regret series and the Exodus End series—crippling loss as I say goodbye to characters that become more real to me than you can imagine. So maybe I'll deal with it better next time. Or maybe not. But I know if I don't let myself get attached to these characters, I can't expect my readers to care about them. So I'll suck it up and deal with it! I just wanted to let my readers know why it took so long to write this book.

Before I leave you, I need to thank the people that helped make this stubborn book a reality. Thanks to Beth Hill, editor extraordinaire and the one who usually talks me off the ledge during my monumental meltdowns; Cyndi McGowen, fantastic friend, concert buddy, beta reader, and the best book-signing assistant (aka bitch-Olivia) I could ever ask for; Charity Hendry, who I'm sure can design graphics in her sleep—she designed Exodus End's logo and the cover for *Insider*; my mom Paula and aunt Pam, friends by blood, fans by choice, beta readers by demand; the Writing Wombats, kindred souls who gave me the courage to self-publish this series; and most importantly, to all my fans, who remind me why I devote my life to making fictional rock stars come alive. Thank you all from the bottom of my heart!

ABOUT THE AUTHOR

Combining her love for romantic fiction and rock 'n roll, Olivia Cunning writes erotic romance centered around rock musicians. Raised on hard rock music from the cradle, she attended her first Styx concert at age six and fell instantly in love with live music. She's been known to travel over a thousand miles just to see a favorite band in concert. As a teen, she discovered her second love, romantic fiction—first, voraciously reading steamy romance novels and then penning her own. Growing up as the daughter of a career soldier, she's lived all over the United States and overseas. She currently lives in Illinois. To learn more about Olivia and her books, please visit www.oliviacunning.com.

Coming Soon

You watched them fall in love in *Double Time*...

Reagan Elliot should be living her dream...

She's touring with Exodus End as their new rhythm guitarist and gaining more notoriety and fame than she ever imagined possible.

She has earned the devoted love of not only one, but *two* spectacular men. Their committed threesome is stable, loving, deep, and satisfying for all involved.

But sometimes the world sees things differently and is determined to destroy what it doesn't understand.

Can Reagan's relationship with Trey and Ethan survive the cruel backlash of the media, her family, and a bigoted public? Or will she lose everything she holds dear?

OUTSIDER
Book 2 of the Exodus End World Tour series!
Coming in 2016

42820160R00269

Made in the USA
Lexington, KY
06 July 2015